Paladin and Necromancer

Adrienne Miller

Copyright © 2023 by Adrienne Miller.

All rights reserved.

No part of this publication may be reproduced, distributed, or transmitted in any form or by any means, including photocopying, recording, or other electronic or mechanical methods, without the prior written permission of the publisher, except as permitted by UK copyright law. For permission requests, contact adriennemilllerauthor@gmail.com

The story, all names, characters, and incidents portrayed in this production are fictitious. No identification with actual persons (living or deceased), places, buildings, and products is intended or should be inferred.

Book Cover by Maxim Mitenkov.

Contents

Prologue 5
Chapter 1 6
Chapter 2 23
Chapter 3 34
Chapter 4 45
Chapter 5 55
Chapter 6 67
Chapter 7 74
Chapter 8 93
Chapter 9 107
Chapter 10 121
Chapter 11 134
Chapter 12 146
Chapter 13 157
Chapter 14 169
Chapter 15 184
Chapter 16 193
Chapter 17 209

Chapter 18	217
Chapter 19	231
Chapter 20	250
Chapter 21	266
Chapter 22	274
Chapter 23	286
Chapter 24	301
Chapter 25	316
Chapter 26	331
Chapter 27	342
Chapter 28	358
Chapter 29	370
Chapter 30	383
Chapter 31	399
Chapter 32	411
Chapter 33	423
Chapter 34	434

Prologue

Seven years ago, the planes of existence split apart. That was rather unexpected for the humans of the realm, but the gods assured them that this happens sometimes. When the army from another plane invaded, the ten deities recruited the more-or-less faithful to save the world.

Many cities were razed to the ground or fell into rapidly opening rifts in the fabric of the Multiverse. But parts of humanity survived when the newly recruited paladins called upon their gods to lend them strength, and the mages cast spells hitherto unimaginable.

The war ended three years ago. It would be overly charitable to say that humanity won, but at some point, the attacks stopped. The enemy had run out of soldiers, dragons, or patience.

The planar rifts stayed open, however. Even the most powerful deities cannot mend the fabric of the Multiverse, so humanity focuses its efforts on creating barriers against future invasions by their extraplanar neighbours.

Understandably, everyone is a little on edge.

Chapter 1

"So, you're telling me the rift just appeared out of nowhere?"

Kass feels a vein on his forehead pulsating. His squire Allen squirms.

"It might have had something to do with the human sacrifices smeared across the walls. But I'm sure the rift came as a surprise to everyone else."

"I take it there were no survivors."

Allen huffs out a dry laugh. The manor, once made of white marble walls and drowned in pastel-coloured, goose-feathered pillows, is now best described as red. And sticky.

"None, Sir."

"Okay, walk me through it. A concerned neighbour calls the city watch because of the …"

"The screams, the terrible screams, Sir."

"Very good. You and the watchmen enter the manor and find that everyone has already died."

"Most horrifically, yes, Sir."

"Very good. You catch sight of a demon fleeing the manor –"

"Which was very scary, I should mention, Sir."

"Very good. And then you find a rift in the basement?"

Kass points at the spiral staircase that leads from the entrance hall into the manor's wine cellar. Someone in the noble family must have thought mixing alcohol and demonology was a great idea.

"Yes, Sir."

"And you find that prospect very frightening?"

Allen looks up.

"Have you been down there, Sir?"

"Not yet."

"Well, it's ... well, it's strange. Pultruding, one might say."

"Pultruding?"

"Yes, Sir."

Kass rubs the back of his neck.

"So, you just had to call her," he mutters.

"Pardon, Sir?"

"Silver. Of all the mages in this town, you just had to go and call Silver."

"She is listed as an expert in -"

"She is a necromancer. You'd think demons would be bad enough. Now you had to go and add the undead into the mix?"

"She's your wife, Sir."

Allen's voice is quiet, and he exchanges an awkward glance with the city watchmen. They move away from their choleric commander and take shelter behind half-torn marble statues and collapsed columns, some clutching their guns. For a moment, Kass is tempted to scream out his frustration until his squire runs all the way back to his backwater home village, sword between his legs.

Then he remembers that he swore a blood oath to the god of justice and temperance and takes a deep breath instead. His squire and the city watchmen relax.

"Very well," Kass says in the voice of someone who is decidedly not very well. "Let's see what my dear wife has unearthed now, shall we?"

Silver is reanimating two corpses, and somehow, none of Kass's subordinates have deemed it fit to stop her. The body of a male teenager, almost entirely torn in two, is hovering in a purple-glowing pentagram. The body of an older woman, perhaps his mother, lies on the ground beside him. She has likewise started to absorb the light from Silver's hand-painted spell.

His wife pays them no mind. She sits beside the rift, her skeletal hand hovering perhaps an inch from its steaming exterior. It is like a tear in time and space, blindingly bright and covered by shifting clouds.

Silver has locked her wheelchair in position and is almost poking her nose into the magic strands holding the rift in place. Her thin, whitish-blonde hair is swaying in a faint breeze.

"Silver," Kass says in place of a greeting. She doesn't turn around when he enters. They get enough of each other at home.

"Great. You're here," she says. "Can you tell me when my friends come to?"

She points at the two corpses she is reanimating. Her voice is raspy and quiet. During the war, she permanently damaged her vocal cords when the enemy tried to torture her to death.

"Is it really necessary to bring them back?" Kass asks. "Some noble idiots opened a rift to one of the hell planes, a lucky demon wandered through, and after it was done here, it decided to stay for a continued killing spree. Just block off the rift so we can get on with our bloody day."

Silver turns around and fixes him with small, dark eyes.

"Think about that again," she merely says, then turns back to the rift. She whispers a short incantation that seems to pass right through its surface.

Kass sighs and steps closer. His squire Allen and the rest of his men cautiously follow him across the concrete floor, still soaked in blood and wine. Dusty bottles, shattered on the ground, soak up the air with the intoxicating stink of grapes. Silver must have drawn up the two pentagrams in the centre of the cellar before returning to her wheelchair. On the right wall are the corpses Allen promised, piled up in a fleshy mess of blood and bones.

Kass sighs internally, then turns back to his squire.

"There any hidden rooms in the cellar?"

He can't see any, but he's never been good at finding trap doors and hidden corridors. Allen, on the other hand, was recruited from the crusades-torn villages where kids had to learn all sorts of skills to survive.

Humanity never had the chance to help the outskirts recover before the enemy's invasion tore them to pieces yet again.

Silver interjects before the squire can answer.

"No."

"And upstairs?" Kass continues.

"Lots of corpses and tasteless décor. But no –"

She interrupts herself to see if he has guessed it for himself. Kass sighs out loud this time.

"No secret laboratory or hidden pile of spell components," he says. "Nothing that could be used to open a rift. Not by a master spellcaster, and certainly not by a bored noble."

"Exactly." Silver turns around, and he sees something like approval in her eyes.

Sometimes, he finds it difficult to look at her, with her torn-up voice, her skeleton arm, and her legs that only work on good days. The war still clings to every inch of her, while Kass feels it has somehow forgotten him.

"We could have missed something," Kass suggests. He turns to his men and commands them to comb through the manor again. They do as he asks, leaving only him and Silver in the basement.

"Waste of time," his wife says. "If a spell of any magnitude had been cast in this house, I could have followed its residual energy. Instead, all I could detect is this."

She points at the rift. Her skeleton hand comes too close to its outline, and a small electric bolt jumps onto her fingers. She doesn't seem to feel the pain.

"Even you've been wrong before," Kass cautions.

Silver strokes her chin. "How about we assume that I'm no bumbling idiot and somehow missed one of our neighbours developing some frankly amazing magical abilities?"

"Very good, Silver."

His wife raises her eyebrows. "First things first. Why would demons enter this manor of their own accord? And why block off their own exit route? In case you hadn't noticed, the rift is sealed. Nobody can pass through it in either direction."

She touches the rift again, this time intentionally. A bolt of lightning springs from its exterior and shoots past Kass's head. It hits the wine cellar's back wall, leaving a sizzling steam residue. He doesn't do Silver the courtesy of flinching.

His wife continues. "This reeks of powerful arcane magic. Powerful enough to make me think that –"

Kass interrupts her.

"There any chance this is a natural phenomenon?" he asks. "Rifts appear all over the bloody place."

Silver thinks about it for a moment. "I don't think so. We haven't had any big ones for a while."

"This rift isn't that big. Not in the grand scheme of things," Kass argues. It is certainly not as big as the ones that appeared seven years ago. The ones that tore the world apart and allowed an army of enemies to cross over into the human realm.

Old Noll, the capital, is still covered in rifts today, their outlines intoxicating and iridescent like the jewellery on a bride's head. They promise the most exhilarating and dangerous escape to other realms in the Multiverse, even if many of them are too small to pass through.

Thank the gods, Kass thinks. *There are enough idiots who would travel the planes just to conjure a bit of pathos into their lives.*

Silver shakes her head. "If this rift came about naturally, why is a barrier spell covering it? Unless the demon chose to block off its own exit. And as far as we know, demons can't cast spells."

"As far as we know. We might as well assume the bloody worst," Kass replies drily. Silver chuckles.

"True, true." She shrugs. "But death cultists and idiot mages have been trying to rip holes into our interdimensional carpet since this whole mess started. Hells, I'm sure some have succeeded by now. My money is on this being the work of a mage. Not demons or chance."

Kass curses quietly. The king has, of course, outlawed any interference with the rifts. But it's hard to enforce rules when it comes to the arcane. Divine energy restores people's health and cures illnesses. The ability to channel it is given to clerics and paladins by the realm's ten gods. Arcane magic, on the other hand, is free from any divine control or oversight. Mages can unravel the very fabric of the Multiverse given enough motivation, talent, and spell components.

Kass thinks giving mages free rein is a powder keg ready to blow. Silver disagrees, of course.

"It could be a coincidence," he reiterates.

"Sure. But a rift appearing here in the capital, Kass? This close to king Ithya?"

"Granted. Big coincidence. Too big."

Silver nods, then taps her nails on the arms of her wheelchair.

"One thing confuses me," she says. "If a mage expended enough energy to open a rift, they wouldn't have bothered butchering a second-rate noble house. No. I reckon the demon has another mission to complete."

Kass sighs for a third time, but he admits she may have a point.

"Could you do a city-wide scrying spell?" he asks. "Find any creature or creatures that passed through the rift."

Scrying allows mages to follow either arcane or physical trails. Many spellcasters who choose to leave the city's mage guild sell scrying spells on the open market, often to suspicious husbands.

Silver hesitates. "I could try, but you're better off asking a diviner. Scrying isn't my specialism."

"I know."

Kass remembers begging her not to go down the path of necromancy. When they first met, Silver was a wide-eyed highborn girl, desperate to protect her home from the invading enemy. Like many nobles, she knew a bit of arcane magic but nothing extravagant or dangerous.

Kass was the son of a tavern owner who swore his loyalty to the first god who would have his services. He never thought he would be chosen as a favoured divine fighter. As a paladin.

In many ways, things had been easier during the early days of the invasion, even as they fought their fears and self-doubt as viciously as the enemy outside the walls. Before they were forced to give up on their youthful illusions.

"Still. Would be better if you tried it first," Kass says. "No point unsettling people before we have more information on what kind of foe is stalking our backstreets."

Silver raises her eyebrows, then smirks. "That, and you don't fancy the paperwork of requisitioning someone from the mage guild."

"I built you a two-floor laboratory. You might as well put it to use for something other than bringing back that damned cat."

"It's your cat, Kassander."

"It was. When it was alive. Now it's an abomination."

Silver rolls her eyes. "That's a pretty big word, husband. Are you sure you know what it means?"

Kass glares at her until she relents.

"Fine, I'll scry for your demon. Let me take a sample." She pulls a vial from one of the pouches strapped to her wheelchair. She holds it close to the rift, using her skeleton hand, then whispers a quiet incantation. The vial closes, trapping some of the rift's air and lightning.

"I assume you can't dispel the barrier on the rift? That way, we could just walk through and track down whoever opened it?" Kass asks instead of a thank you.

Silver shakes her head. "First thing I tried. The rift didn't like that and spat out a whole cluster of lightning. One of the city watch boys is in the hospital up Glengarden Road now. Don't worry, he'll live."

Kass nods, then gets distracted by a movement on his left. The two corpses in the pentagrams have risen and stare at him with unblinking, glowing eyes.

"Ah, finally!" Silver says, clapping her hands. "Their bodies were so messed up, it took ages to bring them back."

Kass suppresses a shudder as nausea builds within him. The divine and the arcane don't mix well, and ever since joining the paladin order of Five, Kass has been susceptible to feeling the aftereffects of magic tearing on the strands of reality.

It's even worse with necromancy. Many gods dislike the undead, but his god hates them with a burning passion. When he first signed himself into Five's service, Kass hadn't predicted this would turn into the single biggest problem of his life.

He fights off the impulse to cleave through Silver's necromantic summons with his Zweihander, a weapon gifted to him by the head cleric of Five. Soon enough, she'll end the spell, and the nobles can be given a proper burial.

"Can you speak, lost souls?" he asks. The teenager manages a nod. The woman doesn't react, but he can't exactly blame her. There is a great gaping hole where her throat should be.

"Tell me what happened here," he demands. The teenager opens his mouth, and a spout of black pestilence falls from his tongue. Kass curses.

"Death," the boy says. "Demon. Poison. Claw."

"Easy questions," Silver reminds him. "Yes or no, ideally."

Kass nods. He knows this by now, however much he wishes he didn't.

"Did you open this rift?" he asks.

The teenager and the woman both shake their head. Hers rolls precariously, but the point stands. Silver mutters, 'Told you.'

"Do you know if anyone else from this house did? Or tried to?" Kass presses.

Again, they shake their heads.

"Do you have any enemies?"

Again, the same response. Kass turns around to Silver, who has narrowed her eyes.

"Predictable," she murmurs.

"Any ideas?" he asks, biting down a twinge of resentment.

Silver rubs her chin, scratching away a bit of skin with her skeletal fingers.

"Were any of you spellcasters? Anyone in your family?" she asks but receives the same response as Kass.

She curses. "The spell is fading. We don't have much time."

"Do you know where the rift leads?" Kass asks.

The teenager shakes his head, but the woman stills, staring at him. Kass turns to Silver.

"Can you make her speak?" he asks. "She might know something."

His wife nods. She raises her skeletal hand and whispers a spell that binds the woman's skin together, twisting around her throat until a temporary flesh shield has formed.

"Speak," Silver commands, her voice even more hoarse than usual.

"Tower. Two towers."

Kass feels his blood run cold. Demons don't build towers. That means Silver is right. Whichever plane the demons came from is inhabited, possibly by an advanced civilisation. And that means the rift was created by a mage.

So, it's a targeted attack. The onset of another war? He utters a quick prayer to Five that it isn't. Humanity won't survive it.

"How do you know that?" he asks. The rift's exterior is covered by clouds and lightning. It doesn't give away so much as a glimpse of what's on the other side.

"I was here. When it opened," the dead woman presses out.

"What kind of bloody demon did this?" Kass demands. But the spell fails before the woman can reply, and the two corpses crash into the ground. He turns around to Silver.

"Can you –?"

Silver raises her hands but, after a moment, lowers them again.

"They are gone," she explains and makes a waving motion that symbolises their souls vanishing in thin air.

Kass sighs. Hopefully, they have passed to a god's plane where they can live out their afterlife. Souls don't need a rift for that. They become one with the fabric of their existence as they sink into peace.

He curses, using terms he tried to forget from his time working in his father's tavern. Silver shoots him a bemused glance but doesn't comment on his outburst. Instead, she twists the vial between her fingers.

"This just got interesting," she mutters. Kass interrupts his flow of curses and gives her a wary look.

"She might have misinterpreted what she saw," he suggests, although his tone isn't very hopeful.

Silver shrugs. "Maybe. But it doesn't sound like it, does it?"

Kass takes another look at the boy and the woman. They belong to a minor house in Old Noll, the realm's second – and now only – capital. Kass knows little about them, so he asks Silver.

"House Karthe? They're mineral traders, from what I remember. They got their titles a few decades ago. They financed a few of One's crusades in the Eastern regions of the realm, if I recall correctly."

As a noble, Silver knows most of the old families and those who amassed enough money to impress her parents. Once upon a time, the D'arrens had been keen to get Silver married off to a promising young lordling or heiress. Kass only met them once before the war turned their home to dust.

Silver's parents had been horrified at the prospect of their favourite daughter engaged to a newly enrolled paladin with nothing to his name except conviction. And then, suddenly, they were dead.

Becoming Silver's replacement family was easy after she lost everyone else. Perhaps that is why divorce is still not a word they dare to utter.

"Right. The way I see it, we have two options," Kass says. "First, House Karthe was targeted specifically for some bloody reason. Second, this is a royal assassination attempt, and the attackers chose a location close to the castle."

He isn't particularly worried when he says that. King Ithya is surrounded by an army of paladins, city watchmen, resident soldiers, and loyal mages. And he is almost always accompanied by Pride, leader of the mage guild and the deadliest person Kass has ever met. She'll crush any demons that so much as breathe near the castle walls.

The rift is worth reporting, of course. But he doubts anyone will take the demon threat seriously until Silver discovers more about their stray invader. The realm has bigger issues to worry about than a single rift. Old Noll alone is currently contending with three active death cults.

"Right," Silver says, rubbing her hands. "Then you and your boys patrol the streets, and I follow our demon's path with a scrying spell?"

"Deal," Kass replies. He is tempted to smile at her, but before he can make up his mind, she unlocks her wheelchair and rolls a few paces back.

"I'll create another seal around the rift. That should prevent idiot city guardsmen from stumbling into it by accident and having their faces fried off."

Kass lets her. He feels a new swell of nausea while Silver is casting. Maybe he should have stepped out of the room when she reanimated the two corpses. He will need to repent at the temple to restore full access to his powers. Ever since Silver pursued the path of necromancy, his god's favour has noticeably dimmed.

Once Silver is finished with the seal, he lifts her and her wheelchair back up the spiral staircase. He is careful not to scrape the metal against the iron railing. Silver feels light in his arms, and he notices that her breathing strains when she is pressed against his chest.

"Do you need me to escort you home?" he asks, his voice a little quieter than he had intended.

She snorts. "I can handle any robbers or stray cultists, husband."

He doesn't doubt it. Even bound to a wheelchair, Silver is one of the city's most formidable spellcasters. And if she wills it, her skeleton hand wilts anything she touches.

"Fair enough," he says, then lifts her back to solid ground. She hesitates for a moment.

"I wouldn't mind the company, though," she finally says.

Kass feels a sting, even underneath the years of silence and resentment. He still loves Silver. It would be easier for them both if he didn't.

He shakes his head.

"I need to file my report," he says.

She does him the favour of not showing her disappointment. "Very well. I suppose I might see you at home."

He nods.

"Don't reanimate the cat," he tells her as she leaves.

Silver laughs.

Chapter 2

Silver takes the inner-city tram to go home and prepare the scrying spell. It's rare enough that she knows what Kass is up to during the day that she's keen to take part. She also doesn't have a lot to do. The standing army has some requisitions, which she ignores, and she firmly refuses to help with teaching duties in the mage tower. Occasionally, she experiments with different types of resurrection spells to improve the fine motor skills of necromantic summons. One of her skeletons recently managed to make her a half-decent drink.

But other than the inane preoccupations of peacetime, she has nothing much going on. Sometimes, she feels like she has forgotten how to exist apart from the all-consuming needs of the battlefield.

Many never returned from the war. Holly was shot in the throat, Melina died from a misfired spell, and Derek was blasted from the top of the city walls. Granted, Derek had wanted to die. He had only joined the army because he thought being killed by the enemy was more honourable than losing his battle to depression. That hadn't made the grief of losing him any less devastating.

Silver sighs and pushes the memories aside as she moves over the smooth stone path through her front garden. One of their friends to survive the war, a former pacifist named Pathas, once joked that the size of their mansion meant that Silver and Kass were overcompensating for something. He wasn't wrong.

Silver doesn't have to get up to unlock the front door. Kass installed the lock at precisely the right height from where she sits in her chair.

Inside, a breath of cool air is a welcome change from the hot temperatures that spread throughout the city. She stays in her chair for a few moments, closes her eyes and enjoys the painlessness and the simple pleasure of being alive. Then, the voice of one of their servants rips her out of relaxation.

"Mistress Silver?" he asks, his voice slightly unsure. Piotr, one of their newest recruits.

"Yes, Piotr," she replies without opening her eyes.

"May I help you?"

"Did I ask for your help?" Silver replies. It's an awful impulse, but like with so many of her impulses, she rarely sees the point in tempering herself.

"No, mistress," Piotr replies, slightly dejected.

She opens her eyes. The manor's entrance hall is clad in dark oak panelling, filled with copies of pictures that were displayed in Silver's old family home. Pairs of shoes lie in orderly piles underneath the coat hangers so as not to obstruct her path.

Kass is a considerate husband. Just not where it counts.

"Would you like some lunch, mistress?" Piotr tries again, having regained his confidence.

"Can you bring it to the lab, please?" she tells Piotr.

Ignoring his disapproving look, she makes her way to the ground-floor laboratory. There, she stores her spell components, books, and workstation, complete with burns and stains. The pentagrams, the dead bodies, and the experimentation chamber are upstairs, past the stair lift. But she won't need those for a scrying spell.

The downstairs part of her laboratory has multi-coloured stained-glass windows adorned with glittering chains and dried flowers. On the side of her alchemy table lie bushels of incense that she lights up with an incantation. None of this improves the potency of her spells. Silver just likes how the light looks when it falls through the chains and gets caught up in the steam of the incense.

Allowing yourself to be distracted is a bad habit that could mess up the composition of your spell. At least Melina always said so.

Melina's parents spent most of their small family fortune to get their daughter an education in the city's mage tower. Trained by the tower's strict teachers, Melina had always been diligent and careful with her spellcasting. When the war broke out, she enrolled before the mages were conscripted.

After Derek died, Melina couldn't think. She messed up the only spell that ever backfired on her. Sometimes, it only takes one.

Silver pulls last month's city map from a nearby shelf and unrolls it on the table. She isn't sure how up to date it still is. Even three years later, they are still fixing holes in the city walls. Tons of open rifts are unregistered. And the mage guild is working on stabilising pylons that supposedly keep rifts from forming. They certainly wouldn't be included on any map for fear of death cultists or other fanatics messing with the construction sites.

Ever since the planes split apart seven years ago, mages have had to ensure the realm's remaining cities don't spontaneously fall into an abyss of nothingness or crash into another plane of existence. It happened to plenty of places already.

The map should be accurate enough for her purposes, though. Silver grabs a handful of knucklebones from an open pickle jar, then tosses them on the table. Then, she takes the vial of rift residue from a pouch strapped to her wheelchair. Whatever passed through the rift in House Karthe left a trail behind. Tracking it shouldn't be difficult, at least not for a mage of Silver's calibre.

She is about to open the vial and smear the bones in the residue of wind and lightning when a knock on the laboratory door breaks her concentration. It is Piotr, and he carries a tray of cheese, oat biscuits, torn-up pieces of chicken, and some buttered rosemary bread.

"Just put it on the table," Silver says, pointing to the only free corner. Piotr's gaze glides over the bones atop the paper map and the various half-closed vials and reagents on the shelves.

"Are these supposed to be open?"

Silver has a terrible habit of not closing lids properly. Still, she nods with unwarranted confidence.

"Don't worry about it," she assures him. The really dangerous stuff is closed, she thinks. Anyway, the worst thing that can happen is a minor explosion, and they're all used to those.

"The drawing room has a nice table I made up for you earlier, mistress," Piotr continues.

"How lovely," Silver says drily. No, she hears Melina's voice, you shouldn't eat in a laboratory, especially not next to spell components. Especially, especially if you haven't opened the windows in a while. Her friend would have a fit if she were alive to see this. Holly and Pathas would laugh, and Derek would start paying attention a little too late and miss the moment.

She thanks Piotr for lunch and chews on chicken flakes and oat cakes as she coats the bones in wind and lightning traces. Then, she mutters the scrying incantation and watches the bones start to glow and move across the map. They break apart to form a trail that represents the demon's path.

The trail starts at House Karthe. So far, no surprise. It snakes around the house as if the creature is looking for something. Then, the trail breaks in three. One moves straight to Old Noll's castle, another towards the mage tower. The final one stops in the plague quarters. Citizens who suffer from magical diseases have been quarantined there ever since they first got infected during the war. There are powerful energies to be unearthed if you are desperate enough to look for them.

All three trails drop off, and Silver snaps her fingers to lock the bones in place so they do not roll off the table. Old Noll is host to semi-regular earthquakes. An interdimensional rift is forming about five kilometres underneath the earth. The mages have tried to contain the rift's outlines, but occasionally, a shift in the tectonic plates allows it to break free from the previously defined borders of the spell. There's not much anyone can do about it.

Silver nibbles on some cheese and stares at the bones some more. The trail could signify all sorts of things. Most likely, they are dealing with three demons. Or maybe one demon that is fast enough to confuse the scrying spell. The trail stopping could mean that the creatures are still there. Or that they started to protect themselves against scrying magic.

Moving towards the castle supports Kass's assassination theory, but there are alternative explanations. After all, the castle is in the middle of the city. Approaching the mage tower could mean the demon was looking for a vantage point. Going to the plague quarters could signify all manner of things, none of them good.

The bones don't lie. They're just hard to read.

If Silver had chosen a different specialism, she wouldn't use bones for scrying. For instance, if she was a conjurer, animal remains would help her cast her spells. But necromancers are most attuned to the energy of dead things, so that is what she uses.

She doesn't think it's a big deal. It's not like knucklebones are expensive.

Silver spends the rest of the day reading a book near the pond in the garden. Sat in her wheelchair, she catches flecks of sunlight that fall through the heavy-leaved willows Kass planted. At some point, Piotr brings out a blanket to put over her legs, and they talk about the frogs that moved into the tall grass next to the pond. He helps her spot one and promises to put out some food.

The cats join, dozing in the sunniest spots they can find. After the war, Kass and Silver adopted any strays they could find, acquiring a proud household of seven uneasy bedfellows. Most prefer Kass and sleep in his gigantic bed, but Silver has her favourites, too. A little black cat with a white spot above his right eye and a mean ginger tom that brings her dead birds and mice.

Silver hears sounds emerging from the manor and turns around to see the servants switch on the lights in the downstairs kitchen. That means Kass is home. Only now does she realise how late it is. The sun has mostly set, barely reflecting against the softly rippling water of the pond.

She never knows what kind of mood Kass will be in when he comes home from the barracks. He was almost cordial this morning; he didn't even give her a piece of his mind about reanimating the nobles' corpses. But if past patterns are anything to go by, they are due to another one of his famous periods of grumpiness. And Silver is an easy target for his ire.

So, she stays by the pond and summons a few mage lights that allow her to continue reading. If he wants to talk, he has to come to her.

She doesn't hear the footsteps until Kass stands behind her and hands her a cup of tea. She doesn't flinch at the sudden intrusion. Unlike Kass, she had no problems regaining a measure of tranquillity after the war. Where he is woken by every raindrop knocking on the windows, Silver can sleep through almost anything.

"I went to your lab. Saw the spell you cast," Kass says. His voice is quiet yet penetrating. Like whatever he says carries some implicit weight.

"Any thoughts?" she asks.

"Probably three demons. I'll dispatch some watchmen to check out the spots near the castle and the mage tower. I'll go to the plague quarters myself."

"Do you need help?"

Kass looks her up and down. "I don't think you'd enjoy the experience, Silver."

She doesn't argue. She's never been there, but she can't imagine that the place is particularly well laid out for wheelchair users. Nowhere in the city is, except for their house. Still, she knows it's an excuse. The reason he doesn't want her to come is that he doesn't want her to come.

"Let me cast some protection spells on you in the morning," she suggests. "Might hold off some of the diseases."

"I can just go to the bloody temple afterwards," Kass protests.

Silver shrugs. "Penitence is better than prevention, then? Suit yourself."

Kass looks like he wants to reply something cutting but chooses to hold his tongue. He quietly sips his cup of tea and watches the ripples on the water as the sun fully descends on the horizon.

"I closed a bunch of lids in the lab. Hope I didn't break something" he finally says.

Silver raises her eyebrows, but the admonishment she expects for the messy state of her laboratory does not come. After a moment and another has passed, she thanks Kass. He looks surprised.

"You're ... welcome," he replies, his voice heavy.

"If you have such a penchant for cleaning, you're free to go in there more often," she teases.

Kass glowers at her. "If I fancy a week-long rash after standing near those damned skeletons of yours, sure. I'll let you know."

"A rash? Really?"

"Yeah. Plus, I get nauseous."

Pointedly, he takes another sip of tea. Silver shakes her head.

"It's absurd that it would affect you this much. It's not like you're running the experiments."

"No, but we live together."

They look at each other. Silver knows Kass doesn't understand why she can't just stop being a necromancer. He doesn't get that when she lost everything during the war, magic kept her safe. Kass couldn't save her from the enemy soldiers when they tortured her. She saved herself.

Silver loves life. She may have a messed-up pair of legs and a fucked-up arm, and a voice that doesn't work properly. But she can still do the important stuff, like watch the sunset and eat a good meal. She will never give up on her powers, not when they are the only thing between her and the abyss. The world is still broken, and it probably always will be.

"I'm sorry," she tells Kass. She is sorry he is suffering because of his god's stupid rules. She is sorry that after so many of their friends died, they couldn't find happiness in each other. She is sorry that he doesn't understand her.

Kass doesn't believe her and tells her as much. She is tempted to argue, but this is still a good day, and she doesn't want to ruin it. When she doesn't respond, he finishes the rest of his tea so quickly he burns his lips and stalks back to the manner. Like every night, they eat separately.

Chapter 3

Kass wakes in a cold sweat. The cats give him angry looks that tell him he once again made for an uneasy bedfellow. His heart is racing, and his throat hurts.

Fucking war. Sometimes, he thinks it'll take a second invasion to make him forget everything that happened during the first. He throws off his wet covers, grabs Five's Zweihander that leans beside his bed and prepares for the day.

The plague quarters are locked off on every side. West, the city walls block out the sky, while the rest of the district is surrounded by hastily drawn-up barricades, barbed wire, collapsed buildings, and magical barriers. There are only two points of entry, and usually, visitors need an official warrant to be allowed inside.

They don't give a shit when it comes to paladins and war heroes. Kass is waved through with nothing but a mild warning not to linger inside for longer than necessary. He has taken both his squires, Allen and Andrea, who shift nervously as they enter the deathly quiet streets of the district. Dark blue shadows lurk between the buildings and suck up every breath of air.

Kass leads them down a few streets, then pulls out a district map on which he has marked the demon's path. Allen leans over his shoulder, completely unaware of the boundaries of personal space, while Andrea hangs a little further back.

"Either of you ever been here?" he asks.

"Nope," Allen mutters. "Thankfully not. Erm, Sir."

"No, Sir," Andrea replies quickly. They are trying not to let their nervousness show.

"Right," Kass grumbles. "Ground rules. We're not entering any buildings unless we have to. Many illnesses here are airborne, and we don't want to take any chances. And for the love of Five, don't touch anyone."

He glares at them. Andrea has been with him for two years. He never thought he would pick a squire, but Andrea changed his mind. They come from one of Old Noll's wealthier family who are considered favoured by the gods. When Andrea was twelve, they fell out of a window. Five resurrected them a few minutes after the accident, as the gods are wont to do with children and teenagers.

Allen is new. He only joined Five's order half a year ago. He is a country boy through and through, in a way that sometimes bemuses and often infuriates Kass.

Allen and Andrea are best friends. Kass isn't sure if they are ready for a real fight yet, but life doesn't tend to wait until you're ready.

"All clear?"

They nod. Kass looks back at the map and plots a path in his head. The plague quarters used to be a market district for foreign traders who visited Old Noll. It was home to many inns, and Kass remembers his uncle often complained at their tavern losing custom to the establishments here.

At the outset of the invasion, the market district took in refugees from the surrounding villages and small towns. Nobody knows if the refugees were already infected when they first entered Old Noll or if that happened later. The going theory is that during the invasion, the enemy spread extraplanar germs which are highly infectious to humans. None of the clerics' healing spells work on them now. So, the sick remain quarantined here.

There are some silver linings to the war, Kass supposes with a twinge of cynicism. Custom at his family tavern really picked up after the plague quarters were locked down.

As they walk through the quiet streets, Kass and his squires are chased by the sounds of windows slamming shut. Sometimes, Kass thinks he hears quiet breathing just behind them, but he resists the impulse to turn around. He doesn't want to give into paranoia and risk unsettling his squires.

Allen quietly turns to Andrea.

"Why don't they just heal the people here?" he asks. "Don't we have enough clerics in the city?"

Kass sometimes forgets how recently Allen arrived in Old Noll. Andrea shakes their head.

"They can't. Once the infection has settled in, the divine miracles don't work."

"Well, why did they leave it so long?" Allen asks.

Andrea hesitates. They don't want to repeat the old government's rationale as if they endorse it. Kass speaks up instead.

"Because the army decided to reserve all divine magic for active combatants. I can promise you that no cleric in the city was allowed to set foot in here until it was too late."

"The queen –" Allen starts, but Kass interrupts him.

"The queen couldn't have given less of a shit about all this. She left all the decision-making to her generals and told them to see us through the war, no matter what."

"She died for us," Andrea says quietly.

"She was killed. There is a difference," Kass says, then shakes his head.

"Nothing any of us can do now. Come on."

The trail stops at an old square. Part of the city wall collapsed on top of a fountain. Broken pieces of frolicking dolphins stare up at them. The adjoining houses turn away their empty grey faces, blank facades of stone unadorned and silent. All shutters are closed, and the doors are barricaded.

One of the houses stands out. A pub with a sign too faded to read, whose shutters have been partially ripped out. When he steps closer, Kass sees dried blood on the glass, black in the day's pale light.

Andrea's hand instinctively goes to their sword.

"Sir," they breathe. "There may be survivors."

"Don't get your hopes up," Kass grumbles.

Allen gulps.

"Didn't you say that we shouldn't go inside? We could get infected."

Andrea shoots him a sharp look.

"We could help people," they say. "Isn't that why we joined the order?"

Allen puts up his hands in silent defeat.

"Do you have a better idea?" Kass asks him. The edge in his voice remains, but he gives his squire the time to come up with an answer. Allen takes a few moments, but then he nods.

"Let's make some noise and lure the demon out here. We can set up traps, and in an open space, we'll be able to take advantage of our numbers."

Kass takes a step closer and narrows his eyes. Allen pales.

"What?" he asks breathlessly.

"Look at that," Kass grunts. "It's a bloody brain. Well done, boy."

Andrea shouts some paladin nonsense about coming out and taking responsibility for your crimes. Kass is almost sure that it won't work – demons are not known to repent – but the noise Andrea makes eventually causes a stir deep inside the pub.

"Get back," Kass snaps, and his squire obeys immediately.

He approaches the open door, ensuring he is visible from the pub's interior. He sees chairs and tables callously thrown across the floor and some disembowelled bodies hanging over the bar. No lights, and there is no movement.

Until the demon comes into view as suddenly as the onset of fear.

It crawls down a set of stairs at the back of the taproom. The air around it flickers as if beset by a spell. The demon's skin is slimy and white, and dull red eyes stare at Kass with an almost empty expression. There is just a scent, an impulse, and a hunt that has been interrupted.

Teeth grow all over its body, adorning the shifting lumps that promise untold horrors lurking beneath skin and bone. The teeth chatter in anticipation as the demon moves towards Kass. There is a gunshot wound on one of its seven legs, but that doesn't slow the creature down.

Kass draws his Zweihander, made lighter by the approval of his god. He takes a deep breath and tries to calm down his racing fear. If anything will put him in Five's good graces today, taking out a demon should do it.

The creature picks up speed as it realises Kass isn't moving. It takes out the doorframe as it charges into the open square. Wood shatters, splinters rain through the air, then Allen's bomb goes off as the demon's feet break the leather container the squire hid under some stray debris.

A flash of fire shakes the creature and nearly topples it. But it takes more than a homemade firebomb to take out a demon.

Kass uses the creature's momentary disorientation to strike its legs, then dances back. Its skin is hard to penetrate. He will have to get a good angle before attempting a hit that can kill.

He tells his squires to stay back, and Allen is happy to oblige, cowering behind the fountain's leftover debris. But Andrea has to play the hero. They emerge from the side of the pub and stab one of the demon's hind legs with their sword. It does nothing. Andrea uses a rapier, and rapiers are great for taking out humans but not so great against anything creepy or crawly.

The demon turns around, and its tail nearly throws Kass off his feet. It opens its mouth and growls at the young squire. Andrea doesn't move, unsure whether they should flee or attempt to parry the beast's attacks.

The demon lunges forward, and Kass jumps after it, trying to keep it from separating Andrea's face from the rest of their body. He rams his Zweihander into the demon's tail, but the creature is too long, and Andrea is too slow.

Kass feels a burning sensation against his skin.

"Bit late to warn me now," he growls and desperately drags on his sword to draw the demon away from his squire.

Allen curses and throws a stone at the demon's head. It falls a few inches short of its target, softly rolling on the ground until it comes to a halt. The demon's head shoots around, and Kass sees an opening. He raises his hand towards the sky. If Five decides that his paladins deserve divine assistance, he sometimes lends them a mystical weapon.

Most of the time, the gods ignore human pleas. But saving Andrea seems to be a worthy enough goal. When Kass brings his hand down again, he is holding a gold-glowing ethereal sword. It cuts the demon's head clear from its body.

His squires relax, exhaling loudly. Kass feels his heart hammer against his chest and tries not to lose himself to memories of similar, worse battles. He watches the demon's white, slimy head roll on the ground, its eyes empty as it stares at the sky. Kass barely feels the adrenaline coursing through his body. He knows it's there, but all he registers is the damned sluggishness that almost got Andrea killed. It's not their fault. He should have prepared them better. Holly, Derek and Melina flash before his eyes. He should have prepared them all better.

The demon's body twitches, even without its head. Kass blinks and stares at it. One leg slowly rises from the ground, and a second one soon follows.

"Erm, Sir?" Allen asks, but he is too late to react. Quick like a spider and silent like the grave, the demon's body hurries away, its long nails clicking on the stone. Its head crumbles to dust.

"Fuck," Kass cries and races after the creature without another glance at his squires.

He chases it through the streets, and his footsteps echo against the stone-cold walls like the rhythm of the damned. But once the demon climbs a wall and starts jumping from roof to roof, he must admit defeat.

Furious, Kass stalks back to the square, where his squires speak with the survivors who have trickled out of the tavern.

Kass sees a middle-aged, broad-shouldered man – the tavern owner, Andrea whispers – two children, an older woman, and a young man who tries to hide his face beneath a cowl.

None of them know what the demon wanted or where it came from.

"Did it seem more interested in some people than others?" Allen asks, which Kass thinks is a good question.

The barkeep hesitates. After a few moments, he shakes his head. "Not really. Come to think of it, the demon didn't seem that interested in any of us."

Kass raises his eyebrows.

"There's enough bodies inside that would argue otherwise," he snaps. He doesn't like it when people are callous about death.

"Sure, but they got in the demon's way," the tavern owner replies. "I mean, we were all surprised by it suddenly showing up, but we had enough time to run upstairs and hide in our rooms."

"What a great idea," Allen mutters.

"Shut it, recruit," Kass snarls.

"It was a pretty good idea, actually," the old woman says with an inappropriate level of smugness. "The demon didn't even try to come inside. It just crawled through the corridors."

"I reckon it was trying to find the way back outside," the tavern keeper says. "Sounded like it was scratching on the walls a couple of times."

"Interesting," Kass mutters.

Andrea pulls on his arm.

"Sir," they mutter. "In which direction did the demon flee when you pursued it?"

Kass points to the roofs, and Andrea asks him to unroll the map again. Meanwhile, Allen hands out bandages and calls on Five for minor healing miracles to patch up scratches and injured knees. His eyes glow with pride when his god answers his call. Kass remembers that joy all too well. When a paladin or cleric calls to their gods for aid, they become a conduit for divine might. There is no feeling in the world like it.

Kass sees it before Andrea has to point it out. A direction.

"The docks?" he asks, raising his eyebrows. "What in the flaming hells does our demon want there?"

His squire shakes their head.

"I don't know, Sir. But a lot of people live down there."

Kass nods.

"We should hurry."

Chapter 4

Kass and his squires leave the plague quarters as soon as they can. They cover their mouths and hands with cloth until they reach the temple district. Usually, they'd go to the temple of Five, an unassuming building no taller than a merchant family's house. Its walls are grey and speckled, with neither towers nor spires. Kass likes how unpretentious it is. But the temple of One is closer. They approach its white marble exterior and wide-swinging staircase. A long, pretentious quotation from some sage is etched above the door.

One is the god of existence and magic. In addition to the clerics, there are always a few mages inside his temple, recovering after failed experiments or pooling their resources with their divine colleagues. There is still tension between them and the clerics, but less so than with the other gods' followers. Silver often joked that she wished Kass could at least have been a different flavour of fanatic.

Magical lights dance across the temple's wide-swinging roofs, dying their gleaming mosaic tiles, now purple, green, silver, and iridescent blue. Kass walks past a line of queuing supplicants and demands immediate attention for himself and his squires. The clerics visibly disapprove of his bravado, and one of them mutters something about 'upstart brutes'.

But they don't refuse him. It would look bad to butt heads with a paladin, a war hero, and one of the city watch commanders. Especially seeing as in Kass's case, they're all the same person.

The clerics lead Kass and his squires into a secluded room. There, they sit on a naked marble bench, awkwardly close to one another, and stare at empty white walls. Andrea and Allen start chatting over the top of Kass, who sits between them, but the conversation soon dies from the suffocating emptiness of the treatment room.

Kass feels he should say something, which makes him want to do so even less. After a few agonising minutes have passed, though, he turns to his youngest squire.

"Decent work today, 'drea," he mutters. Andrea's eyes widen with pleasure, but they shake their head. "I nearly got killed."

"You fought with passion," Kass responds gently. "Arguably too much of it. Sometimes, the courage will dry up, and you'll hesitate."

Andrea smiles shyly and promises to try and keep a cooler head in the future.

Kass looks away and readjusts his scowl. Allen can't help himself.

"No heart-warming compliments for me, Sir? Nothing on how my trap may have saved the day today, but my hubris will surely be the end of me?"

Kass glowers at him.

"You have a bloody clever tongue on you, boy," he says. Allen shrugs.

"What can I say? I'm a clever lad. Sir."

Kass nods. "Did you feel clever when you sat behind that fountain and threw a rock at your enemy?"

Allen hesitates, his eyes inadvertently darting towards Andrea.

"Not really," Allen admits.

Kass nods.

"You felt helpless?" he prods. Allen nods slowly, and Kass continues.

"You'll always feel helpless. During every battle, no matter how many you fight. The trick is hating the feeling enough that you prepare better next time. You're smart, and you know you're smart. Keep using that to your advantage."

Allen swallows whatever response lies on his tongue and nods again.

Kass resists the urge to sigh. Epiphany after pointless epiphany. He remembers all those hard-earned lessons from the war. But did any of those realisations keep his friends safe? Did they prevent his wife from being tortured? Do they keep the nightmares at bay?

But just because the epiphanies didn't help him doesn't mean they will be pointless for his squires. What in hells did he fight for if not for the next generation to have an easier time?

"Sir?" Andrea asks.

"Hm?"

"What do you think the demon is after?"

Kass rubs his chin. "That's the question. It kept going after losing its head, so we can guess it was summoned by a mage whose spells force it to keep going even after death."

Maybe by a necromancer, he thinks with a shudder. He continues.

"It has a clear target, given that it ignored some of the civilians in the tavern. And Silver thinks the rift it came through was manmade. So, I reckon our demon's a bloody assassin."

"That's ... concerning," Andrea whispers.

"Is she really that strong? Silver, I mean," Allen asks. Andrea's eyes light up.

"Oh yes! She's amazing! Apparently, during the war, she saved the city by ripping a hundred dragons out of the sky."

Kass raises an eyebrow. "Are you done? Or do you want me to go home and get you an autograph?"

Andrea colours.

"And the commander doesn't like it when people talk about her," they explain sheepishly.

Allen mouths the word 'weird', and Andrea looks away to hide their smile.

"It was thirty dragons, not a hundred," Kass mutters, then sighs.

"Our mage commands three demons and probably opened a rift," he says. "I reckon that means they won't bother with the small shit. Love triangles, broken promises, bad reviews in the local paper – forget about it. The target's got to be of a pretty damn high calibre to justify this kind of effort."

"But would someone like that live at the docks?" Allen asks. "No offence, Sir, but when I last went there, I wasn't massively impressed."

"So, could the demon be after someone in hiding?" Andrea asks. Kass nods.

"And I have an inkling of who it could be."

An overworked cleric gives Kass and his squires a once-over with divine healing spells, courtesy of One. He is an expert in curing magical diseases, and much more thorough with his invocations than Kass would have been. The head cleric squeezes into the room and demands to know what the city watch is doing in the plague quarters. Kass tells him in no uncertain terms to mind his own business.

He enjoys pulling rank with this one. Dominik Var'Herren is the second son of one of Old Noll's wealthiest families, and his mother deftly manoeuvred him into the most prestigious position at the most prestigious god's temple. Supposedly, once upon a time, Var'Herren had been a candidate for Silver's hand in marriage. In his less pious moments, Kass wonders why a powerful god like One accepts a pompous idiot like Var'Herren as a conduit for his might. Dominik must have some very deeply hidden qualities.

After some verbal sparring, Kass takes his squires on the tram to the docks. They step on the outdoor carriage just as it starts moving. Even during the middle of the day, the tram is full of people, and Kass and his squires are squeezed into the ink-black railing as they watch the districts fly past.

He spots several horse-drawn carriages transporting the wealthier citizens of Old Noll. The clattering of hooves always makes him feel on edge. Even though he's technically a noble now, he has still not learned how to ride. A stubborn part of him thinks this kind of crap is for people who are too lazy to use their own two feet. And when he's being honest with himself, he acknowledges that he's scared of how big horses are.

A woman with a pram bumps into him as the carriage picks up speed. He watches flower shops and greengrocers and closes his eyes when the smell of the sea fills the air. The familiar bells of ship captains and the shrieks of seagulls chasing after shoreline fish ring in his ears, and he feels a semblance of calm.

Then he opens his eyes and sees Allen struggle to jump off the carriage, and the feeling passes as quickly as it comes on.

Kass gives his squire a hearty slap on the back, then holds Allen by the arm when he nearly falls on his face. They leave the tram tracks behind, then weave into the masses of people hurrying through the dock's labyrinthine alleyways.

The district curves around a steep descent to the shoreline, with viewing platforms peaking atop hastily constructed, rotting fortifications that were supposed to fend off the enemy's naval attacks. Warehouses, watchtowers, and pubs dominate the lower parts of the district, and a small promenade near the water is always chock-full of wooden stalls where fishermen sell oysters, crab, and freshly grilled fish.

And, of course, there are the death cultists. They're having lunch right now, trying not to get sandwich juice on their long robes. Their dress is modelled after mage robes, although few reputable mages would be caught dead anywhere near the cultists.

They try to trap Kass in a philosophical argument about the pre-determined fate of the Multiverse. They argue that the world should have ended seven years ago, and they are merely helping fate continue on its path towards ever-increasing entropy. Why entropy might need human help, Kass isn't sure.

Across Old Noll, death cultists try to expand existing rifts or open new ones. Fortunately for the rest of civilisation, you need magic to do either of these things. So, the cultists mostly just sit around and smear spell components around the edges of rifts.

It's been a while since a high-profile mage joined their cause and actually tried to open a new rift. Said mage was very publicly and rather horrifically executed, together with his cultist friends. The death cultists are begrudgingly tolerated only under the premise that they are an annoyance rather than a realistic threat.

Kass isn't worried about them doing anything to the rift in the docks. The head of the mage guild, Pride, sealed that one herself. Nothing and nobody is getting through her black barrier anytime soon.

Once he is out of earshot of the cultists, Kass orients himself. His family tavern, *The Burning Mage,* is on one of the side streets closer to the top of the district. But Kass isn't going there today. Instead, he asks his squires to fan out and look for signs of the demon.

"Where would we even start with something like that?" Allen asks, still visibly disgruntled after Kass's unceremonious method of helping him off the tram.

Andrea clears their throat. "We could ask the district's city watch for any sightings of demonic activity. Then, we could talk to the fishermen at the promenade and any resident cultists or homeless folk."

Allen scratches the back of his head. "Right. We could do that." He glares at Kass. "And what will you do in the meantime, Sir?"

The 'Sir' is as strained as always.

"I'll go where I reckon the demon's heading." Kass replies, equally testy.

"Where?"

"None of your fucking business. Not 'till I've confirmed my suspicions."

Kass interrupts any oncoming protest by fishing a cleanly polished onyx stone from his pocket. He hands it to Allen, then turns to Andrea.

"Still got yours?" he asks.

The squire nods quickly and presents theirs, bound with a leather strap around their neck.

"What does it do?" Allen asks.

"If any of us are in danger, the stone will start to glow and vibrate," Kass responds. "Heats up when things get properly dicey."

Allen whistles. "Useful. Did your lady wife make those, Sir?"

Kass glares at him, and Allen falls silent.

Once upon a time, Melina enchanted the stones for their group of friends. When she, Holly, and Derek died, the stones emanated such vicious heat that Kass felt them burn through his skin. He still has the scars from that day. He isn't sure if Silver still has hers.

Kass was the one who dealt with their friends' bodies, so he collected their spare stones. He hates using them, but a life is a life. He'd use anything at his disposal to protect those under his command. Annoying as they may be.

Chapter 5

After watching his squires split up, Kass goes to find his former paladin general, Octavia. After renouncing her fellowship of Two, the god of light, and rejecting any honorifics she received after the war, she moved into a little apartment by the sea. Kass is one of the few people who knows where she went.

A few persistent rumours claim that Octavia died during the last thrusts of battle, heroically sacrificing herself for either king Ithya, a helpless orphan, or a stray dog. Kass knows Octavia dislikes Ithya, doesn't care much for children, and is a cat person.

Most of the houses at the docks look the same. They have rough stone facades and low, swinging roofs to shake off the rain. The ones closest to the sea are painted with pastel blue, green and purple colours, which regularly fade under the assault of the elements.

Kass remembers that Octavia's apartment can only be accessed via a backyard full of petunias and yowling cats. There are a lot of small, half-hidden backyards in the Docks. Finally, though, he finds it. He throws a stone against her window like a lovesick youth. He waits a few moments, then throws another, feeling thoroughly idiotic.

Finally, a lacy, white curtain moves by an inch, and he spots black eyes underneath a heap of greying tousled hair.

Octavia opens the downstairs door and gives him a few hard slaps on the back. She is a woman in her late fifties drowning in a pale blue sweater. Her black skin has gained a few more wrinkles since he last visited.

He stands stiff and salutes her, military style. Octavia nods approvingly despite her own informal greeting.

Before they speak, she gestures for him to follow her upstairs. He is greeted by a bizarre sight. Octavia's living room is filled with a pale-yellow couch with a floral print, a hand-made ship in the window, and a shining silver tea service on a small round table. Kass remembers his general cleaving apart the heavens to summon divine fire and lightning onto their foes. Once, she fought off three dozen enemies until help arrived. She never flinched in the face of reality.

"Kassander D'arran," she says. "What's on fire?"

"General," he replies with a slight bow, trying to keep his voice quiet. "There might be a demon after you."

"Oh, good."

Octavia sits down in one of those rocking chairs that look more comfortable than they are. Kass pulls up a hardwood chair from the kitchen. They share lukewarm, black tea that smells of smoke.

"Tell me from the start."

Kass always liked that about Octavia. Her first impulse is never to doubt. He tells her what he knows, and she nods slowly.

"It makes sense to think the creature is after me," she says. "But I haven't seen any demons in this neighbourhood. At least not recently."

"I might have slowed it down. Decapitation tends to do that."

"Hmm. Didn't finish it off, though, did you, boy?"

Octavia is the only person ever to call him 'boy'. He shakes his head, embarrassed.

"No, general. I'm sorry."

"You don't have to call me that anymore. I told you that before."

"I know. General."

Octavia rubs her chin.

"Any idea what triggered the demon's appearance?" she asks.

Kass shakes his head. "Nothing concrete. Silver thinks the rift it came through is manmade, so this is likely a targeted attack."

Octavia's features lighten up. "Oh, and how is Silver?"

Kass groans internally. "She's fine."

"And how are her legs?"

"The same."

"Oh? That's a shame."

Kass sighs again. "The bloody healing spells don't work anymore. I reckon she's stuck with them for the long haul."

"You reckon? Do you not speak to your wife?"

"Generally only when I can't avoid it."

Octavia shakes her head. "Seriously, Kassander. I hoped you would have patched things up by now."

"If you're about to give me a speech about how necromancy isn't all that bad, I swear to Five…"

Octavia chuckles. "Very well. But the girl served under me and sacrificed a lot. I'd like her to be happy."

"Oh, Silver's happy. She's always happy."

"Just not thanks to you, huh?"

Kass shrugs uncomfortably, and Octavia drops the subject.

"So, she thinks someone is targeting me specifically. Do you agree with that?" she asks.

Kass grunts affirmatively. "Our mystery spellcaster may well be one of the enemies that attacked us seven years ago. And if that's true, you make for an obvious target as one of our only surviving generals."

Octavia nods slowly. "If they have something of mine, they can track me to this place."

Octavia has always had a deeper knowledge of magic than most other paladins. Personal interest, she calls it.

She takes a big sip of tea. "But why? Revenge?"

"They might blame you for their defeat."

"There were other high-profile fighters. Pride, for one. Your dear wife, for another."

"Maybe. But you might have killed someone's kid during the war. Who fucking knows what the enemy is thinking?"

Octavia nods again. "Very well. I understand your concern. Every second I spend here is a second I'm putting the people of this district in danger, yes?"

Kass nods with clenched teeth. He doesn't like this. It feels like an admission of defeat to ask Octavia to leave her home. But the thought of Allen and Andrea trying to defeat the townspeople from the white, dripping demon makes his blood run cold.

Instinctively, he reaches for the onyx stones. All remain cold. He should make sure that Silver still has hers. Just in case.

"You could stay with us," he offers. Octavia refused all post-war honours and payments for a reason. She wants nothing to do with king Ithya and she'll hate living in the castle.

His former general laughs, but there is little humour in it.

"And put you and your lovely wife at risk? I think not."

"We can handle ourselves. And Silver would appreciate the company."

Octavia smirks. "That's sweet. But I reckon the only places in this town that could hold off a demon of the calibre you describe are the castle or the mage tower."

"Your pick," Kass says, although he knows the decision is as good as made. Octavia and Pride hate each other. Or rather, the former paladin general hates Pride with a passion Kass finds hard to reconcile with his impression of Octavia as a calm and reasonable woman.

But he reckons that whatever happened between them is their burden to bear and very much none of his business.

"I suppose I shall have to see how much of a grudge Ithya insists on keeping," Octavia says and walks into her bedroom. She takes a leather bag from the top of her wardrobe and throws random assortments of clothes and shoes on her bed. Kass watches her fold her things, then awkwardly returns to the living room, distracting himself with more tea.

"So, little Kass is a bigshot city watch commander now," Octavia calls from the other room. "And how's that been for you, boy?"

"It's a whole lot of bull."

Not all paladins serve the city watch. But Kass wanted to make a difference even after the war. More fool him. Octavia laughs from the other room. Kass elaborates.

"You usually don't get involved until it's too late. The job's twenty per cent dealing with corpses, twenty per cent dealing with assholes, and fifty per cent bureaucracy."

"So, you do it for the ten per cent of the time when you get to save people?"

Kass hmm-s in affirmation. "At least it's a better bloody ratio than we had in the army."

"That is true," Octavia says with a heavy voice. Not many people survived when the rifts in the planes first appeared. In many ways, the world ended seven years ago. Pathas says he feels like a ghost inhabiting a ruined time. Like the world is so much fuller of death than it is of life. Silver disagrees with that. She says she can tell that most of the dead have moved on.

"I get that you left Two's order, but you could join the city watch," Kass says, not for the first time. "I can't say you'd enjoy it, but they could use you. Nobody can inspire recruits like you inspired us."

A long pause. After a few more moments, his former general emerges from her bedroom, packed bag in hand.

"You lead people now, Kass," she says slowly. "You've avoided it long enough, but now you do. How do you feel when you look at your squires?"

"Fucking terrified," he admits.

"That you'll get them killed?"

"Among other things."

"Yes. I felt terrified when I was allocated my first squadron. Half of them died during my first battle. And things didn't much improve after that. Wars are won on surprisingly slim margins, Kass." Octavia's voice is quiet.

"Someone has to be in charge," Kass replies.

"Very true. And I was. For a long time."

"We're not fighting a war anymore, general. Peacetime responsibilities are different," Kass argues.

"Are you so sure we're not at war anymore? Did we ever get a surrender from our enemies? A peace treaty?"

"No, but I'm noticing a distinct lack of armies outside our gates."

Octavia shrugs. "For now. You know that anyone with even a cursory link to the military will be drafted as soon as a scout spots so much as a shadow in one of the big rifts."

"Sure. But you could also slip in the shower and break your neck. The present is the only time that matters."

That's one of Silver's lines, and usually Kass thinks it's bullshit. In this context, however, it works.

Octavia laughs. If she realises where this grain of wisdom came from, she leaves it uncommented. "That's a very wise attitude, boy. Probably too wise for someone as old as me."

She sighs. "I used to live in the future. As a young squire, I was consumed with the unfairness I saw around me, and no effort I made to improve things ever felt like enough."

"And now?"

"Now I can't stop thinking about the past. About all the things I did wrong. All the people I got killed."

She looks him straight in the eyes, but he notices how her back curves inwards and her fingers clench around her wrists.

"None of us are free from guilt," he offers, although the words sound hollow.

"Fuck off with your platitudes, Kass," Octavia replies with a laugh, then shakes her head.

"I made a lot of mistakes in my youth. Fighting in the war, taking on all the responsibilities I could – it was a way to atone. And although I think I can never fully make up for what I did, I would like to think I've earned some peace."

Kass feels his thoughts start to race.

"These mistakes you mention. Tell me if this is none of my bloody business, but could they be why the demon is after you?" he asks. It is a half-hearted question. Too much of him wants his former general to be infallible.

Octavia raises her eyebrows but hesitates momentarily as she takes his suspicion to heart. She shakes her head.

"Not even the gods know of my transgressions," she finally responds. "And they have committed worse sins than I."

Kass frowns.

"What do you mean?"

Octavia hesitates. "No one is blameless, Kass. You know that."

"Sure, we're all monsters," he agrees too readily. But that isn't what she meant, and they both know it. He stares at her until she shifts under his gaze.

"What are you not telling me?" he asks. He has an inkling that this is important. That this might be connected to the reason Octavia resigned from her position as paladin general. Age, peace, and all that nonsense aside, there must be a real reason someone would toss aside everything they ever worked for.

Octavia hesitates again, and that alone is enough to worry Kass. His general isn't one to waver. She didn't hesitate to ask everyone under her command to ride into a burning inferno. What is scaring her now?

"You still serve him, don't you, Kass? Five?"

Kass narrows his eyes.

"Obviously."

"And you're happy doing that?"

"He helped save us. More than any of the other gods. No offence."

"Why do you think that?" Octavia asks.

"Because he gave everyone a fucking chance," Kass says, his voice rising. "When the bloody army closed its gates to common folk who wanted to enlist, Five took us in and made us paladins. Gave humanity an actual advantage."

"A numbers advantage, yes? Even though most of you young paladins didn't make it through your first week under siege."

Kass doesn't appreciate her tone. "He gave us a chance. That's more than anyone else ever did," he snaps.

"Yes, of course. And it was just an unlucky coincidence that the enemy was so strong that our numbers didn't matter."

Kass stretches out his hands. "It was war, general. One side always wins, and lots of people always die."

"Very true. And why wouldn't both sides be powerful if their gods supported them?"

Kass shakes his head. "What are you –?"

"What if I told you it was the same gods, Kass?" Octavia whispers. Her back is bent, and she suddenly carries each one of her years. He sees the light in her eyes breaking underneath the memories.

"The same gods accepted worshippers from both sides of the trenches. They lent out miracles to both armies in equal parts," she says.

Kass feels a hot flash run across his body. His muscles tense, ready to jump into action and defend himself from invisible enemies. He takes a few deep breaths and tries to fight the feeling.

You're okay, he tells himself. The enemy is gone. You're okay. He repeats it like a mantra.

"Why?" he simply asks.

"Why not? It's double the number of worshippers for them. So many more prayers, so many more souls that migrate to their planes and serve them with their afterlives."

"How would you know that?" Kass asks. The last seven years taught him not to use words like 'impossible'. There is no longer any point in doubt, only in hope.

"I saw it with my own eyes. The enemy used invocations to the same effect as our clerics and paladins. Prayed at same shrines, made the same gestures, followed the same rituals."

"Their gods could just be very similar."

"Kass."

"You could be wrong."

"That is always a possibility. But I wouldn't have staked my life on a hunch."

She wouldn't. Kass knows his general. He never doubted her before, and old habits are hard to break. But before he can decide, she asks him to escort her to the castle. They walk the grounds in silence.

Chapter 6

Wartime

When she was first drafted into the army, Silver expected to be revered as the new magister of destruction, her magical prowess swiftly carrying Old Noll to victory. It was easy for her to imagine the enemies that descended upon their world as a horde of idiotic cannon fodder and herself a wizardess supreme reigning over the skies with her newfound powers.

After the fifth battle, she was just happy to still be alive. Somehow, it had never occurred to her that the enemy side would also have spellcasters and that they would be much more experienced at attack spells and protective barriers than she was. Silver was one of three mages in her squadron and probably the least well-trained among them. Kindly old Roland was a master of ice magic, although he needed help climbing the battlements' stairs, and the pedantic diviner Melina taught Silver how to make her spells backfire less often.

Their squadron had shrunk from a hundred and fifty to forty-two. Section commander Octavia told them they had done well not to be wiped out in the last attack. Silver didn't feel like she'd done particularly well. But as she sucked in a breath of air, heavy with the smell of burning wood, she felt grateful. Every moment was another chance.

During the last battle, one of the junior paladins had pushed her out of the way of a mid-sized rock. It had come down so suddenly that Silver hadn't even seen it. She would have been crushed without his intervention, but she didn't have a second to register her shock. More spells needed casting, and more attacks needed dodging. A moment's hesitation meant death, and Silver D'arren refused to die in this stupid war.

The junior paladin was a man about her age, wearing a perpetual scowl. He usually sat with Pathas or the rogue they'd allowed into the army. Whenever she'd seen him in the company of the other paladins, he categorically ignored them.

She might have paid a bit more attention to him than strictly necessary. It wasn't every day a brooding young paladin saved your life, and his propensity to be short-lipped had the positive side-effect that he hadn't said something off-putting yet.

She had asked Melina to swap watch duty, so she'd catch him atop the battlements just when his shift was about to end. Much to Silver's chagrin, every shift had to have a mage on duty in case the enemy spellcasters plotted something. Not that they could see much from the city walls. Plotting mages could easily hide amidst the thousands and thousands of enemy soldiers below. But, as Octavia told her, sometimes looking like you're preventing a problem is enough to lift morale. So, Silver hadn't slept much.

The young paladin stared blankly at the burning torches and campfires.

"Hey," she said and leaned against the battlements. It was loud, even up here. A whole district of wooden barracks, tents, and temporary watchtowers grew next to what was left of the city walls. Before the war, this part of the city had been full of guesthouses and public baths. It had been the first to be levelled by the enemy's surprise attack.

The paladin startled, then stared at her. It took him a few moments to recognise her, a fact that irritated Silver more than she cared to admit.

"Hey," he replied. "You're one of the mages, aren't you?"

"What gave it away?" Silver asked with a grin. She wore long blue robes, and spell components were smeared across her hands and wrists.

"Your inability to dodge projectiles," the paladin responded drily. Silver laughed. The sound rang loud and awkward in her ears.

"Right. That's fair." She coughed. "Thanks for that, by the way. I would be -"

"A bloody mess of crushed bones and sinews? No problem. We don't have enough mages to play fast and loose with you guys."

"Your concern is touching," Silver replied drily. The paladin looked at her for a moment, and she realised he wasn't about to continue the conversation of his own accord.

She took a step closer and held out her hand. "I'm Silver."

He was visibly taken aback but tried to disguise his surprise with an unnecessarily firm handshake.

"Kassander. Kass."

"Nice to meet you, Kass."

"Likewise, Silver. All jests aside, it's good to have you mages on our side. We'd be fucked without you." He looked her up and down. "Even without you noble lot."

"How do you –?"

Kass grinned sardonically. She noticed the scrapes on his armour and the brittle metal of his sword. Both obviously hand-me-downs from soldiers who weren't lucky enough to make it this far.

"You want a list?" Kass asks. "The name, for one thing. No normal person calls their daughter that."

Silver grinned. "Maybe my parents wanted to humble me a little. Make me feel second best at least once in my life."

Kass laughed, but there was a hard gleam in his eyes. "At least she's self-aware."

"Oh, self-awareness will get you anywhere," Silver responds. "I learned that pretty quickly after being drafted."

She leaned further on the battlement, resting her face on her left palm. Kass's smile faded fast. He was clearly not a man who smiled easily.

He looked down at the tents and campfires below, a routine check. Everything seemed calm. Silver didn't think he'd say anything else, and she didn't want to bother him with inane chatter. But when she started to think up a polite way to take her leave, he surprised her by speaking again.

"You were drafted? You didn't join voluntarily?"

Silver shrugged. "It all happened pretty quickly. I considered enlisting, but before I could decide, the army already said that all spellcasters had to join."

Kass hesitated. "I'm sorry they did that."

"Wasn't your call, was it?"

"No. But still. Serving the army should be a choice."

Silver disagreed but thought it was sweet of him to say.

"It's fine," she said nonchalantly. "As you said, we're useful to have around." She winked. "If I wasn't here, who would protect all you meat shields out there?"

"What, from wayward trebuchets? I think I've been doing okay so far."

Kass smiled again, and Silver playfully prodded his arm. "Hey, now. Do I need to save your life for you to stop bringing that up?"

"Sure. Let's say you do. I could always do with someone else watching my back."

He held her gaze, and she felt a bit of heat on her face.

"It's a deal, paladin-man," she said, feeling her voice breaking slightly.

He flinched. She frowned. "Sorry. Not a paladin?"

"No, no, I am. It's just – that whole thing's still new." He shrugged. "At the start of the war, they wouldn't let people like me enlist unless we were serving under a bloody god."

"People like you?"

"Normal people." He noticed her confused expression and sighed.

"People who haven't been combat-trained," he explained. "Stupid fucking rule. Lack of training doesn't mean you can't hold your own when it comes down to it."

He shrugged again.

"At the start of the war, Five allowed everyone to become a paladin. Normally that's a rare honour and involves a whole lot of religious crap, but I reckon Five predicted how bad the fighting was gonna get. We needed more people in the army, no matter their background."

He sighed. "Or maybe it was a stupid idea. Most of the lot who joined with me are dead now." He gestured at himself with an undeniable flourish of irony. "I got lucky."

"All that tavern-fighting must have paid off." Silver noted with a raised eyebrow.

"Oh, it did." He relaxed when she smiled.

"Well, honoured paladin of Five," Silver said. "I look forward to witnessing a whole host of divine miracles from such a devoted follower."

"Oh, piss off," Kass laughed.

"Shouldn't your god sting you for that kind of language?" Silver teased.

"Don't give him ideas now."

Silver tried to think of something else to say, but another soldier climbed to the top of the battlements and relieved Kass from watch duty. The paladin looked reluctant to leave, but tiredness and hunger won out. Before climbing down the ladder, he placed a warm, broad hand on Silver's shoulder.

"Be safe, mageling. Remember, you still have to save my life."

"Count on it, Kass."

Chapter 7

Octavia receives an icy welcome at the castle, and Kass tells the guards that she is to receive the best protection the realm can offer. The castle staff don't take his warnings of demons crawling out of rifts particularly seriously, which pisses him off. He reminds them that he saved their and their parents' asses during the war. Perhaps he gets a little too loud.

The castle staff get nervous and call for reinforcements. Amaya is the only one willing to face off against an angry Kass. She's not technically a member of the city watch, but she is one of the city's highest-ranking investigators. More importantly, Kass likes her. They share a no-nonsense approach that often sees them on the wrong side of courtier approval.

"Kassander D'arren," Amaya says when she finds him lurking outside Octavia's room. She is an inconspicuous presence, and her clothing is elaborate yet unobtrusive. Everything about Amaya is made to fit the way she wants to be seen.

"Amaya Pekka," he responds with a slight nod. Amaya doesn't do handshakes or eye contact. It suits him well enough.

She hands him a cup of coffee made exactly the way he likes it. He takes a deep sip and sighs with pleasure. "You're the best."

"You only say that when you want something." Amaya nods at the two guards, who try not to look like they are listening. "What's this all about?"

"Octavia has a demonic stalker," Kass explains. "Already massacred one household. If she stays at her place, she'll get half the docks killed."

Amaya shrugs. It's been a while since Old Noll has faced an extraplanar crisis, but it is generally hard to faze her. She takes on the goriest cases, seeing as the bloody remains disturb her less than her colleagues.

"Okay," she says. "But the castle is already guarded by a small army of spellcasters, archers, and soldiers. What are two more guards going to do?"

Kass lowers his voice. "My mage consultant believes a manmade rift was created to let this demon through. Or demons. There may be several." He gestures at Octavia's locked door. "If the demon suddenly appears in her room, we'll need a warning system. It could endanger the king, too."

"Is that possible?" Amaya asks. "Could a demon create a rift? Wouldn't you need to use magic for that?"

Kass shrugs. "Even some of those crazy death cultists are playing around with the rifts, and they're high on Five-knows-what. Why wouldn't a bloody demon succeed if it tries hard enough?"

With how many people have been trying to mess with the rifts, the fabric of reality needs a bloody tailor. Still, he knows he's grasping at straws. Amaya is right that you need magic to peel open rifts, whether it is channelled by a rogue cultist or Pride herself. And demons don't have magic. At least the ones they fought during the last war didn't.

He remembers the horned, winged, and tailed demonic mercenaries that fought on the enemy's side. They were strong, quick, and well-trained, often needing more than a dozen soldiers' efforts to take them down. Kass sincerely hopes that in addition to all that, the demons haven't also learned how to cast spells. More likely, an enemy mage created the rift in House Karthe and hired the demons as his personal assassins.

But it's his job to cover all eventualities.

"Whose idea was this? About the rift being manmade?" Amaya asks.

"Silver's," Kass mutters.

"Oh, Silver," Amaya says, her eyes lighting up. "How is she?"

"The same. Fine. Silver's always fine," Kass responds, exasperated.

"Well, you'll tell her hello from me."

"Yeah, yeah. Now, about those guards...?"

"I'll make sure they stick around," Amaya promises. "No bother. I'd also prefer to have a warning if we're going to have demons running around the castle."

"Thanks. I owe you," Kass grumbles.

"No, you don't. Public safety is my job."

"Well. Thanks, regardless."

He takes another sip from his coffee. He should go back to the barracks and meet up with Allen and Andrea. He should follow up with the city watchmen he sent to chase Silver's other demon leads. And after all that, he should go home and rest.

He doesn't want to do any of it, though. He feels Octavia's words weighing him down like a sickness.

"What are you working on right now?" he asks Amaya. The investigator is always happy to talk about work.

Yet another death cult has formed at the corners of the markets and the docks. Kass knows the spot Amaya is talking about. A blue-rimmed rift appeared in the centre of an old clock tower, which once housed impoverished artists and academics. Now, the cultists have driven off everyone who doesn't want to participate in their drug-fuelled sex rituals.

On the last day of each week, they try to throw themselves into the rift stark naked, even though the barrier Pride cast on the rift's exterior shows no signs of weakening. The cultists consider Pride's shield an affront to nature and are trying to dispel it with the rather unimpressive force of skin against magic.

Kass sighs. Death cultists. Maybe one of these days, he'll find himself agreeing with them. Maybe the world *should* live up to its inevitable fate and be swallowed up by an ever-expanding rift. After all, he already has a hard time accepting that humanity survived the war. A bit of eternal peace and quiet sounds mighty good.

Amaya reassures him that the cultists aren't too much of a threat, seeing as they don't have any spellcasters amidst their ranks. Given that, they are unlikely to cause any meaningful damage to the fabric of existence, at least if you discount all the noise complaints. That, and on Thursdays, they perform a bunch of ritualistic sacrifices (all volunteers, apparently), which causes an excessive amount of work for the public cleaners. Amaya is down to the last four cult members she has to track down and bring to trial for the latest series of ritual-related deaths. It is thankless work, but at least it isn't difficult to track down a bunch of robed fanatics screaming about the end of the world.

Kass lingers for a little longer than needed, then he sets off. He can easily walk to the barracks. He just needs to cut through the castle's botanical gardens, which are about to carry their first Spring blossoms. According to Amaya, the gardens currently host a water exhibition by a noble artist who learned a bit of illusion magic in her youth. Iridescent raindrops hang motionless in the air, breaking apart the light that flitters between the still-bare trees and gets caught in the garden's labyrinthine canals.

Silver would like this. She would point out every pretty effect even though she probably knew a thousand ways the spell could have been improved.

The barracks are a nonsensical and impromptu collection of wooden buildings, surprisingly sturdy tents, and a defunct bit of tram that was catapulted into the district during the war. The original barracks were two bungalows connected by a small courtyard and a coffee truck that was somehow never staffed. During the war, said bungalows grew into a distorted mess of a district, swallowing any- and everything in its path. No part of its monstrous body feels permanent, but without a peace treaty, the military buildings can't be removed.

However, after a slew of citizens complained about the lacking aesthetic quality of the district, architects are now trying to upgrade the makeshift offices, training halls, and sleeping quarters. For months now, the barracks have been full of cranes and scaffolding, and their efforts have somehow made things even worse.

Kass was taken to the barracks as a teenager. During a drunken bar brawl, he hit a soldier who insulted his uncle. Neither he nor the soldier admitted to anything when they were taken in for questioning, so the officers begrudgingly let young Kass off. That day, he swore to himself that he'd never come back to this place.

On the way to the city watch meeting hall, Kass finds Allen and Andrea sitting by the side of a building site, drinking green tea and chewing on baked potatoes.

Andrea profoundly apologises when they see Kass, mortified that they dared to take a break. Allen merely greets his commander and offers 'Sir' a bit of potato.

"Found any signs of our demon?" Kass asks, ignoring Allen's offer.

"No, Sir," Andrea confesses. "We were thorough, but to the best of our knowledge, no demon has made its way to the docks."

"Good. Thank Five," Kass says. "I found Octa – I mean, former paladin general Octavia Nwosu, whom I suspect the demon from the plague quarters might be after."

Andrea's eyes widen, and they mouth Octavia's name in reverence. Kass continues.

"I moved her into the castle for now. Security there should keep our extraplanar critter at bay. It can try its bloody claws at the castle's art installation."

"Why would they be after this Octavia person?" Allen asks, chomping down on another bit of potato.

Andrea shoots him an incredulous look.

"Octavia Nwosu was one of our most highly revered army commanders during the war," they explain. "She was responsible for winning the battle of the fire barrels, and –"

They interrupt themselves. "I heard she died."

Kass shrugs. "After she told king Ithya to go fuck himself, there have been many rumours about Octavia. It's best to ignore them."

Andrea silently repeats the words, their mouth slightly open.

Kass lets his squires finish their lunch, then drags them to the city watch meeting hall, where he enquires about the watchmen he sent after the other demons. None of the watchmen spotted any signs of demonic activity, although Kass can tell they are pretty relaxed about the whole thing. Few people fought demons during the last war. The inhabitants of the hell planes weren't the primary force that attacked them, after all. The enemy hired demons to reinforce their ranks, but that was a good while into the fighting. And the demons stopped coming after the paladins took out a few hundred of them.

Some people don't think demons are real. That hell is just a word for a bad day. Kass would give anything to share that belief. To get rid of that endless pressure on his chest. He almost gets used to it, and then it's back, reminding him that no amount of time will let him run from his mind.

Kass gives the watchmen a dressing down about their attitude, then tells them to stay vigilant and patrol their assigned perimeters at least twice daily. Once they're done grumbling and rolling their eyes, he moves to his office and sends his squires home for the day. He sits in a former tram driver's cabin, which came loose when said tram somersaulted across the district and remained permanently attached to the office of Kass's predecessor.

Andrea brings him lunch when he writes his findings into a report for the king. He snaps at them to move their ass home already, and his squire laughs.

When Kass finishes writing his report, the sun is beginning to set. He decides to walk home rather than take the tram or, gods forbid, a carriage. He hopes the walk will clear his head, but his head decides to do the opposite. On the entire way home, Octavia's words repeat over and over in his head, cast into iron by memory.

So many more prayers, so many more souls that migrate to their planes and serve them with their afterlives.

The worst thing is that it makes sense. The gods want to be worshipped and adored. Otherwise, they wouldn't ask humans to build temples and shrines in their honour. Otherwise, they would help people without needing to be asked. Otherwise, they wouldn't care to spread their philosophies and dogmas amongst their followers.

The gods have taken sides in conflicts before. The crusades that shook the human realm a few decades earlier were a culmination of ideological differences between the followers of different gods.

Kass prefers not to think of these days too much, especially since Five was one of the gods for whom the bloodiest battles were fought. More than his god, he blames fanatics who misinterpret Five's ideas of justice. Who don't understand that free will extends to other people.

When the planes ripped apart, everyone assumed the gods were on their side. The clerics healed the wounded and revived the dead, after all. It felt good to think that humanity was fighting on the side of divine righteousness. Often, that belief was the only thing that kept Kass going during the wartime years.

Kass kicks a bit of trash from the sidewalk and sighs deeply. Part of him doesn't want to know if Octavia is right. If she is, it would not just devastate humanity's morale but cause the most devastating form of anger. Helplessness. It isn't like they can punish a god for their lack of partisanship.

But Kass knows that good sense won't stop him from doubting. He pushes open the gate to his and Silver's mansion. A small rift, no longer than his index finger, dances in the quiet evening breeze just above the handle. Sometimes, Kass accidentally grazes it and feels the heat of another plane coursing through.

Part of him wants to look through all the rifts that are scattered across Old Noll to explore the endless hall of half-open doorways. Part of him wants to get to know the world he saved.

But he doesn't. He goes inside without another glance at the gate and plans to disappear into his room and go straight to sleep. The longer he is awake, the stronger his anger festers inside him, as if his consciousness is kindling to his rage.

He lets the door fall shut behind him. A loud bang rings through the hallway, and he hears Silver startle awake in the adjoining living room. He freezes, and then her voice floats into the hallway.

"Kass? Is that you?"

He grunts as affirmation and hopes he can leave it at that. He hears her shuffling on the sofa and the soft thump of a blanket falling to the ground. A fire is crackling, and he sees the soft orange-red light of the flames reach out of the half-open door to the living room.

"Kass?" his wife calls again, this time more hesitantly. He should just go. He should go to bed and wait for the next day when he'll be calmer.

Instead, he follows her voice.

Silver lies on the couch, her back propped up by three impossibly large pillows. Her purple blanket fell on the floor, revealing a simple black dress that rode up her legs while she was asleep. Her light hair is a little frazzled, but she obviously tried to smooth it out before he entered the room.

"Yes, Silver?" he says, ignoring how his chest tightens at the sight of her.

"Did you find your demons?" his wife asks, then rubs a bit of sleep out of the corner of her eyes.

"One of them," he replies, then describes the encounter. Silver is no demonologist, but he hopes she might recognise a description from her general magic studies at the tower. But she is as puzzled as he is.

"If it raced off without its head, that indicates we are dealing with an extremely powerful creature," she says slowly. "That, or the spell commanding it is powerful enough to override bodily impulses."

"Such as death?"

"Such as death."

She rubs her eyes again, then blinks up at him. "And you're okay? Sounds like it was a tough fight."

"I'm fine, Silver."

She nods. She knows better than to prod.

"I'll look at some of Pride's books that describe the hell planes," she promises. "I sincerely doubt there'll be anything more specific than scattered observations by scared researchers, but it might be better than nothing."

Kass nods. Silver cocks her head to the side, then laughs.

"You're welcome."

"Hm?" he grunts. "What, you want a paycheque?"

"I'd like you to say thank you, you brute," Silver says with another laugh. Kass is not in a laughing mood, but he thanks her nonetheless.

"So, who was the demon after?" his wife asks. She angles her legs to make room on the sofa, so he sits down. He can feel his temper boiling from overcooked anxiety, but she moved her legs for him, and he knows that it hurts her to do that. So, he sits down, *just for a moment*, he tells himself.

"Octavia."

Silver's eyes grow wide. "Is she okay?"

"Of course she is. I would have told you if she wasn't."

Silver's doubtful look tells him she doesn't believe that, but she leaves the remark uncommented. Instead, she purses her lips, still pale after sleep.

"Who would be after Octa after all this time?" she asks. "If it's retaliation for the war, Ithya would make for a more obvious target."

"The king?" Kass shakes his head. "Could be a personal revenge quest. Octavia actually fought on the bloody battlefield. Kings don't do that."

Silver hesitates. "I've been thinking about that. If it's revenge our culprit is after, would they send demons in their stead? If you're mad and powerful enough to open a planar rift, wouldn't you just kill your enemies yourself?"

Kass nods slowly. "I see what you mean. But until we catch the demons, all we can do is speculate."

"Hmm." Silver twirls a lock of hair around her slim, pale fingers. "How's Octa?"

"She's fine," Kass grunts.

A short pause.

"She was asking after you," he adds.

"Oh, was she?" She laughs. "I've always liked her. She was never as stuck-up and thick-sculled as the rest of them. No wonder she was the only one with the guts to tell Ithya where to shove his idiotic honorifics."

Kass isn't sure if by 'the rest of them' Silver is referring to the other war officers or the other paladins. Either way, it rubs him the wrong way.

"Do you even know why Octavia resigned from her bloody post?" he asks.

Silver shrugs.

"Well, I expect she came to hate Two for allowing the war to happen in the first place," she says, not matching his sour tone. "That whole philosophical chestnut of 'why are omnipotent gods allowing all this suffering to happen, existential angst, etcetera, etcetera'. And I imagine all the decisions Ithya made during the war didn't help with Octa's general feelings of disillusionment."

Kass scoffs. "And you think we should all do what she did? Give up on our gods and live according to our – what? Desires? Shitty, biased understanding of right and wrong?"

"And what would be so wrong with that, Kass?" Silver snaps. "It's not like Octa has done anything wrong since she resigned. She is just living her life."

"Not everyone is like Octavia," Kass counters, remembering the effortless kindness he had always found in his general's eyes. Where the other gods' chosen excluded him because of his upbringing, Octavia never judged him on anything other than merit.

"And she could be doing more. She could help restore the city," he continues, even though the words feel like a betrayal.

"She has given enough," Silver snaps, and he can't wholly disagree with the sentiment. But these things are never about fairness as much as they are about duty. He tells her that, and Silver scoffs.

"Duty! Duty to whom?"

"People who can't defend themselves."

"Oh, and everyone we saved during the war is a good person, then?" she asks, her voice rising.

"Doesn't matter. Whether they're a good person or not, everyone has a bloody right to live," Kass replies.

"That doesn't make it my duty to look after each and every one of them."

"Not even if you could make their lives better?"

"That's an impossible hypothetical, Kass," Silver responds, shifting uncomfortably. "You're never going to make things right for everyone. Some people will always benefit more than others. You just have to get on with it as best you can."

"And by 'getting on with it', you mean living in a five-bedroom mansion with your parents' servants?"

"You live here too," Silver snaps back. He thinks she's being unfair but bites his tongue. Yes, he could move out. They could live separately and get a divorce and never speak to each other again. Silver doesn't want that. He doesn't either, even though it would be better for them.

Silence settles between them. Silver reaches for her blanket, but her arms aren't quite long enough. Kass picks it up and spreads it over her legs. She smiles, and after a moment of hesitation, she speaks again, her eyes half-lidded and voice raspy.

"It makes you think. A general like Octavia renouncing the god of sunlight, whom she served for her entire life. I suppose there's nothing like war to shake your faith."

She gives him a meaningful look. Octavia's words ring in his ears like a curse. What if she is right? Would it matter? Should he renounce Five and throw away paladinhood, the proudest achievement of his life?

He knows what Silver would say. She has asked him to leave Five's services many times. In her mind, if he no longer has to adhere to his god's dogmas, he won't be punished for being married to a necromancer. He supposes that from the perspective of a spoiled, brilliant, megalomaniacal noble, that passes for a halfway convincing argument.

She doesn't understand that faith operates on free will. That the gods never force their desires on humans. The only punishment Five ever subjected him to was a lack of response to his invocations. Disappointment and disinterest that make his heart crumble to pieces. And what marriage could be built on him bearing that?

"Look, Silver -" he starts, but she interrupts him.

"Yes, yes, I know. I won't try to talk you into anything."

"Good," he grunts.

"Because it's not like you've ever listened to anyone in your entire godsdamned life."

Kass feels a headache approaching. "And why should I listen to you?" he asks. "You don't even follow any of the gods."

"You don't need to listen to me," Silver says with deliberate nonchalance. "I'm well aware that you won't. But Octa -"

"Octavia has her view on things, and I have mine."

"And you don't think that after all her years of serving Two, she might have a clearer perspective than you do?"

The headache reaches him at the same time as a vein on his forehead starts to pulsate.

"You don't know what you're talking about," he snaps.

"Don't I?"

"No, Silver. For once in your life, you don't know bloody everything."

She narrows her eyes, and he guesses that she's now realised that his earlier conversation with Octavia involved more than pleasantries.

"Then tell me, Kass. Tell me why Octa resigned."

"No. Not my place to. If she wants you to know, she'll tell you."

If he tells Silver, she'll bite into the idea like a ripe fruit. He can imagine the juice dripping down her face, and he can't promise he won't lick it from her skin. And then no god or propriety or bitterness will stop him from falling until she consumes him.

Things could be like they were. They could fuck on the couch, and he could hold her in his arms until she falls asleep on his chest.

"Why not?" she asks, her voice shrill.

But he's not ready. He's not ready to acknowledge the possibility that Octavia might be right about the gods, let alone conceive of a world where he might follow in her footsteps.

"It's been a long day, Silver. Can you just let it go?" he asks. She looks like that is the last thing she wants to do, but after a few moments, she pushes down her anger and shrugs.

"Suit yourself, Kass."

She holds onto her blanket and sighs. Suddenly, the sight of her makes him sick. Why does he always have to be the one questioning things? It isn't as though his choices were what caused their marriage to fall apart.

"If you're so disinterested in making a difference, Silver, it's easier to quit a bloody profession than a divine calling."

"You weren't called," his wife scoffs. "You joined Five's order because he was the only one who'd take you. Don't make it sound more special than it was."

She knows exactly how to hurt him. How to eat away at his pride until he feels like an insecure commoner raised far above his station.

"It doesn't have to start as a calling to become one," he replies quietly.

"Whatever, Kass. I'm not quitting magic, and you know that."

"Oh, piss off. When I say I don't want to leave the service of a god –"

"Because magic is just a tool," she interrupts him. "Blindly following the whims of a god – a creature we know almost nothing about – is completely different."

"Yeah, it is bloody different. You're desperate for power. I'm helping to make the world a better place."

He feels like a pretentious ass for repeating the temple's dogma. Silver scoffs.

"And what if you're wrong? What if Five isn't the paragon of virtue you think he is?"

Her words cut like a knife. Kass shakes his head and gets up without another word. Silver does not call him back.

Chapter 8

As soon as Kass wakes up and checks the date, he knows it's going to be a bad day. Today, king Ithya meets with his wider advisory board to discuss current and ongoing threats to the city. To Kass's never-ending dismay, he sits on that board.

When Ithya's sister, Donheira, was queen, she never attended any meetings. Sometimes, Kass wonders if she was onto something. It was supposedly a member of the advisory board who recommended that she go to the enemy's camp and negotiate the city's surrender. Donheira never returned from that parley, although parts of her were seen on black iron spikes outside the walls. Now, nobody wants to remember who gave their former queen that priceless piece of advice.

Ithya takes his royal duties more seriously than his sister ever did. Kass respects him for that. Donheira had been a princess through and through, schooled in the fine arts, charm, and diplomacy, a model dancer and an elegant fencer. None of that had prepared her for seeing a country through a war.

As a child, Ithya's face sustained severe burns during a castle fire. He was left with the leftmost quarter of his forehead sunk inward, painting a permanent fleshy scowl on his features. Afterwards, the prince took few chances not to live up to the gloomy disposition his looks prepared him for. He threw himself into scholarship and studied magic with more dedication than was generally acceptable for someone of his station. Through his love of the arcane arts, he cultivated a close friendship with Pride, and he later supported her in rising through the ranks of the mage guild.

According to several courtiers' reports, Ithya was devastated to find that his sister had been killed and more devastated still to find himself next in line to become king. Still, Kass reckons that the shy, awkward boy more than rose to the call of duty. Crowned with a hasty, bare-bones ceremony, he did what it took to see them through the war. He signed off on dangerous arcane experiments, suicide commandos, and public executions of suspected conspirators. And it worked. Humanity held together. As bitter as the fruits of victory might taste, in his rational moments, Kass can appreciate that it's probably better than being dead.

Kass and Silver arrive at the castle separately. He took the tram, and she took her family's carriage. After their spat a few days ago, they have not spoken. It isn't hard to avoid each other with Kass patrolling the barracks and castle grounds as he hunts for the mysterious demonic assassins.

No luck so far. He feels like the demons are waiting for something.

The wider advisory board consists of distinguished war veterans and the resident army general Markos Alt, one of the few nobles of this city with actual battle experience. Ithya also invites merchants from the trading guilds, supposed 'experts' on rift magic, clerics from the gods' temples, civil engineers, and teachers. Fifty people sit on the board, and although Kass can see the sense in bringing everyone together, he never feels like they get much done.

But maybe Ithya takes something away from the meetings. Kass certainly hopes so, given how much they irritate him.

Kass spots Amaya as he walks up the stairs towards the castle's main gates. She is drinking a cup of coffee and stares at a point in the distance, past the thin line of trees on the first bailey. She doesn't notice him walk past, and Kass suppresses a small smile. There is a reason Amaya is rarely used in field operations.

To his satisfaction, he notes that, as per his request, the number of guards inside the castle has increased. He knows that he isn't the guardsmen's favourite commander – that would be Girah, who Kass finds insufferable – but it is gratifying that his reputation still carries enough weight for his instructions not to be dismissed.

The wider advisory board meet in the second-floor drawing room, the 'blue' room named after the wall tapestries that depict long-faded scenes from sunny seas. A mahogany table spreads across the room, and pale light falls through thin windowpanes. Small chairs sit uncomfortably close together. Only Ithya's chair on the far end is sized to fit an actual adult.

As usual, Kass is early. He lingers outside the room, unsure if he should go inside and risk being forced into uncomfortable small talk or stand out here like an idiot who doesn't know where he's going.

He sees small carts full of meats, cheeses and fruits arranged in the drawing room, complete with pitchers of wine. He rolls his eyes. Someone has ordered far too much food. From the looks of it, they are in for another long, unproductive meeting, full of booze-heavy complaints and impossible suggestions.

People arrive and trickle into the room. Kass stands awkwardly near the food like a servant hired to hand out plates and cups. Silver arrives a few minutes late but before the king. One of the nobles, whose name Kass doesn't remember, pushes her wheelchair, and she laughs at something he said.

He looks away before her eyes meet his, and when he enters the room, she hasn't saved him a seat. He sits between a merchant and one of the elderly civil engineers who has a propensity of falling asleep during the latter parts of the meetings. The merchant shoots him a timid glance and looks like he wants to ask him a bunch of pointless questions. Kass takes a deep breath. He has made it his mission today not to lose his temper.

A few moments later, king Ithya enters the room with six high-ranking guardsmen. He wears a steel-grey breastplate, and his long, dark hair is greasy and in need of a cut. The king has to force himself to look up at them in greeting, and his smile is worse than a poor attempt.

He sits down at the head of the table and takes a few breaths.

"Thank you for coming. I - appreciate your time."

He isn't a man of many words and speaks infuriatingly slowly.

"I have called you here because I received several reports that require our collective attention. We will go through them in order."

Kass hopes his report will be close to the top of the list, given that it concerns not one but potentially three wayward demons. But his hopes are quickly dashed when Ithya starts with various building requisitions and trade agreements. A few hours in, servants distribute wine and food, and Kass feels his concentration waning. He hasn't said a word this whole time. As a war hero and, more importantly, a born commoner, it is frowned upon for him to weigh in on peacetime matters. The same scrutiny is not applied to Silver and the other noble veterans, of course.

Kass is not in the mood to drink, but by the time the servants walk through the room with rich-red wine pitchers in hand, he's desperately bored. He downs two glasses far too quickly and feels a soft cloud of intoxication spread throughout his body.

In retrospect, that was a mistake.

A moment later, a demon bursts through the doors, rips the wood from its hinges and carries a cloud of dust and splinters into the room.

Where the first demon was white and covered in fat-running liquid, this specimen is a fleshy spider. Its skin looks like it has been peeled off by a child, with strips of hairy, grey rind surrounding flecks of soggy flesh. The seven-legged body is crowned by a small head that rotates around its axis as it searches for its target.

An eerie ringing noise fills the air.

The king's guards form a human shield around Ithya. Two mages jump up and summon spheres of ice. They hit the demon but disappear when connecting with its skin, probably repelled by some inborn resistance. Markos Alt takes the king's arm and leads him to the other side of the room. He opens a hidden door with a brief incantation.

Kass would never have guessed the intricate wood panelling was hiding a secret corridor, although, in retrospect, he shouldn't be surprised. This place was built to keep royals safe from attacks. They are probably standing in the middle of a veritable puzzle box of tricks, traps, and secrets.

The demon roars and jumps into the wall of soldiers, piercing through their armour with its steel-hard claws. The mages shriek and one of them tumbles on his back.

Everyone else in the room stays relatively calm. There is little screaming and almost no chaos. They all lived through the end of the world, and they remember how that went.

Some manage to follow the king through the secret passage, but one of the engineers closes the way behind them, lest the demon manage to pursue them. The rest of the advisory board either race out of the room, passing the demon in a wide berth, or shuffle along windowsills, where some fall to an untimely death.

The demon kills a third guard by the time Kass reaches it. He brings down his Zweihander on the leg with which the demon is impaling the young guardswoman's body. But even with his full strength, he cannot break through its flesh. He manages to get its attention, though. The demon's head stops whirring, and its furious red eyes settle on him.

Kass feels his sword heating up. He glances down to see small flames dance on the metal. This is one of Silver's favourite spells. She used it on his and the other soldiers' weapons during the war. It was often the only thing that let them cut through their enemies' scaled skin. She used it on Kass more than the others. Maybe that's why he is still here, and they aren't.

He lifts his Zweihander, ready to make a second attempt, but the demon is faster. It twists its body around its axis, and its legs become a whirlwind of swords. They cut the air, a swell of silver rain. Kass jumps back to dodge the attacks, but two of the demon's legs strike his chest and neck. He curses internally. He should have worn armour to this stupid event.

Silver hits the demon with a spell, summoning a strong gust of wind to blow it back by several inches. Kass doesn't hesitate. Ignoring the pain that burns across his body, he brings down his sword again. The creature parries him, crossing its legs. But this time, Kass's fiery sword cuts through the demon's flesh. The creature jumps back with a pained hiss as its torn skin burns with rage.

Then, suddenly, it stops moving, and Kass's heart clenches when he realises what is happening. In a singular motion, three dead guards grab the demon's legs and hold it in place. Kass suppresses a wince but forces himself to attack. He strikes once, twice, feeling his sword sink into flesh and bone.

The creature screams in pain, but he blocks it out. He hacks at the demon until it lies on the ground in more pieces than he can count, its red, hot blood a sea in which he drowns. He hardly remembers killing it. But when the dead guards drop to the floor, he is still standing over misshapen chunks of demon and choking on his breath.

This endless pressure on his chest. Forming an impenetrable wall between who he was and who he is. He almost gets used to it until the pressure is tight enough that he can't breathe. One of these days, he is convinced it will kill him.

Silver slowly rolls over to him. They are the only people left in the room.

She sits next to him through the seconds and minutes. She knows that any touch might set him off. That his instincts don't differentiate between genuine and imagined threats. He is shaking all over and feels humiliated by his weakness, but the emotion is dulled beneath the thunder of his heart and the blood burning in his chest.

Finally, he manages to calm himself. He rubs his eyes, then nods at Silver.

"Thanks," he grumbles.

"Kass, you're bleeding," his wife says, her voice strained. He looks down at her and, for once, finds nothing but worry in her expression. He shrugs nonchalantly.

"Good. Means I'm still alive."

She rolls her eyes at his fake bravado and motions him to kneel beside her. She takes his hand and moves it to his throat. Her fingers are cool to the touch, and they break through the loudness and terror of the moment.

"Call on him, Kass. Call on Five to heal you."

"I don't know if –"

She lets go of his hand but looks at him imploringly. "Please," she simply says.

There is no arguing with that. He utters a silent prayer to his god, but as he expected, there is no reply. Not that close to the corpses Silver just reanimated, not at the behest of his wife, the necromancer.

He doesn't need to explain it to Silver. He sees the tears of frustration in the corner of her eyes and sighs.

He rips a bit of fabric from a dead soldier's tunic and presses it into his throat to still the bleeding. Silver rolls to the still-open door and screams for help. After an endless minute, someone seems to answer, and she commands them to fetch a cleric. Kass doesn't think she needed to add the threats of damnation and eternal hellfire, but he supposes he's not one to talk when it comes to foul tempers.

Silver returns and touches Kass's chest close to the wound. A black corruption is spreading, and he can feel it poisoning his skin. It is intoxicating.

"Kass," his wife whispers. "The healers are coming. You'll be fine."

"Stop fretting," he laughs. She squeezes her eyes shut.

"I shouldn't have cast that last spell. I should have known it would – fuck, Kass. I'm sorry."

"That's alright."

"No, it's not. You could –"

"We all die, Silver."

"Stop. Stop. You won't die."

In his delirious state, he can almost taste the tears on her cheeks. Silver has always been an easy crier. He feels things more intensely, but she shows it more easily. He has always thought that arrangement was tremendously unfair.

A shuffle of steps makes Kass's head spin, and Dominik Var Herren's face appears in the blurred edges of his vision. His bronze-glowing skin is paler than usual, and he is already uttering a prayer by the time he kneels next to Kass. He says something to Silver, and she moves away.

Var Herren continues his invocation, his voice rising with frustration. Then he suddenly stops. Kass meets his gaze, but the cleric is no longer looking at him. His eyes stopped somewhere just to Kass's side, widening in fear. Kass can hear Silver shouting, then an ice bolt passes over his chest.

He turns his head just in time to see the chunks of demon growing back together. It looks as if they are moved by the invisible hand of a god. Var Herren stumbles backwards, but to his credit, he pulls Kass with him. Silver steps between them and the demon and raises her hands. She stood up from her wheelchair.

She mutters something, but Kass can hear her voice shaking. He has seen it a thousand times before. He tries to force himself to speak, to warn her, but the words won't come. Silver finishes her incantation, but it's not quite right. Her concentration, the words, her fragile hold on the world – something fails her and the spell rebounds. Her chest is suddenly covered in ice that tightens with each second.

"Silver!"

His cry barely makes it out into the open. Kass feels breathless and light-headed. He remembers Melina's spell backfiring, her body breaking under the assault of her own magic. The ice that covers Silver's chest tightens and tightens, and the demon raises its sword-like legs –

Silver barks out a word of command, and the ice melts. With stiff arms, she removes the glove from her left hand, and Kass can see the bone remains of her fingers and ligaments. Her stance is shaky. She can't use her legs for long, and there'll be hell to pay for straining them later.

"Silver, get back," he presses out, but his wife isn't paying him any mind. Just as the demon's head rolls across its back and finds its seat between fleshy red shoulder blades, Silver takes a few steps forward and presses her skeletal hand against the demon's flesh. Kass can hear it squirm and convulse as the flesh rots under her touch.

But even this spell is not strong enough. The demon winds out of Silver's grasp and strikes at her. Silver stumbles and falls, wincing with pain. The demon chitters and raises three legs, ready to impale her. The onyx stone in Kass's pocket burns so hot that he almost faints from the pain.

Silver raises her hands, and a translucent shield appears above her. Kass tries to get up. The room around him is spinning, but he only needs to land one solid hit. He can still hear Var Herren chant behind him, and Kass reaches for his blade, useless on the floor beside him. He forces himself back to his feet, clutching the blade tightly.

The demon stares at the three of them, then turns on its heels and jumps out of an open window. Silver stumbles after it and throws a few spells in its general direction. Kass struggles to remain standing, then Var Herren's snarling voice is in his ear.

"It got away. There's nothing you can do now, fool."

"Fuck off, Var –"

"You need to rest. And I need to not hear your impertinence," the cleric replies nonchalantly, then utters a spell Kass recognises all too well. Technically, it is a healing spell, but one that causes a deep sleep that allows the body to regenerate.

He can feel something deep inside him rejecting the spell, but his body is ready to relent to the endless pressure in his chest. The wounds burn, the stone burns, and he feels dizzy under all that heat.

"No, stop, I need to –"

Whatever else he was going to say is washed away by sweet black oblivion.

Chapter 9

Like every morning, Kass wakes up with a sharp breath and a racing heart. Only, it isn't morning. The rays of the setting sun sit on the window glass like seeping blood. He slept until early evening. He tries to calm his breath as he looks around the room. He is alive. He is alone. So far, so good.

He is still inside the castle, judging from the thick stone walls of the guest room. Sitting up, he can see out of the thin window. The barracks surround the castle like an ever-growing beast. The sea glimmers in the distance, and he longs to have the salt-heavy air fill his lungs again.

He can't hear footsteps outside his room, but he reckons the next guard isn't far away. They should be patrolling the perimeter, given the attack that just took place. Ithya has no heirs, and the royal family's distant cousins died either when they got involved in the crusades or during the war. If Ithya were to be killed, they'd have a civil war, with Old Noll's noble families fighting over the ashes in which the rest of them try to live.

A terrible part of him is gratified this attack happened. At least they'll have to take the demon threat seriously now.

He stretches his muscles, first cautiously, then properly. He can't feel any aches and pains, and from what he can see, the wound on his chest has mostly faded, with only remnants of black corruption lingering around its edges. He expects his body's natural defences will repel the rest.

Kass grunts. Dominik Var Herren is an asshole, but he serves a pretty powerful god. To be granted the same healing miracle, Kass reckons he would have had to pray stark naked on top of a mountain for a straight fortnight. He's lucky most people only come to him with cuts and bruises.

He swings out of bed and gets dressed in the courtier's attire someone left hanging over a nearby chair. He was stripped of his clothing, presumably because he was getting blood on the king's pristine sheets.

The courtier's clothes are ridiculously tight and feature a few too many ruffles, but Kass can't bring himself to care. He rushes out of the room and goes straight to the hall on the castle's top floor, where he knows Ithya holds his small council meetings. On the way, he runs into several soldiers who, for a moment, look like they want to stop him. Wisely, they relent when they recognise their commander's stony yet furious expression.

His legs stiffen as he races up one, two, five floors, then stands in front of the small audience hall. The door is slightly ajar. He can hear Var Herren's nasal tone, occasionally interrupted by Silver, whose voice is even raspier than usual. Kass takes a deep breath, then cautiously pushes open the door.

King Ithya sits half-sunken on a plain wooden chair at the back of the hall. He is surrounded by two dozen guards. The audience hall is a reformed chapel built for one of the now-forgotten gods. Ithya kept the elaborate, dark-stone pillars and the intricately decorated ceiling that depicts exotic birds pursuing a dying moon. On the West side, half-rounded windows show the vast, dying skies and thin curtains flow in a lazy breeze. A faded red carpet lies before Ithya and his not-throne, adorned with filigree gold depictions of spells and alchemy.

Silver and Var Herren stand before the king beside Markos Alt and Girah Embriis, everyone's favourite city watch commander. Amaya hovers at the back of the room with two other investigators Kass doesn't know. Pride and Octavia are present also, standing as far away from one another as humanly possible.

Ithya looks up when Kass approaches and waves him closer.

"The man of the hour," he murmurs with a grim smile. "I suppose I should thank you for risking your life for my sake yet again? Although I'm sure it must sound a little hollow at this point."

"It is my duty and honour, your majesty," Kass responds with a shallow bow. He had plenty of opportunities to defend his newly crowned king during the war. He is glad Ithya is not the type to forget these things.

Ithya shakes his head.

"If only I were a more worthy recipient for your devotion. But I suppose that is what the gods are for, no?"

Kass reaches Silver, whose eyes hover on his chest.

"I'm fine," he mouths, and she abruptly turns back towards the king. She sits in her chair, and from the way her legs are tensed up, he guesses she's in pain.

"So," Ithya says, awkwardly clapping his hands together. "Now that we're all here, I don't suppose anyone knows where this demon might have come from?"

"As I said, your majesty," Silver says. "I suspect it came through the rift in the Karthe manor. And it is likely that two others are afoot."

"Yes, right. Sorry, Silver. I was paying attention," Ithya hastily corrects. "I meant to ask which plane the demon came from."

"Hard to tell," Pride says, pacing up and down beside some re-functioned prayer benches. "Our visitor is clearly demonic in nature. So, we might deduce that they came from what we commonly call the hell planes."

With a glance at the others in the audience hall, she continues.

"I am speaking of planes inhabited by non-anthropomorphic creatures that were used as assassins and warlords during the war. We have long suspected that many demon populations are enslaved by the enemy and forced to fight in their battles."

Kass nods. He remembers the day when terrifying monsters first appeared alongside the scaled but anthropomorphic enemy soldiers. One of the many times during the war when he had been tempted to throw himself off the city walls.

Pride presses a finger against her chin. She is imposing in every regard. Her voice rings in the smallest spaces and demands her listeners' attention.

"But which plane did our demons come from?" she asks rhetorically. "We simply don't know enough about the hell planes to say for certain."

"But we might deduce that they came from different ones," Amaya suggests. Pride turns around.

"How so?"

The investigator does not approach, nor does she look Pride directly in the eyes. Still, Kass notes her subtle enthusiasm at being asked to share her theory.

"Well, if we compare Kass's report from the plague quarters with Silver and Dominik's testimony, we are looking at two different demon species," Amaya explains. "And the third one might be completely different yet."

"Well, we can't assume that all demons on a plane are going to look the same," Silver interjects. Amaya shakes her head.

"As you say, but how would these two demons possibly coexist in the same environment? Today's demon clearly lives in a hot place that constantly burns its skin from its bones. The other had a perpetually moist exterior. I don't see them making for easy neighbours."

"That is a good point. Fair enough," Pride admits with a nod, although she looks slightly irritated.

"But why is this relevant?" Var Herren asks.

"Cause it means our mage was able to travel to different planes. And do so without being eaten up by the blasted critters inhabiting those planes," Kass says. "I don't know about you, but I'm starting to think our attacker wasn't acting alone. This might be a vanguard."

Silver quietly shakes her head. "No," she mutters, although she can't rationally disagree with his conclusion.

Kass's eyes rest on her chair and the way her left glove awkwardly falls around the skeletal remains of her hand.

How much more will Silver sacrifice for the chance of survival? How much does she have left? He will still gladly lay down his life for her, but if they face another invasion, that might count for less than nothing.

"So, what you're saying is that we're fucked?" Octavia asks. Her voice is quiet and soft. Kass is often struck by how different her speaking voice sounds from her shouting commands across a battlefield.

Pride shoots the former paladin general an irritated glare, but Kass notes that she does not disagree.

"We've been fucked for years," Ithya says laconically. "Only now there are demons involved rather than dragons. I can't say I hate that as a development."

"Certainly easier to kill," Kass murmurs with a nod.

"You didn't kill it," Silver snaps. "The demons will be back. Our mage's mysterious powers will bring them back to life until they've killed their targets. And there's still a third one out there."

"Well, we can guess who two of them are after at least," Amaya says. "Octavia and king Ithya."

"We don't know that for certain," Pride protests. "Octa was in the castle the whole time. The demon could have just stumbled across the meeting downstairs while looking for her. It's not like the demons were above massacring house Karthe while looking for their real target."

Kass isn't convinced. Something about the demon simply happening upon king Ithya feels like too big of a coincidence.

He feels a twinge at the back of his mind. Coincidence. Was it really a coincidence that the rift appeared in House Karthe's manor? Had he dismissed the possibility of an attack against them too quickly?

"I suppose at this point it is too early to jump to conclusions," Ithya says with a shrug, then turns to Girah.

"Can we concentrate our efforts on patrolling the streets for our demonic invaders? And have the guardsmen patrol with mages who can try to magically contain the demon's bodies once they are incapacitated."

Girah nods enthusiastically. "Of course, your majesty. Consider it done."

Pride sighs. "I'll give you the names of some of my students, but no promises about their levels of competence once they're outside a lab. I will also need some mages to keep working on the rift in House Karthe's wine cellar."

Kass looks at her in surprise, and she explains. At Silver's behest, Pride has been working to dispel the barrier that blocks access to the rift's other side. If she can pull that off, they can enter the Two Towers the dead woman saw. And perhaps that will let them find the mystery mage who is behind it all.

Kass feels a twinge of relief. If they have Pride on their side, things aren't as bleak as he feared. He didn't interact with her much during the war, but he remembers how many times her tell-tale black barriers saved him and the other soldiers from an enemy barrage.

Markos clears his throat.

"We could pull back some soldiers from riftwatch, majesty."

Part of Old Noll's standing army is permanently stationed near some of the bigger rifts in the realm to keep watch for coming invasions. Many soldiers have learned to live in drifting cities made from ships and on the cliffsides of precarious canyons in the Polainian mountains. All while trying not to fall into the gigantic, convulsing holes in the fabric of reality.

Ithya nods. "I trust you. Do what you think is right."

Markos nods.

"Good," Ithya says. "So, the city watch will round up the demons. Pride, Silver and the rest of the mages will work on ways to open the rift in Karthe manor. Meanwhile, I want to know about any open rifts to hell planes in and around the area of Old Noll. I don't care how small they are."

There are a ton of hidden rifts in attics, backyards, at the back of children's wardrobes or the bottom of wells. There are far too many to catalogue, and most don't lead anywhere exciting. A five-inch rift near *The Burning Mage* opens into the interior of a tree.

Some researchers have been trying to catalogue the rifts' destinations ever since they first appeared; a fruitless yet important task. If they can find an opening to a hell plane, they may be able to cross over and continue their investigation into the demons' origins there.

It is a tall order. No one knows how many planes exist. They might spend an eternity combing through every realm of the Multiverse before they ever stumble across the right one. But it's better than sitting around, so Kass volunteers. So does Amaya, to his delight.

Octavia remains silent, and Kass supposes it's better that she stays within the castle's confines. Still, a small part of him is disappointed that she isn't choosing to get involved. He tells himself she's doing it to keep the citizens safe. This way, the demon won't be tempted to track her down across populated areas.

The last air seems to leave king Ithya's body, and he slumps into the back of his makeshift throne. All things to do with reigning exhaust him. The decision-making, the diplomacy, the careful consideration of everyone's perspectives. That is not to say that he is bad at it, Kass thinks. Donheira, his sister, was perhaps a more charismatic and natural ruler, but she had been known as a distant and disinterested queen who would leave all practical aspects of her rule to Old Noll's noble families. She never interfered with the crusades, no matter how bloody they got, claiming that it was the prerogative of the faithful to serve their gods however they saw fit. Meanwhile, the interests of the merchant and working classes were thoroughly ignored, and unprecedented poverty ravaged the realm. If it hadn't been for the war, the queen would have had a rebellion on her hands within a few years.

If Pride is to be believed, Ithya could have been an outstanding mage if he had been able to devote more time to the craft. But he is the king they need.

When they leave the chapel, Kass finds Allen and Andrea lurking in the corridor, shooting him anxious glances. He suppresses a smile and walks over to them.

"Don't you kids have anything better to do? I thought I gave you the day off?"

"There was word of an attack on the castle, Sir," Andrea says indignantly. "We couldn't just sit at home and hope for the best."

"So, you came here and hoped for the best?"

"I mean, I told 'drea that it wasn't the smartest idea," Allen mutters. "But they were pretty adamant."

Pretty adamant or just pretty? Kass wonders, who hasn't missed the shy glances Allen throws Andrea's way. Andrea remains blissfully oblivious, of course. He likes that about them. No room in their head for nonsense.

"It's not like you were busy," Andrea defends themselves. "When I went to your flat, you were napping. In the middle of the day."

"It's a rest day, Andrea," Allen protests. Have you heard of the concept?"

"I have. It's an opportunity to reset your mind with light religious reading, cardiovascular exercise, or a hobby."

"A hobby?" Kass raises his eyebrows. "Let's hear it, then."

Allen snorts. "Andrea's really into glassmaking. They've got a proper set-up in their apartment. And the vases they make are *everywhere*. It's like the place is tempting you to break something."

"I inherited the tools from my grandfather," Andrea hastens to explain. "I just thought I'd continue the family tradition. I'm not very good at it, but there's something relaxing about working with something so delicate after a day of martial training."

Their voice trails off as their gaze shifts to a spot behind Kass. Allen has the honest-to-gods gall to salute.

"Mistress Silver," he gasps. Kass rolls his eyes, and he hears his wife chuckle.

"Mistress? I'm fairly sure there's only one person you paladins owe honorifics to, and it's certainly not me."

"Well, you are a war hero," Allen mutters, blushing. "I just thought..."

"I am charmed to meet you both," Silver says smoothly and enters their circle. She extends her white hand – the fleshy one, Kass notes with relief – and Allen and Andrea shake it enthusiastically.

His wife flashes her best smile. "So, you're the squires who have to endure my husband's moods? My condolences, I'm sure."

Allen snorts, but Andrea looks a little uncertain.

"Sir Kassander is an amazing mentor," they protest. "I have learned so much from him already."

"I'm glad to hear it," Silver says, and only Kass hears the irony in her words.

"Did you really kill thirty dragons during the siege, mistress?" Allen asks, unable to keep himself from staring at Silver. She laughs.

"I did indeed. The enemy didn't expect us mages to have quite so many tricks up our sleeves."

Kass is horrified at the thought of Allen and Andrea asking for details on how she managed that feat, but fortunately, they don't. They stare at Silver with wide-open eyes as though she's the living embodiment of the spirit of human resilience. And in a way, she is. She has undoubtedly endured more than Kass. He suddenly remembers the tears on her cheeks when she leaned over him after the fight.

"How are you feeling, Silver?" he asks, his voice unusually hoarse.

His wife looks up at him with surprise. "I'm fine, Kass. Why do you ask?"

He glances down at her legs, which he knows must be killing her. These days, Silver rarely stands up unless it's an emergency. Training hasn't helped, and now she says that the temporary mobility isn't worth the pain.

Silver follows his gaze and waves her skeletal hand – still hidden by a glove – dismissively. "I'm fine," she repeats.

"Sure. Just as fine as I am." He shoots her a sardonic glance, and she cocks her head to the side. He turns back to his squires.

"My house. Sunrise tomorrow. We'll start our demon investigation in earnest."

Andrea salutes. "Yes, Sir!" they say before kissing Silver's hand upon their departure. Allen murmurs something about 'gods-damned morning people' before forcing out a 'yes, Sir' and trailing after his fellow squire.

Silver glances up at Kass. He knows she won't ask him to accompany her home. With Silver, it always has to be fair. She asked him last time, and he turned her down. He has to be the one to ask her now. He used to find these little games adorable, a delightful proof that she was overthinking every aspect of their relationship. Now, he just finds them irritating.

But Silver did save his life today.

He'll be good starting from tomorrow. He'll go to the temple, repent, and ask his god for guidance. Five will restore his powers, and he'll be able to perform his duties for the realm.

"Come on, trouble," he says and cautiously puts a hand on the back of her chair. "Let me take you home."

Silver smiles.

Chapter 10

Wartime

Silver told Kass she'd save his life, and she intended to keep her word. The army generals devised a plan wherein a squadron of soldiers would raid the enemy camp under the cover of night and tear down their siege tower. The human mages couldn't touch it, thanks to the enemy spellcasters' protective barriers. So, it had to be taken out by a surprise martial attack.

Octavia hand-selected a group of experienced fighters and two detonation experts, criminals who had been given little choice but to comply. She also enlisted a paladin for the raid, who was supposed to heal anyone who got hurt. Divine invocations worked faster than needle and thread, even if the gods didn't always listen.

Thanks to most of the junior paladins lying in a mass grave outside the temple district, Kass didn't face much competition for the job. Holly and Derek also volunteered for the squad, but Octavia only accepted the former. She didn't want people with a death wish on a critical mission, the general snapped at Derek. The archer stormed off in a fit of rage, Melina trailing closely behind.

The attack on the siege tower was successful. Amidst the chaos of the raging battle, the soldiers remained concealed until the detonation experts could attach the bombs to the bottom of the tower. The human squadron was well on its way out of the enemy camp when the explosion shook the earth, and most of the enemy foot soldiers were too surprised to give them much trouble.

That didn't mean their archers and artillerymen were equally slow to react. Arrows and rocks rained down on the fleeing human commando like a hailstorm. Kass, Holly and the others were racing across the battlefield to avoid the bombardment, but a squadron makes for a big target. Only the human mages' protection spells prevented the soldiers from finding their end outside of their own city gates.

Silver and Pride stood atop a makeshift wooden tower at the barricades outside the walls. A few months ago, the thought of standing shoulder-to-shoulder with the head of Old Noll's mage guild, spellcaster supreme and general Wunderkind Pride, would have caused Silver to break out in unflattering sweats. But by now, the two women had developed a strangely comfortable rapport.

"Still got the left side?" Pride asked, then flicked her hand to change the angle of her protective shield. Pride's shields were black and almost impossible to see through. Silver never managed to get hers to look quite like that.

A bombardment of rocks fell out of the sky and collided with the interwoven strands of magic. Silver could feel her hands shaking in response to the impact.

"Hm-hm," she pressed out. Silver wasn't good at multitasking, at keeping hold of the intricate web of spell craft while continuing a conversation.

"Is that a 'yes' grunt or a 'no' grunt?" Pride asked.

"I'm fine," Silver pressed out, narrowing her eyes in concentration.

She could feel Pride's eyebrows rise, but the mage general did her the courtesy of not commenting on her student's evident struggles.

Silver had never been a master of shielding magic. Before the war, the closest she had come to choosing a specialism was her frequent use of illusion spells to smooth out her dresses, add extra sparkle to her make-up, and make her hair look thicker. Nobles didn't tend to specialise in schools of magic. That was the realm of researchers and combat mages. Silver hadn't known many spells before being drafted into the army.

Protective magic didn't come naturally to her. Pride assured her that it didn't for most people, but they were under a bit of pressure as things stood. The enemy would not wait for Silver to practice until she finally mastered a simple shield wall.

So, when she had the choice, Silver stuck to spells she found easier to cast. Evocation spells that let her set things on fire or summon large icicles. And necromancy, the power of drawing power from the dead. Silver didn't think the former would be much help in the middle of a raging battlefield where she was as likely to hit humans as enemies.

The human squadron was close enough to the palisade that Silver could start to make out their faces. She spotted Kass supporting one of his fellow soldiers, who was limping precariously. Holly was ahead of them but kept glancing back, her movements furtive like a bird.

Silver felt her breath quicken.

It helped to think that she would never have met any of them if not for the war.

So, if they died, there was nothing gained and nothing lost.

But now, watching yet another barrage of artillery rage against her shields, the thought didn't help so much. She felt her concentration strain against the fabric of existence, trying to slide out of her mental grasp. She had rubbed spell components into her fingers, and the edges of the precious stones had broken her skin. Her blood rained on the barricade below.

"Almost there," Pride breathed, and then the squadron broke through the palisade and made straight for the city gates. Between the wooden encampments the humans had put up, they'd be much harder to hit. Pride released her shields as soon as the soldiers crossed the threshold and fixed on the enemy archers and artillerymen she saw in the distance.

"Come on," she hissed at Silver. "Let's finish this."

Silver wasn't sure what Pride imagined they'd finish, but she nodded.

"Here's what I want you to do," her mentor said. "I'll throw fireballs at the top of the enemy's encampment until all the archers move downstairs. And then I want you to work some wonders with necromancy."

Silver hesitated. "Is that even allowed?"

Necromancy wasn't strictly forbidden in Old Noll. But in a realm devout to gods who claimed ownership over the dead, it was frowned upon to meddle with corpses. Pride scoffed.

"As long as we win, nobody will care, Silver. And if anyone gives you shit about it, you say it was my idea."

"Why don't you cast the spell?"

"Because you have a knack for necromancy," Pride responded. "One that should be developed."

"I do?"

Pride gave her an impatient look, and Silver coloured.

"Yes. You haven't seen much death, so you have no real fear of it. Not yet."

That was true. Silver hadn't lost so much as a grandparent. Pride had walked through a horizon full of corpses after a crusade led by Eight ravaged the border towns East of Old Noll. An orphan without a kind word to her name, she had worked her way up to the top of the city's mage guild. Silver sometimes wondered how much embitterment and rage lay beneath her mentor's matter-of-fact demeanour.

However, this wasn't a good time to ask.

"Very well. I will try," she said. She could feel energy radiating from the dead, piled up around the enemy's camps in fleshy walls. Pride cast three gigantic fireballs in short succession, each driving their enemies from the tops of battlements.

Silver whispered incantations that imitated the gods' resurrection calls to their followers.

Most souls quickly fled a desecrated hull, but some lingered close to their fallen bodies, confused by the manner of their death, too scared to move on, or hoping that a god's intervention might revive them. Sometimes the gods interfered in someone's death, albeit not often.

What did the souls have to lose by remaining on this plane? No one knew what afterlife awaited them. That was the prerogative of the gods. Why hurry to nod neon chores when they might yet be revived?

Necromancy relied on souls that could be bound to flesh and commanded to fulfil the spellcaster's wishes. Even after the ravages of the crusades, there had never been this much death staining the world. It seeped into every crack and crevice of existence. And there had never been such a wealth of resources at Silver's fingertips.

She clenched her fist and trapped the souls within the enemies' dead bodies. She imposed her will on their flailing minds, promising she would soon again release them from their newly painful prisons. If they just did this one thing for her, if they just killed their former comrades, they would be free.

She couldn't revive as many as she wanted, and she felt hot and frustrated at the feeling of the souls slipping away.

But the sight of their dead comrades returning to life caused many of their enemies to hesitate. They hesitated long enough to be killed before the deceived souls escaped the battlefield.

In the chaos of the skirmish, Silver and Pride followed their squadron into the city. Behind them, the large iron gates fell shut, and they were greeted by Octavia, who had just finished debriefing her squadron.

"Effective tactics," the paladin general said with a frown. Octavia had celebrated her fiftieth birthday mere days before the rifts opened.

Pride pushed herself in front of Silver. "All my orders," she said calmly.

"They usually are," Octavia sighed, then shrugged. "I suppose this is what we're reduced to in our hubris."

Pride rolled her eyes. "It's just magic, Octa. A tool like any other."

"Don't." Octavia shook her head, then looked at Silver with concern. "Are you okay, girl?"

"I'm fine," Silver said, but she was distracted. Her eyes kept moving to Kass and Holly, who were waiting for her.

Octavia followed her gaze and smiled briefly. Then, she turned back to Pride.

"I want Silver stationed under me. She'd do well in my squadron."

"Out of the question," Pride snapped back. "She's a mage, and I coordinate the mages."

"Don't you have enough on your hands, old friend?"

The words were tense enough to break.

Pride glared at Octavia. "If you want a pet mage, you may choose from the others. I'm keeping Silver stationed under me. She has potential."

"Potential to do what?"

Silver cleared her throat. Both women turned to her. Pride's demeanour softened a little.

"Apologies, Silver," the mage general said. "You must be tired. Why don't you rest and prepare for tomorrow?"

"Yes, Ma'am," Silver responded, eager to join her friends. She didn't mind where she was stationed, although it was gratifying to see two generals vying for her services.

She ran over to Kass and Holly. The rogue locked her in a firm embrace before she could say anything, nuzzling her short, dirty hair into Silver's left ear.

"Another day, another miracle," Holly said, her tone half amused, half astonished. She was a devout follower of Three, the god of night and truth.

"Wasn't a miracle, Hol," Kass said, his dark eyes resting on Silver with burning intensity. "That was the mages saving our lives."

"I keep my promises," Silver replied when Holly finally let go. She and Kass awkwardly faced each other, unsure if they should commit to the same level of intimacy.

"Apparently, you do," Kass said, his voice a little strained.

A stray breeze tussled Silver's hair, and a few strands flew into her face. Kass stared at her for a moment longer, then gently moved them behind her ears. Silver stood stock-still as his fingers caressed her face, and she felt her heart race with every touch.

Once he was done, Kass coloured and looked away, embarrassed by such a blatant display of affection. Holly smirked but didn't comment on it.

"Shall we go and find ourselves a fire? I'm starving," Silver suggested to dispel the awkwardness. Kass and Holly agreed enthusiastically.

When the rogue skipped ahead, Silver and the paladin walked side-by-side through the colony of tents that spread outside the half-destroyed barracks. Silver could tell that Kass was still tense. He walked stiffly and barely responded to the shouts and waves of soldiers who welcomed them back to camp.

"I don't think I've ever seen anyone wearing plate armour run quite this fast," she offered to lighten the mood.

Kass looked down at her, then smiled a forced smile.

"Suppose you would only ever have seen knights at tournaments. Where they subject their poor horses not only to their fat arses but also to fifty solid pounds of steel."

"Just so," Silver responded. "And as you might imagine, there isn't a lot of running done at those events."

Kass snorted. "Let alone any real fighting."

"Oh, they fight," Silver says. "Tournaments used to get pretty bloody before Donna put new regulations in place."

"Donna? Oh, you mean the queen."

Silver laughed. "Who else?"

Kass raised his eyebrows but left the statement uncommented. Instead, he grunted again and patted the sword hanging by his side.

"I've never been to a tournament, obviously," he said. "But I can't imagine any duels fought for public entertainment would even bloody resemble what fighting is actually like."

"Well, it's their reputation that's at stake. Some knights have been said to care about that more than their lives."

"Then they're fools."

Silver shrugged. "I could honestly not tell you if there's much difference between tournament fighting and a real battle. I just stand in high places and launch spells at the largest target I see."

"Oh, but do give yourself some credit, mageling. You do that very well."

She gave him a mock bow. "I'm ever so happy to be noticed."

"That you are, Silver." He shook his head but couldn't entirely hide a smile.

Silver felt a twinge of courage gnawing at her tongue.

"So, now that we've saved each other's lives, what excuse can I use to keep an eye on you?"

Kass barked out an embarrassed laugh. "I'm sure there will be plenty of opportunities for either one of us to get into trouble."

"I was rather hoping for a chance outside of battle."

"You were?"

He looked at her, and Silver found uncertainty underneath his intrigue and gratification. They spent a lot of time with one another, sitting at the same campfires and making jokes with the same group of friends. Still, Silver could tell he remained behind an invisible wall, unwilling to cross over to her.

So, she pushed through and took his hand, cold and dark from the remnants of battle. Kass closed his eyes for a moment, then looked at her again.

"Not sure why you'd bother. I'm no one special," he whispered, and she wasn't sure whether the words were aimed at her or himself.

"Nobody's special. And even if you were entirely unspecial, I don't care," she replied, and Kass laughed again, squeezing her hand with his own.

"Flatter my ego some more, would you?"

"Sorry. I'm no flatterer, Kass."

"No, I suppose you noble lot never are."

His eyes wandered across her mage robes, thick, well-crafted, and dyed in elaborate turquoise colours. Her mother had commissioned them for her after it became clear that Silver would be drafted. Above her breasts a small silver pin displayed her house sigil.

With infuriating slowness, he took the pin from her robes, the tips of his fingers caressing the skin beneath her robes. Silver felt her breath shudder.

"Holly's not the only one capable of theft, you know?" he said, his voice husky. "I'm lucky my god is the forgiving sort."

"Well, you're really showing off your skills now," Silver replied, her voice low. Kass grinned, then took the pin between two fingers.

"I suppose you'll just have to come looking for this."

Silver laughed. "Oh, this is a most exciting quest. I shall employ all the magic at my disposal to assist me with punishing the culprit."

"Punishing?" Kass raised his eyebrows.

Silver grinned. "Oh yes. Most devastatingly so."

"Now I really am intrigued."

128

They stared at each other, and Silver would have been content to keep talking until the sun went down. But Holly called them over to a nearby fireplace for some stew and ale, and the magic of the moment fled as quickly as the wind.

Still. Kass sat next to her all evening.

Chapter 11

The temple district is busy this morning. Word has got out about the attack on the castle, and the people of Old Noll storm to the district in waves. Many carry small tokens and weapons they ask the priests to bless. The temples are surrounded by twisting queues for incense-burning stations and offering spots, where prayers can be burned for whichever god will listen (or, frequently, for whichever god's temple has the shortest queue).

Allen and Andrea are uncharacteristically quiet. As they make their way through the nervously chattering crowds, the unrest in the city suddenly feels real. Their investigation has become a matter of the realm's safety.

Kass feels blinded by the bright day. As if to spite the gloomy mood, the sun reflects against the glittering waters of the small canals below. He keeps bumping into people, although that's more an issue for them than for him. Still, it triggers the tight feeling in his chest. He is sweating in his armour. He has already decided that this is a bad day.

The temple of Five lies in the centre of the district. The most prominent spot right at the entrance is taken up by One, of course. His gilded, exuberant temple is considered by many to be one of Old Noll's best tourist attractions.

Five's temple is small in comparison. Its grey, speckled walls are plain and more similar to a warehouse than the other temples whose towers and spires dominate the skyline.

Kass touches the building's exterior for a moment and remembers the first time he came here. His parents never took him to temples as a child, and he never bothered going as an adolescent. He was helping with the inn, getting in trouble with his no-good friends, and chasing after the neighbours' daughters. He was angry at the gods for letting his father die so young, but it was a poorly defined, elusive anger. Mostly, he just got on with things, and religion was one of those things he never much thought about.

When the war started, Kass came here for the first time. He walked through the abandoned, quiet streets, trying to catch his reflection in the rain-drenched canals overflowing onto the walkways. Almost all the temples were shut, overcrowded with wounded soldiers and refusing to admit any more.

Only Five's doors were open, and pale light shone from the inside. The wounded lay on the steps leading up to the entrance, and the whole place stunk of blood and death. No part of the scene convinced him that serving Five would be any different to the misery he saw before him.

Kass believed there was honour in honesty. He still believes it. And the place still makes him feel calm.

He walks inside, his squires at his heels, and finds himself inside the main prayer hall.

Little light finds itself inside the hall, dominated by a square pillar and fragmented into small booths where supplicants pray. When he took Silver here, she said the darkness was caused by the angle of the windows and the walls. She was keen to leave and feigned hunger as an excuse, so they got sweet potato wraps from one of the vendors outside. She never returned.

A priest in long grey robes comes to greet them. Marlon, no last name, now replaces Emilia Var Herren, who died during the war. He is charitable while having little patience for nonsense, two qualities Kass appreciates. Supposedly, he spent the first fifty years of his life homeless. But he never talks about that.

"How bad are things?" he asks Kass instead of a greeting.

Kass points at one of the private prayer rooms to the side of the hall, and Marlon leads them there. The room is barely bigger than one of his and Silver's storage closets, and still, someone fit a bronze, shining alter against the wall. It depicts an abstract humanoid shape wielding a scale and a hammer. A few specks of light from a ceiling window coat the statue in an eerie, golden light.

"Not sure yet," Kass finally responds once the four are standing in awkward proximity between the walls and the altar. Allen shuffles when he accidentally touches Andrea's back.

"Will there be war?" Marlon presses. Kass shrugs.

"Honestly? I don't know. But I reckon it doesn't matter whether we know about it. If these demons are an honest-to-gods vanguard, we're all going to die."

"We fought them off once. There are things we can do to defend the people here, Five willing," Marlon replies sharply. He is seldom in the mood for Kass's pessimism.

Kass sighs. "Like what? Three-quarters of the people in this realm died during the last attack, if not more. Most of our cities are gone, and we're only just starting to restore our bloody fields and fisheries. And if our attackers are working with demons ..."

"The gods are on our side," Marlon replies. Kass feels a sting in his chest, and he forces his breathing to still. Part of him wants to ask Marlon about what Octavia said. A bigger part of him dreads that conversation. Either way, he won't do it in front of his squires. The next generation needs hope.

"So, are you looking for divine guidance?" Marlon asks when he realises Kass isn't about to respond. Kass nods, and Marlon pulls some incense and a prayer scroll from his robes.

"Thought you'd forget yours," he says with the faintest smile. Kass accepts the gifts and gives the old priest a grateful nod. Their hands touch while they exchange the scroll, and Marlon's face suddenly twists.

"What?" Kass asks.

"There's ... I can feel corruption," Marlon mutters, then raises his voice.

"Is that possible? Did the demon strike you?"

Kass nods and feels his heartbeat fasten again. Marlon is a cleric, and one of Old Noll's most adept ones at that. If he can feel corruption, it is there. Kass curses quietly. He trusted Var Herren's invocations would have cured the demon's poison.

Allen and Andrea help him remove his chest plate, and Kass lowers the top of his tunic to reveal the faint outline of the wound from the demon's claws. The skin around the area is tinged with a deep grey hue. It didn't go away. Kass never checked if it went away.

Marlon glances up at Kass.

"Did you not try to heal it?" he asks.

"I couldn't. Silver had just cast a spell nearby."

Marlon clicks his tongue, but Kass is thankful he doesn't comment further.

"Var Herren started healing me after the attack," Kass continues to explain. "I thought that would take care of it. Much as I don't care for the man, he wouldn't leave me to die."

"Of course not," Marlon agrees quietly, then traces the skin with soft fingers.

He mutters a quiet invocation, but nothing happens. He doesn't try again. The message is clear.

"What does that mean?" Allen asks, staring at Kass's chest while standing on tiptoes.

"It's Five's way of saying fuck you," Kass explains. Andrea coughs indignantly.

"But why?" Allen asks, his voice a little hollow. "Sir," he adds after a brief moment.

"It could be your marriage to Silver," Marlon suggests. There is no judgement in his voice, but he also refuses not to say it. Kass grunts.

"Maybe," he admits. "But why now?"

"Maybe you lost your healing privileges long ago and never noticed?" Marlon replies. "Five doesn't punish people for their transgressions. He simply stops rewarding them. You know that."

Kass grunts again.

"So, you're saying I've used up all my favours? That Five no longer considers me worthy of a miracle?"

In their simple brutality, the words feel true.

"It is possible," Marlon mumbles.

"But the commander is trying to keep people safe. And Silver is a hero," Andrea protests.

Marlon narrows his eyes. "Silver is a war criminal," he says. "The god of justice has deemed it so, and there is no coming back from that. Not from what she's done."

"What –?" Allen starts, but Kass interrupts him.

"Alright, out. All of you." His squires stare at him, and he narrows his eyes. "I need to talk to Five, and, believe it or not, at this particular moment, I'm not in the mood for an audience."

"But –" Andrea starts, but Kass's furious stare makes them think twice about continuing.

They shuffle out of the prayer room. Kass pulls his shirt back up, then smashes the incense and prayer scroll onto the altar, not bothering to light them up. Instead, he fixes on the bronze statue's faceless head, staring at him with what seems like impassionate mockery.

"Okay," he starts. "You're angry. I get it."

Cold silence faces him. Kass sighs, then cracks his knuckles. He doesn't kneel before Five's altars. That has never been the nature of their relationship.

"So, can we talk about it? Or do you insist on slowly torturing me to death? Feels a bit petty, I won't lie."

Silence.

"Look, I'm trying to catch a potential enemy vanguard here. I don't have time for this shit."

Kass wonders what Marlon would think, hearing him speak to his god this way. Maybe he takes the same causal tone. Or maybe he'd take Kass by the ears and dunk him head-first in the canals. You never really know with Marlon.

Finally, there is some movement in the room. The copper statue shifts. An uncanny mouth grows on its face, far too wide and with too many teeth.

"This is no enemy vanguard."

A disembodied voice rings through the room. It is made up of different voices, young, old, male, female, and other. Five has only spoken to him on a handful of occasions before, all of them during the war. Sometimes during those conversations, Kass thought he could hear a dissenting whisper amidst the god's voices, but he was never quite sure.

"Okay, that's reassuring," Kass replies. "So, what are those demons?"

"They are demons."

"Yeah, but what are they doing here?"

"Hunting prey."

"What prey?"

"Human prey."

"Why?"

"They are an instrument of revenge."

"Whose revenge?"

"That need not concern you." The statue hesitates for a moment as if it is listening to another voice from even further afield. "It is justified retribution."

Kass feels himself pale.

"Are you telling me not to interfere?" he asks. His thoughts are racing. He doesn't know if he could obey Five if he told him not to protect his king. Or Octavia.

"I do not dole out commands to my followers. This is not the nature of the divine."

Kass exhales slowly. "Why did the demons kill House Karthe? Was that part of the revenge act as well?"

"No. It should not have happened." The avatar sounds angry. Kass raises his eyebrows.

"So, the demons fucked up?" he asks.

"Yes."

"They killed the wrong people?"

"Yes."

Simple questions. It's almost like talking to Silver's summons, Kass thinks, then banishes the thought as quickly as it arises. It is blasphemy.

"Can you tell me any more?" Kass asks.

The voice hesitates again. Kass reckons he is not speaking with Five directly but rather with a singular extension of the god's consciousness. Five is probably speaking with many of his faithful across the realm at this very moment. Maybe across the planes if Octavia is to be believed. For a mad second, he considers asking Five about it. But he doesn't want to. He is afraid of what the answer might be.

"No," the avatar says after another long pause.

"That's all?" Kass responds incredulously. "No 'stop the demons before they cause more damage'?"

"No."

Of course. No god will ever force a human's hand. Free will trumps everything. Otherwise, devotion turns to servitude. Silver reckons that the gods are simply not powerful enough to force all of humanity to obey their will. And that if they tried to, they would have to war among themselves for control over an army of servants.

Kass never believed that. It is just like Silver to see every part of the world as devious and cruel.

He sighs. Five has given him something, at least. His instincts telling him to look more closely into House Karthe may have been correct.

"Can you tell me why you're so set on fucking me over? Now of all times?" he asks, trying not to sound as furious as he feels.

"I am not punishing you."

"Is it because of Silver?"

"I am not punishing you."

The answer comes quickly and is uttered in the god's uncanny chorus of voices. Except, there is one voice, very quiet and very far away, that repeats Silver's name. Kass can't make out the tone or if anything is said afterwards. And anyway, he must be imagining things.

He'd recognise that voice anywhere, but it doesn't make sense. That voice belongs to Melina.

But Melina is dead, and she wasn't one of Five's faithful, so her soul would not have passed over to his plane of existence.

Kass takes a shaky breath.

"So, what do you want me to do?" he asks.

"You may do as you like."

"Well, not for very long if you're going to allow that fucking corruption to murder me!"

"Your own choices led to your injury."

"Sure, but you're preventing the other gods' healing from affecting me."

"The other gods make their own choices, Kassander."

Kass pales. Have all the gods condemned him to death, then? Silver did horrible things during the war, but punishing him like this seems excessive.

"So, what do I do?"

"You may do what you like."

Kass closes his eyes and exhales a slow breath. By the time he opens them again, the mouth on the statue has disappeared, and he feels that the presence in the room has vanished.

His chest tightens, and his lungs feel like they're no longer absorbing air. He sinks to the ground and presses his face between his legs. One breath, two breaths, three breaths. His heart is racing, and his fingers clench into the armour on his legs. His grip is hard enough that he feels his skin break.

He can't breathe. He can't fucking.

He grabs the onyx stone from his pocket and presses it against his forehead. It is cool and smooth. That means Pathas is alive. Andrea is alive. Allen is alive. Silver is alive. He is alive. He has time to figure this out.

He clings to that thought as he gasps for air and tries to hold on to his heart. The attack is worse than any he's had in years, but eventually, he feels it abating. Just like the enemy finally stopped attacking after it realised humanity was tougher than anticipated.

The world will have to fight to take another piece of him.

Chapter 12

"You look like shit," Amaya tells him when he enters her office.

Kass reckons she's not wrong. Ever since he discovered the corruption, he is suddenly more attuned to its effects. And whenever he tries to ignore the pains in his chest, his squires ruin it by being irritatingly concerned about him. Allen even offered to carry Kass's sword. He nearly threw him off a bridge for such a preposterous suggestion.

"Yeah, well, I'm dying. What's new with you?"

"Nothing much," Amaya replies with her usual literal-mindedness. "Why are you dying?"

Kass explains the situation, and Amaya clicks her tongue. "That seems like it'll keep you from investigating. You should give the job to someone else."

He considers her words for a moment. He knows she isn't speaking from a lack of concern. Work comes first for Amaya, the same as it does for him. But Kass has the strange feeling that he is more connected to this case than circumstances suggest. He tells that to Amaya, and she shrugs.

"Fair enough. Follow your intuition nonsense if you must. Just let me know when you're about to collapse. And once you do, you're off the case, off to a divorce lawyer, and off to a temple, in that order."

"Sure, 'Maya."

He puts a takeaway bag in front of her, and the smell of freshly cooked burgers rises from its open top. Amaya shoots him a thin-lipped smile. She is too picky of an eater to enjoy going out for lunch, but Kass knows how to buy his way into her good graces. There is one food truck in the market district that prepares the meat just the way Amaya likes.

She takes a bite out of the burger and sighs with pleasure. Andrea and Allen sit to the side of her desk and likewise unwrap their orders. Andrea doesn't eat meat, so they nibble on a poorly seasoned vegetable patty. Allen ordered the same thing in a painfully obvious attempt to impress them.

Kass went for the same thing as Amaya. It's pointless to argue with the tastes of a talented investigator.

"Do you reckon there's a reason the rift appeared at House Karthe in particular?" Amaya asks, fixing her gaze somewhere between Kass's eyes.

"If our enemy is after king Ithya, it could have been a coincidence," Andrea says. "They couldn't have opened a rift inside the castle, correct? There are too many barrier spells in place for that."

"Yeah, but they could have opened it just outside the castle gates," Allen argues. "Or, if Octavia is the primary target, they could have opened it at the docks."

"Good point," Amaya says and takes another bite. "All in all, the location was rather inconvenient, at least for the demon who had to trek through the plague quarters to get to the docks. All assuming that Octavia is, in fact, a target."

"Okay. So maybe the Karthes were involved with this shitshow somehow," Kass grumbles. "Question is, how do we find out more about them? Silver told me that they're former mineral traders. Doesn't sound like a family with many skeletons in their closet."

"Former traders? Five preserve us, don't tell me they used to be filthy commoners," Allen remarks with a mocking edge to his voice. He doesn't like nobles.

Kass snorts. Andrea looks a little troubled, but Amaya answers the question with her usual level of seriousness.

"Mineral traders are considered vital to the realm, especially during times of war. A lot of spell components are made from precious metals and stones. Pride even hosts galas for the heads of the noble families involved with the trade."

"Ah, right. So, if you make the mages happy, they might eventually give you a nice title and manor?" Allen asks with a twinkle in his eyes.

Kass laughs. "Don't get any ideas, boy. If you want to get in with the mages, you're in the wrong profession."

"Don't listen to him," Andrea says with a smile. "There is no reason for paladins and mages not to get along. And you know that, Sir. You married a mage, after all."

"Except for several glaring contradictions in ideology and the common propensity for mages to try and destroy the divine order of things that paladins attempt to uphold," Amaya notes drily, then finishes her burger. "No offence to Silver, of course. I don't care either way."

She clears her throat. "But to get back on topic, if we want to learn more about House Karthe, the castle library will have their trade and family history records."

Kass groans. "The library. I was worried you were going to say that."

Old Noll's city library used to be its own building, a wide soapstone structure with thick, plain columns and the world's most antiquated referencing system. It was one of the first buildings to be hit by the enemy's trebuchets. Those librarians who hadn't been flattened by the impact quickly relocated the remnants of the collection to the castle. Unfortunately for them, the only unoccupied part of the castle was the traitor's prison, as all prisoners had been drafted for the front line.

Despite impassioned petitions by the librarians, the collection has yet to be moved back out of the former prison. Many library workers have since learned to cast simple spells to protect the books from dampness and dust. But despite their best attempts to help visitors navigate the different sections, the layout remains labyrinthine, intricate, and often nonsensical, with categories split across various former cells and corridors. Still, given that the space is technically usable, Ithya's advisors consider the matter closed.

Amaya leads the way with unsurprising ease. She enjoys a puzzle, and the library is a remarkably complex and time-intensive one. Andrea also has a decent idea of where they are going, seeing as Kass usually sends them in his stead when he needs to cross-check information. Allen isn't even trying to keep track of where they're going. He's busy thinking of the next in a series of word plays on king Ithya's name in a painfully obvious attempt to make Andrea laugh.

The library doesn't have any books on the history of House Karthe itself, which Kass thinks is not terribly surprising given that they are a pretty minor noble house. Amaya finds them indexed in a series of catalogues on trade deals, though, which she splits between Kass and Andrea. Meanwhile, the family's birth certificates are listed in the annual temple service tomes. She and Kass perform some guesswork to determine how old the Karthe family members might have been before she tells Allen to check the birth certificates.

"What's the point of this?" the squire asks, his voice whiny. Amaya shrugs.

"Just being thorough. Although, wouldn't it be interesting if we were missing a birth certificate?"

"That could just be a clerical error," he responds with a frown.

"You try telling these librarians they made an error," Kass mutters with a furtive glance at the door. "I'm not sure even I could protect you from their wrath."

Allen is not convinced, but he doesn't argue further. They read silently for a few hours.

Although Kass finds a few trade agreements that shift suspiciously high numbers of minerals for suspiciously low fees, none of the information points towards House Karthe having made any powerful enemies. They underpaid their miners but always ensured they gave the mages a competitive rate. The rates were so competitive, in fact, that their house was eventually raised to nobility. Pride herself enjoyed a close relationship with the Karthes once they became the leading provider of diamonds and ruby dust for the guild's spell components.

"All birth certificates accounted for," Allen says in a shit-eating tone, spreading the documents before him. Amaya nods, not taking the bait.

"Well done," she responds absent-mindedly, flicking through her book with a line forming between her eyebrows. Allen crosses his arms and doesn't ask to be given another task. His gaze rests on the documents in front of him, and Kass is about to tell him to get off his ass and get them a round of coffee – library restrictions be damned – when his squire inhales a sharp breath.

"What?" Kass asks.

"Erm, I don't know if this is relevant, Sir, but I think one of these certificates is fake," Allen responds.

"How do you know that?" Andrea asks. Allen colours.

"Well, back home in the village, you sometimes can't get hold of the regional administrator if you need permission to ship – well, anyway, we'd sometimes take a bit of a shortcut ..."

"You have the right to remain silent, boy," Kass says with a poorly suppressed grin.

"Which certificate?" Amaya asks. Allen points at the one belonging to Tade Karthe, the teenager whose body Silver resurrected when this thrice-damned case first began. Amaya takes one look at the document then nods appreciatively.

"Oh yes, that's fake. Well spotted."

She points to the edges of the wax seal on the bottom of the page, supposedly fashioned by the head cleric of the Temple of Four.

"I don't see –" Andrea starts. Allen points at the god's symbol, a polyhedron made to look as though it is spinning around its axis. For comparison, he shows them the seals on two other birth certificates from the same year. All three are from Four's service tome that details births registered at the god's temple.

"Notice anything?" he asks, unable to hide his smugness.

"Hmm, let's see," Andrea says, bending their head downwards. They narrow their eyes in concentration.

Kass is vaguely aware that he is dying from the corruption in his chest, but he'd also gladly take the sweet embrace of the afterlife over interrupting this moment between his squires. Amaya seems to agree and remains silent.

"The edges of the polyhedron aren't as straight on those two," Andrea finally says, pointing at the two certificates that don't belong to Tade Karthe. "The lines are a little uneven. But I'd assume those would be the fakes, then? Not Tade's certificate?"

"It makes sense you'd think that," Allen readily agrees. "But if you keep using the same seals over and over again, the lines become uneven and fade over time."

"Aah," Andrea starts, their eyes beginning to glow.

Allen hurries to finish his point. "The only way for the lines on the polyhedron to be as even as they are on Tade's certificate would be if the seal was completely new. But if we look at the birth certificates immediately preceding and following Tade's, they have the same uneven edges. It's just his that is different."

"Right! Of course!"

Andrea beams at Allen.

"Nice one!" they say, and Allen colours.

"Yeah. I'm thrilled I didn't just hire a country bumpkin. I hired a criminal country bumpkin," Kass says, but his smile takes the edge out of his words. Allen winks at him.

"I am sure your never-ending patience and grace will allow you to forgive my past transgressions, Sir."

Kass smirks and claps the young man on his shoulders instead of a response.

"So. Tade Karthe's birth certificate is fake," Amaya says slowly. "So, what does that tell us? Was he secretly adopted into house Karthe when someone wanted to get rid of an unwanted infant?"

"How did no one notice that?" Andrea asks incredulously.

Kass shrugs.

"Noble mothers miscarry the same as everyone else. It might have been that ..."

He checks the name of Tade's listed mother.

"It might have been that Emilia miscarried but hid that fact from society. Shame, maybe. People like to spout bullshit about divine punishment." He scoffs, then continues. "Then, just around the time of her due date, she's given an infant by someone who can't keep him."

"Why not officially register Tade as Emilia's child at Four's temple? There is no need to fake a birth certificate," Allen counters.

Kass shakes his head.

"If you baptise a child under a god's name, you can't lie when declaring its parentage. You risk divine intervention if you tell an untruth during a holy ceremony."

"What, would Four have swooped in and killed the child?" Allen asks with wide eyes. Kass sometimes forgets that his squire hasn't been a believer for that long. And to an outsider, the gods can be terrifying.

"Well, no," he quickly clarifies. "But Four would have made it clear that she didn't accept the conditions of the child's baptism. Red light, swarms of insects, clouds, a disembodied booming voice... I've seen it all before."

He shrugs again.

"So, the Karthes postpone the baptism indefinitely, later claim that it 'totally happened, so sorry for not inviting you', and eventually bribe someone to add the fake birth certificate into the temple service tomes."

"The question is why. This might all be irrelevant to the demon's appearance at their manor," Amaya cautions.

"Well, we didn't find anything else," Andrea argues. "We might as well pursue this lead if we have nothing else to go on."

They shoot a concerned look at Kass, who feels his blood pressure rise. He hates feeling helpless. His squires should have better things to do than worry about their commander.

Amaya nods.

"Alright. But if we want to uncover Tade Karthe's biological parentage after all these years, we'll need the help of a diviner."

She looks at Kass.

"Your call. I'm happy to requisition someone from the mage guild, but that will take a while. And require you to do paperwork."

Kass sighs. Especially after yesterday's fight, he would prefer to keep Silver out of the investigation. But at this rate, that's probably not going to happen. Right now, his wife is already trying to tear the barrier from the rift at House Karthe at the heels of her mentor Pride.

That, and Kass hasn't forgotten about the third demon that made its way towards the mage tower. He doesn't seriously suspect anyone in Old Noll is aiding the demons, but he also can't completely eliminate the possibility that one of their mages is involved.

"I'll ask Silver," he grunts. "But you all are coming with me. I'll need backup in case my wife insists on doing something altogether heretical."

Chapter 13

The rift looks like a distorted grin. Silver feels mocked by it somehow. It is still impossible to touch its exterior without receiving an electric shock. The barrier, sizzling with power, prevents anyone from crossing to the other side.

She wonders if the demons were ever supposed to return to their master or whether the barrier was intended as a permanent lock. As far as she knows, it is impossible to close a rift once it has been opened, so this might be the best the rift's creator could do to hide their plane of origin. She can't imagine the enemy mage would care much about what happens to the demon assassins. Demons are mindless beasts trained only to hunt and kill. She can't say she would shed a tear for them either.

Pride and three of her apprentices have been working on the force field for the past few days. Spell components are scattered across the floor of the wine cellar, creating a misshapen carpet of diamond dust, bat guano, oak bark, and animal hides. Some city guardsmen are upstairs, busying themselves with a high-stakes game of poker.

Silver is relieved the guards are not downstairs with the mages. With her and Pride in the same room, experiments tend to get ugly.

Sometimes, she wonders what kind of mage she would have become if she hadn't been thrown into a war and moulded by the most ambitious person in the world. She probably would have stopped developing her skills after reaching the high point of mediocrity and spent her life doing nothing in particular. Floating from one party to another while sampling all the sweetness her wealth could offer.

Sometimes, she wonders what keeps her from enjoying the fruits of victory now. The world still tethers on the edge of destruction, but that's not the problem. Perhaps she has grown weary of celebration. It is hard to feel cheery when she is alone in that enormous house. When her worry for people like Pride, Octavia, and Kass cuts through sugar-sweet diversions like a knife.

Pride greets her outside the manor where Silver's carriage drops her off, then casts a spell to levitate Silver's wheelchair down to the wine cellar. Silver knows that spell, too, but Pride is nothing if not courteous. Levitation is a deceptively draining spell, and Silver finds that it seldom is worth the effort when a willing servant or husband can carry her instead.

"How are you?" her mentor asks before they come in earshot of the apprentices.

"So, so," Silver admits. Her legs are so tense that they are in perpetual pain. It will take weeks for the knots to untangle and the tears to heal, but she refuses to take painkillers. She needs her mind to remain sharp, at least until the demons are caught. Until she knows that Kass won't get himself killed on some stupid mission to save what remains of the world.

"Same. I didn't sleep a wink last night," Pride admits and shakes her head. "It was too damn close."

Silver nods. She feels trapped in the terror that gripped her when she saw the demon strike her husband. The scene repeated over and over in her dreams last night, and each time, she was just a little too slow to react. Same as during the war. When Holly was shot in the neck before Silver's protective barrier had risen high enough.

Death is so quick and unspectacular. Really, necromancy is a way to give the whole thing the attention it deserves.

"We can't lose Ithya," Pride continues with a dull voice. "We can't have a civil war when things are finally stabilising. When humanity is finally getting strong enough."

Strong enough for what? Silver wonders but is distracted when Pride's apprentices greet them. There is a young woman from the surrounding villages who had been trained by her grandmother before she sought out the excitement of the capital city. An older woman from the plague quarters who had been evacuated with Pride's special permission. And a former sailor with an unusual knack for pyrokinesis, which turned out to be incompatible with his occupation.

Silver forgets their names as soon as she learns them. Pride shoots her a knowing smile, well-familiar with her mentee's poor memory. But Silver knows she's charming enough to get away with a bit of rudeness.

She takes a sack of bones from a pouch – heart and chest – and scatters them around the rift. They clatter in the silence of the wine cellar, still heavy with the stench of blood and decay.

"So, what have you already tried?" she asks Pride. Her mentor rubs the back of her head. Pride has been bald for as long as Silver can remember. When they won the war, all surviving mages got a small commemorative lily tattoo, which now adorns the back of Pride's head. Silver's is on her wrist, but she rarely registers it.

"Breaking it with sheer force. Displacing it with wind and telekinesis. Funnelling the electricity from the barrier into a pool of water with the hope that its protective force dilutes. All busts."

She chuckles. "The last one was a phenomenally dumb idea, I'll admit."

Silver grins when she sees the pale faces of Pride's apprentices.

"Has anyone else tried to go through it?" she asks.

Pride nods. "The fourth apprentice I brought here. Goro. We loaded him with protection spells and armour and had him walk into the rift."

"And?" Silver asks, although she reckons she wouldn't be here if the experiment had been successful.

"Zap," Pride says and claps her hands together for emphasis. Her youngest apprentice scrunches her face in displeasure at her mentor's callous tone. Silver is used to it.

"Dead?" Silver asks.

Pride shrugs.

"Near as, to be sure."

"Did anything change about the rift's exterior when his body connected with it?" Silver continues.

"The electricity seemed to move towards him," the older female apprentice explains. "Most of the light was concentrated around the centre where Goro stood while the edges of the rift grew darker."

Silver bites her lower lip and glances up at Pride. "So, you want a more durable target, I take it? That will allow us to measure the barrier's behaviour over a longer period?"

Pride winks at her with evident satisfaction. "Great minds, Silver. Yes, please."

It turns out that Pride is already one step ahead of her. At her signal, the city watchmen carry down five relatively fresh corpses, all tall and strong specimen who have been treated with oil to overpower the smell of decay. Silver ignores the looks of disgust on the faces of the watchmen when they lower the corpses to the ground. They wouldn't dare to disobey Pride. And this is for the good of the realm. It always is.

She instructs the apprentices on how to draw resurrection pentagrams, then sits back on her chair and watches them work. Pride runs strands of her thin, white hair through her fingers and tells her meaningless things about her week. Silver could resurrect the corpses without using pentagrams, but it would cost her much more strength than if the spell is funnelled through the intricate lines drawn in the apprentices' blood. And anyway, getting here was arduous enough. She feels like she has earned a brief break.

"You never visit anymore," Silver complains, glancing up at her friend.

Pride looks dejected. "I know. I overwork myself and then don't realise how much time has passed."

"Why are you still working so hard? We won, remember?" Silver replies with a whiny voice.

Pride scoffs. "We won a battle. But a door, once opened, will not remain unused. Even if this no enemy vanguard, sooner or later others will come."

"So, what's the grand idea?"

"To go on the offensive." Pride grins. "With mages like you and I on humanity's side, we could rule more than just our own plane."

When she sees the sceptical look on Silver's face, she hurriedly continues.

"Humanity could carve out a kingdom on a plane that isn't littered with rifts that lead gods-know-where. We could explore what else the universe has to offer. Wouldn't that be worth doing? Wouldn't it be worth knowing what is out there?"

Silver shrugs. She doesn't even feel particularly inclined to travel in the human realm. Pride ruffles her hair.

"Oh, come on, Silver. Dream a little bigger."

"Whatever. I like living in Old Noll."

"You've lived here your whole life. Do you never feel like you want to see other things?"

"Why? I like it here. If I'm bored, I'll read a book." Silver frowns. "Speaking of travelling, though, you still have my good wheelchair. The one you promised you'd fix ages ago?"

"Shit. Sorry. I knew I was feeling guilty for some reason." Pride looks genuinely guilt-ridden.

"Come by for dinner once this is over and bring it over. No excuses," Silver says with raised eyebrows.

Pride laughs. "I promise, I promise."

The apprentices finish the pentagrams and stand back up, their faces a little red and uncomfortable. They have moved the five corpses into the centre of each star and shuffle to the sides of the wine cellar when Silver raises her hands and utters an incantation. The pentagrams fill with eerie light, and the corpses slowly start to float.

"Shall I spread the bodies out to cover as wide an area as possible?" she suggests to Pride. Her mentor nods.

"Good idea. That should draw the energy of the forcefield outwards, leaving a vulnerable spot at the centre. Which the rest of us can focus on."

"What do you want us to cast?" the former sailor asks.

"Force spells," Pride replies. "Silver, can you count us down from ten once your corpses are in place?"

"Yes, Ma'am."

Once the corpses stand upright, Silver commands them to encircle the rift, two on the left and three on the right. Their bodies are still in good condition, and she can see the muscles on their arms and legs shifting with each motion. They should be able to withstand a good amount of electricity before losing their usefulness.

"Ready?"

Pride nods eagerly, but her apprentices are more hesitant. Still, after some encouragement from their master, they take point and raise their hands, heavily coated in spell components. Pride doesn't use any, which Silver notes with some surprise. Her mentor must have gotten ever stronger since the last time she saw her in action.

"Ten," Silver begins, then counts down to zero. Her summons walk into the rift's edges, and Silver winces when the electricity jumps onto soft human skin, and the stench of sizzling flesh fills the room. The summons twitch as though they are trying to escape, and Silver is sure their souls are howling in agony.

No matter. They'll be free soon enough. They're just doing a quick favour to the living. Everyone wants to be useful.

Pride and her apprentices shoot their force spells towards the centre of the rift. Silver feels the room's atmosphere shift, and for a moment, the protective layer is gone. A layer of white, dizzy clouds disappears, and two towers come into view.

They stretch into the sky, tall and elegant like the legs of a dancer. Silver feels a strange sense of anxiety as she looks upon their dark exterior.

The heavens in the realm beyond the rift are almost impossibly bright. The skies are golden and warm, but all Silver registers is encroaching blindness as the air becomes more and more alight. After a few moments, all they can see is the black silhouette of the towers' exterior.

The force field readjusts itself, and Silver's corpses fall to the ground, steaming with heat. The barrier convulses and converges atop the rift. A lightning bolt forms atop the rift, then comes loose, flying towards the mages.

"Shields! Now!" Silver shouts. She raises her own with a mere gesture, then widens it to the pale-faced apprentices who are stumbling over their words in panic. But she is too late. The lightning bolt hits the youngest apprentice before Silver's shields fully cover her.

The girl shrieks and falls onto her back, an angry, steaming wound carved into her chest. Silver feels her die from shock almost immediately, but with a twist of her hands and a touch of the bones on the ground, she compels her soul to stay. The girl might still be revived if they can get a cleric to come quickly.

Pride remains motionless. She keeps staring at the spot where the clouds have parted. Silver can't feel any magic on her. Pride didn't bother to lift her shields. Her eyes are wide, and her lips are moving, although no sound is forthcoming.

Silver shouts at the other two apprentices to fetch a cleric. She moves some of the dead girl's flesh to cover the wound, then turns to her mentor.

Pride is still staring at the rift. Silver knows her well enough to realise that she isn't confused. Pride is shocked. And you can only be shocked by something you recognise.

"What is it?" she asks. Pride ignores her for a moment, then blinks and looks down at her mentee.

"Hm? Nothing." Pride is never short with her. She also usually cares about her apprentices.

"Did you recognise the towers?" Silver asks.

Pride blinks. "No, of course not. Did you?"

Silver raises her eyebrows, then decides to keep the dead Karthe woman's words to herself. Pride nods and looks away without asking any further questions. *She seems relieved,* Silver realises. *Is she relieved that I didn't recognise what I was looking at?*

The apprentices return, a cleric of Five in toe. He takes one look at the dead girl on the floor and winces. Pride promises him a frankly absurd reward if he revives her, and he gets down on his knees and prays.

Silver can feel the girl's soul squirm in her grasp. The dead apprentice is scared. Or maybe she's just sick of the human world. Silver doesn't care. If the girl wants to die, she's not thinking straight. She'll thank her later for forcing her to stick around.

Silver keeps the girl bound to the human plane until the cleric's voice is hoarse from uttering unanswered prayer after unanswered prayer. Pride shakes her head distastefully.

"Come on now. She's young, and she only just died. Revive her already," she mutters. Silver is inclined to agree. Since the end of the war, with humanity's numbers devastated, the gods have often revived the young if they died from accidents or sickness. Just as long as a cleric served as a conduit for the divine powers and tried to resurrect them within the first few hours of death.

The priest is wailing out his prayers now. *Surely*, Silver thinks, *it's more uncomfortable for Five to listen to this than to revive the girl.*

But the god remains silent and unyielding.

Chapter 14

"You are not going to like this, husband."

Silver smiles a thin-lipped smile. They sit in the downstairs kitchen of her and Kass's manor, sharing over-decorated confections and heavy red wine.

Kass sighs.

"You don't have to sound so pleased about it, Silver."

Amaya frowns.

"What do you mean? Can you not do it?"

Silver turns to her.

"What, retrace the familial ties that bind a dead teenager to people he last saw seventeen years ago? No, that part is no problem."

Allen and Andrea stare at her with unconcealed awe, and Kass wants to slap them on the back of their heads.

"So? Stop bragging, Silver. What's the part I'm not going to like?" he grunts.

Silver shrugs. "Well, I need something to anchor the scrying spell to, no? Remember how I could trace the demons' paths by taking some essence from the rift they came through?"

Kass stares at her. Sometimes, he swears she's being deliberately difficult.

"So we get you some of Tade's stuff from the manor," he says. "A jumper or a childhood toy should do the bloody trick."

Silver raises her eyebrows and gives him a condescending look.

"And where exactly do you think that would lead us? Right back to Karthe manor, of course. Tade's possessions have no link with whoever gave birth to him all this time ago."

Amaya clicks her tongue. "Ah. So, you need the boy's body."

"Very good," Silver responds. "Blood begets blood. If it's the boy's birth parents you're after, you'll need to dig up his corpse."

"Out of the question," Kass barks, and his wife laughs.

"See? I told you that you wouldn't like it."

Andrea shifts uncomfortably.

"Would a mage with a ... different specialism have another way of scrying for Tade's parents?" they ask.

Silver shakes her head.

"No. Think about it," she explains. "What links Tade to his birth parents except for the bare bones of biology? As far as I know, he lived at House Karthe all his life. All his memories and interactions would have been with his adopted family. Any part of his life that mattered."

"He could have met with his birth parents in secret," Allen interjects.

"Sure," Silver responds. "But unless you can tell me which fuzzy sweater he wore for each occasion, that doesn't give me anything to go on."

She takes another sip of wine, her cheeks red in the flickering candlelight.

"So," she says. "If we assume that he had no or limited contact with his birth parents, we must rely on his blood. It's the only link we can be sure of."

"Five won't like this," Andrea says quietly. "Disturbing the rest of the dead is an affront against the natural order."

"Maybe he'd understand? We are doing this to save the city from demons," Allen says, his voice feeble. Amaya yawns, bored of any discussions that involve religion.

"Well," Silver says with a strain to her voice. "I am merely telling you what is and is not possible. Whether you want to be rational adults and make progress in your investigation is, of course, up to you."

"Silver," Kass says slowly. "I don't know how to tell you this in a way that will get through to you. I. Am. Not. Digging. Up. A. Corpse. For. You."

"I cannot tell you how much I hate this."

Kass feels a rash spread from the nape of his neck to the middle of his back. Sores sit between his fingers, making it increasingly hard to grab the shovel. And, of course, a splitting headache has made its way to the space between his temples.

Silver can't quite conceal a smug grin as she glances down at him from the top of Tade Karthe's grave.

"You're doing great, Kass. It's so very impressive to see you digging for justice."

"Screw you, Silver."

"Now, now. Is that any way to speak to your wife?"

Her grin widens, and she retracts her head as she leans back on her wheelchair. A few moments later, Allen's head appears.

"Are you sure we can't help you, Sir?" his squire asks. He wears that annoying look of concern as he glances down at the sweat on Kass's brows and the fiery redness of his commander's skin.

But Kass won't let his squires condemn themselves. Disturbing the rest of the dead is pretty high on the list of no-nos for followers of Five. His squires won't be protected from the consequences just because they acted on Kass's orders. Really, he didn't even want to let them come to the graveyard at all, especially not Andrea. Every time they pass by a graveyard, he wonders if they think of their own death and how that Five brought them back to life. If they do, Andrea doesn't ever let it show.

"Fuck off, Allen," Kass replies with a little more enthusiasm than necessary. His squire mumbles something about stubborn old men and is promptly replaced by Andrea.

"I read the information pamphlets from the graveyard keeper's station," they say. "Which state that the coffins are usually buried somewhere between four and six feet deep. Judging by how far you've dug, it shouldn't be much longer now."

Kass takes a ragged breath, then forces the shovel back into the earth.

Five is already happy to let him die. If there was ever a time to piss him off, it might as well be now.

"Try to finish this before morning, Kass. We didn't get a warrant for this, so we'll be in trouble if we get spotted," he hears Amaya from further away.

"Bah! Who needs a warrant? We're war heroes," Silver snaps. "That, and I locked off the entire graveyard with a barrier. Anyone who tries to force their way in here gets catapulted into the crusade memorial fields in the Polainian mountains."

Kass groans internally, then shovels another load of earth out of the hole. He can feel every single muscle in his arm screaming.

The relentlessness of the pain makes him think. Five is probably just mad at him. He is hardly a model paladin, never has been. But still. He glances skyward.

If there's a reason you don't want me to continue on this path, just bloody tell me. He thinks the words quietly, hoping his god might somehow hear him. Clerics and paladins become conduits for their gods' powers through a mere invocation. Who is to say that Five doesn't hear every single one of his thoughts?

Then he shakes his head. He's being stupid.

He puts the shovel back down, and this time, he hits a hard block of wood.

"Here we are," he grunts and frees up the top of the coffin. It still takes him far longer than it should, but eventually, he lifts the wooden lid and reveals Tade Karthe's decomposing corpse.

Kass sighs quietly. He remembers the boy. He died young and probably spent the last moments of his life in horrific agony.

"Is there a way you can not wake him up?" he asks Silver. His wife gives him a long look, then nods.

"Yes. It's just a scrying spell. I don't need his soul to come back for that." She smiles at him, but the motion is a little shaky. "Let's get this done as quickly as possible, okay?"

He nods. The stench of decay fills the hole, and he isn't sure he can stand it for much longer without memories of similar scenes from the war entering his mind.

"I need you to cut his wrists. His blood will serve as an anchor to the spell," Silver says.

Of course. Kass draws a knife from his belt and does as he is asked. The feeling of the boy's limp, thin wrists between his aching fingers almost makes him throw up. But blood, congealed, black, and slow, flows from the blade's silver edge. It is almost like Tade is still waiting to come back to life, desperate for a god's divine intervention. Which never came. The gods' will is mysterious.

He hears Silver mutter an incantation, and the blood shoots upward into the night sky. It spins around its axis as it looks for a target to latch onto.

Allen and Andrea pull him out of the hole as Silver closes her eyes and whispers words Kass doesn't recognise. She has revealed her skeleton hand, which helps her amplify the potency of her spells. Almost as if she is spellcaster and spell component at once.

He promised her a million times that he would get her the best prosthetic money could buy if only she got rid of the damned thing. Perhaps, his foggy mind tells him now, that was an insensitive thing to say.

Then again, the hand is an undeniably disturbing sight. His squires stare at Silver, surrounded by whirring blood and raising her glowing skeleton hand, and for the first time, there is fear rather than admiration in their eyes.

He wishes he could enjoy a bit of righteous indignation, but he just feels tired.

The blood stretches into a line, then starts to glow with a deep-set, internal hue. It settles in the air like it is waiting for them to follow. Then, the spell flickers and disappears.

Amaya coughs.

Silver opens her eyes again.

"What?" the necromancer snaps.

"Did it not work?" Allen asks.

"Hm? Of course, it worked. I'm no amateur, boy," Silver snaps. Kass wordlessly points at the spot where the spell disappeared. Silver glares at him.

"I'm sorry, did you see any of your demons following glowing magic strands through the city? Scrying spells are only visible to the people they are made visible to. Otherwise, the whole process would be far too conspicuous and would also cost the spellcaster far too much energy."

"So, would you mind making the spell visible to us, mistress?" Andrea asks, ever polite. Silver smiles at them and nods. The spell returns to view, just as red and disconcerting as before.

"See? It worked. The spell is anchored to a point on this plane," Silver explains. Amaya frowns. "Just one point? So, just one parent?"

Silver nods slowly. "I felt a pull in two directions, but one was much stronger than the other. I assume that is because only one of Tade's birthparents is still alive."

"Very well. I suspect that will be the more helpful lead. Let's go," Amaya says, and the blood spell unfurls in response to her words.

Kass bids them to wait and wordlessly gestures at Tade's corpse, frail and vulnerable in the open air. Before he can protest, Andrea jumps into the hole and closes the coffin lid, gently folding the boy's wrists across his chest.

Allen pulls them back out, and Kass mutters a quick 'thank you'. He hopes Five will reward them for that. He hopes his god isn't –

Silver's wheelchair struggles with the gravel on the graveyard's small paths, so he grabs the handles on its back and carefully pushes her across the most even-looking sections. His wife waits until the other three have passed them by as they follow the spell that flickers in the night air. Then she turns around to him. Her dark eyes gleam in the night, and memories of a different time fill Kass's chest with a strange spell of longing.

"You're struggling, aren't you?" she asks softly. "Is losing Five's favour hitting you that hard?"

Kass forces himself to glare at her.

"There's no point apologising now, Silver. It's done now."

"I am not apologising. This was necessary for your investigation. You wouldn't have gone along with it if it wasn't." Her dark eyes soften a little. "But you're struggling, and I'm –"

She hesitates for a second.

"I'm worried about you. Everything, the way you breathe, the way you move, it's – off. Even for Five and even for the ever-so-horrific crime of grave robbing, this level of punishment seems disproportionate."

"Does it now?" he huffs, then lifts her gently across a slight dip in the path. "Remember that Five doesn't punish people. The gods don't work like that. I'm just getting weak in my old age."

"You're not old just yet."

"You're just saying that because you're the same age as me."

"Maybe. Although thanks to illusion magic, I'll be forever young and beautiful." She winks. "All for the benefit of my husband, who couldn't care less about all that, of course."

Kass can't believe that she can make him blush even amidst the hot flushes of pain that race through his body.

"Inappropriate, Silver," he grunts.

"You never used to mind that. You never used to mind a lot of things."

"I'm pretty sure even in my wildest youth, I would never have said yes to grave-robbing."

"Kass –"

"Yeah, yeah," he interrupts her. "You're just helping, and I'm rewarding you by being a grumpy bastard. I know."

He sighs, and for a moment, they are caught in the uncomfortable silence that follows Kass's begrudging surrender.

The spell has led them back out of the graveyard and now stretches through empty night streets in the direction of the castle. So far, Kass isn't surprised. To convince a noble family to take an infant, you need connections. The spell might lead them to one of the many nobles living inside the castle after their manors were destroyed during the war.

"You're not telling me everything," Silver says quietly.

"Hmm?"

"Normally, you'd use a divine incantation to heal yourself if you struggled this much. There's a reason you're unable to heal yourself, and I think you know what it is."

Kass sighs internally. Silver knows him far too well for him to be able to brush her off. He has to give her at least a partial truth.

"I don't. Not really."

"Kass."

"I'm not lying to you. I talked to Five's avatar at the temple earlier today. He seems pissed at me, but I'm not sure why. Except for the obvious."

"The obvious? You mean me?" Her expression is amused, but he recognises the frustration that weighs down her tone. "You used to have nicer pet names for me, Kass."

"Silver..." he sighs.

"I'm just saying that a years-long marital crisis is no reason to let your imagination slack off," she says, and the humour is sweet even though it's forced.

"I'll remember that, butter bear," he relents.

"Butter bear!?"

Kass shrugs with a grin. "You asked for it."

Silver playfully rolls her eyes before her expression turns serious once more.

"Do you think Five wants you to stop your investigation?" she asks. "Is that why he's not helping you? Is it an attempt at slowing you down without interfering directly?"

"I -"

He should deny it. He does not want to have another argument with Silver, and he does not want to defend himself against her distrust of the gods. But he also doesn't want to lie to her.

"It's possible," he admits.

Silver nods slowly. She doesn't seem surprised.

"What does that mean?" she asks. "Is our mage affiliated with the gods? Or is our culprit a cleric?"

"I don't know, Silver."

He should tell her. Octavia's accusations are becoming harder and harder to dismiss.

"Are you scared to find out?" she presses.

"I'm always fucking scared."

She reaches over the back of her chair to squeeze his hand.

"Don't be," she says. "I'm here. I'll see us through this, I promise."

"Silver –"

He takes a deep breath and tells her. Although every word burns his mouth, he tells her about Octavia's suspicions that the gods have devoted servants amidst the paladins and clerics of other planes of existence. That they support no people and no side except for their own. He is careful to speak quietly so that his squires and Amaya can't hear him.

Especially Andrea. He does not want them to think that their resurrection was somehow meaningless. Because it wasn't. It never could be.

Silver stays quiet for a little while after Kass is done with his explanation.

"You should have told me," she finally says.

"That's your reaction?" he barks.

"I'm just saying. I could have helped you more if you weren't keeping half the information from me."

"I swear to Five, Silver, I –"

"Well, maybe you shouldn't," she interrupts him. "Maybe you should save your loyalties for someone who will show you the same level of devotion that you have wasted on them."

She shoots him a meaningful glance. He shakes his head.

"I haven't had time to think this all through yet," he says.

"What is there to think through? Foreswear Five. He's punishing you for arbitrary reasons because his loyalties are split between us and our attackers."

"We don't bloody know that!"

"What else could it be?"

Kass sighs loudly.

"I don't just give up, Silver," he says. "Not on a quest. Not on people. Not on my god. You of all people should know that."

Silver stares at him, but for once, she doesn't argue.

"Fine," she says. "But let me just tell you this. It makes sense."

"Hmm?" Kass grunts, his heart racing.

Silver rubs her chin. "Well," she begins. "I often wondered why I was able to revive enemy soldiers during the war. Necromantic resurrection spells mirror the resurrection miracles of the gods. That's why the souls return to their bodies. They hope that they are going to be revived. But why would the enemy follow my summons if they didn't believe in the gods? If they didn't expect to be resurrected by divine intervention?"

Kass remains silent. After a few moments, Silver touches his fingers, cold against the handles of her wheelchair.

"Let's find out what is going on," she says. "Together."

He blinks.

"Al...Alright," he mutters.

"Just don't complain when I'm inevitably proven to be right," Silver adds, unable to keep the smugness out of her voice.

"Silver, if my god turns out to be irredeemably corrupt and somehow involved in summoning demonic agents into our capital city, you get to say 'I told you so' all you like. Happy?"

"Exceptionally so."

Chapter 15

To Kass's surprise, Silver's scrying spell leads them around the castle and through the barracks. As they walk past make-shift offices, sleeping quarters for city guardsmen, watchtowers, and food trucks whose shutters are closed for the night, Amaya points out the outline of the mage tower northeast of the castle.

"Didn't you say the third demon was heading in the direction of the tower?" she asks.

"Yes," Silver replies slowly. "But by now, it could have crossed the city walls for all I know. It's been days."

"If our demon is looking for high-profile targets, the mage tower is a logical place to attack," Kass says. "It could be that the bloody thing has been biding its time. Waiting until it can catch its prey alone."

Silver shrugs.

"It is possible. The mage tower is usually crowded with students, but after yesterday's meeting, quite a few are out patrolling the streets or working on the rift."

"So, if one of the mages is the demon's target, we might have just made the assassin's job a whole lot easier. Fantastic," Kass mutters.

He curses internally. He should have thought of that during the king's meeting. Once more, his mistakes could cost innocent lives. He suddenly feels like the war truly never ended.

Amaya rubs her hands together.

"This is all speculation," she says. "We know nothing definite about the third demon. Let's focus on the assassins' connection to Tade's mysterious parent."

The rest of the group agrees. They continue to follow the spell as it snakes through the narrow alleyways surrounding the mage tower. The tower is built on the foundations of an ancient church dedicated to a god whose name was lost over time. With each generation of mages it housed and trained, an additional level was added to the foundation until it now looms fat and heavy above Old Noll's skyline. Most classrooms and living quarters are inside a granite spire, but wide-ranging wings and extensions have grown out of the stone like tumours besetting a sleeping animal.

As far as Kass remembers, the tower's opal windows are always illuminated with flickering, multi-coloured lights, and a high-pitched alarm bell perpetually rings as city guardsmen hurry towards or away from the building. The mages like their experiments, and Pride very much encourages their ambitions.

So, Kass is surprised to see that almost every part of the tower is coated in deep black, even considering the late hour of the night. Only a few windows at the very top of the building are filled with pale light.

"I told you. Most of the mages have been drafted for patrol," Silver explains. "They're probably asleep, preparing for their rota, or already out walking the streets."

She laughs.

"Girah even tried to get *me* to go out patrolling. That man is nothing if not convincing. By the end of our conversation, I wasn't sure if surveying the streets of Old Noll hadn't, in fact, been my life's long-sought calling."

"Yeah, he's good at that. Best to ignore everything he says," Kass grunts.

"Isn't that your approach to everyone, Sir?" Allen asks with a deliberately blank face. Andrea prods his side.

As they reach the bottom of the tower, the spell begins to glow more intensely. Kass frowns. Are they chasing Tade Karth's parent or the third demon's target? He exchanges a weighty glance with Amaya. Could they be the same person?

Amaya frowns, silently cautioning him not to jump to conclusions. Still, she places her hand on her gun.

They walk up the narrow staircase to the tower's entrance, a half-open amphitheatre hewn out of the former temple's stone foundations. Faintly painted constellations still adorn the floor, whose intricate design Silver points out every time they're here. She also always mentions that the constellations don't match any that exist in the night sky.

Except for today.

Silver casts a levitation spell on her wheelchair and anchors it to Kass, allowing her to follow him. Levitating costs her a lot of effort, but Kass understands why she does it. This tower has a lot of dark corners from which a demon could strike, and if Kass carries her, that might take them both out of the fight.

Once upon a time, Pride promised Silver she'd find a mechanical solution to make the mage tower wheelchair-friendly. But like many of Pride's high-flying promises, its implementation has yet to see the light of day.

The spell leads them up a winding spiral staircase, closed doors framing their path through the dimly lit corridor. According to tradition, every mage paints the doors to their living quarters with motifs that represent either something about themselves or their specialism. Kass passes by colourful meadows, dark caverns with gleaming treasures, and warm taverns full of laughter and song.

However, many mages are terrible artists, so he and Andrea previously made a game of guessing what some of the scribbles are supposed to be.

Upstairs, they pass classrooms marked with the arcane symbols for the different schools of magic. Kass notes, with relief, that there is no designated room where necromancy is taught. He knows Pride wants to train more necromancers and has presumably bought up the subject with king Ithya. He is relieved that Ithya remains, as always, the one voice of reason left in this sorry realm.

The scrying spell leads them to the top of the mage tower, where the mage general moved her living quarters after the war's end. Conversation between the group falls silent when they reach the same inevitable conclusion. Pride's door stands before them, painted with a red bird in flight before an entirely white background.

Kass speeds up when he sees the door is only partially closed. The pale light inside is flickering. He hears a soft groan, followed by the sound of teeth peeling off a layer of flesh.

He curses and charges through the door, all thoughts of pain and slowness forgotten. Pride lies at the centre of her living room. Her stomach is ripped open, and her intestines leak out of a red-gaping wound, wide like a smile with too many teeth.

Her eyes are closed, and soft moans escape her lips as the third demon takes a bite out of her.

This demon is smaller than the others, its exterior a dark, mossy green speckled with softly gleaming spikes. The scent of wet trees fills the room with an intoxicating smell that sends Kass's head spinning.

"Careful," he tells the group as they follow him into the room. "It's probably poisonous."

Silver hovers beside him and raises her hands, spell components already smeared across her fingertips. The demon jumps away from Pride, and its spikes suddenly grow to twice their length. A yellow liquid secretes from their tips, and the smell inside the room becomes even more intense. Kass feels his vision blur, and Silver falls unconscious.

Amaya clutches the doorframe and draws her gun. Allen and Andrea push past their commander and draw their swords. Kass curses. He trusts his squires, but he'll be damned if they get hurt under his watch.

The demon leaps towards Andrea, stubby legs outstretched and spikes growing as it falls through the air. Andrea does precisely what they've been taught. They side-step the attack, then raise their sword to cut through their flying foe. The demon levitates upwards and spits a pale yellow liquid at Andrea's face. The squire screams as the excretion clings to their skin, steaming.

Amaya shoots a bullet at the demon, but its movements are too erratic for her to get a hit in. Kass raises his Zweihander and attacks the demon with a jumping strike, but it flies out of range before his blade can connect. Allen is shaking Silver's arm, but Kass has little hope that his squire will wake her up in time. Since the war, Silver's defences against attacks - or even just a simple cold - have been through the floor.

The demon, now hovering close to the room's ceiling, shoots more of its secretion at Kass and Andrea. Its spikes are almost as tall as its head and continue leaking with softly glowing liquid. Its stench makes Kass dizzy.

Amaya continues to take shots at the demon, but it dodges her bullets with ease. She mutters something under her breath.

Kass looks over to Andrea, whose eyes are wide with adrenaline and worry.

"When I tell you to, jump on my shoulders. You should be able to reach the demon from there."

"Yes, Sir," his squire replies without hesitation.

"'Maya, can you try to chase the demon into a corner?" Kass barks at the investigator.

"Yes," Amaya replies, although her voice shakes with frustration.

Allen mutters a prayer to Five, asking him to slow down the demon's movements. The squire's eyes are squeezed shut in concentration, and he has folded his hands.

Kass has little hope that Five will assist them, but it's worth a try.

Amaya keeps up the barrage of bullets and manages to chase the demon into the leftmost corner of the room. Kass follows, then rounds his back and lowers his head before asking Andrea to jump.

A moment later, he feels his squire's heavy boots pressing against the plate mail on his back. Several disconcerting cracks rattle his spine. He fails to suppress a pained groan, but a squelch and a triumphant shout from above tell him his plan worked.

Groans of disgust fill the room before Andrea jumps back down, and the impaled figure of the demon crashes to the ground.

Amaya runs over to it and starts cutting it into pieces.

Kass feels his vision blur as he straightens up. He can tell that at least part of his spine is dislocated.

"What are you doing?" Andrea asks Amaya as they wipe the demon's secretion from their hair.

Allen opens Pride's windows before he hurries over to the barely conscious mage general. He utters a healing prayer to Five, but like before, no response is forthcoming, and no divine power fills his eyes. Kass feels a stab of guilt at seeing his squire's crestfallen expression.

"The other ones regenerated," Amaya responds to Andrea. "We need to make sure this one doesn't."

Kass nods. She is right. He joins her, and together, they cut the demon into small pieces.

Then Allen calls them over.

"Five isn't answering," his squire says, staring at Kass. His voice is shaking. For most of his life, Allen felt he deserved to be overlooked. Right up until Five chose him as a potential paladin and confronted him with the terrifying realisation that he could do something with his life.

Kass knows what that's like. Being ignored now, when he did nothing wrong, must cut Allen deeper than any knife.

Pride's eyes flicker open. For a moment, there is nothing besides terror in her expression, then she moves her hand across the wound on her stomach.

The skin slowly grows back together as if the mage is turning back time. Her intestines crawl into the comfort of her stomach, the blood snakes underneath her skin, and Pride's cheeks turn back to a rosy colour.

She sighs with pleasure before focusing her gaze on her rescuers. Kass thinks he can read a challenge in her expression.

He feels himself grow pale. He has seen spells like this before, channelled through the hands of clerics and fellow paladins.

What he just witnessed was a divine intervention.

Chapter 16

Kass pushes Silver's chair to an open window. Thin strands of hair have fallen into her face, and he meticulously brushes them behind her ears. He is vaguely aware that his back is killing him, but he barely feels it.

Silver's breathing is strong, and his rational side knows she'll be fine. Knowing and believing something isn't quite the same, though. His heart is beating so hard he thinks it might burst.

Pride slowly approaches him. Her head is carefully polished, as usual, and her eyes are rimmed by lines of coal. They have agreed to postpone all questions until Silver has come to. The parts of Andrea's face where they were struck with the demon's secretion are still steaming. Allen and Amaya are helping them rub out the remnants with water and soap. Andrea is trying their best not to complain.

"Oh, Silver," Pride mutters and bends down to gaze upon her sleeping friend. "She could set the world on fire just to die of a coughing fit."

"I'd rather she didn't set the world on fire," Kass replies.

Pride laughs, then reveals a bottle filled with yellow-glowing liquid.

"I got it from the attic," he explains. "That should help her come to."

"What is it?" Kass asks suspiciously. Pride narrows her eyes.

"It's a potion. Its material composition triggers an adrenaline rush in the brain, forcing it out of a restful state. I can give you the recipe if you want."

Kass takes a deep breath. "We're all on edge, Pride," he says, as conciliatory as he can manage.

"Indeed," she says curtly. "In fact, I don't see your intestines sprawled across the floor."

"Neither are yours," Kass responds.

Pride laughs humourlessly. "Try to be a little more disappointed about that, will you?"

She uncorks the bottle, and the sharp smell of ephedra flowers mixed with lemon and alcohol fills the air. Kass remembers these kinds of potions from the war. He takes a step back even though he feels his head clear with immediate effect. Stimulants don't mix well with his flashbacks.

Silver's eyelids flicker as Pride moves the bottle closer to her face. After a few moments, she stirs. Her eyes fly open as she inhales a sharp breath, and she raises her hands as if she is about to cast a spell.

"Relax, Silver," Kass says softly. "We won."

"We – What? Kass?" Silver blinks at him, and her eyes widen with surprise and pleasure. "Oh, we did? Good."

She coughs and blushes. "Sorry," she adds after a few moments. "What a great help I was."

Pride clears her throat, and Silver shoots around.

"Pride! You're –"

Her eyes wander to Pride's abdomen, where she expects the bite wound to linger.

"You're fine," Silver finishes lamely, then reaches for her mentor's hands. "Thank – well…"

"Thanks to you," Pride replies with the kind of warmth she seems to reserve for Silver and, very occasionally, Ithya. Kass thinks her comment is a tad rich, seeing as his wife spent the entire fight unconscious, but he does not want to ruin the moment.

Instead, he turns around to his squires and Amaya, who are finished with their clean-up. Amaya stands up and marches towards Pride.

"Are you Tade Karthe's mother?" she asks without interlude.

Pride raises her eyebrows.

"I'm sorry, what?" she responds, letting go of Silver's hands. "And here I was assuming you'd ask me about the demon that was taking its fill of my intestines."

"Oh, we'll get to that," Kass grunts.

Silver explains the spell she cast to find Tade Karthe's living parent. Pride shrugs with slight exasperation.

"Well, that's a tale from another time. I suppose I – yes. The boy was my son." She scoffs. "In that, I gave birth to him nine months after a stupid night of frustration and regret. But Emilia and Ernst are – were – his parents in the only way that matters. I must admit that I was never particularly interested in him."

"Why did you give him away?" Silver asks softly. Pride looks at her, and Kass sees the hesitation of someone who fears being judged.

"I never wanted children, you know that," the mage general says. "I had just established myself as head of the tower, and things were finally looking up. What was I supposed to do? Teach classes in between changing nappies? Advise the queen after I put down my baby for his afternoon nap?"

She shrugs. Amaya smiles wryly, even as the rest of them do not react.

"Back then, I was close friends with the Karthes. I purchased most of the guild's spell components from them, and business gets people talking. After I heard that Emilia had lost her child, things fell into place. I knew Tade would have a good life with them. Much better than the life he'd have with me."

"That must have been hard," Silver says. Pride shrugs, looking more uncertain than anything.

"It is ancient history. Why does it matter now?" she asks.

"We think the rift opened at House Karthe for a reason," Amaya explains. "Not only is it at an equivalent distance between Octavia's home in the docks, the castle, and the mage tower, but as we have learned, House Karthe is also indirectly connected with one of the demons' targets. With you."

"Hmm." Pride rubs the back of her head and starts pacing up and down.

"If someone set a demon on you, how would they have done it?" Kass asks.

Pride glares at him. "What do you mean?" she snaps.

But Silver understands what he is getting at.

"Well, they would have used a scrying spell, no?" she says, her dark eyes gleaming. "The demons would be following a bloodline. Or several. And if they did, the spell linked to Pride might also have led them to Tade."

"How would they have gotten hold of Pride's blood though?" Allen asks. He is sitting next to Andrea.

"I fought through a war. I bled plenty," Pride snaps, and the squire falls silent.

Amaya looks at Silver. "How doable would that be?" she asks. "Track down three targets using years-old blood from the war?"

Silver exhales slowly.

"Doable," she replies after a brief pause. "If you're working with blood that old, you'd need an exceptional diviner. But someone like Melina could have done it."

"Melina is dead," Pride says pointlessly.

"Someone like Melina," Silver repeats, her voice dull.

"Do you have any idea why someone might be targeting you, Pride?" Amaya asks.

"What, are you asking if I can think of anyone who might hold a grudge against myself, Octavia, and Ithya?" the mage general snaps. "Hells, I don't know – maybe every enemy soldier who survived the war?"

Amaya doesn't let herself be provoked. "Any way you could narrow that down for us? We're looking for a powerful spellcaster."

"No," Pride responds sharply. "I've had other things to do over the last few years than worry about all the people I might have upset. Isn't that the kind of details work we employ people like you for?"

Amaya stares at her, impatient for Pride's mood to blow over. Kass narrows his eyes and steps in the mage general's way, forcing her to stop pacing.

"'Maya and I are doing our bloody jobs right now in case you hadn't noticed," he snaps. "And don't act like you're playing with an open book here." He gestures at her stomach. "The way you healed yourself. That was divine magic. How the fuck did you do that?"

"What?" Siver whispers. Amaya fills her in, and the necromancer's eyes return to Pride, wide and full of uncertainty.

Pride scoffs. "Divine magic, arcane magic – what is the meaningful difference between them? Both are types of power used to rearrange the Multiverse. And, in the end, power is just power."

"But arcane magic can't be used to alter the human body," Andrea argues. "That is the remit of clerics and paladins."

Healing others is considered a sacred practice. Only clerics and paladins can perform divine miracles by becoming temporary conduits for the gods' will. It is a difficult and intense process that forces the faithful to call upon the gods again and again until the divine can find their supplicant within the vastness of the Multiverse.

Mages just blow shit up. At least, that's the way Kass has always seen things.

"There is a difference between something that can't be done and something that has been implicitly forbidden," Pride replies. "What do you think Silver has been doing for the past seven years? Necromancy assumes the ultimate control over the body. Does it really matter if that body is dead?"

Her eyes flicker over to Silver.

"Restoration is not so difficult once you know what you're doing. I've been working on this spell for years." Her expression softens. "Once I've mastered it, I'll fix your legs. I swear it."

Silver's eyes grow wider still. Kass clenches his fists. So much for hoping his wife might be on his side.

"But healing is the remit of the gods –" Andrea argues, but Pride interrupts her.

"Who decides that? You people can believe whatever you want, but I do not recognise the authority of the gods, especially when their powers aren't that much greater than mine."

"That's heresy, Pride," Kass snaps.

"Didn't you say it yourself? I cast a divine miracle. Maybe you should start praying to me instead of Five. If you're a good boy, I might listen." Her smile is cruel and mocking. Kass clenches his fists until he feels his nails break through his skin.

"How did you learn to do this, Pride?" Silver asks quietly. Pride turns to her former student.

"There is so much knowledge on other planes if you're only brave enough to travel through the rifts. There are people, entities, and consciousnesses willing to teach you anything for the right price."

She scoffs.

"Do you want to know something? Those precious gods of yours aren't even known across the Multiverse. Beyond a few select worlds, I've seen no statues built in their honour, no temples, no devout followers, nothing. They are just -"

"That's enough," Allen snaps. He pulls himself up and glares at Pride with barely concealed disgust. "We risked our lives to save you. The least you can do is not mock our beliefs."

Pride snorts.

"And how are your beliefs serving you? Your god isn't listening to your prayers. I can feel the demonic corruption on Kass from where I'm standing. Why is Five still allowing such rot to spread in one of his chosen fighters? Your so-called god doesn't give a shit about you."

Silver stares at Kass, the shock pale on her features.

"What?" she whispers.

Kass closes his eyes for a moment.

"Fuck you, Pride," he says and means every syllable.

"What is she talking about, Kass?" his wife repeats, her voice high.

"We can talk about this at home, Silver," he says, trying to reach an assuaging tone.

"We'll bloody well talk about it now!" his wife replies. "What does she mean? And why am I seemingly the only person here who doesn't know you're poisoned?"

"Stoic and silent. How very typical of you paladin lot," Pride says with a sly grin.

Silver shoots around to her. "Would you consider, for one fucking second, to cool your enthusiasm about my marital disputes?" she snaps.

Pride shuts up. Kass sighs. "Look, Silver, I just didn't want you to worry. I'm sure Five will heal me at some point, it's just that –"

He interrupts himself. *It's just that my god seems to insist I cut all ties with you.* How can he say that to her? She might deserve to hear it, but life isn't about what you deserve. Silver narrows her eyes.

"It's just what?"

"Five wants the commander to divorce you," Allen mutters. "That's why he's not healing him."

Kass shoots around. "How the fuck do you even know that?" he barks in his squire's general direction.

Allen colours. "Sorry. At Five's temple – I was listening at the door."

"I told him not to," Andrea interjects, their cheeks bright red.

195

"I'm sorry, Sir," Allen repeats. "But, well, you look like you're about to die on your feet. And we need you."

"Allen, I swear to Five, I will throw you head-first from the top of this blasted tower –"

"Fine!" Silver interrupts them and throws up her hands. Her eyes are light with tears. "Fine! Fine. Let's get divorced. If your stupid god hates me so fucking much, I won't – I won't be responsible for your death. I won't poison you with my presence."

"Silver," Kass forces his voice to soften again. "Silver, nobody is saying that –"

"Everyone is saying that!" his wife replies, her voice shrill. "And now even the bloody gods agree."

Kass clenches his fists shut. "I'll be damned if I let anyone decide for us. This is between you and me. Nobody else."

"You will be damned if you don't," Silver replies. "And I won't be responsible for it. Not anymore."

Pride rolls her eyes.

"So melodramatic," she says, then approaches Kass. Before he can stop her, she makes the same gesture across his body that she used to close her own wound. Kass feels a flurry of power rush through him, forcing his spine back into place and chasing away the fever, the rash, and the sores. Air rushes into his lungs, and suddenly, everything feels much clearer.

And yet. A tingling feeling latches onto the depths of his chest, hooking tiny claws into his breastbone. Whatever spell Pride used to cure him, it comes with ties.

Silver stares at him with barely concealed relief, her anger forgotten.

"You're welcome," Pride says with a condescending smile. "You don't need a god's approval to be cured."

Almost as an afterthought, she walks over to Andrea and does the same to their face, still red from the demon's poison. Kass pats down his body. He feels better than he has in years. Even his racing heart has calmed down.

Silver clears her throat.

"Your apprentice died at the rift yesterday. You might have saved her if you used that power then. How could you just stand there and watch her die?"

Pride's tone softens. "You know as well as I do how people get when they're confronted with things they don't understand. To my apprentices and the guards, it would have looked like I was trying to act like a god."

"Because you are," Kass mutters.

"You're welcome," Pride snaps. "Look, much as I wish it were, the world isn't ready to lose its deities. Humans aren't ready to accept that we can become our own saviours. In a few years, when we've fully recovered from the war, when people are doing more than just surviving –"

She coughs. "Hells, I haven't even perfected my divine spells yet. I can't bring anyone back from the dead. I can't even do anything particularly complex. I'd heal your legs right now, Silver, if I didn't think I'd mess it up."

Silver narrows her eyes. "I don't care about my fucking legs. I want to know why my friend lied to me."

"I'm sorry," Pride says, and for the first time that day, Kass believes her. "I was going to tell you. I really –"

"Oh, that seems to be everyone's favourite line today," Silver snaps, her voice full of bile.

Amaya sighs. "None of this is helping us solve the case," she notes. "Although we can now conclude with certainty that Pride is the demons' third target."

"Great," Kass mutters. "So our mystery demon is after two powerful war heroes and our king. As long as it's just bloody that."

"But this time, we actually killed the demon," Andrea says. "And now that we know they all regenerate, we won't be taken by surprise again."

"Easier said than done," Amaya says. "But you make a good point. With increased security at the castle, former general Octavia and king Ithya should be safe enough. And if we station guards at the rift, we might catch the two loose demons if they attempt to return where they came from."

Kass looks back at Pride.

"And you really have no idea who could be after you?" he asks. "You said you travelled across the planes to learn these divine spells. Sure you didn't make any mortal enemies out there?"

"None powerful enough to pursue me here," the mage general replies haughtily.

"Are you sure about that?" Amaya presses.

"As sure as I can be of anything."

Allen cocks his head to the side. "Erm, I've got a question. Now that we have one of the demon assassins diced up, could we use another scrying spell to find whoever hired it in the first place?"

Pride raises her eyebrows.

"If we want to waste our time. In all likelihood, the demon's master is sitting behind that blighted rift in the Karthe wine cellar. And if we could open that, we wouldn't be in this situation, would we? Try to keep up, boy."

"Shut it, Pride. At least Allen is trying to help," Kass snarls. "Also, it's not an altogether dumb idea. The demon lived on a hell plane before it was taken by our mage. So, how did the mage get to hell in the first place? By opening a rift, most likely."

Silver's eyes widen. "And what if that rift is still open? It would have to be, wouldn't it? And it might be unprotected."

"Exactly," Kass replies. They stare at each other. Kass feels a warm feeling spread through his limbs.

"But if you use the demon fragments to cast a scrying spell, wouldn't it still lead you to the rift in the Karthe manor, just like Pride said?" Amaya asks.

"Yes," Pride says slowly. "Scrying spells latch onto the closest link. That's why your spell on Tade found me rather than the corpse of his long-departed father. I was closer."

"Who –?" Silver starts, but Pride shakes her head.

"No. I won't speak of it. Not even to you."

Silver purses her lips but remains silent. After a moment's disorientation, Pride continues.

"Now, if you were already on a hell plane and cast the scrying spell there, the magic would seek the shortest way towards its target. If you're unlucky, it'll lead us straight back here."

Silver shakes her head and continues in her mentor's stead. "But say, we enter the hell plane the demon comes from. If I cast a scrying spell there, it should lead us to the rift that was created by the mage to access his demonic servant. If we make the spell powerful enough, it could even lead us across several planes. As long as the mage's location is closer than our home plane, a scrying spell should lead us to them."

Pride nods, then scratches the back of her bald head.

"This is all assuming you're in a feasible range for the magic to connect, Silver. Don't overestimate the potency of scrying. I imagine few mages can cast spells that take hold across the planes." She hesitates for a moment, then continues. "I could give you spell components that would increase the power of your scrying. And I could –"

"So, we're thinking of going to hell? Am I understanding that correctly?" Andrea asks. Their voice shakes slightly.

"Regret signing up? I sure am," Allen quips with a shaky smile. Andrea shakes their head but looks less certain than usual.

Kass sighs. "Seems like a bloody daft plan, but it is a plan. And with half of king Ithya's soldiers on the lookout for a rift to the hells, it's only a matter of time until we can test this theory in practice."

Amaya raises her eyebrows.

"I assume you'll want to keep this off the books for now?"

"Please," Kass replies. "But Ithya and Octavia will need to be informed."

"I can do that," Pride suggests. Her expression is haughty, but there is also a tethering layer of excitement she struggles to conceal. "If you manage to track down this blasted mage for me, I will stay here to ensure nothing happens to Octa and Ithya."

"What, after all your planar travels, you don't fancy a sojourn to hell?" Silver asks. Kass has never heard her take such a tense tone when speaking to Pride, and he catches a flash of hurt across the mage general's face.

"I have other, more pressing obligations," she says sharply. "I can't waste my time chasing after a single enemy, especially when someone with actual power needs to protect the king. In case you've forgotten, two demons are still on the loose."

"What obligations?" Kass asks suspiciously.

"Things concerning the protection of the realm. Don't trouble your little paladin-head with them," Pride snaps. "But feel free to pop by if you bruise your knuckles or scrape a knee. We wouldn't want you to feel useless now that your god has abandoned you."

Chapter 17

Wartime

The enemy had decidedly too many scales to be called 'human', but their bipedal, four-limbed shape made for predictable opponents. After the war had raged for a few years too many, they had enough of throwing their armies against the city walls and being drenched in the humans' crossfire of spells, arrows, and holy invocations.

So, they called their big brothers. Gigantic, scaled lizards that could fly and spew fire. Some human soldiers started calling them dragons, and the name stuck.

The first time the dragons appeared, they tore down two districts and all the encampments outside the city walls. Pride and her pupils saved the city by creating a makeshift barrier. It lay atop Old Noll like a black, ragged blanket and would only hold for so long. And while some dragons had been felled by arrows, lightning, and the occasional suicidal fighter, there were still at least thirty left outside the city perimeters, waiting for their moment to strike.

Like the other mages, Silver had spent every minute since the last attack trying to devise a spell that could destroy the dragon fleet. Initially, they had been called into the mage tower for an emergency conference, but conflicting ideas and philosophies soon drove the spellcasters apart again. Silver had some ideas, but they felt too dangerous to share with anyone. They sat on her tongue like unuttered acid.

She wanted to talk to Melina. She would tell Silver if she was being crazy. But Melina was dead. Silver had watched her die, then washed her hands in blood, trying to pull her chest together so Kass could plead with his god to revive her.

Sometimes, she still smelled the blood when she moved her fingers too close to her face.

They were out of time. Silver was stationed on the battlements when the dragons rose into the skies, their wings forming a darkening cloud front. After three days without sleep, Silver felt oddly dull watching them approach the city in a terrifying formation. She was aware that her throat was sore, her stomach was bloated, and her sleeves scratched against the skin on her wrists. But she didn't feel scared.

They would either win, or they would lose. More probably, they would lose. At this point, she just wanted to make the enemy's job as difficult as possible. Turning war into a numbers game was the only way to make it make sense.

Others had already rung the alarm. Below, the remaining soldiers were preparing for the assault. There was little noise, little shouting, just the low thrum of booted feet getting in position and hands grabbing well-worn weapons. There weren't many of them left now. Silver's squadron had been merged with two others, and still, there were barely sixty soldiers on this corner of the wall. Silver was the only mage.

What were the soldiers going to do against dragons? Throw their swords at them? Scream, cry, piss themselves, pray to their gods and mothers and beg?

Silver wasn't scared. She was angry. Her friends were dead, and she wanted someone, something, to pay for it. No matter what it cost.

The dragons were close enough that she could see the shapes of their monstrous faces, their mouths wide open and filled with fire. Some, Silver imagined, were still stained with blood from when they bit down on the battlements. Then spat out the remains that poured on Old Noll like red, hot rain.

There were so many corpses outside the wall. Fallen enemies, fallen humans, fallen dragons. Many of the bodies were destroyed, ripped to pieces, set aflame, and exploded by spellcraft.

But there were skin, bones, crusted blood, ligaments, sinews, and nerves. A decaying thread Silver could use to stitch up this broken world. It didn't have to hold for long, just long enough. But it would be insane to ignore the wealth of resources right under her fingertips. The agonising choir of souls still hoping to be resurrected by a divine miracle.

They could still be useful.

She couldn't see Kass amidst the soldiers racing between tents and make-shift barracks. Octavia had assembled a suicide commando of paladins, who would storm the enemy encampment when the city walls fell. They would try to take out their leaders at the same time as Old Noll's new king perished. Kass hadn't told Silver that he had been chosen for it. He didn't have to.

She spread out her remaining spell components. She had so much of everything left. She had been given all her dead friends' and colleagues' resources.

Why shouldn't she use them for whatever she saw fit? There was no one left to make that decision now. Most of the other mages were dead. Silver had watched them die.

Where did the souls of the dead go? Nobody knew. Maybe they just travelled the planes and faded to nothing over time.

And who cared? They were dead. They'd had their chance to be happy, and they never would be again.

Silver was alive. And she wanted to win. She wanted to hurt the enemy with everything she had.

With a flick of her hands, she directed the spell components to face towards the dragons. She didn't bother to separate and re-arrange them in an optimal ratio. The wind of dragon wings was almost upon them, and she was running out of time. She closed her eyes. She needed three spells. Neither was even that complicated on its own. If you were willing to do anything, a myriad of horrifying doors suddenly opened.

She moved her lips and fixed on the piles of corpses outside the city walls. There had to be thousands intertwined in the twisted embrace of death.

Pride had taught her something at the start of the war. A soul can't distinguish between a necromantic resurrection and a genuine, divine one.

Silver activated every spell component at once, feeling the force of the world itself rush through her body, a hitherto unimaginable concentration of magical power. This would undo her in a thousand ways, but she didn't care.

When Silver cast her resurrection spell on the corpses sprawled across the battlefield, the remaining souls chased back to their bodies, believing their silent prayers had been answered and their gods were giving them a second chance at life.

Of course, Silver wasn't strong enough to control every single corpse on her own. No mage in the world had that power. The heap of spell components helped, of course, catalysing her magic with the materials' interior properties. But it wasn't enough.

But more fuel was available on this battlefield of the living and the dead.

A spell was a manipulation of the world's innermost molecular composition. The mage's mind and imagination shaped the way in which this manipulation played out. Spell components were a commonly accepted, if expensive, set of materials that carried energies a mage could use to unravel and rethread the world.

Souls also carried energy. If anything, if you stripped away their memories, souls were nothing but energy. And there was so much energy below that Silver could taste the decay and desperation between the invocations she released from her numb tongue.

With one hand, she was using human souls as fuel, while with the other, she used that fuel to draw the remaining souls into their old bodies. Amidst this whirlwind of power, the souls had no chance to figure out what was happening. Until it was too late. They either vanished into nothing or were drawn back to rotting flesh.

The dragons moved in. They were close enough to the city that Silver could almost hear them heaving, could see the steam rushing out between their teeth.

The souls were bound to their bodies now. Silver could see them writhing on the ground like an army of worms. Most couldn't get up. They were either consumed by piles of dead flesh or found their arms and legs already crushed.

But they were undead, ready for Silver to command. That was the first spell. She still felt arcane energies in the air, tingling on her fingertips. She'd have to act quickly before other spellcasters picked up on the shift in the atmosphere. Power was just power; it didn't just belong to her. The enemy could just as easily use it against Old Noll.

She raised her left hand and uttered a levitation spell. Slowly, the corpses lifted out of the trenches, out from piles of bones and heads and dismembered arms. They flew into the skies, crawling towards the dragons in a race against gravity. But they were too slow.

"More," Silver grunted. "Faster."

It wasn't impossible. Nothing was impossible. But there was always equivalence, something she had to surrender to fuel her manipulation of the world.

It was a numbers game. One she intended to win.

"Take what you want," she whispered senselessly, and she had no idea who she was talking to. The magic tore at her flesh, ripping it from her fingertips, her wrist, her arm. She let it. She let the flesh, so painfully born and grown, dissolve from her bones. And then, the undead bodies shot through the skies, chasing after the dragon army.

Finally, she was winning. She would have beaten them even if all that was left of her were a steaming skeleton on top of the battlements.

The corpses collided with the dragons. The beasts' dark eyes looked downwards, and their wings slowed. Bloody, dismembered flesh stuck to their scales, fitting into every gap and crevice the soldiers' arrows had left.

"Give them hell," Silver whispered and cast her last spell.

The corpses combusted in a single, sky-shattering explosion. For a moment, all Silver could see was white light and power filling the air above her. She wondered if she had used up her entire body to fuel the combustion spells. But the dizziness passed, and she saw that all thirty dragons had been ripped to pieces. They fell on the graveyard outside the city walls.

There was deadly silence on the city walls until one of the soldiers began to clap and shout profanities. Two, three joined in, then suddenly, the entire camp burst into a fire of celebration.

The noises behind her formed the strangest contrast to the deafening silence outside the walls, where she could feel not a single soul remaining.

Silver looked down. The flesh on her left arm was gone, but, perhaps in a twist of irony, the white bones of her skeleton remained. It didn't hurt, but maybe she just didn't register the pain. The rest of her body had been left unscathed. In the grand scheme of it, she couldn't believe how cheap all those souls had come.

Chapter 18

The walk home is slow and silent. It's too early for the sun to rise but too late for public transport to operate. Kass insists on walking both his squires and Amaya home, and Silver falls in and out of sleep as he pushes her chair through the cobbled streets. None of them say much.

Once they've dropped off Amaya at her flat next to a quiet park, Kass and Silver circumnavigate the giant rift in the centre of the markets. As usual, the mages' spells crackle against the rift's exteriors, creating interconnected barriers that bar anyone from passing through. Seeing it makes Kass's hair stand on edge. Silver has explained a thousand times how nothing short of a god could force its way through. But still.

The rift is aglow with a feint blue light, showing the sky in a realm ruled by perpetual sunshine. Kass glances down and sees that Silver's eyes are open, her stare wide and vacant. She has always been worse than him at hiding her emotions.

All he wants to do is fall at her feet, press his head against her chest and hold her until they both feel calm.

He doesn't. But when she catches his gaze, he feels he should say something.

"Are you okay?" he asks.

She shakes her head slowly. "Wrong question. I'm not the one who was cursed."

"I'm not cursed."

"Kass."

He sighs.

"It was a moot point," he says. "I was not about to divorce you over something like that, so there's nothing you could have done to help."

"Why not?" Her voice is hollow. Their steps echo against the tall buildings of the market district. It is the only rhythm that gives structure to the quiet night.

"Silver…"

"Why put yourself through all this for the sake of a broken marriage? We don't talk, Kass. We don't – there isn't much left here, is there?"

Her tone is calm. He recognises it from when her parents died after the bombardment. From when he had first foresworn her after the spell. From when she had learned that her legs would never heal.

He sighs deeply. "Let's talk about this tomorrow, Silver. I'm exhausted."

"Kass. Please."

"You know why I won't leave you. I am not an unfaithful man, and my feelings did not change." He shakes his head, and his grip on her chair tightens. "What's the bloody point in me saying this? What's the point in making it harder than it already is?" he asks.

She turns around. "What's the point in continuing things as they are?"

"I don't know, Silver. If you want to leave –"

"You know that's not what I want." Her tone sharpens. "I love you, Kass. I love you, but I can't live like this forever."

Her words cut through the pressure in his chest like nothing else can. He feels like he is falling and torn open by the rush. This is the feeling he would once have done anything for. He had almost forgotten what it tasted like.

"I know," he says.

Silver sighs quietly.

"I know," Kass continues. "But if you want things to change, it will be your choice. I will never leave you. I swore you that oath, and I will swear it a thousand times more."

He feels the words heavy on his tongue. It helps to say them out loud, unexpectedly so. Silver's eyes fill with tears, but she shakes them away.

"I –"

She stares at her left hand, still uncovered. The skeletal remains gleam in the night, and tears flow down her cheeks. Her hand starts to shake, and Kass realises how much the thought of giving up her powers terrifies her. In Silver's eyes, things will be alright only because she has the power to make them so. Take away her powers, and the world is relentless and cruel.

"Ask me again," she says, impossibly quiet. "Ask me to stop my necromancy, and maybe I will. Maybe once all this is over, I can live like that."

But Kass has lived under Five for too long. He would never demand anything of Silver. Any concession must be a gift. And even if Silver still means her words in the morning, she'll resent him for the sacrifice she would have made for his sake.

He presses his face into her shoulder and closes his eyes. Silver cries while he embraces her with heavy arms.

A week passes without news as the city guard combs through every part of the city and tries to determine which rifts lead to hell planes. Although Kass gets involved in the search, he spends too much time inside the manor to be around Silver. Both feel a temporary euphoria after the moment they shared near the rift. Silver started wearing her pin again. But tentative hopefulness turns to irritation once it is burdened by the weight of expectations.

So, they do what they do best. They bicker.

"I cannot comprehend how anyone can stand their eggs being so overcooked," Silver complains, poking her fork into the scrambled egg, piled on a slide of bread.

Kass knew having breakfast together would be a mistake. But he somehow never gets to enjoy being right.

"Undercooked eggs aren't good for you," he echoes his uncle's words. The man runs a tavern for sailors. He should know.

"We all die eventually, Kass."

"Your body is a temple. It behoves you to take care of it as best you can."

That's one of Five's dogmas. He can't hide the smile that dances around his mouth. It's not like Silver can't ask the servants to cook her eggs differently from how he likes them. She's just grumpy because she forgot to.

"I'm pretty sure this temple is mostly out of commission," she replies drily and gestures at her legs.

"Silver."

"Oh, I'm sorry. Are you uncomfortable with my war trauma?"

"Yes, actually. Can't we just have a normal conversation over breakfast?"

He sighs, and she rolls her eyes. "What, you want to talk about the weather?" she asks.

"For instance," he replies. "Look at the lovely sunshine."

Rain is drumming hard and fast against the window. Silver smirks, and Kass uses the opportunity to shovel two forkfuls of eggs into his mouth. His wife drums her skeletal hand on the table.

"Well, health-related issues won't be a problem for much longer if Pride comes to fully control this divine magic of hers," she says thoughtfully.

Kass flinches as he remembers the tiny claws hooked into his chest. He didn't tell Silver about it. Maybe he should have, but it always feels like there is already too much going on.

"You know," Silver continues. "I wonder if the clerics lied to me when they said the damage in my legs couldn't be healed. Maybe the gods refused their prayers like Five does with you now."

Kass always suspected that this might be the case. But saying it wouldn't have helped matters. He never feels like it does with Silver.

"Are you sure accepting Pride's help is wise?" he asks instead. Silver narrows her eyes.

"Why? You're fine, aren't you?"

"For now."

"Stop. You'll be fine."

Kass scoffs. "We all die, Silver."

She rolls her eyes. "Very good. I knew I didn't just marry you for your looks. The grim existentialism has always been a welcome bonus."

Kass coughs an embarrassed laugh, and Silver grins before seriousness returns to her.

"There's a reason you said that about accepting Pride's help. What is it?"

Kass hesitates. "I'm not sure. But something about all this doesn't sit right with me."

"Beyond the rogue demon assassins, you mean?"

"Yes, Silver. Beyond that." He shakes his head. "Do you remember Pride being happy to stay on the sidelines during the war? I sure don't."

Silver shrugs, and Kass continues.

"If she already has experience traversing the bloody planes, why would she insist on staying back while we track down this mage? I don't buy this bullshit excuse about her protecting Octavia and Ithya. They have enough people watching out for them in the castle."

Silver drums her hands on the table again. Her eggs lie before her, forgotten.

"That's true. I was thinking that, too." She frowns. "There's another thing. It might be nothing but..."

Kass nods encouragingly. Silver looks down.

"Well, when we investigated the rift at House Karthe, we managed to create a hole in the protective barrier. Only for a few moments, and I didn't recognise the realm behind it, but..."

"Of course not. Where would you have recognised it from?"

"That's the thing," Silver says. "I'm pretty sure Pride did."

Kass raises his eyebrows. "How?"

"I don't know," his wife replies. "Maybe she went there as part of her planar travels? Or maybe she's read about it? I've been looking through travel testimonies from the library to cross-compare with what I saw, but I've found nothing."

When the rifts first opened, many people fell through them, often alongside their houses, relatives, or least favourite pets. Some even returned, sometimes years later, to tell the human realm about their travels. Most of the stories are so ridiculous that Kass is convinced they are made up. Not many people feel particularly inclined to fact-check, however.

"How would you know that she recognised the place? Did she say something?" he asks.

"I know Pride, Kass."

Kass nods slowly. "But if she's not telling even you –"

"That is exactly the part that worries me."

They stare at each other for a moment, and despite the ever-present tension, Kass feels his chest fill with warmth.

Kass meets Amaya for lunch on the steps to Old Noll's least popular art collection at the intersection of the temple and market districts. Amaya does not care for pre-Medieval paintings, but the place is within convenient walking distance of the food truck she likes. To his surprise, it is not just Amaya who greets him burger in hand. His two squires are already sat by her side, happily biting into soft, white buns. The rain has let off, and the three blink into the sun's warm rays.

"'Sup, Sir," Allen says, handing Kass his usual order.

"'Sup," Kass responds with all the ire the word deserves.

"How are you, Sir?" Andrea asks with a cautious look at their commander's chest. Kass sighs internally.

"I'm perfectly fine, Andrea. No need to worry."

"Worry is a sign of care. There is nothing wrong with it," they respond. Now, Kass's sigh makes it to the surface.

Amaya clears her throat.

"I've got news on the investigation," she says without interlude. Kass nods and takes a bite out of his lunch. Amaya isn't one for courtesy catch-ups, so he expected as much.

"Did we find a rift?" he asks.

Amaya nods, then pulls up her shoulders.

"We found a ton of them. After going through existing catalogues and surveying previously undeclared rifts, the city watch found that twenty-four per cent of all rifts in the city lead to a plane inhabited by creatures that could be described as 'demonic'."

"What even makes a demon?" Allen asks. "How many tails, wings, or teeth do you need to qualify?"

Andrea laughs, but Amaya nods earnestly.

"That's becoming increasingly difficult to answer," she replies. "When the first rifts opened, we thought that only one of them led down to what we used to think of as 'hell'. Fire, brimstone, rivers of lava, you can picture it. Drawing on references from folk tales, we called the inhabitants of that plane demons."

She shrugs.

"But now it's become a descriptor of anything sufficiently non-human. In my opinion, such a loose definition doesn't help anyone."

"Okay," Kass says slowly, hoping to get the conversation back on track. "So, we've found a crap ton of rifts to hell planes. Any way to narrow that down so we don't have to jump through all of them?"

"Technically speaking, yes," Amaya replies. "Remember anything about our diced-up demon friend?"

Kass shivers when he remembers the flesh he still carries with him. The pieces keep trying to grow back together, but one of Silver's spells permanently pries them apart.

"Yeah. Green, spiky, ugly, and poisonous. Why?"

"Well, from that, we may deduce quite a bit about the kind of environment the demon originated from," Amaya explains. "Nothing too arid and hot, so its secretion can form without drawing vital liquids from other areas of the body. Given the creature's agile nature, I would also assume it would thrive in a jungle-like habitat."

"Alright," Kass replies, already feeling himself losing patience. "Did we find a rift to a place like that?"

"No," Amaya replies, her tone perfectly level. "And most of the rifts we found are unusable anyway."

Kass curses. "Okay. Why?"

Amaya ignores his foul temper. She is very good at that.

"Because they are either tiny or they lead to the bottom of an ocean, a wall, or into another type of obstacle. Mind you, most of the time, that's lucky for us because we certainly don't have enough mages to cast barrier spells on every single rift that opened in and around the city. Someone has to uphold those spells, after all. But, right now, it is unlucky for us specifically."

"Alright," Kass sighs. "So, how many hell plane rifts are actually operational?"

"Three."

"Perfect. Of course."

He groans and finishes his burger with an angry bite. "So, what are our options?"

"You're going to love this," Allen mutters. Amaya clearly already filled his squires in. Andrea tries to summon an encouraging smile, but they are uncharacteristically fidgety.

"Option One," Amaya begins. "The city watchman who drew the short straw describes it as a desert surrounded by mountains. Hot winds, sundown, and floating skulls in the distance. He didn't see any demons per se, but the mage who accompanied him claims she could feel some non-human energies nearby."

"Love it," Allen mutters.

"Option Two," Amaya continues. "A beach full of drowned sea creatures. The sea creatures periodically come back to life to fight demons that shift in and out of the visible sphere."

"What do the demons look like?" Andrea asks.

"The best description I got was 'creepy'," Amaya replies sourly. "But apparently distinct from the sea creatures."

"And Option Three?" Kass asks, feeling a headache approaching.

"Well, the city watchman couldn't describe the third plane very well, given that the other side of the rift was perpetually dark. But she did get attacked by a creature whose claws left a similar corruption to the one that afflicted you."

"Send her to -" Kass starts, and Amaya interrupts him.

"Already sent her to Pride."

"Good. Good."

Kass is not keen on word of Pride's divine spellcasting spreading, but caution is never worth someone's life.

"So, how do we choose? I mean, how do we make a meaningful choice here?" Allen asks. Amaya shrugs.

"I don't think we can," she responds. "Even if we choose the plane with the most similarities to our demon's presumed home, that's no guarantee that the demon came from there."

She ignores Allen's crestfallen expression and continues.

"There's also no guarantee that a rift connects the plane we enter with the demon's home world. Where and how rifts appear seems random."

Kass massages his temples.

"So, we just go through each of the rifts and have a mage cast a scrying spell on the demon's remains?" he asks. "And see if the spell picks something up? In essence, hope for the bloody best?"

"And if there's no connection on either of the three planes, we're fucked," Allen notes.

"And if there's no existing rift between the plane where we enter and the one we're trying to reach, we're equally... in trouble," Andrea adds.

"This sounds like a fool's errand," Allen mutters.

"Sounds like my kind of mission," Kass sighs. Amaya nods seriously.

"One last thing," she adds, looking at Kass intensely. He sighs.

"No," he responds before she has the chance to ask.

"We need a mage to cast the scrying spell," Amaya says.

"Any mage will do," Kass responds sternly.

"It would help if they didn't suck," Allen notes, but Kass can tell he isn't insisting. Seeing Silver's necromancy in action has finally dimmed his squires' enthusiasm for his wife.

"I suppose there are other powerful mages in Old Noll," Andrea says.

"Ones with Silver's combat experience? Ones who would drop everything they're working on to accompany us to a hell plane?" Amaya asks. "And ones we implicitly trust with all the details of the investigation?"

"We can find someone else," Kass says stubbornly.

"We won't allow her to get hurt, Sir," Allen says slowly.

Kass closes his eyes.

"You don't fucking get it," he mutters. The thought of Silver in her wheelchair chased down by a demon and impaled by its iron claws makes his heart burst with terror.

"She'd be furious if you left her behind," Amaya cautions. Kass barks out a laugh. "She's always already furious with me."

"Sir," Andrea softly says. "Your protectiveness honours you, but this should be your wife's decision. We would force her to stay behind if we withheld information that she has earned the right to know."

"Fuck off," Kass whispers. "Fuck this. Fuck Five and his dogmas."

"Kass," Amaya says quietly, but no more words are forthcoming. Kass buries his face in his hands to cool his pulsating temples.

"She's one of the city's most powerful mages, Sir. I'm sure she is more than capable of defending herself," Allen says in an unusually level voice.

Kass groans. "You didn't live through the war. After the enemy captured her, you didn't see – her legs. Her throat, her –"

He interrupts himself when he feels tears rise into his eyes. All of this is his fault. Silver would never have resorted to necromancy if he had been able to save her that day. If she didn't feel so deathly afraid to be left without her powers.

"Fuck," he repeats, this time louder. But they are right.

Chapter 19

The first rift they try is the dark one. It lives in the backyard of a pub close to the city walls, full of overgrown ivy, damp-smelling wooden tables, and long-empty bird feeders. During the war, the innkeeper learned some simple barrier spells to lock down the rift, and he never bothered to register it with the city watch.

Kass isn't too pressed about it. People have learned to live with the rifts, and for most of them, the terror of looking the Multiverse in the eyes is gone. Some people have been known to fall into unprotected rifts because they became too good at ignoring their presence. Some people jump into them for fun or out of despair. But they are a quickly depleting minority.

Silver rips the innkeeper's protection spell apart with a flick of her wrist. She is wearing the turquoise robes her mother gifted her at the start of the war. Her silver pin sits near her collar. Kass feels his chest clench every time he looks at her.

Silver's skeletal hand is unconcealed and already holds the demon flesh, coated in a potent mixture of spell components. A dagger is tied to her belt, and several pouches dangle from her chair, filled to the brim with bones.

The rift looks like a cut in the fabric of reality, leaving only nonexistence under the touch of the knife. Kass has the terrible feeling that when they reach the other side, they will fall and never stop falling.

Andrea and Allen are wearing full armour, although Allen's is lighter and made from more leather than steel. He has yet to catch up to Andrea in both strength and discipline. Kass knows he lets him get away with too much. Yet another thought that keeps him awake at night.

The squires check their swords and tug on their cloaks. Kass convinced Amaya to wear loose-fitting leather armour, although she is notably uncomfortable with the unfamiliar pressure on her skin.

They surround the rift, their breaths creating an uncanny rhythm.

"Are you ready?" Kass asks Silver. She nods silently. Her eyes are hard as steel. They both remember how to push aside every feeling to get the job done.

But he doesn't want to be like that anymore. He hasn't for a long time, and he isn't sure Silver realises that. When Allen, Andrea, and Amaya slowly reach through the rift, he squeezes his wife's hand.

She looks up at him, and he smiles.

"Just like old times, huh?" he asks.

She laughs and keeps hold of his hand for a moment longer.

On the other side of the rift, the ground is soft enough that it moans. Silver's wheelchair sinks in, and she curses. She could cast a levitation spell to free herself, but she can't do that at the same time as she is scrying. Levitating both herself and her chair depletes her magical energies dangerously quickly.

The air is freezing, and Kass smells something acidic that sits heavy on his lungs. The sound of wings is audible in the distance. They shouldn't spend too much time here.

Silver clutches the flesh and casts the spell. Her hand begins to glow, but the light remains entirely concentrated on her. No part of this strange, heavy world allows itself to be illuminated.

Allen flinches when he hears a noise just behind him. The sound of two pairs of wings shuffling against one another, a heavy breath, a shuddering intake of air.

Andrea draws their sword.

"Don't attack unless they attack first," Kass cautions. "We need to buy Silver as much time as possible."

His squires nod, their faces pale and lips drawn. Amaya's shaky hand rests on her gun. She desperately tries to catch a glimpse of the figures surrounding them in the dark. Kass utters a silent prayer to Five but hears no answer.

Silver keeps chanting, her voice rising in intensity. A hiss emerges from the darkness. Kass stands before his wife, his plate mail gleaming in the remnants of her spellcraft.

Then, with a flicker and a rush, a demon rams its hooked claws into his chest plate, scratching with a desperate need to find skin. Andrea does not hesitate. They draw their sword, hack off the demon's feet, and stand back-to-back with Kass. Allen curses and moves in front of Amaya.

A chorus of cries emerges from the darkness, surrounding them with a furious sound. Amaya shoots a round of bullets into their midst, but she is too late. With a terrifying sound, the demons' wings catapult the bullets into the air. Kass raises his sword and meets hard bone and rough skin. Beaks try to tear into his skull, and ear-piercing shrieks disorient him in the dark.

Then, not a moment too late, a ball of fire rushes past him and explodes above the demons, tearing the wings from their bodies and setting them aflame. *Silver.*

Her eyes are wide, and her hands still gleam with power. She says something, but Kass can only make out two words. *Not here.*

"Back! Go back!" Kass yells, gesturing at the rift behind them.

Amaya is closest to the rift and jumps through it without hesitation. Andrea and Allen stand equidistant, and Allen frantically motions at Andrea to go first. They move towards it when Allen is suddenly grabbed around the waist and pulled into the dark wall of demonic shapes.

Kass roars his name and starts to follow his squire, but Andrea is faster. With all the force of youth and desperation on their side, they throw themselves after Allen, sword outstretched and arms flailing.

Silver curses and casts a spell that illuminates Allen's outline even amidst the deepest dark. Kass can see blood dripping from his squire's midriff, where the demon's claws tore through the leather of his armour. He is shaking with panic. With a jump, Andrea cuts off one of the creature's legs, then Kass reaches his squire and swings his Zweihander into everything he can reach.

The demon's head flies from its body, and Andrea pulls Allen towards them, slinging his arm over their shoulder while Kass's wide sword strikes hold the rest of the demons at bay.

"Thank –" he starts, but Andrea interrupts him.

"Always."

A scream interrupts them. Kass turns around in horror to see Silver surrounded by a circle of demons. The only thing keeping them at bay is a wall of flames that Silver summoned. It licks against her pale skin. The creatures slowly move their hooked claws and wings through the fire, their thick skin resisting its impact.

And Silver's chair is still sinking into the ground. She is trapped. Just like –

Kass howls and races towards them, beckoning his squires to follow. He tears through demon after demon, feeling their hot blood fly into his eyes and run over his arms. He breathes in tandem with his racing heart, and every swing is rewarded with a cry and a death. Silver is just behind him, casting spells of doom and destruction, and for a moment, it feels like no time has passed.

"Kass!" His wife's voice barely registers. Every thought that isn't a prediction of the enemy's movements is unnecessary. Dangerous. "Kass! Your squires are through the rift. We need to go!"

Silver. He forces himself to move towards her. She is hovering next to the rift, the back of her wheels already crossing over to the human plane. She cast a levitation spell, and he can see that her brows are soaked in sweat.

"Go!" he bellows, but she hesitates.

"You first."

She doesn't trust that he'll stop fighting. He screams with frustration, then races towards the rift. He feels claws and wings pull on his face, and blood runs across his cheeks, but his arm connects with Silver, and he manages to pull her through the rift with him.

They fall to the other side, smashing into the hard stone of the inn's backyard. Kass glances up and sees that his squires and Amaya have surrounded the rift, weapons at the ready. Silver forces herself on her back and raises her hands, still glittering with the remnants of spell components.

"Out of the way," she demands, then makes a swiping motion. A soft-glowing barrier appears across the rift's exterior, hardening with each breath they take. After a few moments, she closes her eyes and leans back her head. Her wheelchair has collapsed on top of her, and her legs are twisted underneath the metal. Kass forces himself to stand so he can help her.

Now that the danger has passed, Allen moans and holds his stomach. Kass can see that the cuts aren't particularly deep. Andrea leans over him. They ask Five for healing, but even their calls remain unanswered.

"Are you alright?" they ask Allen, their voice very soft. "Can I do anything?"

Allen coughs out a laugh. "You already did. I would be dead if you hadn't –"

His voice breaks, and he grows pale when he realises just how close he was to never leaving the dark plane.

"It was nothing," Andrea replies firmly. Kass shakes his head.

"No. You showed some real bravery in there, 'drea. I'm bloody proud of you."

Andrea blushes profusely, and Kass isn't sure he has ever seen them so happy.

Amaya turns to Silver, who is straightening out her robes with shaky hands.

"Did the spell not work? Or did you not find anything?" the investigator asks. Her tone is softer than usual. Silver glances up at her friend and takes a breath before responding.

"The ... latter," she presses out. "The only anchor I found for the scrying spell led back home."

She takes another deep breath, and her voice grows calmer.

"I don't think our demon has ever been anywhere near that dark plane."

"Good," Allen says, a little too loud. "That means we won't have to fight through these hordes. Again."

"Agreed," Kass says, then puts his arm around his squire's shoulders.

"Are you alright?" he asks quietly. Allen scoffs, but the tension in his body dissipates.

"I ... guess I will be."

"I take it you can't heal yourself?"

Allen shakes his head. "Five's not been answering my prayers for a little while now. When I call him, there's just – nothing."

He tries not to cry, and Kass clenches the young man's shoulders a little tighter.

"Okay. Here's what's going to happen," he decides. "We're going to Pride's to get some more of that miraculous healing. We'll use the tower's luxury baths to get cleaned up. And afterwards, we're all going to a pub near Allen's sad little flat and getting drunk at my expense."

Silver laughs, and Allen's eyes light up a little.

"Commander's orders?" he asks incredulously.

"You bet your ass these are orders," Kass replies with a smile.

Pride is her usual unpleasant self when she sees them back at the tower. She does not hesitate to mock their lack of progress in finding the demon's home plane. To her credit, however, she also does not hesitate to heal Allen's wounds. After a few moments, Kass's squire is back to his old self.

As before, seeing a human channel divine magic makes Kass uncomfortable. But now that he's had a week to sleep on the idea, he cannot stop imagining the possibilities. For all her hubris, Pride has earned her title of war hero. The enemy would have overrun them without her defensive barriers, and during her time as the leader of the mage guild, she undoubtedly made the realm a better place.

She will not hesitate to heal Silver's legs once she feels confident in her healing abilities. Further down the line, she might even cure sicknesses and ailments the gods remain deaf to. She might finally end the quarantine in the plague quarters. Maybe she'll be able to bring back the dead.

Kass understands that in a finite universe, life must also be finite. The gods teach that only when a soul has shed its physical constraints it can live a limitless existence on one of their eternally blissful planes.

And how could he, with his limited human perspective, understand the gods' decision over who lives and who stays dead? Maybe the demons' crusade against Pride, Octavia, and Ithya is justified somehow, and he shouldn't interfere with it. And maybe Five is right, and he should finally take a bloody stance in his relationship with Silver.

But why punish Allen by not answering his prayers? He saw his squire's shame and sadness to so suddenly be rejected. Where is the justice in this?

He ends his silent deliberations with a sigh and leads everyone to *The Burning Mage*. Allen lives close to Kass's family tavern, which makes it a convenient pit stop. And it is hard to argue with familiarity and good company. Allen's spirits improve with every step away from the mage tower and towards the chance of out-drinking his commander. Amaya doesn't join them for this part of the evening as she hates both the feeling and taste of alcohol. They agree to meet at the next rift the next day.

The Burning Mage is half empty, as usual. His uncle's less-than-sunny disposition does nothing to promote repeat custom, so Kass easily secures a booth next to the grimy, steamed windows. He lifts Silver from her chair onto a bench filled with old, stringy pillows. Before he can walk up to the bar and order drinks, his uncle spots them and walks over.

Kass's mother left the family when he was a child. That was a few years before his father was killed during a robbery. Kass's uncle Elijah, who never married and had once dreamed of being a painter, took over the tavern and parental duties. He did his best, and now, years later, Kass can appreciate that.

After his marriage to Silver, Kass offered to buy him a painting studio and outsource the tavern's day-to-day to someone else. Elijah just laughed.

'In life, there are some things you have to see through,' he said. Perhaps he didn't want to let go of his brother's biggest achievement. But Kass expects his hesitation to let go of the *Mage* also has to do with the fact that Elijah is madly in love with the barkeep he hired for the Monday through Thursday shifts.

Anders, said barkeep, is such a kind man, and so obviously reciprocates Elijah's feelings that, of course, nothing ever came of it.

"Kass."

Elijah greets him with an awkward hand on the shoulder and a movement that indicates that he'd like to embrace his nephew but doesn't wish to impose.

Kass buries him in a firm hug, then gently slaps his back instead of a greeting. He suppresses a momentary frown when he looks at his uncle. Elijah has always been thin, and the later years of his life have exacerbated this to the point where the swollen veins on his forearms stand in stark contrast to his feeble wrists and arms.

Silver beams at Elijah, and he takes her hand.

"My darling," he says with genuine warmth. "It's been too long."

Like everyone else in Kass's life, Elijah can't understand the source of their marital difficulties. In fairness, Kass never told him about any of it, and Elijah never asked.

"It has," Silver says, then glances around the taproom. "I love what you've done with the place."

To Kass, the *Mage* looks the same as it always does, but from his uncle's pleased half smile, he guesses that he might have exchanged the grimy old curtains or hung up some more of his homemade artwork. His uncle loves drawing ships caught in sudden and violent storms. In Kass's opinion, all ships look the same.

Kass introduces his two squires, and Elijah looks at them with the same baffled pride that made him choke up whenever Kass was being honoured at post-war ceremonies. When he catches Kass's exhausted expression, Elijah forces the emotions down and grins.

"Is he running you two ragged? Do you need me to have a word with the boy?"

"Yes. Please," Allen says immediately, causing the rest of the table to erupt in laughter.

"The commander is a wonderful -" Andrea starts their usual spiel, but Kass raises his hands in mock surrender.

"Mercy, 'drea. I can take Allen's vicious mockery, but if I hear one more genuine compliment from you, I might spontaneously combust."

"An interesting psychological deficiency to perhaps unpack at the temple?" Silver says in a sly voice. "All that time you spend there has to be good for something."

Elijah laughs, and Kass's squires join in. Kass glowers at Silver, and she shoots him a triumphant grin. After a few moments, Elijah claps his hands together.

"Alright, alright. What are we all drinking?" He turns to Silver with a gentle smile. "I remember your order, of course, darling."

Ever since Silver first visited the *Mage*, Elijah kept a case of her favourite wine at the back of the pantry. Just in case the beautiful, noble girl returned. Just in case idiot Kass didn't fuck things up between them.

And she did return. Many, many times after.

Kass shakes his head and tries to dispel memories of a young Silver seeking out his company whenever she could, without any pretence or embarrassment. Eventually, she spent more time at the tavern than her parents' manor. That was why the enemy's attack didn't kill her. She hadn't been home.

His squires go with Elijah's recommendation of a fruity ale, and Kass sticks to his usual lager. Once Elijah brings over the drinks, Allen downs his in one swig and immediately orders another.

"Oh, here we go," Kass mutters. Silver laughs.

"Did you say this was going to be at our expense?"

Kass grins. He takes a few big sips and can feel it going to his head. He hasn't had much to eat today. "Not like you can't afford it, butter-bear."

Silver snorts. Andrea tries their drink and nods with approval.

"What a lovely flavour profile," they decide. "Just a hint of spice to keep the fruit from becoming too overpoweringly sweet. A lovely composition of astringent and umami flavours."

Allen stares at them, and after a moment, they burst out laughing. "I have no idea what I just said," they confess with a cheeky smile.

Allen blinks, then laughs a little louder than is strictly necessary. Kass and Silver exchange a glance, and Kass rolls his eyes good-naturedly. Silver raises her eyebrows and grins.

Once their next round of drinks arrives, Allen raises his glass.

"A toast. To stepping onto another plane and not dying immediately."

"I'll bloody drink to that," Kass mutters.

"To heroic actions," Silver says with a smile in Andrea's direction.

"And heroic spell craft," they respond with a blush.

"It's so crazy," Allen says once they've all taken a sip. "Back in the village, we heard about the rifts, but I never actually saw one until I got to the city. Now, the more time I spend here, the more rifts I see! And now I've stepped through one."

He shakes his head. "Crazy."

"We all felt like we were going crazy seven years ago," Silver reminisces. "All mages were conscripted to put barriers on the rifts, so I saw some of the worst of it. Whole houses were swallowed out of existence, random weather phenomena burst out of holes in the sky… I don't think I slept for a month when we suddenly had to figure out how to seal all that."

"A bad time to be important," Kass nods.

Silver scoffs. "It's always a bad time to be important."

"I've been wondering –" Allen starts, then clears his throat. "Sorry. I'm being annoying."

"It's fine. We've spilt blood together, so that makes us friends. Ask what you like," Silver replies with a smile. Allen nods.

"Okay. It's just – in the village, we were told that the rifts just appeared one day. That there were no warning signs or anything. And at the temple, they say they're a natural phenomenon, like the seasons or earthquakes." He shakes his head. "But why now? Why not a hundred years from now or a millennium ago? It seems so random."

"That's the way all people feel who have to live through interesting times," Kass grunts.

"If this is what you call interesting, Sir, I shudder to think what you'd classify as thrilling," Andrea says. The comment teases another laugh from their commander.

Silver leans her head on her hand and sips her wine slowly.

"If you're hoping the mages have a better explanation, I'm afraid I must disappoint you. It's not like we withhold some arcane knowledge from the public because we think it would scare you. Seven years ago, we were just as baffled as everyone else."

She gestures at Kass.

"In fact, paladins and clerics used to do far more theorising about other planes and the journey that souls take after death. The divine miracles had to come from somewhere, after all."

Kass nods.

"Gen – former general Octavia once told me about a theory," he says. "A theory from before this all happened, that is. Some clerics believed the gods' had their own planes of existence where souls materialise after death. People called them bloody heretics for believing the gods were anything but ethereal."

"I remember that theory," Silver nods, her eyes glowing. "When I first studied at the tower, I went to one of Pride's lectures where she mentioned it. She seemed compelled by the idea of several physical planes coalescing into a Multiverse. Still, I don't remember the mage guild ever performing experiments to put the theory to the test."

She swirls her wine around to catch flickers of light.

"Then again, how would you even begin to test something like that? Unless you know what you're doing, how would you tear a hole into reality?"

"Could you?" Allen suddenly asks, his eyes wide.

Silver blinks. "Excuse me?"

Kass groans internally, but Allen isn't deterred.

"If you wanted to, could you open a rift? Like, what those death cultists out in the docks are trying to do?"

Silver raises her eyebrows. "I am a necromancer, not a lunatic. Believe it or not, there is a difference."

Allen pales. "Sorry, sorry, that's not what I meant. I was just wondering if you knew how to. Because -"

He chews on the inside of his cheek, and Kass finally understands what he's getting at.

"Because you think she might have to," he says.

Allen nods slowly.

"I've been thinking about this. Imagine we get lucky, and Silver's scrying spell picks up a connection to the demon's trail on one of the hell planes we visit. But unless a path of open rifts exists to the mage who hired it, we get stuck." He gestures at his waist. "I don't think we want to get stuck."

"I won't let anything happen to you," Kass promises, but he feels the words ring hollow in his ears. Andrea frowns.

"The universe is fragmented enough as it is. We shouldn't make things worse."

"What is one more hole going to do?" Silver counters and nods at Allen.

"You make a fair point. I'll think about this before we set out tomorrow."

"Silver..." Kass says quietly, but his wife shakes her head.

"I don't want to argue about this. I won't act recklessly, but I won't have us die on some gods-forsaken plane for the sake of propriety."

"It's not about propriety, Silver," he protests. "Some rules –"

"Does your precious god's dogmas say anything about opening rifts?" Silver asks, turning to Andrea. The squire bites on their lower lip, but they shake their head.

"Very well then."

She turns back to Kass triumphantly.

He shakes his head, but he knows she'll leave if he pushes the issue. She'll leave, she'll be angry, and they'll be right back at the point where any word uttered between them is drenched in poison.

The candlelight makes Silver's skin look like it's glowing. The silver pin shimmers against her robes. He's tired, warm, and so relieved that they're all still alive.

So, he relents and takes another sip of his lager. Silver places a hand on his leg.

"I won't be reckless," she promises him with a low voice when Allen and Andrea start talking about something else. Kass feels a shiver run up his spine, and for an infuriating moment, he feels drunk with desire.

241

Their eyes meet, and Silver's lids flutter when she looks up at him, searching for any signs of his tell-tale irritation. He holds his breath for fear of revealing too much. After a moment, Andrea distracts Silver with something, and he slowly exhales.

For the rest of the night, he talks little and drinks too much.

Chapter 20

Silver stays until midnight, but when Kass and his squires show no signs of slowing down, she orders a carriage home. Kass walks her outside, and she kisses his cheek when he lifts her inside the cabin. For an insane moment, he considers following her, but the cool night air forces just enough sense into him that he remains.

He lingers outside the tavern, staring at the spot behind the streetlights where the carriage disappeared.

His squires hold out until just before Elijah closes for the night, so Kass and Andrea half-drag, half-carry Allen into his flat. As usual, Kass insists on walking Andrea home. They live East of the castle at the edge of the same affluent district where their family has their estate. Kass knows Andrea struggles with money, but they refuse to move further away from their family. Despite everything.

Just before Andrea closes the door, they hesitate.

"Sir... if Silver does try to open a rift tomorrow..." they begin, then take a deep breath and look at Kass, unwilling to even utter the words. Kass feels the knife twist in his chest, but they're right to be concerned.

"Leave it to me," he tells them, and Andrea agrees with obvious relief.

On the way home, Kass passes by the castle again, cast in the last remnants of darkness. One of these days, he'll have to get into a sensible sleep rhythm. One of these days, they will all have to find some kind of routine.

But until then, there are too many unanswered questions. He sighs and gives in to the impulse. He cuts through the barracks and makes it onto the castle grounds past a city watch nightshift, who are visibly confused at seeing their commander out that late at night. He races up four flights of stairs until he is out of breath and hears the echo of his steps ringing in his ears.

His heart is going too fast again, and he knows it isn't from the drink or the exercise. He should sit by himself and close his eyes until he has calmed down.

But he won't. Not tonight.

No light shines out from under Octavia's door, but Kass doesn't let that deter him. From his time in the army, he remembers his former general is a notoriously light sleeper.

He knocks on the door, and, true enough, Octavia opens it not a minute later. Her curtains are open and admit the light of a full moon, sitting heavy above the skyline of Old Noll. Octavia is wearing a long nightgown and has a thick cloak draped across her shoulders.

She clearly doesn't think her visitor is a threat. Kass can see her armour and sword untouched in the corner of the room.

"Demons don't knock," she answers his unasked question.

"Fair enough," he mutters, and she steps aside to let him in.

Kass procrastinates by catching his breath, then finds the least awkward spot to hover in. Octavia sits at her desk and turns towards him, her dark eyes unreadable.

Finally, Kass sighs. "Sorry. This is stupid. I should let you sleep."

"You came here for a reason, Kassander. Ask your question," she says with all the strictness he remembers from serving under her.

Kass closes his eyes for a moment. "I can't get it out of my head. What you said about the gods," he admits.

Octavia waits. She makes him say it.

"That they helped both sides of the war," he whispers. "That humanity isn't chosen."

"I did not lie to you," she responds.

"I know."

"But you don't believe it."

Kass hesitates. His chest hurts, and he struggles to concentrate.

"I don't know what it would mean if I did," he admits.

"Why?" The word cuts deep despite the outward calm of her tone.

"Because," he begins slowly. "I don't know how I would justify it."

Octavia shakes her head. "No. You know that you cannot justify it."

The distinction is heavy, if true, and Kass doesn't know how he could shoulder another weight. How much stronger can he grow to ensure he doesn't break?

Octavia continues.

"There is no justification for the wanton cruelty of fuelling two sides of the same war. Of making people fight each other like pawns in some cosmic game."

"Even if that is true, what about all the good the gods do for the realm?" Kass responds, his voice rising. "They heal our wounds and perform miracles when our children are sick. They grant us free will and allow us to repent when we have done wrong." He shakes his head. "The world would be a worse place without them."

"Do you think people would lose their kindness and propensity for love without their divine overseers?" Octavia's tone is still level, but Kass tastes the note of irony within it. He shakes his head.

"Not everyone. But people are fundamentally self-centred. Without being promised a reward, most people won't bother helping those who need it."

"And are the gods doing that? Helping those who need it?"

Kass narrows his eyes. "They are."

He never curses around Octavia, but he feels bloody close now.

"Are they?" his former general asks. "Did they revive every soldier who died in the war?"

Memories of his dead comrades flash before his eyes. A mountain of blood-soaked corpses, their limbs at strange angles, almost as if they were waving at Kass to join them.

"Octavia –"

"Did the gods cure your wife's legs?"

Kass clenches his fists. "What would life be without an end?" he says. "The Multiverse would burst at the seams, over-full of its apathetic inhabitants. You told me that when I first joined the army."

It's a tenet from Five's dogmas, appropriated to fit Kass's mood. He sighs, forcing himself to continue.

"And Silver... Silver made her choice. She can't expect the gods to grant her miracles after she –"

He shakes his head, and Octavia raises her eyebrows.

"Is any of this fair?" she asks. "The arbitrary choice of whose lives are saved, of whose wounds are healed?"

"What does fair have to do with it? Choice is necessary for the kind of life we want to live."

He thinks of Andrea. They were revived from the dead when so many weren't. He is desperately happy that they were, but how many Andreas rots inside the earth?

"We?" Octavia asks. "Do we truly want this? Or are these divine rewards and retributions only necessary for the kind of society the gods want to create? For the realisation of the dogmas that they want to spread across the planes?"

Kass shakes his head as he feels his thoughts spiral. He takes a deep breath.

"Did you know about the planes before the rifts opened?"

He asks the question on a whim, but he seems to have hit a nerve. Octavia's eyes widen, and for the first time, she seems surprised by something he said.

"I believed in the clerics' theories of divine material planes," she finally admits, but Kass feels like she is holding something back.

"Theories?" he presses.

"They were well known across the temples, Kass. I'm not telling you anything new."

"And were you right? Were the planes what you imagined them to be?"

"What are you getting at, Kassander?"

He doesn't know. He feels the words drip from his tongue like a swell of rain. His body is shaking, and his hands are searching for something to hold onto.

"What did Ithya do, Octavia? Why did you reject all your medals and honours? What happened at the end of the war?"

Octavia stares at him for a few endless seconds.

"Nothing," she finally says. "All of my decisions were made before the war began. The path I took was inevitable."

"That doesn't answer my question."

"No," she admits. "I suppose it doesn't."

She sighs.

"I exchanged my old gods for new ones. I was a fool, and they turned out just as flawed as the ones I served before."

Kass tries to think of his next question, but Octavia abruptly rises.

"Enough of this. I know you are doubting your faith, but I won't stir up these old wounds. Not even for your sake, Kassander."

Kass sleeps in the barracks and meets the others at the rift the next day. Silver gives him a long look but doesn't ask him where he spent the night. Despite Allen's complaints of a headache, his squires and Amaya seem well-rested. None of them want to put this mission off longer than necessary.

They are better prepared this time. Amaya brought more bullets, and Allen exchanged his armour for plate mail. Pride has lent them more spell components to fuel Silver's scrying magic. The minerals already sparkle on her wrists.

Kass can tell the others are more nervous than last time, but no one hesitates when he gestures for them to follow him through the rift.

They step into the middle of a desert. Dim red light and a sand-heavy wind force their eyelids to flutter. There is tension in the air, the pressure close to an uprising storm. The winds caught in the mountains on the horizon produce an eerie choral chant. A thick layer of fog covers the skies above, impenetrable beyond the all-consuming red glow of the place.

"What in Five's name is that?" Andrea points at a circle of skulls that levitate in the air, completely motionless even amidst the winds that race across the desert. They are turned towards each other as if in silent deliberation.

"Something we best avoid," Kass grunts, then looks at Silver.

"You casting already?" he asks his wife. In the deep red light, it is difficult to see whether her hands are glowing. She shoots him an irritating glare that says, 'What the hell do you think, genius?'

Fortunately, this time, they are not immediately beset by demonic attackers, and the skulls appear content to hover menacingly in the distance. Amaya lifts a fistful of sand and lets it fly through her fingers. There are grains of black and white stone set amidst the fiery-coloured sand, and the investigator frowns as she twists and turns them between her fingers.

Allen shuffles nervously, his hand resting on his sword in a stance that protects his stomach. Andrea stands an inch before him, their eyes shifting with every turn of the wind.

Finally, Silver exhales slowly.

"I have something, but it's very weak," she says.

"What does that mean?" Kass asks.

Silver gestures towards the desert and the mountains looming in the distance.

"I can feel the spell pulling us in that general direction. So, I assume our demon friend has spent some time in a mysterious location I can only describe as 'over there'."

She snorts, but there is little emotion behind it.

"Thing is," she continues. "The pull is weak enough that I cannot guarantee whether it originates on this plane or on a plane that is close by. And, if the latter is the case, I can't say whether there is an open rift that will take us there or whether this plane and the other just lie very close together. I don't understand how these things work in the geography of the Multiverse."

Amaya clears her throat.

"From what we already discussed about the demon's physiognomy, I consider it highly likely that we'll need to travel through another rift to find the beginning of the trail. Look around you. A creature like the one we killed couldn't survive in this heat."

Kass nods. He feels his head swirling. "If the bloody trail starts on another plane, wouldn't there have to be an open rift for your spell to connect?"

Silver shrugs. "I hope so."

"But you're not sure?" he presses.

She throws up her hands.

"Look, Kass, we only learned about the planes seven years ago! It's not like we've had time to test all of this. All I can tell you is that when I tried the spell yesterday, I felt nothing, and now I feel something. That leads me to believe there is a connection between this place and wherever the demon came from." She blows out some air. "Make of that what you will."

"It's your call, Kass," Amaya says, rubbing the last few grains of sand between her fingers. "But I believe this might be the best lead we're going to get."

Kass closes his eyes for a moment.

"Everyone happy to proceed?" he asks. Everyone nods, albeit with varying levels of enthusiasm, so they make their way through the desert.

Kass pushes Silver's chair ahead of the group. They follow a faintly glistening strand of air interwoven with a few specks of blood Silver managed to coax from the demon's flesh. His wife's fine hair moves in the breeze, and Kass can tell she struggles to breathe in the heat.

They move excruciatingly slowly. Even though the sand is dense, their heavy boots and Silver's wheels keep getting stuck. The wind feels as though it is pushing them away from the mountains.

They pass by more circles of skulls, all immobile and deathly silent.

"Why the hell are they here?" Allen mutters when they pass by the third bastion of dead heads.

"Maybe they are the remnants of travellers who failed to cross this desert," Andrea suggests with a nervous glance towards the rift they departed from. They can no longer see its outline glimmering in the distance.

"Then who's keeping up the levitation spell?" Allen asks.

"It could be that gravity works differently on this plane. Maybe anything lighter than, say, ten pounds isn't tethered to the ground," Andrea replies. Amaya shakes her head.

"That wouldn't work. How do you imagine the sand remains underfoot if that is the case?"

"Ah. Right," Andrea responds with a slight blush. Amaya narrows her eyes.

"No. Someone or something is levitating these heads on purpose. Perhaps for some kind of ritual."

Allen shivers despite the heat. Kass sighs.

"Maybe, and just hear me out here, it doesn't fucking matter," he grunts.

"Where's your curiosity, Kass?" Amaya asks. Kass grunts once more.

"At home, right where I bloody left it. I'll be more than happy to leave this hellhole behind and never learn any more about it." He glances at Silver. "How much longer?"

"Seventeen minutes, thirty-eight seconds," his wife responds drily.

"Very funny, Silver."

She shrugs.

"I try my best." She turns around and glares at him. "The pull is marginally stronger than before, but we're nowhere near the trail's origin. I'll let you know if that changes."

Kass gazes upon the horizon. The light shows no signs of dimming. The skies are strangely foggy above the ever-roaring winds, and he can't pinpoint the sun's location. Eventually, they will need to rest.

The closer they get to the mountains, the more skull circles surround them. Superstitiously, they avoid walking through the centre of the circles, but at several points, one of them nearly bumps into a floating head as they attempt to avoid another.

Kass thinks he sees movement on the mountain's cliffsides and crevices but convinces himself that he is imagining it. They've been walking for a while with few breaks and little water to spare, so they're probably dehydrated.

But when Amaya keeps staring at the same spots his eyes are drawn to, he begins to worry. Finally, Andrea silently points to a lion-shaped shadow as it disappears into the depths behind a large platform, and Kass motions them to halt.

"Silver, is your spell leading us towards the mountains?" he asks. His wife frowns. Perspiration has gathered on her forehead, and her hands are shaking. As he remembers from the war, casting a spell over a prolonged period is strenuous for mages.

"I think so."

She points at a wall of stone before them, vast and impenetrable. No valleys or dales cut into its magnitude as if it had never been touched by time.

Kass shakes his head. "I'm not sure that's going to work."

Silver clasps her hands together.

"I've been thinking about this," she says. "If I manage to extend a levitation spell to all of you and use a conduit to strengthen the spell's intensity, I could lift -"

"You would bloody wreck yourself, Silver, but that's not even the bit I'm worried about," Kass says with a sigh, then turns to the rest of the group. "Who else has seen the unfriendly-looking beasties skulking on the cliffsides?"

"Erm, what?" Allen asks with wide eyes, but Andrea and Amaya nod with shifting glances towards the mountains.

"Right," Kass says. "And even if your levitation idea was feasible, Silver, we can't risk being ripped down by those monsters in mid-flight."

His wife nods slowly. Amaya's eyes once more rest on the sand.

"The black and white stones, and the skulls... it's almost like this plane used to be inhabited," she mutters.

"How could anyone live here?" Allen asks with raised eyebrows.

"They couldn't. And yet, it looks like people did. Why carry all the skulls here from elsewhere? It doesn't make any sense." The investigator frowns. "And I'm not convinced they were left here as a warning. Why go to all that effort?"

"Then what are they here for?" Allen asks.

"Maybe they're a memorial?" Andrea asks, and the rest turn around to them. They shrug. "The circles have different numbers of skulls, but none of the groups I've seen contain more than ten heads. They could represent families."

"So, did the demons suddenly arrive? And kill them all?" Kass asks with a nervous glance towards the dark shadows creeping atop the mountains. They are showing themselves more frequently now, gaining confidence.

"It's possible that they came through a rift. Or through several," Silver says. Amaya shakes her head.

"I don't think the demons are the ones who suddenly arrived. The skulls are humanoid, but this climate doesn't support human life, at least not for a prolonged period."

She rubs her chin.

"In fact," she continues. "The elements of this plane have ground everything to dust. Think of the black and white stones amidst the sand. Those could have been buildings."

"So, how'd they end up here?" Kass asks, growing tired of speculating.

Silver glances up at the sky.

"Oh no," she whispers. Amaya catches on a moment later and blinks.

"I guess it's possible?" she mutters.

"I'm sorry, what are we talking about?" Andrea asks and exchanges a confused glance with Allen. Kass follows Amaya's gaze, then groans loudly.

"Oh, fuck," he groans.

"There might be a rift in the sky," Silver explains. "Which would mean that the people of another human realm fell through it. Together with their cities, their possessions, their – everything. The demons of this plane killed them all, and any signs of their civilisation eroded into dust."

Allen's eyes widen.

"Is that where we have to go?" Andrea asks.

"I bloody hope not," Kass groans, but Silver shakes her head.

"I feel the pull from the mountains, not from the sky. Plus, we're not looking for a human realm," she says.

"Thank Five for small mercies," Andrea mutters. "I never thought I'd be happy to be looking for a hell plane."

"Would it kill you to be a bit more specific on how close we are to the demon's trail?" Kass asks, although his tone doesn't match the severity of his words. Silver glares at him.

"I'm trying. The longer I work at it, the more clearly I can feel the path before me; it's just -" She opens and closes her fists, trying to capture something elusive. Kass nods, then sighs.

"None of this solves our bloody problem," he says. "We don't have a good way up those mountains, and I'm not keen on fighting a whole horde of demons. Again."

"We... might not have a choice," Allen says, his voice suddenly hollow. He stares at a spot behind Kass, and the paladin shoots around. The shadows have climbed down the mountain and now race towards them at full speed.

The demons are quadrupedal, with long-swishing tails, dark grey skin, and horned faces with far too many teeth. Their skin seems to shift from moment to moment, from one horrifying shape to another.

Kass pulls his sword and shouts at everyone to get behind him.

Chapter 21

Wartime

Silver used to enjoy receptions. For her, there was great satisfaction in playing the role of the dutiful and demure daughter, a prize to be desired by a thousand men who would never be considered worthy of her. She enjoyed floating around the grounds of her parents' estate in long, ethereal gowns, guessing at her suitors' opinions, tastes, and interests, and sampling them as one would sample a delectable selection of wine.

Now, she was married, and her parents' estate was levelled beneath a barrage of rocks. The reception celebrated the end of the war rather than a birthday or a trade deal. It was held in one of the remaining halls of the castle, which the servants had hurriedly liberated from a layer of dust and the presence of uninvited insects.

There was no official peace treaty, but there had been no attack in almost a month. People were in the mood to celebrate, and honouring war heroes was an obvious occasion for a party. After her destruction of the enemy's dragon squadron, Silver was an obvious candidate for an honouree. It helped that almost none of the non-mages understood how her spell worked. People didn't care to, either. They were keen to congratulate her on her ingenuity and self-sacrifice (yes, they had heard about the hand, but no, no one wanted to see it) but less interested in asking how she was.

Kass knew, though. Or so she guessed. There wasn't any other reason for her husband to avoid her and the rooms they shared. For a few days, she wondered if he was dead but was too scared to check, too caught up in the numb realisation of what she had done. Then, she saw his patrol on the battlements. Kass stared straight at her, unashamed of his anger. She met his gaze, her expression nothing but tired. It occurred to her then that they had never argued before – incredibly enough, given Kass's temper.

Someone had forced her husband to attend the event. He stood next to one of the tables burdened by opulent plates of canapes and fruits and by glass containers filled with brightly coloured alcoholic concoctions.

He was scowling at anyone who tried to approach him. The reception was attended mainly by courtiers and politicians starved of war-time gossip and excited to hear stories of heroics and virtuous sacrifice. None of the actual veterans had much of either to share, but most made more of an attempt at politeness than Kass did.

A shame. Silver had hoped for at least one friendly face at this event. Pathas had killed too few dragons to be considered a war hero. Octavia had thrown her medals at king Ithya and had taken off to gods-know-where. And Pride was nowhere to be found. Maybe she was with Octavia, trying to reason with her.

During the ceremony, Ithya touched Silver's head with the tip of his sword, light as a kiss. Everyone had clapped, and nobody had whispered about necromancy. But people's smiles had been thin, and they were disinterested in witnessing the reward of sacrifice and labour. All they wanted was juicy stories, overrunning with blood, soil, and sweat. Silver had enough of selling her memories for cheap, so she ignored the courtiers. Instead, she walked over to her husband, wineglass in hand.

She tried her best to ignore his cold stare. Pathas had fixed up her legs for the day. It was a temporary solution, he'd emphasised, but today felt normal enough for her to forget his cautioning words. Fundamentally, Silver still thought the world was going to be all right.

"Hey," she said, leaning against the table to take the weight off her feet. Kass stared at her for a few moments. Then he grunted instead of a greeting.

"Still mad?" she asked, her tone light-hearted. He stared at her some more.

"Well, just for today, could you not be?" she continued. "I'm not sure I can get through this shit show on my own."

She groaned. "You know, earlier, someone asked me if I drank the blood of my enemies to absorb their strength. Got really excited about the idea, too."

She shook her head. "Sometimes I wonder if we fought on the correct side."

"Silver." Kass pressed out the word. "Stop it."

For a moment, she wondered if someone was approaching who wasn't privy to their conversation. When she saw no one nearby, she looked back at her husband's pale face.

"What?" she asked.

Kass narrowed his eyes. "I'm not in the mood."

"Well, tough shit. In sickness and in health, my friend."

"This isn't a joke," Kass said sharply.

"What isn't?"

She knew he was mad about the necromancy, but they could talk about that later. They just had to get through this event, and then he could growl, he could shout, and they could work things out.

He stared at her, and suddenly Silver thought she could see hatred in his eyes. The look of it terrified her. Kass was gruff and choleric, but he was also one of the kindest, most thoughtful people she knew. He would never hurt her unintentionally.

He turned away.

He meant this.

"You don't want to do this here," he whispered. "Trust me."

Silver took a deep breath. Anxiety flared up in her stomach, and suddenly, she wanted nothing more than a quick horse to ride out of town so she could forget any of this had ever happened. She twisted the plain wedding ring on her right hand and sipped her wine.

"I saved us," she said pointlessly. She could anticipate Kass's response, but she had to hear it from his own lips. Part of her hoped the blow would be less brutal if she knew it was coming.

It wasn't.

Kass poured himself a glass of something dark and strong. He downed it with a single sip.

"You doomed more humans to a fate worse than death than our enemies ever managed," he said quietly. She thought he was exaggerating, but this wasn't the best time to debate specifics.

"The dragons would have killed us all."

"You condemned a thousand souls to nonexistence. A thousand dead waiting to pass over to the afterlife, and you used them as fucking fodder for your spells."

He stared at her, and she saw the hurt behind his eyes. His shock at what she had done.

"You've made it so those people never existed," he continued. "No trace of them remains on any planes of existence. How could you do it, Silver? How could you even think of doing something like this?"

"They were already dead," Silver replied. "I chose to save those of us who are still alive, Kass."

He shook his head. "Even if we all died, our souls would have passed over to the afterlife. To join the gods on their planes of existence and to finally experience some bloody peace. We wouldn't just be – gone, Silver."

"You don't know that," she protested.

"I know what the gods tell us."

262

"And you think the gods never lie to us? We know that some souls linger on this plane. Just because the others disappear doesn't mean they pass on to the lands of wine and honey."

She saw his eyes narrow, but she wasn't willing to concede on this point. Not then, and not later.

"Look. If we think about this rationally, we can't know what happens to the souls of the dead. Maybe they fade into nothing."

"Something that exists doesn't just disappear, Silver. There has to be equivalence."

"Why? How would you know that?"

"I have faith."

"Well, I don't." She shook her head.

"I know what the gods teach us," she said. "That if we pray to them and follow all their rules, we get to go to their pretty realms after we die. But the gods didn't tell us about the rifts. We didn't even know their planes were a real place before all this! What makes you think they wouldn't lie to us about anything else?"

"Because I choose to believe that our actions have meaning, Silver. That there is some grand cosmic scale that keeps track of the things we do."

"What I did has meaning. I saved us."

"You doomed yourself," Kass said, his voice cold.

Silver felt tears behind her eyes.

"Maybe in the eyes of your god," she replied quietly. "What about yours?"

"There is no difference? Murder is murder."

"It wasn't murder!" Her voice rose. When people turned around to look at them, Kass pulled them out of the reception hall behind a large vase filled with lilies.

Silver repeated the last thing she said, even though the words felt just as hollow as they did the first time. Kass just stared at her. He looks like the avatar of Five, she thought. Tall and impenetrable and unforgiving. Justice undiluted with emotion.

"You used those souls up like they were nothing. And now, they no longer exist because of what you did," he said.

Silver felt her legs starting to hurt again. The pain turned to frustration, then to anger. How dare he?

"Don't act like you would have been fine to die," she snarled. "I know you were afraid. I saw your face when Holly died. You want to live."

"Everyone wants to live, Silver. That doesn't justify –"

"It justifies everything. Without life, we have nothing. Are nothing. Everything else is secondary."

Kass shook his head. "And now?" he asked. "Can you live with yourself, Silver? Knowing how many people you sacrificed for us to be at this bloody reception, drinking and feasting and talking about fucking nothing?"

Silver did him the favour of looking inward. She waited, a breath, then another. Then she nodded.

"Yes. I think I can. They had their chance at life. I want mine."

Kass stared at her.

"You're a monster," he finally said.

Silver felt her blood turn cold. Kass never said things he didn't mean. It was one of the things she liked most about him.

She pleaded, even if she didn't feel like it. Because they were still married, even if everything had somehow become twisted over the course of this gods-forsaken war.

"Please, Kass. I didn't want you to die. I didn't want anyone else to die," she offered, then reached for his hand. "I'm so tired of all this pain."

She could see his resolve straining, just for a moment, then he pulled away.

"I know," he muttered. "I know why you did it, Silver. It just doesn't make it better."

Chapter 22

The demons attack as soon as they reach the humans. There is no warning, no hesitation, no battle cry cutting through the heat-soaked air. They fall upon them like shadows. They move fast and whip their tails across the dunes to create shifting walls that block Kass's line of vision.

Initially, he fights at the helm of their group, blocking the demons' attacks and preventing them from reaching his companions. But, quickly enough, they are surrounded, so his squires fan out to cover the ground before Silver and Amaya. Amaya has drawn her gun and fires with abandon, her shots echoing widely across the empty planes. Silver summons giant icicles that materialise inside the demons' bodies and split them apart.

They are holding out. But more demons are pouring from the mountains, like a dark stream from a spring.

A demon tries to jump over Kass's head to get to Amaya and the source of the noise. Kass rips up his Zweihander at the last moment and peels open the beast's stomach. Innards and blood rain down, and the demon's body collapses on top of him. For a moment, all hell breaks loose when the demons take advantage of the break in formation and try to reach the two women.

An icy wind crashes into the attacking horde and rips the demons into the dusty sky. Amaya shoots wildly amidst their tumbling bodies. Kass shifts out from under the corpse and forces himself back up to his feet. He glances back at Silver, whose body is glowing in an eerie white light. Her skeletal hand is uncovered and coated in Pride's white-sparkling spell components. She is panting heavily but has the gall to wink at him before he turns back into his defensive position.

The attacks are unrelenting. He is sure half an hour must have passed. The onyx stones in his pockets are burning hotter and hotter. Amaya has run out of bullets and stands beside Silver's wheelchair, ready to defend the mage.

For a while now, his wife has stopped casting spells to fend off the demons, and Kass isn't sure whether she's run out of energy or preserving her resources.

He would certainly not mind a bit of a reprieve. His arms are burning every time he swings his sword, and from his squires' loud panting and cursing (on Allen's part), he knows they are not faring much better. The dead demons are piling up around them, creating walls of flesh that block out the horizon.

A demon jumps at an unexpected angle and hits Andrea in the shoulder. His squire manages to shake the creature off and decapitate it, but he notices that their movements are slowed after the attack. Allen picks up speed to take the pressure off them, but after a few minutes, he starts to heave uncontrollably.

Kass clenches his teeth. He can't keep the demons at bay by himself. Not without Five's help, not when they have the group so tightly surrounded. Not in the demons' territory, with never-ending reinforcements raining down from the mountains.

"Silver," he calls. "Get ready to levitate us out of here."

He has seen how high the demons can jump, but they have to risk it.

Silver ignores him. He repeats himself, but still, there is no reply.

He runs his sword through one, two demons, then there is a brief break in the fight when the reinforcements have to climb over the corpses of their predecessors. He glances over his shoulder.

A blinding light surrounds Silver, and her eyes are closed. Her skeletal hand twitches as if it's searching for something. A feeling of utter wrongness spreads throughout his body when he looks at her. The stink of decay, hot and all-consuming, sits on his tongue.

"Silver," he roars. "What are you doing?"

Silver's eyes fly open, and she mouths two words. *Found it.*

The dead demons rise in a single horrifying motion, ripped into the sky with their limbs softly swaying from side to side. Silver clenches her fist, and their flesh bursts apart. Blood rains across the horizon until the droplets freeze in the air and congregate at the centre of their defensive hold.

Everything, *everything* feels wrong. Kass feels his own blood drawn towards the centre of Silver's spell and buries his feet as firmly into the ground as he can. The closest attacking demons are ripped apart by the force of the magic, their blood rushing towards Silver as her spell breaks their skin and bones.

Then, the universe moans in pain. The blinding white light leaves Silver's body and settles in the blood-soaked air. Amidst the brightness, Kass sees the world they entered reflected a thousandfold: the rolling hills of its deserts, the towering mountain ranges, and scaled animals hiding in caverns far, far away.

Silver twists her skeletal hand, and the demons' red blood gets caught in the web of spell craft, forming an intricate pattern that becomes more insoluble the longer Kass looks at it. Then, the white spell components on Silver's hand fizzle and dissipate, and his wife rips her hands apart. The blood and magic tear away from each other, the pattern stretching and groaning. In the gaps between the red and the light, he can see another realm appearing, full of green foliage and the smells of musty forests.

"It's a rift," Amaya shouts.

"What do we do, Sir?" Allen asks, his voice shaking.

Andrea is pressing their hands against their temples, and Kass wonders if they feel the corruption of the spell even more intensely than he does.

Silver screams as she tries to widen the rift. The blood pulls on the fabric of reality, but the world's inertia is strong, and the gap between the planes threatens to fall shut with each of her shuddering breaths.

"Silver! Stop this!" Kass roars. "You don't know what you're doing!"

She doesn't respond, but her eyes are wide and full of fury as she holds her hands outstretched. But it's not enough. Even with all the blood from all the corpses, the rift is too narrow for them to fit through.

Then, she utters a single word. Kass knows nothing about the language of arcane commands, but he remembers this one from the war.

It's the word for dissolution.

"NO!" he screams and jumps towards his wife, blood and magic be damned.

But he's too late. The small finger on Silver's skeletal hand crumbles into dust, and the rift widens with an earth-shattering sigh. Amaya doesn't hesitate and jumps through the gap.

"Fuck! Go! Go," he screams at his squires, who are hesitating at the edges of the rift. They follow his command.

Silver's eyes are white and blank, and the spell reaches her next finger. Kass can see the edges of the bone falling to the ground like flecks of snow.

He reaches her and grabs her skeleton hand between his own. The touch burns through his skin, and he can feel his flesh begin to scald, but he doesn't care.

"Silver!" he calls, but she isn't reacting to his voice. The spell sucks on her remaining fingers and thins them out against the relentless air. If he doesn't do something, she will be consumed by it, body and soul.

"Come on, mageling! Don't fade on me now!" he yells, squeezing her hand between his. He feels the spell jump over to him, burning the skin to the bone. Wet blood congeals around the wounds.

Silver starts to blink, but her eyes are still white and empty.

"Silver! *Please*!"

He presses his forehead against hers and repeats the words over and over.

"Kass?"

His heart stops at the sound of her voice.

"Stop the spell!" he cries. "The rift is open!"

"Wh -"

"Stop casting your dissolution spell! You're killing yourself!"

Silver takes a deep breath, and her eyes return to their normal dark colour. She mutters a few words, and he feels the dissolution fall from her hand.

For the first time in minutes, Kass takes a breath and feels his legs almost buckle from underneath him. But life isn't that gracious. He can already hear the next horde of demons approaching in the distance.

Silver blinks again.

"I - I did it," she says, sounding as stunned as he feels. "I opened a rift."

"If you want a gold star, I'm afraid it'll have to wait," Kass grunts, although he doesn't have it in him to be mad at her. He's just happy they're both alive.

He glances down at Silver, pale and shaking. Then, he takes the back of her chair and pushes her through the rift.

They arrive in the middle of a forest, cool compared to the arid desert heat and with air so humid that it's hard to breathe. The first thing Silver does is seal the rift behind them with a simple barrier spell, for which she uses a few bones from a pouch by the side of her wheelchair.

Andrea and Allen watch her from the ground, with horrified looks painted on their faces, while Amaya is already pacing through the nearby surroundings, looking through the gaps between the thick-stemmed trees and touching the wet, green leaves with the tip of her dagger. The leaves are full of viscose, yellow moisture that escapes the plants' skin at the slightest touch.

Kass can still feel the onyx stones burning against his skin. He is sure his thighs will have red, angry marks tomorrow. He doesn't mind. It'll be nothing compared to the state of his hands.

It's not dark yet, but the light from the realm's two suns is pale and slowly disappears into the horizon. Kass sinks down and pulls a set of bandages from another pouch on Silver's chair. At some point, she had made some disparaging comments about being relegated as a 'packing mule'. Now, she looks concerned as she takes note of the state of his hands.

She doesn't seem to realise what caused the wounds, which he is grateful for. He doesn't need her feeling guilty. Not now, and not for this.

"What the ... what was that?" Andrea finally asks.

It takes a moment before Silver realises the comment was aimed at her.

"Excuse me?" she asks. She is visibly shaken from the effort of casting her spell, and she keeps glancing down at her missing finger as if she is only now realising that it has truly disappeared.

"The spell. *What was that?*" the squire repeats.

"It was ... an experiment," Silver stammers. "To open a rift."

"Yes, I saw that," Andrea snaps, their voice uncharacteristically sharp. "But what in the name of Five was that blood spectacle?"

"Do you really want me to go into details of arcane theory?" Silver asks, anger growing pale on her features.

"I –" Andrea starts to raise their voice, but Kass steps towards them and glowers down at his squire.

Allen shakes his head and mutters something along the lines of, 'At least we're still alive'. But Andrea isn't as easily assuaged. They take a deep breath, then meet the necromancer's eyes again.

"Mistress Silver, forgive me, I don't understand how magic works, but ... am I understanding correctly that you used the demons' blood to fuel your spell?"

Silver nods slowly. "Yes. Opening the rift required an extraordinary amount of power. The fabric of reality was already thin, but breaking through it was not easy." She rubs her fingers together absent-mindedly.

"Even with all the demons I used as fuel, I couldn't have done it without Pride's spell components. Or without ..." She glances back down at her hand.

"Resourceful," Amaya says with an appreciative nod. Silver smiles at her.

"You owe me dinner for this, 'maya."

"Well, you know where I like to go."

"I can do burgers."

Andrea clears their throat, their voice shaking. "You used the ... demons as fuel, you say?"

Silver nods and takes a lecturing tone.

"Everything in the Multiverse can be reduced to a form of energy in motion and countermotion. Shifts of power, you could say. So, if you want to cause a significant transformation in the Multiverse's structure, you have to offer a significant energy shift. So, I shifted –"

"The demons' bodies? Or their souls?" Andrea asks, hitting at the core of the issue. Kass feels a sigh rising in his throat.

Silver glares at Andrea, then, for a moment, at Kass.

"I used everything I had," she says. "Blood, heat, air, souls – all that is energy."

"Souls are sacred. Five teaches us that they must be preserved at any cost so that they can join him after death," Andrea replies, their voice shaking.

"I don't think those demons were devout followers of a human god, Andrea," Silver says, her voice strained with irritation.

"I don't think it matters," they respond. "A soul is a soul."

"A soul is energy," Silver responds. "We don't know what happens to it after death. And I needed them. *We* needed them."

"I didn't – I don't want this," Andrea mutters, horror settling behind their eyes. "I don't want this on my conscience."

"It was just demons," Amaya says with a hint of an eye roll. "There is no reason to assume they are any more intelligent than animals."

Silver glances over at her and remains silent.

Kass puts a large hand on his squire's shoulder.

"This isn't on you, 'drea. It was Silver's decision. Let her live with the guilt or the lack thereof. You didn't know. And you couldn't have stopped her."

He sees tears glimmering in the corners of his squire's eyes. Allen narrows his eyes.

"You seem very... calm about this, Sir," he notes. Kass hesitates.

"It's not like he hasn't seen it before," Silver says and glares at him. "It's not like this is anything but a drop amidst all the guilt I already carry. Right, Kass?" She scoffs and turns her chair until she no longer looks at them. "Now, if you're done complaining about me saving your lives, I'm going to see whether I even opened a rift to the correct plane."

She picks out a fresh pile of bones and scatters them around a piece of demon flesh. Amaya nods appreciatively.

"Chances are good. This climate and environment seem more conducive to our dead demon friend's needs."

Silver looks at her. "I hope so. Once I tracked the demon's trail to this plane, I interwove the scrying spell with the force I used to open the rift." She shrugs. "Still. A lot of unknowns. It could have gone disastrously wrong."

Kass takes a long breath. Guilt is tying up his stomach whichever way he turns, so he reckons he might as well do what he bloody feels like.

"You did fine, Silver," he says. "Even if it's the wrong plane, we can find other rifts. The important thing is that we survived."

Silver's eyes fly towards him and widen with unexpected pleasure.

"I... yes. I agree," she replies, cheeks colouring. Kass feels Andrea's gaze burn on the back of his head, but he busies himself checking and re-tying the bandages around his hand.

Silver weaves together another spell, and blood slowly seeps out of the dead demon's flesh. Allen cracks a joke about trees and people who are named after trees, but nobody laughs. They are all exhausted.

Finally, Silver gently clasps her skeletal hand over the demon's flesh and nods with a self-satisfied smile.

"Yes. The scrying spell works. Our third demon has spent a lot of time on this plane."

The group sighs with relief.

Chapter 23

They camp before following the trail, using coats and piles of leaves as make-shift beds. Silver and Allen fall asleep immediately, and although he can see Andrea continuously stirring, Kass hopes they nap a little. Amaya can't sleep outdoors, so she offers to watch over them while she cleans the inside of her gun. She has used up all her bullets but doesn't let that stop her from maintaining proper weapon hygiene. You can find bullets in the strangest places, she says.

Kass lies down in full armour, expecting his racing heart to stop him from resting. But he falls into a black, deep sleep almost as soon as his head hits the ground. For once, he does not dream.

When Silver wakes him at dawn, he feels like he is climbing out of a well. The world spins, and he is struggling to focus.

"Relax," she says, correctly interpreting his hazy movements. "Your squires are still asleep. You've got time."

She knows about his night terrors and the panic attacks that follow. She probably figured he wouldn't want his squires to see him like that.

He gives her a thankful nod and props himself up on his elbow. Silver is already sitting in her chair, and she is close enough that he could put his head in her lap and rest a little longer. She would probably let him.

"Are you okay?" he asks with a glance at her finger. She shrugs with deliberate nonchalance.

"You always said the thing was creepy. Maybe it's less creepy now that there's less of it?"

"I'm sorry, Silver," he says, not entirely sure what for. But another knot of guilt in his stomach loosens when he realises the sentiment is genuine.

She smiles. "It's okay. We all say cruel things sometimes."

Repentance to Silver is certainly easier than repentance to Five.

She bites down on her lip. "I don't remember much from when I opened the rift, but your hand - you ripped me out of a trance, didn't you? And hurt yourself?"

"I don't give a shit about my hand, Silver," he says. She laughs.

"Then that makes two of us."

Kass grins. "Look at us and our fake bravado. All to spite a terrible world."

"It's not all terrible," Silver says and gently touches the bandage on Kass's hand.

His squires stir soon after, and Kass forces himself to stand. His head still swirls a little, but he can feel that the sleep restored his energy.

They only brought meagre provisions so the weight of their packs wouldn't slow them down, but they manage to scrape together enough for breakfast. The group is silent, still reeling from yesterday's tensions, although Kass thinks he can see some guilt in Allen's eyes whenever he glances at Silver. Andrea looks tired, and Amaya yawns throughout the meal.

"Do you have any idea how close the start of the demon's trail is from here?" Kass asks his wife. She raises her eyebrows, and he hurries to explain.

"I know this is an imprecise science, love, but how does this compare to you casting the scrying spell in Old Noll's graveyard?"

"Love?" she mouths. He feels his cheeks colour. What an odd time to slip back into that old habit.

Silver is gracious enough to stay on topic.

"It feels a little further than that, but certainly not by much," she says. "Why? You all getting tired?"

Her mocking smile is soft around its edges. Fundamentally, Silver wants to be liked. She has always wanted life to be easy and fun.

Allen chuckles when Amaya nods emphatically.

"I'm wondering if we'll need to hunt for food. And find a stream to refill our water pouches," Kass explains. "We're running low, but in a place like this, I'd rather not risk exploring the bloody scenery unless we have to."

"Ah," Silver makes, then shrugs.

"I can tell you that we should reach the trail within the day. But I can't promise what we'll find when we get there. It might be that there's nothing but forests in this realm."

Amaya nods.

"It doesn't strike me as likely that this demon species constructed any great architectural feats," the investigator says. "Why bother? The trees make for excellent homes and hiding places, and the creatures can probably sustain themselves with the dew that gathers on the leaves below."

"I did not bring the right clothes for this," Allen complains. He is already sweating under his heavy armour.

Kass nods. "Very well. We still have enough water for today, but tomorrow night, we should use a tarp to gather more liquid."

"What if the water in this place is poisonous, Sir?" Andrea asks quietly. They don't look at him. Bad sign, Kass thinks.

"Then we die," Amaya says laconically. "It's not like we have much of an alternative, do we?"

Allen looks at Silver, but the mage shrugs.

"I could test the water's composition if I could access one of Pride's labs. Out here, though ..."

Kass slaps his knees.

"Enough of this," he says with forced elan. "Let's go."

The air in the jungle heats up quickly as the realm's two suns reach their zenith. Thick-leaved plants grow up to their calves and knees, and a few times, Kass is sure he catches them moving.

The trees provide shade from the sun, as Silver's spell navigates them through the untouched forests. Kass carries his wife in his arms and tries not to think too hard about the way her body feels against his chest. Andrea wordlessly strapped Silver's wheelchair to their back and ignores every one of Allen's offers to take over.

Amaya insists on taking frequent breaks. The constant brushing of tree bark and plants against her clothes has her head spinning from overstimulation.

Nobody complains, however frequent the interruptions get. Allen is sweating buckets, and Kass and Andrea aren't doing much better.

But Kass just knows that as soon as any of them take off their armour, they'll be beset by some mysterious, extra-planar monster with swords for hair and teeth on top of teeth. And he's not in the mood for that.

Finally, the jungle stops. The trees, their crowns thick with branches, cease, and the undergrowth is replaced by a freshly mowed lawn.

They do not spend even a second looking at the perfectly manicured grass below. Their gazes are captivated by what looms before them.

"Erm, so much for a lack of civilisation," Allen says, his voice hollow.

"Even I have been known to be wrong," Amaya responds in the same tone.

Several massive structures lie at the centre of rolling meadows, their exterior almost perfectly reflective of the bright blue skies and the green grass surrounding them. The buildings are made of what looks like interconnected spheres, round, stacked atop one another, and occasionally rotating to catch more of the shifting sunlight. No doors or windows are visible from the outside, but Kass feels strangely watched. As if the building's inhabitants all turned towards him with a single motion.

"Silver?" he asks.

His wife's eyes are large when she looks at him.

"Yeah," she says, her voice husky. "The demon comes from this place."

When they walk closer, Kass sees movement in the forests surrounding the strange structure. Nothing emerges from the shifting green seas, but still, he rests his hand on his Zweihander.

"What do you make of this?" he asks Amaya.

She narrows her eyes.

"I'm not convinced our demon built this. From an ecological perspective, its species is perfectly adapted to this world, so I'm not sure it would have developed a need for structures to protect it against the elements."

Kass frowns.

"So, what? Are you saying these people might have come from another bloody plane?"

"Why not?" the investigator replies. "We did, after all."

"We have Silver," Kass grunts. "That's a pretty unique asset. Plus, I don't see any open rifts nearby."

"Rifts don't have to be above ground," Silver replies. "If the structures continue under the earth, there might be a rift down there."

"Oh, fantastic," Allen mutters. "I was getting sick of this world anyway. What's next? A realm where everything is made of goo?"

"Hopefully, we won't have to go through yet another rift, Allen," Andrea cautions him with a mild smile.

"We kind of do," he reminds her. "This is where we're hoping to find a rift to the mage culprit's home, remember? So, we have at least one more world to visit."

"Ah, right," Andrea says, shaking their head. "Well, if it is a world full of goo, you may depend on my sword for any cutting services you require."

"So gallant," Allen replies with a grin, and Andrea laughs.

Kass is happy to see his squire's spirits picking back up, although they still avoid looking at Silver.

As they approach the strange building, a door melts out of its reflective exterior. The air vibrates, and Kass thinks he can trace the outline of two beings with a dozen long, soft limbs. Their bodies grow around a gaping hole at their core, a swirling vortex of dark, liquid flesh. Then, the air shifts again, and the hazy vision disappears. Only an empty doorway remains, and the knowledge that its inhabitants remain unseen.

A voice fills the air, but Kass can't make out the meaning of the thin sounds. Allen is shaking, and Kass places a quick hand on the squire's shoulder.

"Sorry," he responds to the air. "I don't speak your language."

He wants to draw his sword. Every impulse from the war tells him to, but he forces himself to stay still.

"Be greeted," the disembodied voice responds. "We speak the human tongue."

"Oh, human!" another voice says. "I should have figured."

The voices feel like they are surrounding him. Kass can't pinpoint where they are coming from. This is bad. Their attacks will hit if he doesn't know where his enemy is. They will hit, and he won't be able to –

"Greetings," Silver responds with her usual politeness. "We apologise for dropping by unannounced."

She reaches out for Kass's arm and squeezes it. He immediately feels himself get a little calmer.

"Thank you, dear customers, for visiting us in this remote outpost," the first stranger says.

Kass tries to calm down and register the words that are being spoken. Customers? Outpost? At least it doesn't seem like a fight will break out.

The second voice speaks. "Please allow me to escort you inside. You may wish to rest and bathe before we show you the merchandise."

Kass and the rest of his group exchange a look, but in lieu of a better alternative, they follow the strangers into the shifting structure.

The interior is made up of brightly lit, white corridors made for taller beings than humans. There are no doors on any of the walls, but Kass wonders if they will simply melt into existence at the wish of their mysterious hosts.

He can feel an incline as they follow the voices of the two strangers, who introduce themselves as Z'kett and Eduard M. Karenin. Kass is sure the names are poorly translated, imperfect equivalents of their own tongue.

Although the corridor continues on an incline, there are no stairs. Amaya quietly muses if their hosts struggle with sudden altitude shifts and theorises what that might say about their physiognomy. Z'kett and Karenin politely ignore her comments.

"So, merchandise, huh?" Allen asks, breaking the silence. Kass groans internally.

"Yes?" Z'kett responds, although there is some hesitation in their tone. Kass hopes they'll be able to chalk up most of their conversational faux pas to 'cultural differences'.

"What my idiot squire means to ask is what kind of, erm, developments you've had in your merchandise production," Kass interjects.

If their hosts assume they are here as customers, they better start acting the part. At least if they want to avoid fighting an undefined number of magically gifted, invisible foes.

Karenin hmms in response.

"Yes," they respond. "As you are no doubt aware, we're a specialised facility. We focus exclusively on specimens of the –"

They utter a word whose syllabic composition Kass can't even begin to register.

"This way, our genetic experiments are much more productive," Z'kett adds. "As it turns out, different species of demon show rather different responses to the procedures."

Their steps echo between the white walls, and Kass notices how much louder their hosts' movements are than his own.

"I always said so, of course," Z'kett continues. "Two years ago, I told the research board to consider the physiological differences between the species and to go for undiluted sampling groups. But did they listen to me? Did they?"

"Here we go," Karenin mutters.

"So, your ... organisation breeds demons elsewhere?" Silver asks.

Their hosts repeat the term 'demon', then exchange a few words in their own tongue.

"We have facilities across five planes, with plans to expand to another thirteen," Karenin finally responds.

"Five have mercy," Andrea breathes. Amaya coughs.

"And, of course, you rent out the demons to your customers," she says slowly.

Neither of their hosts protests this assumption, and Kass exhales a slow breath.

"Is this very profitable?" Amaya continues. "I imagine not many people are experienced planar travellers."

"It took a few years for business to pick up," Karenin agrees. "The first year after the rifts opened, we only saw corpses falling through the rifts. Then, of course, came the human from your realm. And after that, custom slowly trickled in."

The human from your realm. Kass starts to guess why Z'katt and Karenin speak his language.

"Word of mouth makes for wonderful advertisement, especially when your customers are satisfied. And who doesn't love a mute 'demon' assassin who can't betray your secrets?" Karenin adds. His pronunciation of the word demon is strained, but Kass hopes they are talking about the same thing.

"So, you people have been doing this since the rifts opened?" Silver asks incredulously.

Z'katt's voice drops slightly.

"We didn't have much of a choice. A lot of worlds got lucky when it came to the planar split. A rift here or there, most of them too small to use."

They stop for a moment. Kass can see a faint outline of a bent spine vibrate against the white walls.

"Our world split apart at its core," they say quietly. "It became completely uninhabitable."

"You couldn't step anywhere without falling into another realm," Karenin agrees in a far more callous tone. "It was most unpleasant. All my cats disappeared."

Z'katt takes a shuddering breath.

"Our elders decided that we would move what was left of our people to another realm. The one they chose just so happened to be inhabited."

They straighten their back, then their outline disappears from the reflections on the wall.

"It ended up working out for the best, of course," they continue. "We captured most of the creatures in the nearby area and enslaved them to do our bidding. Predictably, many influential houses started training them as assassins to take out their competition."

"Barbaric," Karenin mutters.

"Sure," Z'katt agrees a little too quickly. "Anyway, to keep down casualties, the elders introduced a law stating that we can only sell the creatures to outsiders. And here we are."

"And here we are," Karenin sighs. "Tale as old as time."

"Are you people fearsome warriors, then? If you enslaved a whole realm full of demons," Allen asks.

Z'katt makes a noise that sounds like a snort. "Don't be absurd. We use arcane magic. The building blocks of the Multiverse."

"A much superior art," Silver agrees.

"None other is worth pursuing," Z'katt says. "Not if you want to make a difference in the world."

"There are divine miracles," Andrea mutters. "Those actually help people."

Karenin's voice approaches.

"Divine? What do you mean, sorry? Is that a service you require?" they ask.

"No, no," Kass quickly explains. "Andrea means miracles performed by gods."

"Gods?" Karenin responds, still confused.

Z'katt clicks their tongue. "Ah, I remember. The other human also spoke about 'gods'. Supposedly all-powerful, transcendental entities that rule the Multiverse. Superstitious nonsense, of course."

"Z'katt." Karenin shushes them. "That is not very polite. Everyone is entitled to their beliefs, however stupid they might be."

Kass and his squires stare at each other in stunned silence.

"About that human from our realm," Amaya says with deliberate nonchalance. "Did you ever meet them?"

"Yes," Z'katt says. "When they went to pick out their creature. They wanted one with scales, I remember that. What was their name again...?"

Karenin makes a noise. "Don't ask me. I never met them. Although we should probably thank them for spreading the word about our services."

The air moves, and Kass wonders if their host gestured at him and the rest of his group. Kass tries to summon a pleasant smile.

Before them, the corridor suddenly ends, and five doors melt out of the wall, revealing simple but clean chambers. Kass can see a bed, a chest, and even a tub filled with steaming water. All are illuminated by the strange white light that fills the rest of the compound.

"Feel free to rest and bathe," Karenin says with a bow. "When you are ready, we will show you the merchandise."

Silver thanks them, but Amaya holds up her hand to stop their hosts from leaving.

"Did that human seek you out on purpose?" the investigator prods. "Did they already know about the services you provide?"

Z'katt makes a strange gargling noise. Only after a few moments Kass realises it might be laughter.

"Did he ever!" they say. "From what I've been told, they fell out of a rift head-first, screaming like an infant. The poor fool had no idea where they were."

"But nobody can resist our incredible deals and customer service," Karenin adds.

Paladin and Necromancer

Chapter 24

Kass falls asleep in the bath and wakes to find his clothes, washed and folded, on a chair beside his bed. He puts on his trousers and shirt but leaves the armour, even though he would feel safer with steel and metal between him and his strange hosts.

His heart starts racing at the thought of Z'kett or Karenin finding him exposed in the bath when they came to wash his clothes. He wonders if they are in the room with him right now. Holding their breaths and stretching out their strange, long limbs towards him.

But he can't do anything about it now. Instinctively, he touches the vanished corruption on his chest. Pride healed that, of course. He shakes his head. Whatever he will owe the mage general in exchange for her service doesn't even bear thinking about.

Silver trusts Pride, but Silver would do well to trust her instincts less.

But who is he to speak of instincts? Part of him still wants to kneel and pray for guidance from Five, even when he knows none will be forthcoming.

Part of him wants to curse his god and tell him to go to hell. He knows the gods are involved in this mystery somehow. Why else would Five abandon not only him but also his squires?

Perhaps Silver has always seen things more clearly than he has.

He wants –

He hears a scratching, then a gentle prodding. He hurries to the wall. A moment later, a ray of light traces the outline of a door that didn't exist a moment ago. Kass pushes against it. The wall swings open and reveals Silver sitting on her bed, idly shaking her bright-glowing fingers.

"Oh," she makes, then smiles bashfully. "I wasn't sure if that would work."

Kass shrugs. "Our creepy hosts use magic. You're a mage. Seems like an obvious overlap in skills."

"Very good, smart-ass," Silver laughs, then waves him into her room. She evidently bathed as well, and she only wears the short tunic that usually sits underneath her robes.

"How are you feeling?" she asks.

Kass turns around. The room looks identical to his own. There is nowhere to sit except for the strange white bed and the chair beside it. Kass opts for the chair, a fact that Silver quits with an amused eyebrow raise.

"I'm fine," he grunts and cracks his knuckles. "Beats sleeping in the jungle."

"I quite agree," Silver says. "After the war, I swore I'd never spend another night outside my warm, fluffy bed. Oh-so-many oaths I'm breaking for your sake, husband."

"You wanted to come along. And along you bloody came," he says, giving her a low-lidded smile.

"Well, didn't our marriage councillor say we should look for a shared hobby?"

A few years ago, they had tried couples counselling. It didn't go well.

"I'm sure this is exactly what she had in mind," Kass laughs.

Silver leans back her head and exposes her pale neck.

"It's interesting what our hosts said about the gods, no?" she asks.

"Silver," he grumbles. "I'm in no mood ..."

"Maybe you should get in the mood," his wife says and snaps her head back to look at him.

"These people haven't even heard of them," she says. "Which is rather strange, given that we are talking about omnipotent and omnipresent beings, no? Why wouldn't they have made themselves known to such an advanced race of magic users?"

"I don't know, Silver. There are atheists, even among humans. You can't force people to believe even when they are surrounded by divine miracles. That's the whole bloody point of free will."

"And all of them just so happen to be atheists?" his wife responds. "Isn't it much more likely that they have never seen a god? Or, rather, that the creatures we think of as gods are nothing but powerful magical beings whose reach extends only so far?"

"You sound like Pride."

"Good. Because I'm starting to think that Pride is right."

Kass groans. "Well, I don't know the fucking answer, Silver. I would ask Five if I could, but you know. He isn't answering."

"Because you're too close," Silver whispers. "You're too close to a truth the gods don't want us to discover."

He sighs. "Maybe. And then what?"

"What do you mean?"

"What if you're right? What do I do then?"

Silver lowers her upper body until her face is desperately close to him. He can feel the movement of her skin, smell her scent. He feels light-headed.

"Then you renounce them and come back to me," she whispers.

Kass feels his tongue loose and heavy in his mouth. So many days and sleepless nights spent agonising about the most important question in his life, and still there are no answers.

And his god remains silent. It is infuriating. It is agonising.

Silver places her hand on his chest, and the agony intensifies a thousandfold. He closes his eyes. She must know what she's doing to him. And, for once, he won't coddle her by pretending otherwise.

For once –

"I know," she whispers nonsensically, her voice even raspier than usual. He feels her pull herself from the bed onto his lap, slowly and deliberately. Her legs straddle him, and he can feel her warmth spread across his body.

He opens his eyes and takes in her dark, half-lidded eyes, heavy with desire, the strands of thin hair that hang across her face, and her tunic that rides up her legs, exposing her white thighs.

He groans and feels himself grow hard. He knows Silver can feel it, and a moment later, she sighs and moves her face closer to his.

"Let me –" she starts, then stops just before she kisses him.

Let me make it better.

Let me make it worse.

Let me undo you in a thousand ways.

Let me corrupt your very soul as you cry out for me to keep touching you.

For once –

Kass exhales, then inhales and the air flutters inside his chest. Silver waits, her body pressed into his, heat spreading between them. It has to be fair. If she is to continue, he has to reciprocate. He has to throw himself at her feet and beg for mercy.

He stares at her for a moment longer. Then, he grabs her arms and pulls her into him. Silver smiles with pleasure as his mouth devours her, and the knots in his chest burst open.

She groans when he grabs the back of her head, runs his fingers through her hair, and tastes the inside of her mouth.

She whispers something – his name, probably – but he doesn't listen. His hands move down to her thighs, then he pulls the tunic over Silver's head until she sits naked before him. He briefly opens his eyes and drinks her in with his gaze.

He closes them again and moans when she bends down to kiss his throat. She runs her tongue down the side of his neck, and he can't help but shiver.

The pressure becomes unbearable the lower she moves, and he gently forces her back up to kiss him. For a moment, everything is pure sweetness as he breathes against her lips and feels her fingers softly against his chest.

Then he lifts her from the chair and lowers her on the bed, placing her head atop the pillows. Silver closes her eyes and rubs her thighs against each other with a soft groan.

Kass undresses slowly, a desperate part of him hoping he will think up a reason not to do this. That the rational part of him will convince him not to give in to his impulses and make everything worse.

Then Silver opens her eyes, and there is a touch of fear and insecurity in her gaze; fear that, like so many times over the last few years, he'll reject her.

And he realises he won't stop. He won't hurt her again, and he'll never again make her feel unwanted.

He moves down until he is hovering just above her. Silver moves up to kiss him and drags on his lower lip until she draws a tinge of blood. Kass moves his hand between her legs, and she moans at the lightest touch.

"Silver," he mutters, the syllables like heavy wine on his lips. Then he whispers her name again.

"Please," she asks, and he loses the last bit of control he was holding onto.

He lowers himself into her, and the sensation is like a flood of darkness. Silver spreads her legs further, and he moves far too fast and far too deep.

But neither of them cares to slow down, their bodies responding almost of their own accord.

Every moment feels like a betrayal, and he never wants it to stop.

He leans down to kiss her again and again, caressing her lips between every breath and after every stroke. Lust, desire, and love become one, and he falls.

As Silver had predicted, the structure continues underground. Their hosts' voices lead them down a winding corridor past more white-glowing walls. How Z'katt and Karenin don't get lost here is beyond Kass. Maybe they exist everywhere at once, forcing their consciousness into a physical shape whenever it suits them.

Like his squires, Kass is wearing armour. Silver helped him put it on. Completed in tense silence, that routine felt almost as intimate as their lovemaking. She has not helped him dress since the war ended.

Finally, the light dims as if to indicate that they have reached a lower level. After another few steps, a door appears that opens into an underground showroom. Once they are inside, Karenin mutters a brief incantation that sounds both familiar and unfamiliar to the arcane speech of human mages. Windows open inside the walls like the slow-lidded blink of a giant spider.

Behind the window sit a dozen copies of the demon they killed in Pride's rooms.

"Holy shit," Allen mutters, and Andrea frowns.

"How interesting," Amaya says and bends down to examine the demons from all angles. "Is this a monomorphic species, or do you only have specimens of one sex?"

Z'katt makes what Kass interprets to be an appreciative sound.

"Monomorphic. They lay eggs which any specimen can inseminate."

Amaya nods. "And which trait is responsible for their regeneration abilities?"

Their hosts hesitate for a few moments before they respond. Kass imagines their limbs growing with the tension in the room.

"Say that again, please?" Karenin asks. "Who promised regeneration?"

Z'katt makes a sound that might be a scoff and mutters something unkind about their colleagues in sales.

Kass blinks.

"So, the demons don't regenerate?" he asks.

Z'katt repeats the same scoffing noise as before.

"They are extremely hard-wearing and adaptable. Plus, they undergo a months-long training regime depending on your specific requirements. But they bleed and die like anything else."

Karenin assures them that this rarely happens and adds something that sounds suspiciously like 'Customer satisfaction guarantee'.

Silver blinks slowly and turns back to the rest of the group.

"So, the demon in Old Noll was enhanced by magic," she mouths.

Kass clears his throat.

"We encountered one of your demons before," he explains. "But that one was able to regenerate."

Z'katt moves closer. Kass can feel their body vibrating just inches from his armour, and he tries not to breathe in too deeply.

"Would you mind describing these features in detail?" Z'katt asks, and Kass shivers at the sound of their voice. "I'm always trying to improve my specimen."

"I can do you one better," Kass responds slowly. "We have some of the demon's flesh with us. It is still trying to grow back together. Or it would be if my wife's spell wasn't keeping it apart."

He looks in the direction where he imagines Z'katt's head might be. It's the strangest feeling speaking into nothing while knowing he is surrounded by a dozen outstretched arms and legs.

After the war, there were a few months when he suffered from hallucinations. This is making him remember all his worst moments.

"I'll give some to study if you tell us who hired the demon in the first place," he promises his host before he can lose his nerve.

Z'katt breathes in, perhaps in half a mind to accept, but Karenin interrupts the deal.

"I'm sorry, that will not be possible," they say sharply. "Anonymity is a guarantee we provide for obvious reasons, at least for recent contracts. I'm sure you understand."

Kass raises his eyebrows and pats the pouch full of demon flesh that hangs on Silver's wheelchair. But it's no use.

"I'm sorry," Karenin repeats, and when the tension in the room becomes sharp enough to taste, and his squires' eyes dart from corner to corner, Kass quickly relinquishes.

They spend the remainder of the evening pretending to be interested in Z'katt's introduction of the demons and the minute differences between their build, speed, and secretion abilities. Kass promises that they'll decide on their purchase after sleeping on it.

Karenin serves them a dinner of mystery meat, a potato-adjacent plant, and something green on the side. Amaya politely declines, but the rest brave the strange cuisine, which somehow tastes like underseasoned chicken.

They eat in a small, warmly lit dining room that Karenin assures them is right next to their sleeping quarters. Apart from a long table and chairs, there are no decorations or other items of furniture. The lack of windows is becoming less disconcerting the more time they spend inside the alien structure. Kass can see himself losing years here, stumbling from room to room without any remaining conception of time. All the while feeling invisible strangers hovering just out of reach.

Karenin and Z'katt claim to retire for the night but assure them that in case of an emergency, they'll probably wake up. It is strangely reassuring to know that they sleep.

Still, for minutes after they said goodnight, the group eats in silence, unsure whether their mysterious hosts have actually left. Perhaps they remain inside the room, breathless and unblinking.

Amaya pulls loose strings from the floral tablecloth on the dining room table. Finally, she frowns.

"So, if those demons don't possess natural regeneration features, and they weren't added by our hosts, who would have given them these powers?"

She turns to Silver.

"Could it be a spell?"

Silver shrugs before she shoves a piece of meat into her mouth. She has never been a picky eater, despite her noble upbringing. One of the many reasons Elijah adores her is that she loves his cooking.

"It must be, but I wouldn't know how to even begin constructing a spell like that," his wife replies. "One that doesn't fade over time, heals all wounds, gathers up loose body parts, and works at a seemingly impossible range."

She makes a face.

"Our hosts are clearly part of a civilisation of mages whose powers are more advanced than ours. If they don't even know how to do it -"

"There could be stronger mages out there yet," Kass notes. "The Multiverse is a bloody big place."

Silver nods.

"True. I'm just saying that I can't even imagine getting to that level of power. All of this –" She gestures at the structure that surrounds them. "This place is amazing, but I understand how its topography works. Kind of. A regeneration spell of that potency, however ... no clue."

"It's a miracle," Andrea mutters softly.

"What did you say?" Amaya asks.

Andrea looks up. It's the first time they've done so since dinner started. "Oh, sorry. I just meant that –"

Amaya cuts them off and turns to Kass.

"Is that something gods could do?" she asks. "Cast a regeneration miracle of such potency?"

Kass shrugs. "Probably. I mean, the gods bring back the dead, so anything's possible."

Andrea flinches at the comparison, and Kass feels a flash of guilt for his insensitive words.

"Not ... anything, exactly," Silver says slowly. "The dead must be recently deceased to be revived. Amaya's question makes sense."

"But it's not like a cleric would have set those demons on the king, Octavia, and Pride. Right?" Allen asks with a laugh.

"Not a human cleric anyway," Kass mumbles.

"Are there others?" Amaya asks, cutting to the heart of the issue. Kass hesitates and glances at Silver. His wife's gaze is hard to read. He feels fear tensing up his chest.

At this rate, he can no longer hide Octavia's suspicions. At this rate, he is fine to no longer protect Five's secrets. But he doesn't want his squires to realise how deep his doubts have already grown. How distrustful he has become of his god.

Silver turns to the rest of the group.

"Pride told me that during her travels, she found out that our gods have worshippers on other planes," she lies. "So it could have been a cleric from another realm who set the demons on us. Our culprit isn't necessarily a mage."

Kass feels a slight twinge of relief. Silver squeezes his hand under the table.

"But then how would they have opened a rift? Clerics can't do that," Andrea protests.

"That we know of," Amaya retorts. "Let's keep an open mind."

"I just ..."

Andrea turns the food around on their plate.

"Clerics heal people," they say quietly. "And paladins protect the innocent. We aren't the kinds of people who hire demon assassins or attack other realms."

"I mean, we don't really know anything yet," Allen tries to reassure them. "All of this is speculation."

Amaya looks like she wants to protest, but Kass shoots her a stern glance, and she falls silent. He turns to his wife.

"I'm guessing that our demon friend was born and bred in this facility. The trail we've been following started here, right?" His wife nods, and Kass continues. "So, whoever purchased him exited this plane through another rift and took their bloody demon with them. There any way you could track that rift down?"

Silver clears her throat.

"Yes. In fact, I had the same idea and was going to have a look for such a rift earlier. And then I ... fell asleep." She catches her breath. "Once everyone is ready, I can cast another scrying spell. See where else the trail leads us."

Kass slaps his knees and rises.

"No time like the present."

Chapter 25

Silver feels the trail all around her. It's like the walls are screaming at her. The demon crawled and bled over every fold of the alien structure. She feels its pain and hatred, and it makes her want to burn the place down. She wants to kill Z'katt and Karenin for the pain they cause to living, feeling creatures.

But, of course, in the eyes of people like Andrea, she's a monster, too. Perhaps she shouldn't be so quick to judge.

The strongest trace of the trail, which Silver hopes represents the most recent path the demon took, leads back downstairs.

Initially, she feels a pull towards the perverse showing hall where the demons are kept behind dull glass panes. But instead of proceeding back into the hall, they follow the corridor as it snakes deeper into the earth.

The air grows colder with each step, and the light from the walls fades into nothing. Silver summons a few mage lights that float beside them. She can tell that Kass is remembering the dark plane from a few days ago. He is probably wondering if there are more monsters in the dark. She increases the potency of the light, and his breathing stabilises a little.

"What do we do if our hosts find us down here?" Allen whispers.
"Maybe they're already here."

"We tell them we wanted to take another look at the demons and got lost?" Kass suggests.

Silver raises her eyebrows.

"I'd buy that for approximately two seconds, husband."

"We could kill them," Amaya says.

The rest of the group silently turns around to her. The investigator shrugs.

"Their operation poses a risk to our national security. I'm pretty sure I could get retroactive clearance for any force we enact here."

She hesitates.

"You know. If we want to."

"I'll ... keep that in mind," Silver says and hears Andrea suck in a sharp breath of air.

She sighs internally. As useful as it is to have two additional meat shields between her and the demons, Kass shouldn't have brought his squires on this mission. Get them accustomed to bloodshed and bad choices, then drag them on a trans-planar crusade. Not the other way around.

Pride would have been a far more useful ally, but for some gods-forsaken reason, the mage general insisted on staying behind. Silver knows her friend is holding something back. She hopes Pride has a bloody good reason for letting her trudge through the dimensions alone.

"Hmm. Stop," she says.

Kass has been pushing her wheelchair, and she can feel his broad hands brush against her neck; whether accidentally or on purpose, she's not sure.

The walls show no signs of a door, but Silver is wise to this trick by now. She raises her hands and uses a spell to trace the outline of an entrance before them. A door materialises, and Kass carefully pushes it open.

They are greeted by a small room, dark and empty. Empty except for a blindingly bright gap in the dimensions, covered by a layer of air and lightning.

It is a rift. And it is covered by the same protection spell as the one in Karthe manor.

The group sit around the rift, bored and full of defeat. Silver has cast spell after spell against the rift's protection spell, but apart from occasionally provoking it to shoot lightning at them, she has had no more success than she did in Old Noll. She feels numb, her head heavy with circling thoughts.

"Well, I suppose we knew this was a possibility," Amaya finally says. "It was pure speculation to assume that our culprit wouldn't cover their tracks at every step."

She shrugs.

"Shall we head back then?"

Allen stares at her. "After everything we went through to get here?" he asks incredulously.

"Sometimes missions fail, Allen," Kass says quietly.

Her husband doesn't seem as disappointed as she expected him to be. She feels his gaze resting on her more often, and there is a softness to his expression she had almost forgotten.

"But Sir -" Allen protests, but Silver doesn't listen. She grabs another handful of bones and summons yet another gust of wind. She slams it into the rift's centre while surrounding their party with a barrier spell.

Nothing happens. Of course not.

The spell shifts to absorb her arcane force, revealing nothing but a small, tantalising glimpse of the realm behind the rift. Silver is sure it is the same place she saw in House Karthe's wine cellar. The two dark towers held together by a bridge that sways in a soft breeze.

For a moment, an eerie sound emerges from the portal, then disappears again.

Kass frowns but doesn't say anything.

"Could you create another rift?" Amaya asks. Silver stares at her.

"What do you mean?" she asks.

Amaya shrugs. "Well, you know how to do it now," the investigator explains. "Couldn't you simply open a rift to the mage's home?"

She nods toward the showroom. "Plenty of fuel to be had around here."

Silver blinks. "I -"

She feels out for the demon's trail as the room explodes into arguments.

Andrea protests wildly, and Kass tries to calm them down. Allen, love-stricken like a puppy, tries to offend no one and say nothing of substance. Amaya is confused about why her suggestion produced such a reaction when it was clearly a sensible consideration.

Silver sighs. No joy. The demon's trail and the mage, are hidden behind the protective spell. It feels as if it was cut off by the hand of a god. She can't open a rift to follow it because the rift would have no anchor, nothing for the spell to connect to. She might as well look for a sole lantern in the depths of the night sky.

She explains this to the rest of the group, which seems to quell the fighting.

"Well, even if we wanted to go home now," Allen says. "We are stuck here, aren't we? Unless we go back through that desert plane."

"With enough fuel, I could open a rift back to Old Noll," Silver says. "If I anchor it to someone at home. To Pride or –"

"We should go back through the desert," Andrea says, their features pale. "We've caused enough damage to the Multiverse already."

"Not yet," Kass interjects. He strokes his chin. "Remember our hosts mentioning a human visitor? That person fell through a rift. If we can find that, we might be able to go back to our realm from there."

He glances at the rift again, and Silver is almost sure he's working out something. She is tempted to push the issue but knows that would do nothing. Kass won't share his thoughts until he's ready.

"Is that before or after they realise we're not here to buy anything? And either kill us or put us in those little glass cages of theirs?" Allen asks nervously.

"We can take them," Silver says. "I reckon they're both spellcasters. I block their magic, and Kass swings his big sword until he's cut off both their heads. Easy."

Allen and Andrea both stare at her, but Amaya nods.

"Very well. That sounds like the most sensible path forward. Kass?"

Kass startles out of thought. "Huh?"

"C'mon," Silver says and waves the rest of the group to follow. "Let's rest up while we can. We might need our strength tomorrow."

She and Kass sleep in separate rooms, which feels strange considering the desperate urgency with which they held each other just hours before. But Silver doesn't feel like forcing a conversation, and her husband is distracted enough that it probably doesn't even occur to him to invite her to his room again.

She sleeps well and wakes to a freshly drawn bath. Z'katt and Karenin join them for breakfast, partaking in the same yellow goo they serve their customers.

Karenin keeps asking if they have narrowed their considerations to a favourite demon, but Kass derails the conversation when he asks about the human from their realm.

"I don't remember much about them," Z'katt confesses impatiently. "And this was almost six years ago."

Six years ago. That was during the war. They still had a queen, and Silver still had her voice, her hand, and her legs. She and Kass had just kissed for the first time. Pride had selected her as one of her favourites. Her parents were still alive.

They were angry that Silver had fallen in love with a commoner, but they were alive. Life felt terrible, but it would never be that good again.

"You mentioned that the human wanted a demon with scales?" Amaya asks. "Do you remember why?"

"Hmm," Z'kett says. "I think they wanted the demon to look like a member of another species. They showed me sketches they made. Apparently, an enemy force was invading the human world, and the demon was supposed to look like one of those enemies."

They hesitate for a moment, and Silver hears a disconcerting shuffling noise to her left.

The other voice – Karenin – mutters something, presumably admonishing Z'kett for revealing too much about past clients.

Silver feels her eyes grow wider once the implications of their hosts' words begin to sink in. Someone had hired a demon to look like one of their enemies. Someone had used the chaos of the invasion to make an assassination look like a casualty of war.

"Clever," Amaya mutters.

Silver digs her fingers into the arms of her wheelchair. Whoever hired the demon must have done it to kill a high-profile target. Someone whose death would have been suspicious if they had been killed by human assailants –

"Six years, six years ..." Kass mutters, then he grows pale. "Six years ago, we had those bloody peace talks."

"What?" Silver narrows her eyes. She doesn't remember that. Just endless nights on the city walls, launching spell after spell into an immovable mass of foes.

Kass stares at her.

"Well, they never really got started," he clarifies. "But do you remember the queen going into the enemy encampment to parlay for peace? The only time she showed even a hint of spine?"

"Donna?" Silver asks pointlessly. She feels her fingers cramp on her legs. She and Donheira had been the same age. As children, they sometimes played in the castle gardens, getting lost in the green labyrinths when they played hide and seek.

Later, she hadn't seen much of her anymore, but Silver still grieved the queen's death and the memories of her childhood friend. She had never seen Donna's body as it had been put up on spikes around the city walls.

"No," she says, the thought too horrific to conceive.

"Think about it, Silver," her husband continues. "Who benefitted from the queen's death? Who could have advised her to go to the enemy encampment and initiate peace talks? Her council members and –"

"Are you saying it was Ithya?" Amaya asks sharply. "Her own brother?"

The two squires gasp.

"Ithya!" Z'katt exclaims. "Of course! That was the human's name!"

Karenin coughs indignantly. Z'katt mutters something in their language.

The group mutely stares at each other until their hosts leave them to finish the rest of their breakfast in peace. Silver feels a strange sense of pressure expanding in her stomach. Her breathing goes flat, and her head feels light.

"I can't believe that," Andrea says slowly. "It doesn't make any sense."

"Everyone says he's a good king," Allen agrees. "He faced the enemy even against impossible odds. Even though he never wanted to rule."

He shakes his head.

"Are you saying that was all made up? That he killed his sister for the throne and then pretended he didn't want it?"

"It makes sense," Amaya says slowly. "By fabricating such a seemingly dire situation for himself, none of us suspected him of having any hand in queen Donheira's death. Plus, her death happened during the war. Who could have suspected a third party of interfering with the peace talks when the much more obvious conclusion was that the enemy killed her?"

Silver blinks.

"Does this mean we could have had peace?" she asks, her voice so hollow it might break. "If Ithya hadn't interfered, could Donna and the enemy have agreed to a treaty?"

The words feel like ash in her mouth. She tries to touch the little finger on her skeleton hand and feels nothing. "Does that mean the war could have ended six years earlier?"

She feels her chest convulsing. There is nothing except fury keeping it all together.

"Does that mean that *none of this* had to happen?"

She doesn't realise she's crying until Kass embraces her from behind, his arms tightly pressed against her chest. She feels like she's suffocating.

"No," she screams. She wants to run into the past and gut Ithya. She wants to drag up his organs and eat them, then spit them out and burn them until there's nothing left.

She wants to escape to a realm where the last six years did not happen.

She wants to run.

"Silver," Kass says, his voice calm and low. "I know. It's okay."

Her legs twitch under the table, and she grips the sides of her chair until the bone-white of her knuckles peaks out from her flesh.

"I'll kill him," she whispers nonsensically. "I'll kill the bastard."

"I know," her husband says soothingly. "Love, I know."

She feels him push her chair out of the room and through the corridors. She imagines their hosts standing in every corner, watching her with wide, unfeeling eyes. Finally, they reach the spot where they first entered the building.

"Silver, can you make us a door?" Kass asks, his tone ever-so-careful. As if the mere sound of his voice might break her.

Silver does as he asks, as if on impulse. She blinks, and they are outside in the cold, wet air. Kass pushes her a little way into the meadow, and the moisture caresses her skin like a gentle swell of rain.

She screams and cries until she feels empty inside, the winds howling through the jungle like the chorus of the dead. Kass sits by her side, his head pressed against her legs, and his eyes closed as he holds her tight.

Later, she wants to apologise, but Kass won't hear of it. He says he knows what it's like to be beset by invisible enemies. The only reason he was holding it together was because she needed him. Otherwise, things may well have happened in reverse.

Silver squeezes his hand and feels shivers crawl up her arm as they touch.

"I will kill him," she promises again. Kass shrugs.

"But then, who rules the realm?"

"Someone who didn't commit mass murder?"

"That's an increasingly small list, Silver," he says with an attempt at light-heartedness. She can tell he isn't ready to have this discussion yet. She isn't either, not when they both know that with Ithya gone, the realm may well descend into civil war. But for now, she just wants to repeat her threats until the anger stops eating her up.

Kass pushes her around the structure on an aimless walk.

"Do you think whoever hired our three demons knew about the queen's death?" Kass asks. "Is this an attempt to punish Ithya?"

"It would have a poetic ring to it," Silver replies. "Hire a demon, then get killed by one."

Kass barks out a laugh. She turns around to him, her expression serious.

"But why also kill Octavia and Pride? Surely those two weren't involved?"

"Not Octavia, to be sure," Kass says. "But Pride? Who knows with that woman?"

"That woman? You mean one of my closest friends?"

"She lied to you before," Kass replies, his voice soft.

"Kept things from me. That's different."

"Is it?"

"If it isn't, you've lied to me more times than I can count, husband," Silver snaps half-heartedly.

He sighs. "So I have. Do you forgive me?"

"Hmm," she says and smiles. "After yesterday, I'm almost inclined to say yes."

Kass coughs out a laugh.

"Glad to hear I haven't lost my touch," he mutters. When she turns around, she can see that he is blushing.

She considers torturing him a little longer, but he changes the topic before she has the chance to.

"Down at the rift," he begins slowly. "Did you hear any voices? From the other side?"

Silver tries to think back to it. "There was a noise, I think."

"Did it sound familiar to you at all?"

Silver shakes her head. She had been too focused on trying to break through the barrier.

Kass hesitates, and she turns around to him. "Come on, husband. Out with it."

"I - you're going to think I'm losing it."

"More than usual?" she says with a quick smile.

"Funny, Silver."

"You always thought so."

"Hmm," he says. "Pretty sure I just thought you were attractive and loaded with a fantastic dowry."

"Oh dear. My whole life is a lie," she says drily, and Kass laughs again. After a few moments, sadness returns to the creases under his eyes and the lines around his mouth.

"It was Melina's voice," he whispers. His voice is so quiet that she almost can't hear him.

"Melina," she repeats, caressing the word she so rarely speaks.

Her friend from Octavia's unit. There had been three mages at first. The old man they had to help on the walls, whose name she forgot. Silver, the noble turned necromancer. And Melina, the diviner.

She and Melina had been the closest among their group of wartime friends. She had seen Melina's unhappy attachment to Derek and had foolishly encouraged it. After Derek died, Melina lost control of herself and died from a misfired spell.

It had seemed impossible for Melina, diligent and dutiful as she was, to die. But she did. She, Holly and Derek all died. A realm full of ghosts she can't help but summon into the present again and again.

Kass never says Melina's name in Silver's presence unless she does so first. There is no way he's making this up.

"Show me," Silver says.

Chapter 26

Kass hopes nothing terrible will happen when he and Silver return to the rift. He is counting on his squires and Amaya to keep their hosts occupied and tries to ignore the little noises he imagines in the empty corners of the white-glowing corridors.

The rift stares at them, bright and raw like a cut right through the centre of the Multiverse.

"I made something like that," his wife mutters, and he isn't sure if she sounds amazed or regretful. He squeezes her shoulder.

"Right," she says, raising her hands. "So, you said you heard Melina's voice when I made the protective layer move?"

"I did," he says, then shakes his head. "I don't know. I'm probably going mad."

"I believe you, Kass. If you say you heard her, you heard her," she reassures him. "There are many strange phenomena connected to the rifts that we don't yet understand. But I'd never assume you're just making this up."

"Thank you," he mutters, feeling his neck heat up.

Had he ever received such unfaltering support from Five? He can hardly remember now. Being a paladin made him feel important and powerful, but –

A word from Silver tears down a wall of fear.

His wife casts a protection spell, then scatters a fistful of bones before the rift. She is slowly but surely running out of spell components, Kass realises. Somehow, he is no longer revolted by the sight. Really, what's so terrible about it anyway? It's not like the souls of the dead take their knucklebones on their journey to the gods' eternal realms.

Silver casts the same wind spell she used yesterday, and the rift's protective layer shifts and realigns under the pressure. Kass steps as close to the rift as he dares, and before he can think better of it, he shouts.

"Melina!"

The word carries all the fragile hope he preserved in his heart. He suddenly remembers why he always clung so tightly to his faith. Because it let him believe that everyone he lost could be found again in the afterlife.

"Kass!"

He flinches.

That voice came from behind the rift.

"Melina!" Silver cries, moving towards the rift as fast as she can. Her hands glow brightly and shake under the sustained effort of the wind spell.

"Silver?"

The voice is fading now. Kass can feel tears streaming down his face. He remembers Melina and Silver huddled together next to campfires at night. He remembers asking the diviner, in jest, if she could foresee whether Silver would accept his proposal. Melina had slapped him on the back a little harder than necessary and said there was no way Silver wouldn't.

He remembers burying her body so that Silver didn't have to. Feeling her limp, soft arms in his own and smelling the burns that had raided her skin.

He still sees her in his dreams sometimes, always in death and never in life. He roars her name again.

"Give me time," the voice answers, almost as quiet as a whisper. "Wait, and I will ... open."

Then the voice disappears. Kass can see Silver's face, pale from exhaustion, yet his wife refuses to stop casting the wind spell. Her magic moves the protective layer from side to side, desperately searching for an opening.

He softly touches her back. "You heard her, Silver. Preserve your strength."

It takes her a few moments to react, but finally, she stops.

"I ... was that real?" she asks, her voice as frail as a child's.

"I think it was," Kass responds, stunned. "It might be ..."

He wonders if the rift they are trying to cross might lead to one of the planes where souls find their afterlives. But that would mean ...

He shakes his head.

"You heard her. Stay here and watch for any movements on the other side. I'll get Amaya and my squires, and we'll meet you here. If Melina thinks she can open the rift from her side, we need to be ready."

It turns out that leaving Allen near salespeople is a bad idea. He has signed his name under several binding legal documents by the time Kass manages to track him down. Andrea is gently trying to guide him away from financial ruin, but they are a bit too literal in adhering to Five's tenet of allowing his subjects 'free will'.

The demons claim to retreat to process Allen's pretend orders, and Kass leads the rest of his party back down to the rift room.

"What were you thinking?" he snaps at Allen on the way down the dark corridors.

"I figured contracts wouldn't be binding across different planes," the squire defends himself. "And they were asking where you were. I had to distract them somehow."

Kass considers reminding his squire that demon ownership may conflict with his aim of becoming a paladin, but then he notes a hint of fear in the young man's expression. He feels it, too. Even though Zikett and Karenin announced they were leaving, they could just as well be following them.

He can never know. He can never be sure. The walls are teeming with invisible eyes.

"Just don't ask me to loan you money when they track you down for repayments," Kass replies with a sigh, and his poor attempt at levity makes his squire chuckle.

Silver is tense when they find her in the rift room, her eyes still fixed on the rift. She has pushed her chair so close to the boundary that Kass can see the electricity caressing her skin.

"Anything?" he asks.

His wife shakes her head.

Amaya leans against the wall. Kass has filled them in on the way down, but the investigator is sceptical. Like Silver, she does not believe souls travel anywhere after dying. She probably thinks Kass is losing it, unable to deal with the reveal of Ithya's betrayal.

Maybe he is, Kass wonders. If he is going insane, would he be able to tell? After the war, when anxiety started to destroy his sleep and fill his days with paranoia, he found comfort in the belief that Five would protect what remained of his mind.

But now? He has never been further from home, and his god has abandoned him.

Suddenly, the protective layer atop the rift shifts enough to free up a sound that travels across the planes. It is Melina's voice. It calls Silver's name through a hole forming atop the rift's surface.

"Melina," his wife cries and scatters her remaining bones on the ground. Raw, unfettered power shoots from her fingers and hits the rift.

Kass feels his body move, but he stops himself. The gap in the protection spell is not large enough for them to cross over safely. If their experiences at Karthe manor are anything to go by, any touch of the protective barrier will result in death.

Melina shouts something Kass doesn't catch. Perhaps it's an arcane incantation. Perhaps it's a warning. Either way, Silver nods imperceptibly and moves her skeletal hand closer to the rift.

"Silver ..."

Kass isn't shouting this time.

She doesn't look at him. Her hand glows in the same eerie light that surrounded it when she opened the rift in the desert. But he doesn't feel any corruption this time, smells no death nor decay. He stares at her in awe as her ring finger crumbles into dust.

It's fine. He can just buy her jewellery for a different finger.

The protective layer grows translucent and moves to the edges of the rift. Behind it, Kass sees a world drenched in golden sunlight, illuminating the dark outlines of two towers. Just behind the rift –

Stands Melina.

His heart crumbles at the sight of her.

The diviner's eyes are narrowed just as they always were when she tried to cast a particularly strong spell. She has that little line above her left eyebrow that appears whenever she frowns. Her casting stance is still too narrow. She won't be able to dodge –

She is wearing the robes he buried her in.

He calls her name, and her gaze flickers over to him. Her eyes fall, softening at the edges, and she intensifies her casting.

"Come on," Silver mutters between incantations. "Piece. Of. Shit!"

Melina closes her eyes and steps closer to the rift. Kass can feel the mages' power sizzle against its outline.

Amaya screams. Kass shoots around and sees her slowly lifted off the ground. She is convulsing uncontrollably, her face a white mask of panic. Andrea draws their sword and stabs the air next to Amaya, but their attacks fail to connect. Allen's eyes rush across the room, looking for the slightest flicker.

Kass draws his Zweihander and runs towards Amaya. He will rip her out of the enemy's claws if he has to.

"Traitors."

The voice echoes over and over in the small room. It is impossible to tell where it comes from, and instead of growing quieter, it rings louder and louder in Kass's ears. Silver tries to ignore the commotion and keep the rift open, but Kass knows she can't do that for long.

Amaya has screamed herself hoarse by the time Kass reaches her. He runs his sword through the areas Andrea can't get to with their sword, but neither of them feels any resistance to their strikes.

"They're mages," Allen screams. "They don't need to touch us to attack! They just need to -"

An invisible force picks him up before he can finish his sentence. He screams in terror, and his eyes turn inside his skull. But Kass understood what his squire was trying to say.

Of course. Their hosts don't need to touch them to cast spells. But maybe they need to be able to see them. And where would a mage stand to keep themselves as well-protected as possible?

He races towards the door, then rams his Zweihander into the corridor outside. His blade connects with something soft and yielding, and he hears the softest exhale of air. The stench of wet decay consumes him, and for a moment, he feels his consciousness slip.

A primal scream fills the air beside him. Then Andrea is by his side and thrusts their sword into the nothingness ahead. None of their hits connect, but back in the room, Kass can hear Amaya and Allen's bodies hitting the ground.

"Hurry," Silver groans.

His wife has moved her chair closer to the rift. Kass can see her raise her hands, and he isn't sure if she is trying to test the rift's outline or planning something more dangerous yet.

Allen pulls Amaya with him, careful not to touch her more than necessary. The investigator is visibly shaken but largely unharmed.

"We need to leave this place," Andrea says, their eyes gliding up and down the corridor. There could be a hundred other hosts ready to kill them for their betrayal. Their long limbs could be stretching towards them at this very moment, their spells ready to force the air out of their lungs.

"Silver! Wait," Kass calls, and his wife hesitates.

Kass pushes past her and forces his shaking hand into the rift before he can think better of it. His body convulses as shocks of electricity race through him. But he remains on his feet. Agonising as this is, the magic isn't killing him.

"The barrier is gone!" Allen shouts. "Go, go!"

Kass feels Allen and Amaya rush through the rift, pulling him with them as they go. Behind him, he sees Andrea grabbing hold of Silver's chair, then he feels the planar winds gently brush away the heat radiating from his body.

He is pretty sure his insides are cooking, but for the moment, he feels calm.

Then they are on the other side, and he falls to the ground, face colliding with sweet-smelling long grass.

"Kass!"

It's still impossible that this is Melina's voice. She turns him on his back and places her soft hands on his chest. Immediately, the pain abates. His squires gasp.

"Like Pride," he hears Andrea mutter.

"Thank Five," Allen says.

"You could say that," Melina mutters, then blinks up at Silver.

"He's fine," she pre-empts the necromancer's question. "I managed to heal him."

"You ..." His wife starts, but words fail her. She takes a deep breath. "You've branched out," she finishes lamely. Melina laughs a desperate laugh.

"That's the thing about being dead. It gives you plenty of time to pick up new skills."

Kass wants to laugh in the face of all this pain, but all he manages is a pathetic sputter. The skies above are more golden than blue, and he feels blinded by the beauty that surrounds him.

Silver rolls to his side, her wheels struggling against the uneven terrain.

"You're a fucking idiot, Kassander," she says and runs her cool hand across his forehead. "Even in its weakened state, that barrier could have killed you."

"Can't let you hog all the glory," he says deliriously. He can feel his senses fading.

Silver turns around to Melina.

"I thought you healed him?"

"His body is going into shock," the diviner replies. "It isn't used to hosting that much magic."

"So, what –"

Kass doesn't hear the rest when sweet unconsciousness rips him into darkness.

Chapter 27

Kass wakes up with a start and shoots up, his heart racing.

"Relax."

Silver sits on the end of the bed, a steaming cup between her hands. Kass feels something inside him relax and forces his breathing to slow. He looks around.

He is inside a small wooden cottage filled with plants, flowing linen, and paintings of Old Noll. His squires and Melina sit on a small table in the middle of the cottage. He and Silver are on a bed in the corner of the room. Amaya is cooking something that smells suspiciously like sausages over a small fire.

An open window admits the still-golden sunlight and the fading song of birds.

For a moment, Kass wonders if he's dead.

"You're not dead," Melina says. She was always good at predicting what he was thinking. A diviner's privilege, he used to jest.

"I am, though," she adds, not without a twinge of humour.

"That seems like a pretty pointless distinction at this point," Silver says, and Kass gets the feeling that the two women have been arguing about this on their way to the cottage. "Given that we're all here."

Andrea and Allen stand up and approach their commander.

"Are you alright, Sir?" Allen asks carefully. Kass nods and gives the young man a grim smile.

"It'll take more than some fancy spells to take me out, boy."

Andrea nods seriously. "Good. Because we need your guidance, Sir. This place -"

They gesture at the air in the cottage, and he sees the confusion behind their eyes. He can feel it, too. The entire realm is alive. It feels like they are sitting atop a slowly breathing beast.

"This is Five's realm," Melina explains. She walks over to the kitchen and fills a blue-painted cup. She hands it to Kass, and the scent of camomile and lavender fills the air. She remembers that this always helped him relax.

Kass takes a deep breath. "Say that again?"

"Well, not quite," Melina corrects herself. She remains standing by his side as if she's worried that he might collapse again. "This whole plane *is* Five. Your god is the consciousness that inhabits this part of the Multiverse."

Silence fills the room, only interrupted by the sizzling of Amaya's sausages and the investigator's muttering of 'not quite done yet'.

Kass closes his eyes and tries to call on his god. He feels life crawling in every inch of the place, filling his chest with a strangely vivid tension. Many times in Old Noll, he felt Five's distaste settle inside his bones, like a shifting layer atop his body. Sometimes, he feels him inside Andrea, deep-set inside his squire's bones. Despite the strangeness of the sensation, it always made him happy to feel his god's presence.

This place should fill him with the ultimate sense of euphoria, no matter how things stand between them. Kass is still Five's paladin, and that still means something.

But he doesn't feel joy. He feels power pressing down on him from every angle.

He opens his eyes again and meets Silver's glance. His wife shrugs.

"Your squires seem to think she's telling the truth." She blinks. "Sorry, Melina. Not that I'm doubting you, it's just so -"

"I get it, Silver. I never worshipped him, so I can't say that I was expecting to end up here either," the diviner replies with a hollow laugh.

Kass looks over at his squires. At closer inspection, they look strange. They are filled with an inner glow, their smiles wider, their edges sharper. He doesn't ask them what they feel, afraid that he is already too far removed from their naïve, uncorrupted faith. Part of him wants to bury himself in the very soil of this realm to feel closer to his god.

He shakes his head and forces himself out of bed.

"Kass," Silver cautions, then interrupts herself when he is able to stand without effort. He shoots a questioning glance at Melina.

"I was able to draw on Five's powers to heal you. I was assuming you'd be too disoriented to do it yourself," the diviner explains.

"So, are you a cleric now?" he asks. "Or is this a spell?"

"Neither," the diviner replies. "All the souls Five calls here become part of him. All of us are cogs in an ever-running machine."

Kass remembers speaking to Five's avatar. Hadn't he recognised the sound of one of the voices amidst Five's chorus? It must have been Melina's voice. He should have trusted his instincts back then, impossible as it might have seemed.

"How long have you been here?" he asks carefully.

Melina shakes her head.

"I don't know. It feels like an eternity. There's not..." She gestures around herself aimlessly. "There isn't much out here. I made this house by drawing on Five's power, but however far as I've walked across this world, I've never seen any other settlements. I know the other souls are here, I can feel them, but ..."

She shrugs, but Kass can see a deep sadness in the downward turn of her eyes.

"Something is keeping us apart. Or perhaps it's me. Perhaps they avoid me because I wasn't one of the faithful."

Kass looks out of the window. Golden light glitters on the dew-heavy tips of high grass and meadows. In the distance, he can see orchards full of cherry blossoms. Rivers and lakes, whose ripples reflect the gold that melts from the sky.

Everything within him wants to immerse himself in the majesty. Sink to his knees and pray for forgiveness, pray for annihilation.

"I should –" he begins, then stops, unable to find the words.

"Go," Melina says gently. "Your squires had the same reaction. Go and be with your god."

Kass barely feels Silver's gaze on his back as he steps outside.

Kass was the one who buried all their friends. He looked for Derek's body amidst the piles of flesh and blood outside the city walls. He put his friend back together piece by piece and laid him into a bed of earth. Derek had told him that he might give living another try once the war was over. That existence was a torment, but one he was finally starting to get used to.

He buried Holly, too, hiding the wound on her neck with one of Silver's favourite scarfs. Her eyes refused to stay closed, so he felt like she was watching him the entire time. Maybe she was. Holly had believed in the afterlife, after all. Maybe her soul remained near the misshapen wooden coffin he made for her. Coffins were hard to come by at the end of the war, but he tried his best.

He buried Melina between them, her burned, brittle remains wrapped in a white cloth. He had wept over each of them, then locked their memory into the realm of his dreams. He hadn't slept well a single night since the war, and peace had felt like a distant fantasy he realised only for others.

Until now.

Kass steps into the wide-open air, and the wind's gentle touch feels every bit like memories of childhood. Warmth spreads through his body, and his head is empty except for thoughts of pleasure and rest. Long-fingered blades of grass caress his legs, and suddenly, he isn't wearing any armour to keep him locked away from the rest of the world.

The two black towers split apart the skies, giving him a destination to walk towards. So, he does.

He feels desperately at ease with himself and his surroundings. He closes and opens his eyes with each breath, moving from dream to reality to an iridescent liminal state in which everything is suddenly clear. He can breathe when he thinks about the future. Humanity won. They fought for their survival, and they survived.

He is alive, and so is his wife, and so is Pathas, and so is his uncle, and everyone who died is with the gods who beckoned them home.

Melina is alive. She is here, and her soul is aglow in the same gold that is draped across the endless horizons.

Kass looks at the lakes that sparkle in the distance, and his legs start to carry him towards them. The grass parts as he steps through it, and the wind enraptures his body more gently even than Silver's softest touches. His thoughts are clear and unafraid. This is what happens after death. This is the afterlife he fought for. This is the peace that was promised.

The sun sits between the two black towers, resting atop a bridge that sways softly in the breeze. Here, the world is still in its cradle, all possibilities born anew with each morning. Every mistake can still be amended.

He reaches the lake and steps into the water. The waves feel like the touch of another, parting and returning with each stroke of his desire. He is naked against the clear air, and when he closes his eyes, he remembers Silver's gaze, dark and intense, as she lay on his heaving chest, covered in warmth.

"Trust me," she said. "If you trust me, I will unravel all of this. You don't need the approval of a god when you have my love."

This entire world feels coated with love. Drenched in golden beauty, softness, and light. It feels fair. Kass fought and killed and bled for others for so long that this feels like the only recompense that could make up for his suffering.

Will he truly have to decide between the love of his god and Silver's? He can still feel her affection in every look, every touch they exchange as they dance around each other, bashful like children in the dark. But the emotions will never not be strained with memories. Memories that push away reality when his foolish heart thinks it can take another bite out of life.

This world has none of the darkness that sits between him and Silver. This world is warm, beautiful, and it permits no doubt. He wants to sink into the grass and grow into Five, just as his soul was destined to. Another appendage on an eternally travelling god whose touch will spread justice across the Multiverse.

There would be purpose in this path. But Silver would never follow him here. Silver will fight and die before she lets herself become part of something other than herself. Kass admires her for that, even amidst all the despair he feels when he imagines her soul, cold and alone amidst the emptiness of the Multiverse.

She will never know the embrace of a god. Somehow, that makes him want to hold her closer.

"They've been outside for a while now," Silver notes, taking a sip of sickly sweet coffee as she glances out of the window. Andrea and Allen left shortly after Kass, each carving their own path through the gold-drenched fields. Amaya had no interest in exploring the outer shell of a god just yet, so she laid down for a nap in Melina's bed. Silver and the diviner sit around the kitchen table, steaming mugs between hands close enough to touch.

Melina shrugs. "Time is funny here. You have to keep track of the days. Otherwise, they slip away from you."

Silver looks at her friend, at the faint lines on her forehead and the side of her mouth. Melina looks just the same, her dark skin, soft curves, and gentle eyes unchanged by the years. But her body is just as unreal as the cottage around them. Silver can feel the strains of magic in everything. As if Five is a spell come to life around an unstable core. When she looks closely, she can see Melina's edges fraying when the diviner loses concentration. Kass didn't notice it because he didn't want to. But Silver isn't afraid to see the truth.

"How long has it been?" Melina asks. Silver closes her eyes for a moment.

"Four years and twelve days."

"I take it we won?"

"Barely, but yes." Silver raises her eyebrows. "You can't see into our plane?"

During the war, Melina grew into one of the strongest diviners of Old Noll, perhaps of the entire human realm. She had to develop her skills quickly. Most of the other diviners had been eliminated early on, and there was always another enemy attack to look out for.

Melina shakes her head.

"I can't look through the barriers that cover the rifts. Those were put there by Five's avatar, and my magic is not strong enough to dispel them." She gestures at Silver's hand. "I would have never been able to break through without you. And your sacrifice."

"It's just bone, 'lina. It doesn't matter."

"One day, you'll have nothing left."

"One day, we all die," Silver responds impatiently. "What's the point in holding on to unimportant things?"

"I suppose Kass has always been the sentimentalist between the two of you."

"Kass." Silver lets the word run out on her tongue, and glances outside again. Part of her feels like she is watching her husband take another lover as she imagines him completely immersed in his god's body. She knows she shouldn't feel like that, but she has long stopped caring about what she should and shouldn't do.

"It's nice to see that you two are still married," Melina says. "Despite everything that happened, you made it work somehow."

"We're hardly a happy couple, 'lina," Silver replies. She has no illusions that a single night of passion has changed Kass's mind about her. Especially now that he is drenched in his god's warped sense of justice, reassured in all his restrictive dogmas.

Silver hates this place.

"Happiness is overrated," Melina says with a laugh. "But I can tell you still love him, even after everything that happened. I wish -"

She sighs, then follows Silver's gaze that lingers on the window.

"He'll come back. I always do, even when I wander this world and get lost for years." She touches Silver's hand. "All the magic that keeps the souls locked inside Five ... it messes with your head. Can you feel it?"

Silver nods. She felt the amalgamation of souls as soon as they stepped through the rift. Human and other, all aglow with a strange conviction and force. Five's faithful, all woven together, fuelling the gigantic monstrosity that assimilated them. Little more than firewood for the immortal powers of a being that calls himself their god. But perhaps this is what the souls wanted. Helping Five realise his dream of bringing justice to all the planes of the Multiverse.

"It's awful, isn't it?" Melina says, her voice little more than a whisper. "I wish I could leave. I've tried so many times. I've walked between the rifts, but they always remained close. Ultimately, all I could do was sit beside the one near my house and stare at its cloud barrier. Hoping for the impossible."

"Five is keeping you here? Why?"

Melina shakes her head. "To do his bidding. I should have refused to serve him. But I fell for his avatar's lies when he said I'd be free to leave this plane once I had done my part."

"What did he ask you to do? Why does he keep you in this place, 'lina?"

Silver feels her voice rise, her vocal cords straining with excitement. Melina scoffs.

"He asked me to cast a scrying spell. Stupid, right? One of the first spells we learned at the mage tower, and a god had to get my help to cast it."

"Why?" Silver asks, breathless.

"Because the gods are great at harnessing souls, but they are neither omnipotent nor omniscient. Their magic is powerful but hard to control. I always thought people made a bigger deal of the gods than they really should." Melina scoffs, then suddenly laughs. "I hope Holly never finds out about this. She'd be so pissed."

Silver joins in on the laughter even though she feels more like crying.

"She would be fuming," she says.

They laugh for a little longer, basking in the warm rays of an old friendship. The steam from their mugs coats the window with a white film.

"What was the scrying spell for?" Silver finally asks. Melina bites on her inner cheek. She hesitates. Whatever she is about to say is important, Silver realises. Horrifying. And that horror will confirm to her that it is true.

"The rifts across the Multiverse aren't a natural phenomenon, Silver," the diviner whispers. "Someone opened them."

"What?"

Silver feels the air squeezed out of her lungs. Suddenly, it is like a host of enemies suddenly appeared before her, ready to drag her back to their tents and finish what they started. Her hands begin to shake.

"The rifts were opened for a reason. Five's Avatar thinks it was done to kill the gods," Melina says quietly.

"Kill ..."

The word tastes sweet and forbidden on Silver's tongue. She imagines the feeling of conquering this entire realm with nothing except her magic and mastery over the fabric of existence.

"And was he right? Five's Avatar?" she asks.

"I don't know," Melina replies. "The first rift appeared here, at the very core of Five's body. So, his Avatar asked me to cast a scrying spell to track down the people who opened it. Then I was supposed to let three demons follow the trail."

Silver nods slowly.

"We found those demons. They were after –" She frowns. "Are you sure your spell worked properly?"

Melina shrugs.

"Not entirely. The rifts opened years ago, and I could only work with a trace of essence that remained on its exterior. That, and the rift is sealed from the other side. Whoever opened it doesn't want to be found."

Silver nods slowly. She doesn't want to think about what this means just yet.

Surely, not even Pride would do something so monstrous?

"Did the Avatar say anything else?" she forces herself to ask.

"Nothing. Just that I was helping to punish a horrendous crime. Of course, he'd say that." Melina sighs. "I know it sounds horrible, but I don't care what happens to the people the demons are tracking down. If they opened the rifts on purpose, they deserve everything that happens to them."

Silver wholeheartedly agrees. Melina smiles at her friend's bloodthirsty response. That has always been their dynamic, one they slide back into as easily as breathing.

"I thought that once I did Five's bidding, he'd let me go wherever my soul is destined to go," Melina continues. "I wanted to search the Multiverse until I found –"

She sighs. "But he never loved me, did he? Not like Kass loves you."

"I don't know, 'lina. I'm sorry."

"It's okay. Maybe the version of him I imagined was always superior to the original."

Silver nods slowly, unsure what to say. She loved Melina and Derek like her own flesh and blood, but Derek had never seen Melina's quiet, uncomplicated warmth. Not like Kass had seen Silver, had grown to read her like an open book.

"But Five won't free you?" she finally asks. Melina shakes her head.

"Perhaps it was foolish to assume he would. There will always be another task that needs a diviner. Another instance of make-belief justice that needs enforcing. I'm far too valuable a prisoner to release."

Melina's face shifts for only an instant, but Silver knows her well enough to recognise what the change in expression means. Time has done nothing to make her forget about those all-important markers of closeness.

"Tell me," she says, a small line between them that tells Melina that it's okay to say the horrible thing she is ashamed to think.

"I hate it, Silver," the diviner says after a few moments. "I was terrified of dying, but this is worse. There is nothing here and no end to the nothingness. I'm alone all the time."

Her voice is shaking.

"I can feel the other souls inside Five's body, but I don't want to join them. I don't want to lose myself within that chorus of supposed justice. But -"

"But joining them is starting to feel inevitable?" Silver asks. There is no point in looking away from the truth. No point living in gold-coated fantasies. Melina nods.

"I have to concentrate on staying me all the time. Sometimes, I feel like I'm gliding into the ground and disappearing somewhere under the earth." She shudders. "I know that if I give in, even for a second, I would lose my mind. And then I truly will be gone. But with each passing day, it's starting to feel like that would be worth it, just to no longer be alone."

Silver slowly reaches for her friend's hands and holds them between her own. Even now that her soul has only haphazardly manufactured a shell for itself, Melina's skin is warmer than Silver's bone and pale flesh.

"What can I do?" Silver asks, her voice a mere whisper.

Melina shakes her head.

"The only way to free me is to kill Five," she replies, making no more attempts to speak quietly. "And that is impossible."

"I don't care if it's impossible," Silver promises. "If that's what it takes, I will kill a god."

Chapter 28

When Kass returns, he doesn't know how much time has passed. The sun hasn't set, although the skies are drenched with dark red streaks. In the shifting clouds, Kass can see half-realised righteous knights and valiant steeds riding into battle.

Silver greets him outside the cottage door. She is sitting at the top of a small flight of stairs.

He can read the worry in her eyes.

"Nice walk?" she asks. "Your squires came inside a little while ago."

He smiles at her forced nonchalance. It is easy to smile in a place like this.

"Nice walk," he grunts. "You'd have loved the lakes."

"You didn't ask if I wanted to join."

"Did you?"

"Hardly."

They laugh, and Kass keeps moving until he stands awkwardly beside her. Part of him feels like he should bend down and kiss her to honour the feelings that linger between them. But the invisible wall between them likewise remains. Loving Silver was never easy, even during their happiest times. Any emotion between them was hard-fought amidst the raging war.

And when he looks at her, he remembers every battle he ever lost.

"This place –" Silver starts, then hesitates.

"How do you feel?"

Kass isn't sure how to respond. He doesn't want to hurt her feelings by telling her he is more at peace here than he ever was in Old Noll.

He doesn't want to give her false hope by telling her that none of this beauty compares with the grip she has on his heart. That none of this lightness comes close to the desperate passion he feels for her, the flurry of emotions that brings as much euphoria as it does despair.

So, he doesn't say anything. He stands by her side and places a hand on her shoulder.

"I don't like it," his wife finally says. "All this magic twisting the fabric of existence according to Five's desires. It's unnatural."

"Didn't think that would bother you, Silver," he gently admonishes her.

"I don't mind it when I control the unnaturalness. When someone else does it, I get suspicious."

Kass laughs, and Silver responds with a self-aware half-smile.

"I'm sure everyone has a million bloody opinions they want to share," he says. "I can't wait to hear them out with my usual calm levelheadedness."

"Oh, you'll love some of the things Melina has to say about Five," Silver mumbles.

"Is it bad?"

"Bad is an understatement."

Kass sighs and kneels by her side. He feels the grass tickle his legs and leans his head onto the armrests of Silver's chair.

"So, should we take a few more minutes until we go inside and fight?" he asks.

"That sounds delightful," Silver says and softly runs her fingers through his hair. "Just five more minutes."

"So, Pride opened the first rifts," Amaya says, drumming her hand on Melina's kitchen table. They sit in a circle of chairs, trying to pin down food that flickers in and out of existence. Melina says that the magic of the plane lets her change reality; turn air into meat and grass into vegetables. But the food seldom feels nourishing, and the drink has little effect on her mood.

"We don't know that for certain," Silver protests. "All we know is that the demons picked her, Ithya, and Octavia as their targets when they followed Melina's spell. For all we know, the spell failed, and the demons just went for the highest-profile targets."

"I doubt the demons possess that level of intelligence," Amaya responds with a frown. "What concept would they have of political power?"

"How would Pride have gained the power to do something as monstrous as opening the rifts?" Andrea asks. They sound absent-minded, still basking in an inner glow.

"Exactly. Pride is powerful, sure, but she's no -" Silver interrupts herself and glares at the glass of thin, red wine before her.

"But you yourself opened a rift, mistress Silver," Allen says quietly. "It seems like any mage with sufficient power might be able to."

Silver glares at him. "That's different. I knew it was possible, plus I used some immensely powerful spell components I got from –" She interrupts herself again. Kass remembers that Pride gave her the spell components.

Amaya continues to drum her fingers on the wooden table, creating a rhythm that tightens the atmosphere like a noose.

"Consider this, Silver," the investigator says. "Pride was aware of Octavia's theories about other planes of existence. It would make sense that the two collaborated on opening the rifts, then drew on the resources of an overlooked prince – Ithya – who harboured an interest in magic."

"But why?" Kass asks. "Why open the rifts? Why do any of this?"

His thoughts feel sluggish, even amidst the revelation of all this madness. The discussion feels as though it is led by a group of strangers.

"Did you say that there is a rift at the centre of this world?" Amaya asks Melina. The diviner nods.

"Yes. It lies below the Two Towers. I can feel hostile energies pooling out of it." She shrugs. "I don't think it'll be enough to kill Five, but it's limiting his powers."

"Maybe that's why he's not been giving us access to divine spells? Because Pride or whoever is weakening him?" Allen asks. He sounds relieved.

"So, Pride is trying to kill a god?" Andrea's eyes are wide. Silver glares at them.

"We still don't know that she is responsible."

"But who else would it be?" the squire responds, their voice unsure. "She is the most powerful mage in our realm. And she already thinks she's on the same level as a deity."

"What we need to ask ourselves is this. Why would Pride want to kill a god?" Amaya asks. "Why would Octavia? Or Ithya? What are their motivations? If they have sufficient cause, this theory becomes much more probable."

"Lots of people hate the gods, 'maya," Silver says quietly. "They spearheaded enough battles to burn the countryside to the ground. Pride isn't the only child who lost her home to the crusades. She just survived."

"What do you mean?" Andrea asks.

"Pride's home was destroyed in a crusade between Five and Eight," Silver explains. "The entire south side of the Polainian mountains was destroyed when the armies of the faithful clashed and set swathes of villages on fire."

Allen nods. "It was horrible. Some of the folk in my home village are refugees from back then."

"Why did that happen? Eight is the god of redemption. What was her justification for the crusade? What was Five's?" Andrea interjects. Amaya shakes her head.

"Who knows? It was a religious debate. You'd have to ask one of the clerics responsible for coordinating the faithful. The crown didn't involve itself, as far as I know. Then again, I didn't become an investigator until later."

"Did nobody care?" Allen asks.

"It was just one crusade among many," Kass mutters quietly. "And they were easy to forget after the war."

Silver nods gravely. "Indeed."

"That might explain why Pride hates Five. But what about Octavia? She was a paladin just like Kass," Andrea says, frowning.

"Well," Kass begins, feeling his squires' eyes burning on his skin. "Octavia was disillusioned with the gods before the war even began."

"Why?" Andrea asks. They sound breathless.

Kass doesn't want to respond and break their heart. He wants to stay still, close his eyes, and sink into the ground until he doesn't have to think anymore.

"Because the gods have never been on our side," Silver says. "They've always been fickle patrons, and I think Octavia has realised this for much longer than she let on. We all saw her publicly disavowing her king and her god."

"And that gives her a motive," Amaya says, rubbing her hands together.

"And Ithya?" Andrea protests. "Why would our king have any interest in opening the rifts? When he fought so hard to keep the enemy at bay?"

"Well, he probably killed his sister, remember?" Allen says with a half-glance at his fellow squire. "I don't think we're working with someone who's wholly honest about his motives. More likely an asshole with a god complex."

"But –" Andrea opens their mouth but then lets Allen finish.

"Ithya could have wanted to create an opportunity for him to take the throne," he says. "Nobody expected him to betray his sister in the middle of an extraplanar war." Allen's voice is firm, but he refuses to look anyone in the eye.

Silver shakes her head impatiently. "What is the point of this speculation? We won't know for certain until we leave this place and confront the three of them in person."

"About that," Kass says, then takes a deep sip of wine from Silver's glass. He frowns at the taste. None of the food or drink feels quite right. It's all hollow, like a shell empty of imagination.

His wife shoots him an amused look that says, 'I told you so'. Melina sighs.

"You want to leave," she says matter-of-factly. It sounds like she is pronouncing her own death sentence.

"How do we do that, 'lina?" Silver asks softly. The diviner shakes her head.

"I'm not sure. I can feel all three rifts on this plane, but the ones I visited are covered by that blasted protective barrier that was put there by Five's avatar."

"How about the rift below the Two Towers," Amaya clarifies. "The one where Pride's spells are attacking Five?"

Melina nods. "That rift lies at the centre of this world. It is like a blade piercing the heart."

She points outside. The skies are blood red, the colour dripping from the sun that sits between the towers like a self-satisfied spider. Kass notes that Andrea and Allen's expressions aren't nearly as disgusted as his or Silver's. Maybe they are seeing something else.

"Have you seen the rift for yourself, 'lina?" Silver asks softly. Melina shakes her head.

"The pull on my soul is too strong when I'm near the towers. The few times I approached, I nearly lost myself. It felt like I was like I was everywhere at once, and a whole chorus of voices assaulted me. I wandered the planes for an eternity until I felt like myself again." She smiles self-consciously. "A strange feeling for a diviner. The sense of disconnect from your own body is what we strive to achieve when we first train at the mage tower. But everything about it just felt –"

"Wrong," Kass says. Melina nods and shoots him a long look.

"Yes. It felt like I was being consumed by a stronger soul. Which, I suppose, I was."

"So, if we manage to reach that rift, it might lead us back to Old Noll," Amaya muses. Allen blinks.

"Why? Because Pride is probably the one who opened it?"

"Yes," the investigator replies. "And if Melina feels hostile energies emerging from the rift, it is likely that this rift isn't protected by the same barrier that has hampered our progress so far."

"A compelling point. Let's hope that these hostile energies don't pose equally as problematic as Five's barrier," Silver says drily. Amaya shrugs.

"It's worth a try, given that we have no other plans."

"Just as long as we don't lose our bloody souls in the process," Kass notes with a glance at Melina. Andrea shakes their head.

"This is Five's realm, and we are his servants. Why would he seek to harm us when all we seek is the truth?"

"I don't know. Why do the gods do anything?" Melina snaps at the squire. "Why keep me locked up here? Just in case I might prove useful again in a few centuries' time?"

"I – I don't know," Andrea says slowly, their expression softening.

"I don't know either!" Melina says, her voice rising. "I don't know why I'm here even though I never prayed to this stupid god! I don't know why barriers are blocking every path out of this hellhole! I don't know why I can't enter the Towers even though they are the only thing in this bloody place that is *real!*"

She is shaking with rage. The last time Kass saw her this mad was at Derek. The archer stayed on the battleground after he used up all his ammunition. He lingered at a broken city gate, unarmed and unsure whether to advance or retreat. They only found him because of Melina's scrying spells, a minute away from being surrounded by the enemy.

Andrea covers her hands with theirs. "I'm sorry this is happening to you," they say, and the platitude sounds nothing but sincere.

Melina shakes her head. "So am I," she replies, her voice cracking under the burden of resignation.

Kass can see Silver clenching her fists underneath the table.

"I'll fix this, 'lina," she mutters. "Mark my words."

"I trust you, Silver," the diviner replies, and for a moment, there is no doubt in her voice. Just the same quiet confidence that saw her through each day until she lost it in a second's despair.

They say their goodbyes quickly and quietly. Melina tries not to let the sadness reach her eyes, but Kass can see it in each movement of her head. He buries her in a tight embrace and tries to remember every one of her features that he tried to forget when he first laid her to rest.

"I miss you," he whispers.

"I miss you more," she replies and kisses his cheek. "I'll keep thinking about all of you for every day that remains."

"If you stay here, I'll find you again," Kass promises. "After I die."

The thoughtless words fall from his tongue instead of something more comforting. Melina gives him a sad smile.

"Don't," she says, then nods at Silver. "Look out for her. She isn't as strong as she thinks she is. We both know she'll keep getting herself into trouble."

"Don't I ever?" Kass says a moment too quickly, and they both laugh. He places a hand on Melina's shoulder.

"Look. If there's anything I can do –"

Melina hesitates for a moment, and he knows she's holding something back. But when her gaze returns to Silver, she shakes her head.

"I just want you to get out of here alive and well."

She turns towards the faded sun, each movement more strained than the last.

"Maybe you won't be able to pass through the rift at the Two Towers. Then you'll have to stay for tea, wine, and card games until the end of times."

"I can imagine a worse fate, 'lina," Kass says sincerely.

Melina smiles, and he turns away.

Chapter 29

The Two Towers are black and shapeless, rising from the ground like a pair of swords that pierce Five's body. Their outline is sharper than the soft grassland surrounding them, their colour more striking than the eternal sky's gold.

As they approach, the landscape bends and stretches, and Kass isn't sure if they are being led towards the towers or away from them. Silver struggles on the uneven terrain, but she refuses to let him carry her as long as she can manage on her own. As usual, they fall back into well-learned distance.

His squires are radiant, their skin translucent as their souls resonate with the world's core. They speak little and spare fewer glances for each other than usual. Their eyes are dull as they glide across the windswept planes. Even Amaya seems disconcerted at their changed mood and remains close to Silver.

Finally, the world relents and allows them to reach the bottom of the towers. There are no windows and only one door. Its outline is etched into the right tower's stone facade. No other signs of craftsmanship mar the perfect terror of the structure.

Kass feels a strange pull to enter, even though he wonders if doing so would be heretical.

"Can you feel it?" Andrea asks him quietly. His squire is standing right next to him, their eyes unusually light.

"Yes," Kass says quietly. He hates how sluggish their voice has become; all of Andrea's unbridled determination vanished. Perhaps he sounds the same to Silver, judging from the worry in her expression whenever she looks at him.

He wants to drag Andrea away from this place and shake them until they return to what they were. The naïve, passionate, impossibly brave squire who looks to him for all the answers about honour and justice. But maybe he's as much a fraud as Five, his unfaithful god. What right did he ever have to claim that his guidance is a replacement for that of the creature they are standing on?

He takes a deep breath, feeling the air heavy in his lungs.

He can feel the same pull towards the towers that Melina described. He wants to lie down, sink into the ground and listen to the call of a thousand voices ring in his head. It feels right. Can't it be enough that it feels right?

"I can feel a sort of lure," Silver admits, her voice raspy. She runs her fingers over the tower's outline. "Fascinating. It's pulling on our souls even while we are still alive. We are lucky they are anchored to our bodies; otherwise, we would have no defence against Five's assimilating force. How Melina can remain herself amidst this – this gravity, I have no idea."

"Is that what this is?" Allen asks, his voice thin and unsure. He isn't glowing as brightly as Andrea, the light flickering around his body.

"Well, Five's voice is commonly known to be a chorus, correct?" Amaya says. "Not unlike the other gods, now that I think about it. I suppose now we know why. He is speaking with the voices of his followers' souls."

"The souls of the faithful are assimilated into Five? We would become part of our god?" Andrea asks. Their voice has no emotion except for the faintest note of desire.

Kass shakes his head. "We don't have time for this. We need to find that damned rift, and then we need to have some bloody words with Pride."

"Agreed," Silver says, then pushes against the door. When she meets resistance, she looks up at Kass.

"Mind making yourself useful, you big hunk of metal?"

Kass raises his eyebrows, but he does as she asks. He isn't sure if he is surprised that the door opens without protest. Darkness looms. He takes a step inside and finds that none of the light finds shelter within the tower's confines.

Then, a gust of wind pushes them forward, and the door falls shut behind them. Silver screams, and Kass runs to find her in the all-consuming dark. But the terrain shifts, and he stumbles.

He falls for what feels like an eternity, air rushing from his lungs as he struggles to breathe. His senses fail him.

Kass glances over the rims of champagne-filled glasses with iron-clad judgement weighing down his gaze. They drank beer around the open gravesite at his father's funeral, then returned to the *Mage* and sat around a table. The evening passed largely in silence until sunrise coated the wooden benches in soft golden reds. There were some of his dad's old friends. And Elijah, of course. Kass's mom had sent flowers, but Kass threw them down the drain. No grandparents. Kass's father hadn't spoken with them in years.

It was an agonising affair, but there had been a sort of honesty in sitting with the awkward brutality the passing left behind.

Silver's parents were more superficially popular. There are hundreds of people in attendance at their funeral. Old Noll's remaining noble families and even their newly crowned king Ithya, who hides behind his advisory board and dodges as many people as humanly possible. Pride, of course, hasn't left Silver's side all night. She hovers beside her friend and tries to send away whichever supplicants are most greedy for a glimpse at the nearly orphaned daughter's grief. Octavia drops by briefly and leaves a bouquet of white lilies on the gravestones.

Silver's parents sleep next to one another in the Castle graveyard and face the rising sun. They wanted to be buried in the backyard of their family manor, but there is nothing left there except for a gaping hole in the ground, still filled with blood and dust.

Kass hasn't talked with his wife all night, except when they agreed on which carriage they'd take to the castle and when Kass made a derisive comment about the number of people attending the funeral. He feels hot and irritated, clad in the agonisingly restrictive suit he is expected to wear, and forced to make small talk with nobles who are still flabbergasted that Silver D'arran deigned to marry a commoner.

Silver did well throughout the ceremony. She read her mother's favourite poem, cried at the appropriate times, and said something about her father's martial prowess in his long-gone youth. She quickly identified Dominic van Herren's inability to hold the crowd's attention and proceeded to lead the ceremony herself. She smiled wistfully, then ruefully, nodded solemnly, and Kass knows that all of it is a fucking act.

He knows his wife. All she wants is to burn the damned castle to the ground until there is nothing left but cinders.

He watches himself stand in a small circle of people, surrounded by nobles whose names he doesn't remember, desperately trying not to say something offensive.

Silver hurries past him, exploiting a rare moment of inattention from the crowds who remain desperate for a moment's glimpse behind her facade.

In the past, Kass shot her a look but stayed inside the circle of nobles, unwilling to move out of his commitments, however much he despised honouring them.

Now, he finds himself floating within the scene, a spectre existing within and out of time. None of the other guests see him. He cannot touch any food or sample any drink. He could stay here and wait for the scene to play out, unseen and unheard.

He knows how it ends. The funeral concludes. He and Silver go home separately that night. They don't talk for a few days, then she cracks a joke over breakfast and makes him laugh.

They talk for a little, then things die down again.

Explosive fights suck the air out of every room until neither of them can breathe. A cycle that repeats for years.

A just punishment for the sin she committed. Or so he thought.

Kass leaves his past doppelganger behind and hurries after Silver, who disappears into an empty corridor in the eastern wing of the Castle. The wing is in disuse after it was hit by a flurry of enemy spells. Restorations still haven't finished, not even here at the heart of the city. Ithya sent the workers home so they would not disturb the funeral. His wife lingers inside the wrecked room, alone.

She stands there like a doll. Her legs are shaking from the strain of the day. She has probably overused Pathas's medicine, Kass thinks. She'll pay for that dearly.

Kass knows she wanted to look strong today. But now she's alone. Her legs buckle, and she falls. The rest of her body remains tense. She doesn't break the fall, so her arms and chest collide with the floor. Dust rises from the ground.

Kass runs up to her. Silver's face is twisted into a pale mask, eyes narrow with fury.

She doesn't look at him. She was so far away, and he didn't take a single step to follow. What an empty, pointless vow he took the day he married her. How easily he fell apart after she saved the world. How quickly his idea of justice turned into a weapon when it could have been a bandage he could wrap around a broken, disillusioned soul.

Silver opens her mouth, and a weak, pathetic sound crawls out. Her throat is still hurt from the torture and probably always will be.

He kneels by her side and brushes a strand of hair from her face. Her dress is covered in dirt, and there are bruises on her arms. He doesn't remember any of this. How did he not notice? What did his absence speak to, if not callousness?

"Silver," he mutters. She blinks up, suddenly seeing him. The first emotion in her eyes is relief, shortly followed by suspicion. Fear.

"I'm just –" she stammers.

"I'm sorry," he interrupts her. He lifts her until she's sat on the ground, then gently folds her against his chest, placing his hand over her collarbone. Silver's breathing slows down, and she utters the same strained noise as earlier.

"I know," he mutters.

"They're gone, Kass. They're really gone," she whispers. She's shaking like a leaf in the wind. Whose duty is it to anchor her if not his? And he never came. He stayed in that reception room until he felt it was acceptable to leave. He never saw any of this.

Silver clings to his arms, scraping her nails into his flesh, and weeps for parents who died for nothing.

"I'm sorry," he repeats pointlessly. "I'm sorry I wasn't here. I don't know what I was trying to prove."

Silver isn't listening. He knows what it's like to lose control of yourself like that. To fall into the depths of your thoughts only to awake, exhausted and embarrassed, hours later.

"There was no justice in leaving you," he whispers, kissing her head. "I'm sorry, love. I'm so sorry."

The dream vanishes, and he wakes up in a dark room.

They are inside the tower, and flickers of light fall through the slowly forming cracks in the walls. Silver, Andrea, Allen, and Amaya are floating beside him, lined up inside a circular room. Their lifeless bodies are slowly flying upwards. Kass cranes his head, but he can only see blackness above, an endless whirlpool filled with a strangely disconcerting warmth.

He tries to wake his companions, but they don't respond. He is disoriented and nauseous. It feels like an invisible hand is trying to tear his soul from his body. He calls out the names of his companions but to no avail. Andrea is floating somewhere above the rest, their face tilted upwards and wearing a serene smile. Kass wonders if their body is rising as their soul is sinking into the ground.

Allen and Amaya's faces are blank, encased in an eerie serenity. Silver, though, is struggling against invisible bonds, her legs kicking the air and her features twisted in pain. Kass races towards her and puts his hands around her waist.

"Silver," he groans. "Come on, love. Wake up."

She doesn't respond with anything but fearful moans. He shakes her, and her head rolls around on her shoulders.

"Silver," he repeats, this time louder. Her fingers twitch, reaching for invisible enemies. Her fingertips start to glow with magic, a bright light in the darkness of the tower. Impulsively, Kass grabs them, expecting a host of pain to shoot through his limbs.

Instead, he finds himself somewhere else.

He is in a half-open tent littered with crosses. The mages of Old Noll are strung up like puppets, some dead, some unconscious, some struggling against their bonds. Outside, battles are raging like the tide, with shouts and blood wafting in from a sea of barely distinguishable bodies.

Silver is hanging from a cross, her legs broken in several places, and bleeding from cuts and scrapes across her face and arms. She is missing several fingernails and looks exhausted and malnourished.

"Silver," he whispers. He knows where they are. During the war, a group of mages were abducted during a failed raid. They were supposed to follow a squadron of scouts through hidden tunnels into nearby forests and strike the enemy from behind. Physically circumnavigating the enemies' magical shields was supposed to allow the human mages to take down the invaders' war machines.

Kass doesn't know what went wrong with the plan. Silver had sounded confident when she told him about it the night before. She had been proud to be chosen for the mission. And while worry had eaten away at his heart when he lay in the tent beside her, fear took a bite out of him every night. Nothing about the mission had been unusual. Not until his lover didn't return to him the next night or the morning after. Not until a quiet panic spread across Old Noll once everyone realised they had lost most of their spellcasters.

Kass remembers that Silver was one of the only mages to escape confinement. She managed to resurrect the bodies of her dead comrades inside the tent where she was kept. Using necromancy, she compelled them to carry her and the other survivors to the city gates.

Against Octavia's orders, Pride, Kass, and some others had rallied the remaining human soldiers to make a futile attempt to reach the enemy's base camp and liberate their fallen comrades. It had ended only in death and failure. But inadvertently, their attack had created the distraction Silver needed to cast her resurrection spell and escape.

Kass floats inside the tent, crowded with the sickly sweet stench of blood. Silver strains against her bonds, ripping the skin from her wrists and ankles. She is trying to steady her breathing through the panic. She knows the enemy might come back at any moment. She knows she only has one real shot at this.

On her way back to the city walls, she will find Kass, Melina, and Holly by the side of a road, disappearing underneath a mountain of rotting flesh. She will resurrect more bodies with a flick of her wrist and have the dead carry the living back into Old Noll.

Kass didn't acknowledge her necromancy back then. He still doesn't know if he should have. He had tried to convince himself that it was a one-time thing and that it was justified because Silver used it to save their lives.

Silver breaks her wrist by slamming it against the cross. With her bones loosened and bruised, she forces the hand out of its bonds, scraping off the first layer of skin.

Kass can imagine what comes next. He knows that she can use the blood as a spell component and that even with just one hand and a fucked-up voice, Silver is still formidable. She saved herself. Utterly abandoned by everyone she trusts, Silver will save herself again and again.

The enemy were fools to leave the mages alive, even at the risk of losing any secrets they might betray about Old Noll's fortifications. Silver will tear them apart with fire and magic, and revenge will be the only justification she needs to kill whoever gets in her way.

She cries at the pain, unable to utter the incantation between heaving breaths and sobs that burst from her ruined throat.

There is no justice in throwing an untrained young woman at an impossibly large horde of enemies. There is no justice in later chastising her when she uses every means available to beat the odds. There is no justice in the fact that her paladin lover failed to save her from all this torture.

Silver must think there is no justice left in the world at all.

Kass knows this is a dream. Some strange, magically constructed reality seeping out of the body and consciousness of Five. And he knows that the past is the past and that time is a river that flows only in one direction. And yet.

And yet, he finds his hands gathering strength and rips the bonds from Silver's body. He catches her when she falls from the cross and slings her into his arm, pressing her against his chest.

She glances up at him like he is a spectre that appeared out of darkness. She mouths his name in the cautious, hesitant manner of someone who thinks they are going insane.

"I'm here, Silver," he whispers. "I came to save you."

"You did?"

She sounds surprised. She had fully expected the Multiverse to tear her limb from limb.

He doesn't know if reaching her in time would have made a difference. If she would not have resorted to necromancy to tear down the dragon horde. If she would have been less desperate to hold on to her powers during the years of peace.

If she would have believed there was justice in this world except for what she carved out with her own vicious hands.

But even so much as hoping to be rescued helps Silver relax. She clings to his chest and presses her head into him as she closes her eyes.

The scene fades to black.

Chapter 30

When Kass finds himself back inside the tower, Silver stands beside him, fully awake. She is holding on to his arm to limit the burden on her legs, and Kass can't see her chair anywhere.

"Are you –?" he starts, but his wife interrupts him.

"It's a strong illusion spell that feeds off our deepest-held conceptions of justice. Fitting for a god such as Five."

"Why –?"

"It is most likely part of the process of assimilation Melina spoke of. Our bodies are pulled upwards, but our souls are drawn into the ground." She sits on the floor, straightening her robes with shaking fingers. "This place must be where Five's powers are concentrated."

"Hence the big-ass monument?" Kass asks, gesturing around the black walls that surround them.

Silver shrugs.

"If this entire realm is Five, it would make sense to interpret its geography metaphorically." She winks. "Sorry if that prospect is a little intimidating for someone as straightforward as yourself, husband."

"I'll live," he grunts, then moves towards his squires and Amaya. Andrea is almost too high up to reach now.

"Could you tell you were in a dream?" he asks Silver. "Is that what your spellcasting was about?"

Silver nods.

"Yes. It was watching myself in an out-of-body experience. I couldn't figure out a way to tear down the illusion, but using what remaining awareness I had of my real body, I was trying to work against it as best I could." She shrugs and blushes. "Apparently, all I needed to snap out of it was for you to be a little compassionate. Who knew?"

"Very good, Silver. You are welcome, by the way."

She winks with a smirk playing around her lips. Kass feels something burning inside his pocket. He takes out the two onyx stones that are linked to Allen and Andrea. Both are hot against his skin, Andrea's more so than Allen's. He exchanges a silent look with Silver.

His wife reaches for the bottom of her robes and pulls up the fabric. She must have fallen, as there is a bloody scrape from her ankles to her left knee. She flinches as she coats her human hand with the blood, then gestures towards Andrea. Tiny flickers of white appear on the squire's body, offsetting the golden glow that still radiates from within them.

Kass looks at Silver. "Any idea what I'll find?"

His wife shrugs. "Some recreation of a memory, no doubt. But as to what that memory will be?" She slowly exhales. "They're your squire. You know them better than me. Who knows what thoughts on justice they have when nobody's listening?"

"Well, I suppose I'm about to find out," Kass grunts, then stretches out his hand to touch Andrea's foot. Silver sighs.

"Don't get lost in there, now."

"I found my way out first, remember?"

"I suppose you did. Try not to be too smug about that."

Silver frowns as if a thought had just crossed her mind. Then she smiles, shakes her head, and remains silent as Kass enters his squire's dream world.

The room is quiet. It is a child's bedroom, not changed for the tastes of its teenage inhabitant. Andrea sits on the bed, blanket wrapped around their shoulders. They are so still that Kass takes a few seconds to confirm they are breathing. The curtains are drawn, and the bookshelves on the narrow walls are cast in darkness. An army of stuffed animals sit on the bed and stare at Andrea in a quiet show of support.

Downstairs, Kass hears the voices. They are loud and intrusive. Angry at themselves and each other and, more than anything, at Andrea.

"What in Five's name is wrong with that child?" a male voice bellows, again and again. It's like a song stuck on repeat. The female voice comes up with excuses and explanations that will not fit. They should know it has nothing to do with the death, or with school, or with books Andrea did or did not read.

Andrea stares blankly ahead. Kass can tell they're listening to every word. Taking each accusation seriously even if they know the sentiment is untrue.

They want to do the right thing. They think that's the same thing as pleasing the people around them. But they also know it's wrong to lie. Five's doctrines make this very clear. And they owe their life to Five.

They can't lie, but the truth makes everyone unhappy. The bind it puts them in is impossible. It demands stillness when every action is wrong.

"What did we do wrong? Nobody else has to deal with this. How will the temple ever accept –?"

Kass knows that Andrea's parents are religious. Their mother used to be a cleric for Five before her dementia made it impossible for her to keep up with the work. Andrea's older sister looks after her now while their father hides inside the manor and drinks.

Andrea is not welcome at home, but they still try to visit once a month. Looking after their parents is a duty, and they have always been good with duty. They understand it as the most radical form of equivalence. Bestow kindness onto a world where there is none. Sit in silence when every word would create disharmony. Forge your own justice from nothing.

Do all this alone.

"But that's not quite it, is it?" Kass whispers. He sits on the corner of his squire's bed and brushes a strand of hair from their face.

"You hate being alone. You love it when Allen comes by your flat and spends time with you. You love working because it drowns out the bloody silence."

Andrea's eyes flicker towards him. He sighs.

"You love the certainty of Five's doctrines. But still –"

The words burn on his tongue. Perhaps he shouldn't say it. But the dream doesn't feel like a place where lies would stick.

"But still, you look at me for all the answers. And, deep down, you know there's a difference between what Five and I believe. You know that I'm bloody flawed. Just like everyone else in your life." He sighs again. "You know that I'll let you down. And then you'll be on your own again."

Andrea's lower lip quivers. They say nothing.

"I'm sorry, 'drea," he whispers. "I wish I was stronger. I wish I could be what you need. Your rock, your certainty, your father. The human incarnation of your god. Your saviour, who gave meaning to your life."

The voices below are a whirlwind of anger and aggression. Andrea clutches their arms, and Kass can see streaks of red amidst black and blue bruising.

"It's not fair. The world gave you nothing, and you asked for nothing. Nothing other than the chance to make things better."

He meets his squire's gaze, and their eyes are swimming with tears. He knows they won't speak. It's too hard to move, and their parents might hear.

"I'm making you doubt, aren't I? The way I'm acting, the things I'm saying. It's tearing at your soul. I know. I fucking know."

He shouldn't say it, but he does.

"Maybe you should follow me, 'drea. I can't promise you mercy or happiness, but you won't have to walk that path alone. I swear it."

Andrea stares at him, but their eyes, full of fear, show no crack in their resolve.

Kass nods.

"But you've been alone for too long to be convinced. Not even by me. Five's justice is the only light you've ever seen, and now it marks the only path you'll take."

He buries his squire in a tight embrace and feels their body shaking under his touch.

"I'm sorry, 'drea," he mutters. The darkness remains, and the voices shriek and burn below. Then, he finds himself slipping out of the dream.

"What happened?" Silver asks impatiently. She still sits on the floor, holding her onyx stone between her fingers. Kass doesn't need to reach for his own to know Andrea's is still burning up.

"I don't – I can't convince them," he says quietly. "Five's justice is who they are. They won't question it."

"Ugh! Stubborn –" Silver lets out a long string of curses. Kass lets her, but his eyes keep flickering back to his squire's lifeless body, slowly rising towards the black vortex at the top of the tower.

His wife interrupts herself and reaches towards Kass. He kneels next to her, and she runs her fingers down the side of his face. He shivers.

"I'll think of something to rip them out of their trance," she promises. "In the meantime, you handle Allen and Amaya."

"What if we shouldn't stop them," Kass whispers, even though the thought of losing his squire terrifies him.

"Huh? You want this ... creature to assimilate Andrea?" Silver asks incredulously.

Kass shakes his head. "I don't. But it's their bloody choice. And Five has been the only constant in Andrea's life. The only thing they believe in."

"This is no meaningful choice. They don't know what's happening to them, and they can't know what assimilation truly means. None of us do."

"No choice is ever made with full knowledge of the consequences," Kass responds, feeling Five's words interweave with his own. "But free will still matters. Why did Five resurrect Andrea if not for them to act on their own will?"

"Spare me your platitudes," Silver snaps. He shakes his head, but Silver interrupts him before he can speak again. "It could kill them. Assimilation. It could crush everything that makes them who they are. We don't let children jump off cliffs just because they want to."

"The gods do."

"Perhaps we should start to question the gods' dogmas at this point, no?" Silver shakes her head. "I don't even know if I can free Andrea from their trance. If I manage, I suppose that will have been my choice. My free will."

"Silver –"

"My choice, husband. Not yours. You focus on rescuing the people who want to be rescued."

Allen sits at the carriage station, blinking into the remaining rays of sunlight. He arrived hours ago, all his possessions crammed in the brittle suitcase beside him. Ripe pickings for any thief in the big city.

Kass remembers that Allen sat here for hours, petrified of leaving the questionable comfort of the carriage station. The bustle of people arriving, horses whinnying, and wheels creaking is enough to make him too nervous to move.

Sometimes, Kass wonders if Allen would still sit there if he hadn't come along that day.

"You lost, boy?" Kass asks, rehearsing the line from the memory. He knows what he must look like to Allen. A tall, armoured paladin, carrying a giant Zweihander on his back, chased by the admiring glances of the citizens passing him by.

"Erm," Allen manages, then closes his mouth again.

Kass raises his eyebrows but recognises the young man's awkwardness as genuine. He sits down and stretches his legs as far as his armour will allow. He doesn't remember why he had been at the carriage station that day. It certainly hadn't been to pick up Allen. Meeting his future squire was a complete coincidence.

"Crazy busy, isn't it?" he asks Allen. "I'm not the biggest friend of crowds."

Allen stares at him.

"Why are you talking to me?" the young man asks, then blushes at his lack of politeness. Kass barks out a laugh.

"Want me to piss off?" he responds with a gentle smile.

"No," Allen says a little too quickly. Kass laughs again.

"No," Allen repeats after a few seconds. "Sorry. I don't really know what I'm doing here."

"What do you mean?" Kass asks.

"Well, I came here on a bit of a whim," the young man explains. "Things back home weren't going anywhere, so I thought I'd come to the capital to do something ... different. Become someone else. I don't know."

He looks around himself and flinches. "It was stupid. I don't know why I thought I could do that."

"Nothing stupid about that," Kass grunts. "We all end up somewhere other than where we started."

"None of the people at home do," Allen says. "Farmer's sons become farmers. They marry the Violets of the world and have five thousand children with her. I'm not – I just can't ..."

He stops himself and throws a sheepish glance at Kass. "Sorry. You didn't sign up to listen to my soppy little life story."

"No." Kass sighs, then continues. "But I'm not moving until this bloody place quietens down, so you might as well keep me company."

He smiles. "Tell me. What kind of person do you want to become?"

Allen shrugs. "I don't know. Is that stupid? I thought I'd just see what's out there. But now I don't know where to start."

Kass sighs. "That's ... one approach, I suppose." He glances up and down at Allen, taking stock of his worn-out clothes, his small suitcase, and the dissolving soles of his shoes.

"You look like you could use a place to rest for a while," he says, then hesitates. Back in the real world, he had taken Allen to the temple of Five. He had found lodgings and food for the young man and introduced him to some of the clerics. He had also introduced him to Andrea, and the two somehow never stopped talking.

Allen had requested to become Kass's squire a fortnight later. Kass was known for being picky with his squires, but something about Allen's openness, his vulnerability, and his willingness to change won him over.

He now realises that he never told him that.

He had always been hard on Allen because he thought he could take it. He had not understood that Allen's humour was as much a shield against the world as his own anger. And he had always treated Andrea more gently because he knew more about the demons that gnawed on their mind.

Kass sighs.

Allen must think that becoming his squire was one big fluke. That it had nothing to do with him wanting to become more than he was. That it was chance, not justice.

"I like that," Kass says.

"Hmm? What?" Allen responds, blinking up at him.

"You moved away from home to be true to yourself. You looked at the path laid out for you and said, 'fuck that'. Takes guts. I respect that."

Allen stares at him like he's going crazy, but Kass knows him well enough to realise what these words will mean to him later.

"Paladins of Five need that. They need to keep questioning themselves and think about what justice really means. That's why the gods don't impose their will on us. We have to use our bloody heads and make decisions." He smirks. "And I think you have a pretty decent brain, boy."

"Erm," Allen repeats. He colours furiously. The carriage station slowly fades to black, and Kass finds himself slipping out of the dream.

Silver catches Allen with a levitation spell when he falls. The squire is disoriented but otherwise fine, making quips to cover up his embarrassment. Soon enough, Allen's eyes turn to Andrea, who floats far above their heads.

He calls their name to no effect.

"Why aren't they waking up?" he mutters quietly.

"I'm working on it," Silver says without looking at him. She painted a small pentagram on the ground beneath Andrea, using her own blood.

Kass suppresses the urge to sigh. It is surprisingly easy.

"Please just – don't hurt them," Allen asks the necromancer. He is fidgeting.

"I think they want to join Five. I suppose it should be their choice if they want to – I mean, I'd miss them like crazy, but ..."

"Oh, for the love of –" Silver snaps. "Can you people all not wait to die? If you're right, your stupid little souls will join the big divine factory soon enough. But right now, we have a mission to complete."

"She's right," Kass tells his squire. After a moment, he places a hand on the young man's shoulder and feels Allen relax. "If Andrea stays faithful to Five, they will lose nothing except time. But Silver and I will need all the help we can get when confronting Pride and the others."

"Yes, Sir," Allen says, sounding a little more cheerful. Kass nods, then turns towards Amaya. Silver already cast the silver-glittering spell on the investigator. He squeezes Silver's shoulders before he gets back up.

Amaya sits in the council meeting room. All fifty chairs are filled with people with identical features. No hair, no wrinkles, no distinguishing features. Ithya sits at the end of the table, surrounded by slowly moving bodies that prevent Amaya from fully catching sight of him.

The room is hot, and everyone is talking at once. The sound filling the air is deafening. It sounds like the human tongue, but it is alien enough that Kass only catches glimpses of words and can't puzzle together their meaning.

Amaya sits in her chair, trying to evade the exuberant movements of her neighbours. Kass can tell that she's trying to listen to the conversation. From the steep line on her forehead and her shallow breathing, he can tell she's overstimulated and frustrated.

He moves the figure to Amaya's right out of his chair, and he disappears. The investigator's eyes move to him. She doesn't seem surprised that Kass is in her dream.

"Is this what it's always like?" he asks. Amaya shrugs.

"In big meetings, yes. It's less bad in smaller groups. One-on-one is best. But then, you know that." She shrugs again. "I wish I didn't have to attend these meetings to give my reports. I'm good at what I do, and what I do prevents harm to the city. Subjecting me to this nonsense does no one any good."

"They aren't considering your needs?" Kass asks softly.

"Look at the state of the world," Amaya scoffs. "People have barely enough time to consider their own needs, let alone those of others."

"Do you think that'll ever change?"

Amaya shakes her head. "No. The self is always more important than the other. It's just how people are. It took me a long time to realise and even longer to accept, but knowing it helps."

"Does it bother you?" Kass presses. "Do you think it's unfair?"

"Fair?" Amaya's gaze is hard. "I like you, Kass. You're probably what counts as my best friend in this city. But your obsession with fairness and justice gets in the way of real solutions. I don't care what's fair. I care about what works."

Kass laughs even though the words cut him deeper than he lets on. "You've never been one to mince words, 'maja."

"What would be the point? It's hard enough to know what other people mean without everyone lying about how they feel."

Kass smiles, then hesitates as he tries to figure out how to change Amaya's conception of justice and break her out of the dream. Before he has the chance, the investigator stands up.

"Well, if you're here, that means this is a spell, right? I distinctly remember you skipped out on this meeting to go home and have one of your fights with Silver. So, this reality is false."

Kass raises his eyebrows. "You remember that?"

Amaya rolls her eyes. "How do we get out of here, then?" she asks instead of answering.

Kass looks around. The edges of the dream are dark and frayed.

"Maybe you just move out of the scope of the dream?" he proposes.

"Why would that work?" Amaya asks. Kass struggles to give reason to his intuition, but for his friend, he tries.

"The purpose of this dream is to keep you trapped by your sense of justice," he explains. "To distract you with your memories until Five has taken hold of your soul. So, if you leave the realm of memories –"

"I can just walk out of the trap?" Amaya raises her eyebrows, then tries to get up. She is visibly surprised when she is able to. "I assumed I couldn't just stand up and leave."

She barks out a small laugh.

"This is quite liberating."

She grins and walks towards the edges of the dream. When she disappears inside the wall, Kass feels himself fall.

Chapter 31

When Kass comes to for the third time, Silver's pentagram is glowing in an eerie red light. The same silver strands that opened everyone's dreams are wrapped around Andrea, tying them to the corners of the blood-painted symbol.

Their body twitches as it tries to float upwards, but Silver's spell holds them down. Allen flitters around the pentagram like a nervous bird, and Amaya leans against the wall of the tower, her eyes shining in the dark.

"What are you doing?" Kass asks, trying to keep his voice as level as possible. Silver won't explain anything if she feels he will shout at her.

"Well, necromancy is the arcane school of souls," his wife says, her gaze fixed on Andrea. "Binding souls to bodies even when the soul is unwilling to return to life."

She narrows her eyes. "Andrea is hell-bent on sacrificing their soul to the altar that is Five. So, instead of letting that happen, I'm forcing their soul to remain bound to their body."

She gestures at the red-glowing pentagram. Upon closer inspection, Kass notes that it looks remarkably similar to the resurrection pentagrams she used in House Karthe.

It feels like an eternity ago now.

Allen turns to the necromancer. "Will it hurt them?" he asks, his voice very quiet. Silver shakes her head.

"Not nearly as much as having their soul ripped out of their body."

"Can you hurry up?" Amaya asks. She has been pacing the tower's confines but found nothing except impenetrable walls and darkness. She doesn't think they can proceed without Silver's spells.

"Almost there," Silver says with an exasperated sigh. Then, with a low moan, she scoops more blood out of the wound on her leg and splatters it across the pentagram.

The red glow intensifies, and Andrea begins to scream. Their body twitches. Kass feels something inside him long to float upwards and dance in the open air, but the feeling passes quicker than he can submit to it.

Andrea screams. The light from the spells vanishes, and they fall.

Kass catches them before they hit the ground. For a long, horrifying second, he thinks his squire is dead, but Andrea slowly starts to breathe again.

"Five," they whisper, their eyes still closed. "Where -?"

"It's fine," Kass says slowly. "I'm - you're okay."

Andrea opens their eyes, and the glossy film has lifted. What remains is sadness. Silver stretches to catch a glimpse of Andrea's face. She is still sitting on the floor. Wherever her chair has gone, it is not in this room.

"Are you alright?" Silver calls. "I didn't mess up the spell, did I?"

"What - spell?" Andrea asks sluggishly.

"They seem fine," Kass tells Silver, which seems to be enough to assuage his wife's worries. He lifts his squire on the floor, where they are greeted by an anxious Allen. The two speak quietly, and Kass steps away to give them some privacy.

Silver pokes against the metal encasing his leg.

"What now?" she asks. She wears the kind of distracted expression that tells him she is passively feeling out for magical strands, but he doesn't expect that she will find much. This whole world is magic. Five's body – and Five himself – is made from the stuff. If Silver is looking for magically hidden doors or corridors, she is looking for a needle in a haystack.

"Your friend Melina," Amaya starts slowly. "She could feel the rifts, correct? Because she is already in the process of being assimilated by Five?"

"She's still resisting," Silver snaps.

"Not my point," Amaya responds calmly. "What interests me is that she was talking about a rift at the centre of the world."

"Yeah, and?" Kass says. "We walked pretty far to get to this place. Depending on how big this ... how big Five is, we may have reached the centre of the world by now."

Silver frowns. "Centre," she mutters.

"Exactly," Amaya confirms. Kass understands a moment later.

"Of bloody course. The rift is underground," he says with a sigh.

"Nobody's to say that this tower is a – well, tower in the way we understand it," Silver responds, her eyes gleaming. "It may be an axis that Five's body grew around. Meaning that the construct may continue underground."

Amaya stomps on the ground. "It sounds hollow under there," she says.

"Right," Silver says, then scratches her head. "A detonation spell for the floor and a levitation spell for us. I'll need –"

Her eyes glide to the sword on Kass's back, then flicker back to her leg. He shakes his head.

"No way, love. You've used up enough of yourself."

"Well, who is going to do it if not me?" Silver snaps. He kneels next to her and offers up his wrist.

"You may be the well-trained and impressive necromancer among us, but you're not the only one with blood running through your veins. Accept the help when it is given."

Silver stares at him wordlessly. Kass realises the whispered conversation between his squires has ended, but he doesn't turn around. He holds Silver's gaze like something fragile.

Finally, his wife nods. "That would work. Thank you, Kass."

Silver blows up the floor, and they fall into darkness. The levitation spell breaks their fall as they tumble through sluggish bouts of air. Two mage lights, summoned by Silver, are the only flickers of light left in the dark tunnel.

The whole place feels stale and unused. There are no arcane symbols painted by long-lost civilisations or signs of alien architecture. The tower is bare and eternal. It lowers itself into the Multiverse as if it is the only constant to exist across space and time.

Kass feels like it is heretical to breathe. Humans are not supposed to see the building blocks of the world. Perhaps, in reality, this place looks entirely different, and what he sees is just what his limited human perspective allows him to perceive.

He grunts. It probably doesn't matter. Silver meets his eyes, and she grins when she guesses what he's thinking.

Finally, they reach the bottom of the tower, which widens into a dark cavern. Darkness lingers at its edges, shifting in and out of view. It's like the boundaries of the plane are constantly redefining themselves around this spire.

At the centre of the cavern is a rift, its surface aglow with flickering candlelight. A black protective layer shifts across its surface, occasionally letting out a beam of pure energy that crashes into the cavern walls. Kass can feel the force of the spells and instinctively takes a few steps back.

"Candlelight," Amaya muses. "That makes me think the rift connects to a human plane. I don't know of any demons that use candles."

"Pride's quarters?" Kass suggests with a sideway glance at his wife. Silver bites on her lower lip and says nothing.

Andrea's eyes are wide, and they take a step closer to the rift.

"She's attacking Five, isn't she?" they ask. They reach out their hand just as a beam of energy shoots out of the rift and hits the wall. The cavern convulses in a motion that looks strangely like pain, and Kass feels sick seeing the space move around them.

Kass pulls Andrea back. "Careful, 'drea. You don't want to touch that."

They turn around to Kass, and he sees their eyes are swimming with tears. "Why is she doing this?" they ask. "Five is a god. She can't just –"

"Five is the reason Pride's family is dead," Silver mutters. "It is her right to avenge herself."

Andrea turns around to her.

"*People* are the reason Pride's family is dead. *People* who interpret Five's doctrines to mean that they should go on a holy crusade. I don't agree with that. I don't think Five ever wanted anyone to die in his name."

They take a deep breath. "But if the gods didn't give us free will, we wouldn't be human. We would be machines. And if the gods didn't exist, people would suffer more than they already do."

"I don't believe that," Silver snaps. "We've never been free from the gods. Who knows what we might be capable of without their dogmas and miracles tempting us away from progress?"

She scoffs.

"They lied to us, making us believe that divine and arcane magic are separate. Convincing us that we could never heal one another without their permission. So, people like me live in perpetual agony for the sake of some god's arbitrary system of justice."

"I would be dead without Five's interference," Andrea says, their voice very quiet. Silver hesitates for a moment, but then she continues.

"Pride has healed all of you without hesitation. She will be the one to heal my legs. Sometime in the future, she might also be able to bring back the dead."

Kass hesitates. He can still feel Pride's hooks inside his chest, ready to snap. But a woefully optimistic part of him wonders if he might be imagining the sensation. Perhaps Pride really is humanity's salvation.

Andrea doesn't think so.

"People are free not to believe," they say, their voice resonating against the dark walls of the cavern. "Other people's faith is no reason to kill a god."

"Other people's faith has turned our realm into a living hell," Silver snaps.

"Enough," Amaya says. "None of this is helping us get home. If you want to stop Pride's spells, Andrea, you will have to get to her first."

Andrea takes a deep breath and nods.

"You are right. I apologise for my outburst."

Kass feels a layer of cold settle in his squire's expression. It is unfamiliar, yet it somehow fits them. Allen places a silent hand on their back, and they sink into his touch.

Silver asks Kass to lift her closer to the rift. The nearer she gets to the black protective spell atop its surface, the heavier her breathing becomes. Kass knows why. Even he remembers Pride's tell-tale black barriers from the war. The truth that Pride stands at the centre of this conspiracy is becoming undeniable.

He squeezes Silver's shoulders. He can't think of anything to say to make her feel better. They will have to make their own decision on how to handle this revelation. But, deep down, he knows he will stand by Silver's side until the end. He doesn't want to break his heart for the sake of a cold and unrelenting world. Not again.

So, instead of speaking, he gently turns Silver until she faces him.

"What?" she asks, her thoughts elsewhere. Kass's lashes flutter, and Silver's gaze softens.

"What?" she repeats, her voice a whisper.

Kass leans in and brushes his lips against hers. Electric currents shoot through his chest, and his breath catches. Silver freezes and clings to his arms as if they are the only things to stop her from falling. Kass sighs, and she opens her mouth and licks across his lips. He squeezes his eyes shut and struggles to hold onto himself amidst the intensity of the feeling.

Silver disentangles herself from the embrace far too quickly.

"Damn it all. I love you," she whispers.

"Damn it all," he echoes. Silver smiles.

"Can you get rid of Pride's barrier?" Amaya asks. They surround the rift, careful to anticipate the destructive beams that shoot from its surface at regular intervals.

"If Five didn't even manage, what chance do we stand?" Allen asks, scratching the back of his head. "It's not like any of us are gods. That we know of, anyway."

Silver sighs. "That's different. The rift lies at the centre of Five's own body. He probably isn't able to close it without hurting himself." When she sees Allen's confused look, she shrugs. "You try using your fingers to close a wound that runs across your own stomach lining."

"But the gods listen to our prayers," the squire protests, then interrupts himself. "Well. Sometimes. And for that, they channel their powers into a precise location."

"Yes, but for them to listen, you call upon them," Silver explains. "By praying, your will guides the gods to their makeshift conduit. But this rift? Pride's barrier deliberately hides it, if anything."

"So, what's the hold-up?" Amaya asks. Silver frowns.

"In case you forgot, Pride is our realm's most formidable spellcaster. I can't just break through her barrier. Except for my and my husband's blood, I am all out of spell components." She shrugs. "Don't get me wrong, there is plenty of fuel to be had around here. But Five is made up of the souls of his faithful. And I feel like some of you would have a problem with me using those to tear open this rift."

Andrea pales again. She mutters something that to Kass sounds strangely like 'he will punish me.'

"Y-yeah, let's not do that," Allen stammers.

Kass squeezes Silver's shoulders.

"Do we have an alternative?" he asks quietly. His wife turns around to him, her eyes flashing in irritation.

"If I could think of something, I would have done it already."

Amaya steps closer to the rift, following the barrier's opening as it shifts across the surface. "Hello," she calls. No response.

"This is Amaya Petra from the city watch's investigations department," she continues. "We require immediate assistance with leaving this plane. If you can hear us, you are legally obligated to let us back to the human realm."

Silence. Kass grunts. "Optimistic, 'maya."

The investigator shoots him a blank stare. "They *are* legally obligated to help us, Kass."

They are interrupted when the rift starts to sizzle. Allen has thrown a stone against the surface that slowly melts into the black barrier. He looks at the others and shrugs.

"It could have worked?" he says sheepishly. Andrea seems to agree as they search for bigger rocks to throw against the barrier.

Silver rolls her eyes. She knows this won't do anything, but she lets them try anyway. She and Kass sit down and stare at the rift's expressionless surface while they hear the plane around them moan with each one of Pride's attacks.

His squires lose their motivation to attack the protective barrier, then regain it when Andrea finds a particularly promising pile of stones further into the cavern. Amaya looks at the rift from every angle and searches as much of the cave as the shifting reality of the plane will allow.

Silver stares at the rift, biding her time until desperation will allow her to justify her consumption of the dead. Kass wonders how many of Pride's attacks it will take to kill a god. Even if it's a million, he doubts she will ever stop. Suddenly, he hears movement on the other side of the rift. Silver interprets his expression correctly and leans further towards the surface.

"Do you think these bloody rocks actually did something?" Kass asks quietly. Silver ignores him.

"Pride! Let us through!" she shouts.

The noise intensifies, and Kass feels himself relax. Despite everything, Pride loves Silver. There aren't many things in this world that he's sure of, but this is one of them. His wife will get out of this place, even if Pride lets the rest of them rot here.

"Pride," Silver cries, her voice breaking with unfamiliar strain.

A blinding light shoots from the rift, and the barrier vanishes. Pride stands on the other side of the rift, her robes flowing in a wild breeze. Her large eyes fix on Silver, and her hands reach for her.

Amaya jumps through the rift first, perhaps fearing that Pride will recreate the barrier once Silver has passed through. Kass commands his squires to go next. Finally, he lifts his wife and prepares to cross back onto the human plane.

Just then, the cavern around them convulses. The ground stretches, and it feels like an enormous beast has awoken. Rocks rain from the ceiling, and the air shifts into something bloody and cruel. Silver clings to Kass's shoulders and looks around with wide eyes.

"Hurry," Pride calls from the other side of the rift. "Before he kills us all!"

Kass feels the world shake with a vicious growl.

"Kass!" Silver cries, and he feels her shaking against his chest. Without another moment of hesitation, he launches himself through the rift as the cavern around them collapses.

Chapter 32

Kass feels his heart racing in his throat. When he fell through the rift, the world expanded and gained an edge. He feels it cutting into his skin, confronting him with a blinding sense of reality. He holds on to Silver, who gasps under his grasp. Noise explodes around them, with Pride casting, Amaya making accusations, and his squires surrounding him with their blades drawn. A spell rushes over his head, and the rift behind him sighs. Silver moves from underneath his touch. He forces himself to stand up to stand at her side.

They are standing in a vast room filled with precious stones, bones, and skin. Anything that can be used as a spell component to fuel the barrier atop the rift and the destructive magic that shoots through it. The roof curves upward into a labyrinth of stone beams. There are a few windows through which Kass sees Old Noll's skyline. They must be at the very top of the mage tower.

Kass has never been up here. Now, it occurs to him that Silver hasn't either. The attic is connected only to Pride's quarters.

Pride stands beside the rift, breathing heavily as her hand connects with the black film covering its exterior. She isn't alone. Behind her stand Octavia and Ithya. Kass stares at his former general. Octavia's face is twisted into a mask of sorrow and barely concealed guilt. Fear bends her spine towards the ground as if she is bowing.

Ithya isn't admitting any emotions. He stares down at Kass as if he's seeing him for the first time. He wears a simple set of leather armour, and his fingers are coated in silver-shining metals.

They came here ready to fight, Kass realises. He draws his Zweihander.

"Enough," Pride barks, then disconnects her hand from the rift. Her skin steams, but she looks unharmed. "There is no need for this nonsense. We are all on the same side here."

She walks over to Silver and offers her hand to the necromancer. Silver stares at her.

"Remember when I told you I'd fix your old wheelchair?" Pride asks.

"You promised a lot of things," Silver responds, her voice dull.

"I suppose I deserve that," Pride whispers and makes a motion with her hand. "But I did remember."

A wheelchair moves from one of the corners of the attic and slowly rolls towards Silver. It creaks slightly as if it has been standing up here for far longer than it should have.

Kass remembers making it for Silver. He had felt insulted when his wife chose to ask Pride to fit it instead of him. But, those days, he had been busy and distracted.

Silver pulls herself into the seat and rolls a few inches back and forth. She sighs.

"Thank you," she says quietly.

Pride nods with a barely concealed smile. Kass grunts and takes a step forward.

"You have a lot of explaining to do," he says. "All of you."

Octavia nods slowly. "Ask what you will, Kassander. We owe you the answers you seek."

Ithya throws her a disgusted glance. "Hardly. We will answer what we see fit. No more, no less. Consider yourselves privileged that we're even giving you this much."

His voice has changed entirely from the shy, uncertain monarch Kass had grown to respect. There is a cold calculation in his tone that makes the hairs on his skin stand up.

Amaya clicks her tongue.

"King Ithya, first of his name," she says with an unwavering voice. "The investigations department hereby accuses you of using demonic assassins to murder your sister Donheira during the second year of the invasion. Do you deny it?"

Ithya narrows his eyes.

"No," he simply says. Amaya falls silent, having expected him to argue. Ithya fixes her for a few moments, then continues.

"Donna was not interested in ruling. Under her, we wouldn't have survived the war, simple as that. My actions were justified if you consider how many lives I saved."

"But isn't it right that you funded Pride's experiments to open the rifts long before the war even began?" Amaya asks. Ithya shrugs.

"Call it academic curiosity. I had always wondered where souls travelled after death. I didn't know it was possible to travel to other planes, let alone that opening one rift would tear open the Multiverse. How could we have foreseen that?"

Silver narrows her eyes. "I don't care about the past times of a bored princeling," she says with her gaze fixed on Pride. Her voice is very hollow. "You were the one who opened the rifts. Why?"

Pride stares at her. She tries to look confident, but Kass can see her hands shaking.

"Because I don't want to live in a world in which our fate is ruled by the gods," Pride responds quietly. "I want to kill them, Silver. For what they've done to me and what they're doing to all the souls they've trapped."

"You doomed millions of people!" Andrea says, their face twisted with anger. "For some crazy, heretical delusion! You –"

They struggle to catch their breath. Kass wants to place his hand on their shoulder, but he remains by Silver's side. His wife needs him more.

"You never told me," Silver says quietly.

"How could I?" Pride asks, her voice wavering. "The war killed your parents. It took your legs, your voice, your friends. And it was a war I started."

"So?" Kass asks, his voice dangerously low. "Was it worth it?"

Pride shakes her head. "It will be. Once I kill Five and the rest of these divine parasites."

Kass turns around to Octavia. "And you? Is this what you wanted? All this death? All this suffering?"

Octavia takes a step towards him, then hesitates.

"Never. I never wanted this. You have to believe me," she says.

Ithya scoffs. "Bullshit, Octa. You lost faith years in the gods long before any of this started. You had all these ideas of the Multiverse and its planes, and once you started wondering if humans weren't the gods' only creations, you started to resent them. As if the gods were your parents who dared to have another child."

"It wasn't like that," Octavia protests. "I - after decades of service, after decades of trouncing through all the shit the believers leave in their wake, I could no longer close my eyes to what the gods truly are. Not after meeting people like Pride, not after seeing the devastation of the crusades."

Her voice grows louder.

"I realised how fickle our gods are, how arbitrary and self-serving their actions, how many people's cries they are deaf to, and I wanted to -"

"And you resented them. You resented them for not living up to your impossible expectations of omniscient, omnipotent parents," Pride snarls.

She paces around the rift. "Both of you wanted to peek behind the curtain of the Multiverse. Both of you wanted to know if a god could be killed."

"I didn't know we would be invaded," Octavia protests.

She looks at Kass pleadingly. "You have to believe me. For me, this was only ever about meeting a god. I wanted to confront them and tell them about all the suffering they ignored ... I never wanted anyone else to be caught up in it."

"Did you really think the gods would listen to you?" Kass asks, incredulous.

Octavia shakes her head. "By that point, I didn't care. I had wasted my entire life on a lie. I just wanted to look someone in the eye as I screamed out my rage."

"And now we have to pay the price," Allen says quietly. He is pale, and his grip around his sword is far too tight.

"None of us knew that one rift would cause a chain reaction," Ithya responds impatiently. "The only place we wanted to reach was Five's realm. But once Pride cast her spell, the Multiverse split apart." He shakes his head. "We couldn't have predicted it."

"And that makes it okay?" Silver screams. She rolls towards him, her legs twisted at an unnatural angle.

"Is the fact that you were ignorant children playing with forces far beyond your control supposed to make me feel *better* about all this?"

"It will be worth it," Pride promises, stepping between her friend and Ithya. "Trust me, Silver. One last time. I have yet to lead you astray."

Silver stares at her.

"You have yet to do a single thing to improve my life," she says. "*Old friend.*"

Pride flinches. Kass shakes his head.

"How do you live with yourselves?"

The words feel heavy on his tongue. He barely lives with his memories of Holly, Derek, and Melina, and all he did was survive the war.

Ithya shakes his head.

"I saw us through the invasion. I do my duties, I listen to the people, and I make the realm a better place. I atone for our joint mistake with every day I serve as king."

Pride nods.

"If ... if you think the war doesn't haunt me, you couldn't be more mistaken," she admits. "Why do you think I oversaw the sealing of all these rifts? Why do you think I'm recruiting mages from across the realm? Why do you think I work to obtain the powers of a god? I am trying to make up for what I did. I am trying to ensure we are never again as powerless as we were."

Her eyes gleam.

"But we cannot be ruled by trauma and regret. We have to look forward. We have to stop being passive subjects. Humanity will only thrive once it has been freed from the gods' tyranny. We will be unstoppable."

"And how would we do that?" Silver asks. "How would we gain access to divine powers? How did you do it?"

Pride hesitates, but from the tension in Silver's body, Kass can tell that his wife already has her answer.

"The spells with which you're attacking Five," she whispers. "You are drawing power from him somehow, aren't you?"

"You are stealing Five's powers?" Kass echoes. He hesitates. "So, when you say that you want all of us to have access to divine powers, you really mean -"

"Heresy," Andrea whispers horrified.

Octavia lowers her head.

"I thought about killing myself many times," the former paladin admits. "And I thought about killing them, too. But they are atoning for their sins by helping people. And once they stop doing that ..."

She places her hand on her Zweihander and glares at her two companions. Ithya rolls his eyes, and Pride ignores her.

Kass clenches his teeth.

"So, that's it?" he asks Octavia. "You were resentful, and the princeling was bored? And you both followed the call of a madwoman who wanted to avenge herself on the bloody gods?"

Octavia takes a long, shaking breath but says nothing. Silver slowly moves her wheelchair over creaking wooden floors to reach Pride.

"Forgive me, Silver," Pride whispers. Silver spits on the floor before her.

"Fuck you," she responds. "You took everything from me."

"I know. I know. But I can give you so much more," Pride responds. She kneels before Silver so she can look her friend in the eyes.

405

"Who knows what I can do once I take all of Five's powers? Once I have killed all ten gods? Maybe I can bring back the dead. Would you like that, Silver? Would you like me to bring back your parents?"

Silver shakes her head. "The dead are gone. Life is for the living. You are the one who taught me that."

"The world lives on exceptions," Pride responds. She shakes her head. "I need you by my side. The rest of these goons I can do without, but I need you. I need you to understand why I am doing this."

"I understand –" Silver takes a sharp breath, and Kass isn't sure whether she is going to add another word or not.

"Please," Pride whispers, the word barely audible.

"I can't –" Silver responds, almost as quietly. The words sound like they are scraping against her throat. "I don't know how I can forgive you. I don't know how I can justify fighting alongside the person who destroyed the world."

Kass can see Pride's heart break as all tension escapes her body. Just for a moment. Then, ice fills her eyes, cold and impenetrable. She closes her fist, and Kass feels a sharp sting in his heart as invisible hooks sink into his skin. His squires fall to their knees, clutching their chests. The spell Pride wove into the divine healing she bestowed onto them is finally taking its toll.

"You can," Pride says. She places her other hand on the armrest of Silver's wheelchair, grazing the necromancer's skin.

"I can make this easier on you. I can take the choice away. Fight by my side, and no harm will befall these foolish cretins you ally yourself with. You can feel like you've done nothing wrong." Her voice falls to a husk. "Because you won't. You're perfect, Silver. I always –"

Silver gently moves her hand on Pride's arm. For a moment, Pride looks deliriously happy, then her face twists into a mask of pain. Steam rises from their point of connection, and the stench of burnt flesh fills the air.

Pride screams as her arms rots away before her eyes. After a moment, Kass realises that Silver is touching her friend with the remains of her skeletal hand. She is corrupting Pride's flesh, twisting her skin into black soot.

The spell tugging on his heart relents, and he forces himself to take a few deep breaths before he pulls his squires back on their feet.

"You sacrificed the world for your revenge," Silver snarls at Pride. "It's only fair if I sacrifice you for mine."

Pride staggers back, struggling to stand. Ithya rips her up by her shoulders and raises his left hand to form a barrier before them. Octavia glances at her former companions, her eyes wide. Kass pushes himself before his squires and Amaya as Silver rolls away from Ithya's protective barrier. Pride raises her hands, her dark eyes cast in fury.

"Silver! Get over here!" Kass shouts, and his heart begins to throb as Pride's spell grabs hold again. Ithya raises both hands. Fire engulfs his fingers and shoots upwards like a snake.

407

Silver is too slow at getting back to him. Kass wants to run to her, but his legs give out after a few steps, and black spots dance in his vision. Ithya's spell roars above the protective barrier and descends towards Silver.

The necromancer stops to summon a protective barrier, but her movements are hazy and uncertain, with heat already eating at her skin. Her spell might misfire, Kass thinks with horror.

Octavia jumps in the way of Ithya's spell before it can hit Silver. The fire engulfs her and rips the skin from her bones within a flash. Silver screams but manages to roll out of the impact zone. Kass forces himself through the vertigo and half-stumbles, half-crawls to his wife. When he finally reaches her, he pulls her behind him.

He nearly faints. The stench of Octavia's flesh is all-consuming. The terrifying certainty that his former general is dead makes him feel so numb that he can barely move. At the same time, his heart races as if it is being pulled out of his chest.

"Not now," he whispers. "Please, not now."

But it's no good. The fear creeps deep within his bones, liberated by the world's assurance that it will always be as terrible as it was. He loses control of his breathing, and his blood roars within his ears, drowning out reality.

He is going to die here. Silver is going to die here. Andrea, Allen, and Amaya – he can't save any of them. Octavia is dead. He might as well –

"Five!" Andrea's voice cuts through the madness and terror. "Five, aid your servants! Help us fight to protect you! Let us regain your favour and bring justice to these sinners!"

Divine light floods Kass's vision. A soft, golden glow settles in his bones and rips Pride's spell apart. His heart stills in the embrace of his god, in that perfect certainty he once grew so addicted to. Andrea stands by his side, holding Five's golden sword in their hands. Their eyes are glowing.

"Let us finish this," they say and raise their sword.

Chapter 33

Pride and Ithya stand on either side of the rift, protective barriers whirring in the air. Silver stares down Pride and wordlessly raises her skeletal hand. A dust cloud of spell components ascends from the corners of the room and latches on to Silver's arms, forming an intricate pattern on her skin. Kass realises that the mages will have access to nigh-on infinite fuel for their spellcraft here.

He feels the warmth of Five's armour sitting on his bones. It makes his sword lighter in his shaking hands. He remains next to his wife, facing their old mage general. Pride is at the height of her power, far stronger even than during the war. Pride raises her hands, and several balls of fire manifest before Silver and Kass. Before they can connect, Silver summons an icy wind that puts out the fire and smashes the remaining spell force into the attic's stone walls.

Silver twists her hand, and a giant icicle appears behind Pride, racing towards the mage's back. Pride's protective spell swallows the ice, but Kass can hear the pained sizzle of the barrier breaking under the attack. Pride narrows her eyes, and a gust of wind blows Silver's wheelchair backwards. Kass grabs onto its handles and plants his feet firmly into the ground to prevent his wife from moving.

"Bitch," Silver growls, then summons seven icicles at once, all shooting towards Pride from different angles. Pride presses her hands into the air, and a ring of fire manifests around her like a gigantic halo. It swallows Silver's icicles within seconds.

Kass takes a deep breath as his hands shake around the handles of Silver's wheelchair.

Silver is trying to kill. Pride is not. But with any more time, he is sure that will change.

His eyes instinctively dart over to his squires. Andrea storms at Ithya, followed by Allen. Amaya takes out her gun and shoots a bullet at the king's barrier. It ricochets off an invisible force field and hits the ground a few inches from the investigator's feet. Amaya curses.

Andrea's sword collides with Ithya's barrier not a moment later. An explosion of force shakes the tower as divine and arcane magic meet, one crashing into the other like the raging sea against tall cliffs. Ithya takes a step back, then summons another snake made of fire. The manifestation winds around itself in the force-filled air, lashing its head against the world.

Andrea stands their ground, slowly raising their sword. The snake strikes, and the squire parries its attack. Sparks fly where the spell meets the divinely infused metal, and the Multiverse groans as the sheer force of the attack threatens to tear another rift into its thinned-out tapestry.

Allen pales, his eyes darting around the room. He settles on a spot below Ithya's feet and shouts something at Amaya that Kass doesn't hear over the noise of battle. But before he can see the investigator's response, a cry beside him rips his attention back to Silver and Pride's duel.

Silver managed to hit Pride with a lance made of ice. Streams of water melt out of Pride's midriff as she bends over in pain, the remains of her barrier crackling in the air.

Kass sees his chance. He storms past Silver and raises his sword. If he can decapitate Pride now, this will be over before anyone else gets hurt. Ithya is a strong spellcaster, but he won't be able to take all their attacks at once.

Pride sees him coming, and her pained expression twists into malice. She smashes her left hand into the ground, and blood breaks from her skin. She does it again. Again and again, until the boards at her feet are sprayed with blood. Kass has almost reached her and starts to bring his sword down when a vicious force throws him back into the air.

A sudden light blinds him, and he feels sick and disoriented, with magic rushing through his body.

"Kass," he hears Silver shriek, and her magic lifts him back onto his feet.

He gasps for air and stares at the spot where Pride just stood. A rift splits apart the floor, already closing around the area where she disappeared. Silver rolls towards it, her eyes wide as she stares at the seam of the Multiverse unravelling and resewing itself before their eyes.

"Oh no, you don't," she whispers. She approaches the remains of the rift, now no bigger than one of the wheels of her chair. She bends down and touches its outline with her skeletal hand. It must feel like touching a wound on the body of the world, Kass thinks.

"Can you open it back up?" he asks.

His wife's eyes flicker towards him.

"Yes," she says. "But I don't know what opening a rift up here will do to the rest of the tower."

Kass hesitates. He knows how many mages and apprentices live here, their bedroom doors painted with little pictures. If the tower collapses, they might not all get out on time. The debris of the fall might bury houses in the nearby districts just like the enemy's barrage buried Silver's parents.

But none of them would be here if Pride hadn't started the war. And she may well start another.

"Do it," he says, and Silver doesn't hesitate. She balls her skeletal hand to a fist, then rips at the brittle seams of the Multiverse until they break. The rift stretches until it runs across the room, and this time, it doesn't stop. It is sinking its claws into the sky.

They fall.

They fall into a world made of clouds. Kass feels his eyes water as air presses into his lids, but after a few moments, he slows down. He blinks and sees Silver holding onto her chair. She raises her glowing, skeletal hand. Ithya has hidden himself inside a black-glowing sphere. Amaya shoots bullets at its exterior, and Andrea tries to force their gold-glowing sword through it. Allen has smeared ruby dust across his hands and mutters quietly.

Pride falls below them, barely visible beneath soft clouds. Open cartons full of spell components fly through the air, spilling their contents. Precious metals, dust, skin, and pelts create sails of power in the air.

Silver narrows her eyes once she spots her former mentor.

"I'll have to stop breaking our fall," she tells Kass. "Get ready."

"We won't catch her like this," he warns. "She's going too fast, and we don't even know if this plane has a bottom."

"Got a better idea, husband?" Silver snaps, but there is no edge to her voice.

Kass gestures at the spell components. "Take us elsewhere. Somewhere with solid ground, where I can help you battle Pride."

"Open another rift?" Silver's eyes widen for a moment, then she nods. "Very well. At this point, I suppose it hardly matters."

She raises both her hands, and the spell components start encircling her. Glittering dust clings onto batches of skin, reflecting the plane's muted sunlight. Silver sighs, and a rift splits the skies, reaching down to Pride.

The former general breaks her fall to look back, and even at this distance, Kass can see she is afraid.

She should have expected Silver to be precisely as ruthless as she taught her to be.

Silver shakes under the strain of the spell, and Kass presses his hands on her shoulders. He forces some of Five's divine energy to flow into her, strengthening her body as it reels under the magic's strain. The energy tries to resist his will, but he forces it to obey. It's just energy, he thinks, the same as any arcane spell. It is his to do with as he wishes.

The rift glows, then stretches outwards. Pride tries to escape its reach, but it widens in tandem with her flailing arms.

They fall into yet another world.

Kass crashes into solid ground, and the impact is almost forceful enough to wipe away his consciousness. As he blinks against the pain, he sees that they are inside an ancient arena. The world drips with grey as only the skeletal remains of columns and arches remain, trapping them inside a half-closed circle. The ground below them is made of a mosaic of stones, bare of any colour or motifs. Heavy rain clouds hide the skies overhead.

Ithya's shell crashes into the ground, and cracks appear on its side. Andrea and Amaya fall on the mosaic, and the investigator seems to be unconscious from the impact. Allen glides to the ground more slowly, next to Silver. Silver's levitation spell seems to have connected with the spell components stuck to Allen's hand, and the squire uses the connection to tap into her spell. For a moment, he looks as though he is going to run to Andrea, who lies moaning on the ground, their gold-glowing sword dissolving with each moment.

But instead, he races to Amaya's unconscious body and picks up her gun. Before Ithya can restore his magical shell, he forces the gun's barrel inside and points it directly at the king's head.

"Surrender or I shoot," he says, and although his voice is shaking, Kass can tell that he means it.

Ithya slowly raises his hands until the black shell crumbles into dust.

Pride floats at the centre of the arena. Her levitation spell is strong enough that it looks like she is swimming through the air. When Silver's wheelchair connects with the ground, Pride still hovers above them, her hands glowing with an eerie red light.

"You cannot stop me," she says.

The clouds above like they are ready to burst. They are surrounded by mountains, and Kass wonders if it will rain long enough for them to drown inside this ancient place.

"Fuck you," Silver says. She forces the silvery glow back onto her hands, but it is flickering with effort. She has been casting spell after spell for days now. She must be exhausted, Kass realises.

"I've taught you everything you know. You would be nothing without me, Silver D'arren. Just a noble girl with no purpose, living according to the whims of others."

"I was happy," Silver says.

Pride scoffs. "Happiness is for children. I gave you power. I gave you knowledge. I gave you a new life."

"I didn't want any of that. I just wanted to -"

"What?" Pride interrupts her. "Sit inside your mansion all day and hide away from the world? Bend yourself to the will of your husband? You are wasting your life, Silver."

"I like my life."

"You're living a lie. You sacrificed your marriage the day you saved Old Noll. You're just lingering in its graveyard now, too scared to move on."

Silver hesitates, and Kass gently touches her back.

"It's not true," he mouths. "We can rebuild. We will."

"He is lying," Pride snaps. "How many times did you think things would get better? How many times did you come to me crying? He is never going to change, Silver. Most people aren't capable of it, especially those who serve an oppressive god."

She shakes her head. "And you waste your life on that? When you and I could explore the Multiverse together? When, together, we could become gods?"

"I don't want that. I never wanted that," Silver says, although Kass hears a note of hesitation in her voice. He wants to say something, to remind her of all the suffering Pride caused the world. But he forces himself to be silent.

This is Silver's decision, and he will stand by her. She has been right every step of the way. He trusts this will not change now.

"You are lying to yourself," Pride says gently. "I know you, Silver. I know you crave power. I know you seek to change the world when it doesn't bend to your will. Together, we could change so much. We could save –"

Silver raises her hands and rips Pride out of the sky with a sudden burst of spellcraft. Pride has no chance to lift her shields or dodge the attack.

She smashes into the ground like a puppet, her limbs twisted from the impact. Blood flows into the gaps between the mosaic, and for a moment, Kass thinks she is already dead. But then she groans and turns towards Silver, bending her head at an impossible angle.

"Please," she mouths. "You know I'm right."

Silver looks at Kass, and he pushes her chair towards Pride without a word. She looks down at her former mentor. Her best friend. She gently reaches down with her human hand.

"I know," she whispers. "You're right. Now that I've tasted it, I would never give up the power I have."

She hesitates, then speaks even quieter.

"And you understand me," she adds. "You have always understood me better than anyone."

Pride stares up at her, her dark eyes swimming with tears.

"I'm sorry," she says. "I'm sorry about your parents and your friends. About your legs and your –"

"I know," Silver repeats. She closes her eyes for a moment and breathes out slowly.

"I believe you. But I can't forgive you."

Her human hand assumes an ungodly glow, and Pride's face twists with pain.

"Silver," Kass simply says. She looks up at him, and he can see the silent plea in her eyes. He raises his Zweihander and severs Pride's head from her body.

Silver turns the head over, drenching her hands in blood. She looks for Pride's faded lily tattoo. A shared memento among all mages who survived the war. She rubs the skin until it is clear from blood and kisses it. The silver pin on her robes gleams in the dark.

Chapter 34

The clouds above the arena burst, and the grey world is drenched with rain. Pride's blood seeps into the cracks of the mosaic. Kass faces the sky. It is strangely silent. Silver has stopped crying. She let go of Pride's head. It stares at the ground with an empty look in its eyes.

Amaya woke from the fall after Andrea used a divine invocation to heal the wound on her head. The investigator has confiscated Ithya's spell components and bound his hands behind his back. The king has not said a word since Allen threatened him with the gun. Kass isn't sure whether he has accepted that he lost or is still plotting the next step.

It doesn't matter. If Ithya shows even the slightest sign of resistance, Kass will decapitate him, too. At this rate, all he wants is to go home.

"We should kill him," Silver mutters, not bothering to look at the king.

"Why?" Allen asks. His voice is hoarse, and his hand around the pistol still shakes. "He hasn't done anything."

Ithya stands stock-still, staring at Pride's dead body. Maybe he had thought she was as immortal as the gods she tried to defeat.

"He's done plenty," the necromancer snaps.

Kass stands at her side. The smell of all this blood is making him sick. That, and the magic from Silver's spells clashes with Five's blessing that still courses through his body. He wonders if that's how Pride felt when she was casting both divine and arcane spells. Nauseous and disoriented. Maybe she got used to the feeling.

He refuses to look at her decapitated body.

"He will stand trial," Amaya says firmly. "That will suffice as punishment."

"Trial?" Kass repeats, then glances down at Silver. His wife still stares at Pride's head, swaying softly under the rain. Her dark eyes are empty as she tries to dissociate from what she has done.

Kass sighs and tries to force as much air out of his lungs as possible.

"A trial would make all this public, 'maya," he explains in a low voice. Amaya meets his gaze even though he knows it makes her uncomfortable.

"It should be public," she says. "People have a right to know where the rifts came from."

"They do, but – wouldn't they go a bit crazy, knowing that it was a mage who opened the rifts in the first place?" Allen asks.

Kass nods. "It would be horrendous for morale. And it would almost certainly lead to the persecution of mages."

421

He imagines what it would do to Silver to go from a war hero to a refugee in her own country. Kass never learned a trade, and neither did Silver. They would struggle to survive on the road, even assuming the disabled noble girl with white hair and a skeletal hand wouldn't be immediately recognised.

"Perhaps rightfully so," Andrea says quietly.

"You need us," Silver snaps. "We're the only ones capable of sealing the rifts to other planes. Our world would be overrun with enemies if not for us mages."

"And Ithya ... is a good king," Kass says slowly. Ithya stares at him with an unreadable expression.

"He was right with what he said," Kass continues. "He saw us through the invasion and has kept the realm safe. Thanks to him, Old Noll is probably doing as well as it can. And who would rule in his stead? We'd have a bloody civil war if we executed him."

"So we just let it go? Conceal the truth because it's more convenient?" Amaya asks. Her voice stays perfectly level, but Kass knows her well enough to detect the fury in her posture. He shakes his head.

"What's more important, 'maya? Justice or human lives?"

The investigator stares at him, then looks away. She mutters something under her breath that Kass doesn't hear. But he knows what she said. Amaya doesn't believe in justice. This is the ultimate proof of it.

Andrea shakes their head.

"I don't like this either," they say quietly. "But it's like Allen said. We can't trust that people will do the right thing. If the masses find out that the gods can be killed, or at least that Pride thought it was possible —"

"There are a lot of crazy people in the world," Allen says. "Death cultists. Megalomaniac mages. Disillusioned paladins." He points at Ithya. "Bored nobility, I guess. Someone might give the god killing another try."

"I don't think Five wants this information to be known," Andrea agrees. "That's why he didn't set his paladins and clerics on Pride. He used demons to conceal the truth about her crimes."

"Oh, and because Five doesn't want us to do something, we should just go along with it?" Silver asks with astonishment clouding her voice. "What will it take for you to lose faith in your god?"

Andrea stares at her.

"Many people hate the gods," they say. "That doesn't mean they are right. Pride was a heretical madwoman. Octavia and Ithya were misguided. I don't have to agree with the things they say."

"You are delusional," Silver snaps. "You only see Pride's madness but not its cause. How far can the gods push people before we hold them accountable for their cruelty?"

"People are free not to believe," Andrea responds, although their voice is tired. Kass can see rings under their eyes and a dull sadness in their expression. He is sure Andrea will recover from this, but he isn't sure what doing so will take from them.

"Was Pride free to not get caught up in the crusades?" Silver's eyes are flashing fire. "You act like the gods' actions don't affect us nonbelievers when few tragedies in our lives are unrelated to their hubris."

"What happened to Pride was a tragedy," Andrea responds, their voice heavy with sorrow. "But tragedies happen with or without the gods' interference. A few bad outcomes don't change the fact that the gods guide us on the right path."

Silver scoffs. "You are incapable of seeing how much potential the world holds once the gods stop interfering."

"And you are incapable of seeing how evil the world would turn out without the gods' aid," Andrea responds. They hesitate for a moment, then continue.

"Five resurrected me all those years ago. He didn't have to, and yet he did. I have to believe there was a reason for it. I have to believe that I am not the product of an evil god who wants to control the world for his own pride."

They look to Kass for support.

Kass feels his heart hammer against his throat. They are right. The world would be a worse place without Andrea in it. Without the gods healing the weary and the sick. Without people believing in a cosmic scale that encourages them to be kinder.

But even a world filled with divine grace was awful to people like Pride. To people like Octavia. To people like Silver. To people like him.

He spent so much of his life making the world better for people he will never meet. All at the detriment of those who remained by his side. He never knew about Octavia's secret, even though she had been the closest thing to a mother he ever had. Could he have noticed her guilt and sorrow if he had been less preoccupied with the day-to-day grind of the streets of Old Noll?

The thought of serving Five makes him feel sick to his stomach. It will drive him from Silver's side. It will force him to bury his doubts, just like he buried his guilt after surviving the war. He doesn't know if he has any space left in the gravesite of his heart.

He doesn't know if he can still live like this. And he doesn't want to. He casts his sword to the ground and raises his face to the sky.

"Hear me, Five," he calls. "Hear your servant for one last time."

The group falls silent. The rain drenches his skin with tears. Silver stares at him, and he can feel every bit of fear and anticipation that tears at her heart. He continues to speak.

"I renounce your justice. I renounce my service to your false ideals and your treacherous deeds. No longer will I be held to your hypocritical standards of righteousness, and no longer will I believe that duty equals blind faith."

"No," Andrea mouths. "Please, Sir. Please don't."

Allen stares at Kass. For a moment, he looks like he is about to join him, but then the squire's eyes flicker back to Andrea. When he sees the horror on their face, the squire freezes. He won't abandon them in Five's order. Regardless of his doubts, he would follow them to whichever hell they chose.

Kass knows the feeling.

"I renounce you, Five," Kass repeats, and a flash of lightning shoots from the sky and splits his sword in half. The warm feeling inside his body disappears, and he suddenly feels every one of his years. His armour is wet and heavy on his back, and he thinks he might sleep a thousand years once this is over.

But the look in Silver's eyes makes it worth it. They are shining with the same light as the day he married her. She looks utterly beautiful, with her light hair flowing around her head like a halo and a wide smile spreading across her face.

"I love you," she mouths. He leans down and presses the top of his head against hers. He can feel her heart beating against her throat. Her breath is going far too fast, and she gasps for air to capture the life they fought for.

"I love you, too," he says. "I will never again leave your side, Silver. This, I swear."

Silver levitates them back to their world. In Old Noll, they find that the rift in Five's quarters has caused the mage tower to collapse. As they float down towards the darkening streets, they see that the debris spreads all the way to the docks, with police carts, rescue squadrons, and volunteers struggling to pull bodies from the rubble. The remnants of the tower are burning with multi-coloured fires that the remaining mages are struggling to put out. Amidst the chaos, Kass hopes the two remaining demons will be forced out of hiding and caught by the city watch. That, or they will dig themselves even deeper into the skeleton of Old Noll.

Andrea shakes their heads, staring at the destruction below.

"Never again," they mutter. "Never again will I allow something like this to happen."

"Pride is already dead," Silver responds blankly. "Spare us your bravado."

Andrea stares at her and says nothing. When they reach solid ground, Ithya clears his throat.

"I will need help restoring order after all this chaos," he says. Kass shrugs.

"You have plenty of people on your council. Take your pick."

Ithya scoffs. "I don't care about bootlickers and administrators. I am talking about someone with real power. You cannot fathom the things that Pride did for the realm. Without her, we are far more vulnerable than we were."

"So, what? You want us to pray to Five to bring her back?" Silver scoffs. Ithya shakes his head.

"No. I want you to replace her."

Kass stares at him. "What?" he asks, feeling the word ring in his ears. Ithya gives him a haughty look.

"I need a powerful mage by my side to oversee the sealing of rifts and gather intelligence on extraplanar attacks. And if we want to stand any chance of surviving another invasion down the line, we need to recruit new mages."

He shrugs.

"Seeing as you killed my last advisor, it behooves you to fill her place, Silver. In fact, you have little choice. After Pride, you are probably the strongest mage we have left. You want the realm to remain safe? Then work with me."

Kass and Silver stare at each other. He can see the apprehension in his wife's eyes, but deep down, there is also intrigue. He knows that she sees a chance to gain more power. To amass more control over the world.

Silver looks up at Kass, shifting in her wheelchair.

"I want to free Melina," she says. "I can't rest while I know she's trapped on that plane."

"I know," Kass replies. The thought of the diviner slowly being consumed by the creature he once prayed to makes his stomach turn.

"I have to – I have to find a way to do that," Silver says, looking down. Her skeletal hand is half gone now. Kass gingerly touches the bones.

"You'll find a way. I'll help, whichever way I can."

"I wouldn't ask you to do that," Silver whispers. Before Kass can ask her what she means by that, she continues.

"I'll need resources. Tons and tons of resources to figure out how to separate Melina's soul from Five. So –"

"So, you'll do it. You'll become Ithya's head mage." Kass shrugs. "It makes sense. This way, we can keep an eye on him, too."

Ithya glares at him but does not protest. Kass looks at the rest of their little group. Amaya doesn't meet his gaze, but then again, she rarely does. He trusts that she will let pragmatism win, just like she always does. Allen awkwardly approaches him and cocks his head to the side.

"The temple will be awfully boring without you, Sir," he says. Kass grins.

"I'm sure you won't miss me giving you a hard time."

"Definitely not. But I know you did it to keep me alive." The squire shrugs. "It didn't always make me like you more, but I did respect it. I do, I mean."

Andrea watches their interaction with their face set in stone. Despite all odds, Kass hopes they will say something. But they know each other too well for that.

"Look after 'drea for me, will you? Don't let them get into too much trouble," Kass mutters in Allen's direction.

"I won't, Sir. I promise."

"And if any mysterious or menacing demons are giving you a hard time, I want you to come to me."

"Yes, Sir."

"And stop calling me Sir."

Allen grins.

"Yes, Sir."

The End.

Thank you so much for reading Paladin and Necromancer!

If you liked it, **please rate and review it on Amazon, Goodreads, and Storygraph**. As an indie author, that really helps me out.

To keep up with my work and gain exclusive access to drafts and Advanced Reading Copies (ARCs), **join my mailing list**:

https://docs.google.com/forms/d/e/1FAIpQLScnZb6vA0eSMBPMxTg773uzmiHCUn-0UpUN2TFAcPL9xL-T6g/viewform

If you want more stories like *Paladin and Necromancer*, check out my debut novel, *The Travelling City,* on Amazon:

After a hundred years of watching humans make bad decisions, anyone would be sick of their job as peacekeeper. Reihan, a seaver created to deal with humans who lose control over their manifestation abilities, is no exception.

Worse still, virtually all humans in the Travelling City can manifest. That is, they shape reality according to their more or less well-formed and often poorly thought-out designs.

That alone would be enough to keep her busy, but then there are people like Phillippe.

Phillippe, who drenched himself in the city's collective subconscious to strengthen his inborn powers. Even though he shouldn't be, he seems fine, crowned as the new star escort in the Brothel of Transformative Curiosities. But Reihan has seen this story play out before. And Phillippe is far too charming, far too kind, and far too inconsolable for her to simply look away.

The Travelling City is a dark fantasy mystery packed with romance and even more existential dread, set in a whimsical, bizarre and ever-changing world. You'll love *The Travelling City* if you're looking for:

Character-driven fantasy books

Genderqueer characters

Fantasy with dark themes, set in a painfully beautiful world

A Grumpy and Sunshine romance dynamic

A magic system that is a reflection of the characters' psychology

Ensemble pieces with clashing, ambiguous, but ultimately lovable characters

Moral and existential philosophy

Epic Indie review: "Wielding a psychedelic array of bizarre imagery and space-distorting magic, The Travelling City boasts a truly fantastical setting for readers to dive into. In a world where humans can manifest new realities for themselves, Adrienne Miller tests the limits of how weird and unfamiliar she can make her debut world, and it's in this uniqueness that the book finds its shine [...] the indie space is blessed to have another author trying new things."

Author Bio

Adrienne Miller (pen name) lives in the UK. She has loved Fantasy literature ever since her dad read her Tolkien's *Hobbit* when she was five years old. *Paladin and Necromancer* is the first novel in the Paladin and Necromancer saga and her second published novel after *The Travelling City* (2023).

Printed in Great Britain
by Amazon